C000000758

Irish Gothics

Also by Christina Morin

CHARLES ROBERT MATURIN AND THE HAUNTING OF IRISH
ROMANTIC FICTION

Irish Gothics

Genres, Forms, Modes, and Traditions, 1760–1890

Edited by

Christina Morin
University of Limerick, Ireland

and

Niall Gillespie
Trinity College Dublin, Ireland

First published 2014 by
PALGRAVE MACMILLAN

Palgrave Macmillan in the UK is an imprint of Macmillan Publishers Limited,
registered in England, company number 785998, of Houndmills, Basingstoke,
Hampshire RG21 6XS.

Palgrave Macmillan in the US is a division of St Martin's Press LLC,
175 Fifth Avenue, New York, NY 10010.

Palgrave Macmillan is the global academic imprint of the above companies
and has companies and representatives throughout the world.

Palgrave® and Macmillan® are registered trademarks in the United States,
the United Kingdom, Europe and other countries.

ISBN 978–1–137–36664–1

This book is printed on paper suitable for recycling and made from fully
managed and sustained forest sources. Logging, pulping and manufacturing
processes are expected to conform to the environmental regulations of the
country of origin.

A catalogue record for this book is available from the British Library.

Library of Congress Cataloging-in-Publication Data
Irish Gothics : Genres, Forms, Modes, and Traditions, 1760–1890 / edited
    by Christina Morin, Lecturer, University of Limerick, Ireland and Niall Gillespie,
    Lecturer, Trinity College Dublin, Ireland.
        pages cm
    Summary: "Variously described as a 'canon', 'tradition', 'genre', 'form', 'mode',
    and 'register', Irish gothic literature suffers from a fundamental terminological
    confusion, and the debate over exactly which term best applies has been
    both heated and, ultimately, inconclusive in the past thirty years.
    The dominant theorization of Irish gothic literature to emerge in late-twentieth
    and early-twenty-first century scholarship has been driven by
    psychoanalytic readings of the literary gothic in Ireland as the fictional
    representation of the repressed fears and anxieties of the minority Anglo-Irish
    population. Such definitions of Irish gothic literature, however, both overlook
    the gothic literary output of authors who were not members of the Anglo-Irish
    Ascendancy and suggest that gothic writing in the eighteenth and nineteenth
    centuries was confined solely to fiction. This collection of essays challenges these
    assumptions, exploring the rich and varied gothic literary production of a large,
    multicultural selection of authors working across the genres in eighteenth- and
    nineteenth-century Ireland"—Provided by publisher.
    ISBN 978–1–137–36664–1 (hardback)
    1. English fiction—Irish authors—History and criticism.   2. Gothic fiction (Literary
    genre), English—Ireland—History and criticism.   3. Literature and psychology.
    I. Morin, Christina, editor of compilation.   II. Gillespie, Niall, editor of compilation.
    PR8807.G67I75 2014
    823'.087290989162—dc23   2014018637

Contents

List of Illustrations

Acknowledgments

This book had its origins in discussions and ideas emanating from the 2011 International Gothic Association conference held at the University of Heidelberg. We wish to thank the organizers and participants of that conference for providing a truly stimulating and productive scholarly environment. We are also extremely grateful for the financial assistance of the Irish Research Council for the Humanities and Social Sciences (IRCHSS; now simply the Irish Research Council), a postdoctoral research fellowship from which was awarded to Christina Morin in 2010. It was under the auspices of this fellowship, held at Trinity College Dublin from 2010–12, that this collection was begun.

Christina Morin and Niall Gillespie
September 2013

Notes on the Contributors

Luke Gibbons is Professor of Irish Literary and Cultural Studies at the School of English, Drama and Media Studies, National University of Ireland, Maynooth. He formerly taught at the University of Notre Dame, USA, and Dublin City University. He has published widely on Irish culture, film, literature, and the visual arts, as well as on aesthetics and politics. His publications include *Gaelic Gothic: Race, Colonialism and Irish Culture* (2004), *Edmund Burke and Ireland: Aesthetics, Politics and the Colonial Sublime* (2003), *The Quiet Man* (2002), *Transformations in Irish Culture* (1996), and, with Kevin Rockett and John Hill, *Cinema and Ireland* (1988). He was a contributing editor to *The Field Day Anthology of Irish Writing* (ed. Seamus Deane, 1991) and is co-editor of *Re-inventing Ireland: Culture, Society and the Global Economy* (with Peadar Kirby and Michael Cronin, 2002), and 'The Theatre of Irish Cinema' (with Dudley Andrew), a special issue of *The Yale Journal of Criticism* (2002). His research interests include film, modernism, romanticism, aesthetics, visual culture, critical theory, and cultural history, particularly as they bear on developments in Irish culture.

Niall Gillespie completed his PhD on the imaginative literature of the Irish Jacobins at Trinity College Dublin in 2013. His teaching interests center on the late Enlightenment, with a particular emphasis on the Irish Revolution Controversy and Irish Romanticism. He is currently working on a monograph on Irish Radical Literature from the Fall of the Bastille to the Reform Act.

Richard Haslam is Associate Professor of English at Saint Joseph's University, Philadelphia. His explorations of Irish Gothic have been published in *Éire-Ireland* (Fall/Winter 2006), *The Irish Journal of Gothic and Horror Studies* (March 2007), and *The Routledge Companion to Gothic* (2007).

Diane Long Hoeveler is Professor of English at Marquette University, Milwaukee, Wisconsin. She is author of *Gothic Riffs: Secularizing* *the Uncanny in the European Imaginary, 1780–1820* (2010), which won the Alan Lloyd Smith memorial award from the International Gothic Association, *Gothic Feminism* (1998), and *Romantic Androgyny* (1990). In addition to publishing some 65 articles on a variety of literary topics, she coauthored a critical study of Charlotte Brontë, and edited the Houghton Mifflin volume of *Wuthering Heights*. Her 13 co-edited volumes of essays include *The Blackwell Encyclopedia of British Romanticism* (3 vols); *Approaches to Teaching* Jane Eyre; *Approaches to Teaching the Gothic* (both for the MLA); *Interrogating Orientalism; Comparative Romanticisms; Romanticism and its other Discourses; Romantic Drama; Romanticism and the Law; Women of Color; Women's Literary Creativity and the Female Body; The Historical Dictionary of Feminism*.

Jarlath Killeen is the author of *The Faiths of Oscar Wilde* (2005), *Gothic Ireland* (2005), *The Fairy Tales of Oscar Wilde* (2007), and *Gothic Literature, 1825–1914* (2009). He lectures in the School of English at Trinity College Dublin, where his teaching focuses on the areas of Children's Literature and Gothic Literature. Dr Killeen's primary research interest lies in the literature and culture of Victorian Ireland and England.

W. J. Mc Cormack is the author of *Sheridan Le Fanu and Victorian Ireland* (1980), and editor of Le Fanu's *Uncle Silas*. He has published biographies of J. M. Synge (2000) and W. B. Yeats (2005).

Anne Markey teaches in the School of English, Trinity College Dublin. Her research focuses on intersections between Gaelic traditions and Irish writing in English, and on the representation of childhood in a variety of texts from the seventeenth century to the present day. She is editor of *Patrick Pearse: Short Stories* (2009), *Children's Fiction 1765–1808* (2011); co-editor of *Vertue Rewarded; or, The Irish Princess* (2010) and *Irish Tales* (2010); and author of *Oscar Wilde's Fairy Tales: Origins and Contexts* (2011).

Christina Morin is Lecturer in English Literature at the University of Limerick. She is the author of *Charles Robert Maturin and the Haunting of Irish Romantic Fiction* (2011) and is currently at work on a monograph titled *The Gothic Novel in Ireland, 1760–1830*.

Jim Shanahan lectures in English literature at St Patrick's College, Drumcondra, Dublin. He has a particular interest in fiction written about the 1798 rebellion. Amongst his previous publications is an essay in *Ireland and Romanticism*, published by Palgrave in 2011.

Elizabeth Tilley is Lecturer in the English Department at NUI Galway. She publishes on nineteenth-century Irish periodicals and is Associate Editor and contributor to the *Dictionary of Nineteenth-Century Journalism* (2010).

Introduction: De-Limiting the Irish Gothic

Christina Morin and Niall Gillespie

The essays collected in this volume present a variety of new perspectives on an area of Irish literary production that has received much scholarly attention in recent years – 'the Irish Gothic'. The inverted commas that so naturally seem to envelop this term suggest its contested nature. Variously described as a 'canon', 'tradition', 'genre', 'form', 'mode', and 'register', Irish gothic literature suffers from a fundamental terminological confusion, and the debate over exactly which term best applies has been both heated and, ultimately, inconclusive in the past 30 years. Richard Haslam – a contributor to the present volume – has ably traced the history of the term 'Irish Gothic', pointing out the ways in which, from the term's introduction in the 1980s, literary scholars have struggled to find 'an adequate critical language' with which to discuss a body of literature that seems so resolutely to resist definition and categorization.[1] The dominant theorization of Irish gothic literature to emerge in late twentieth- and early twenty-first-century scholarship has been driven by psychoanalytic readings of the literary gothic in Ireland as the fictional representation of the repressed fears and anxieties of the minority Anglo-Irish population. In other words, what underwrites Irish gothic literature of the eighteenth, nineteenth, and early twentieth centuries is a mixed 'fear and desire' expressive of what Julian Moynahan calls the 'ineluctably haunted' nature of the 'Anglo-Irish literary imagination'.[2]

Such readings have been offered by Margot Gayle Backus, William Patrick Day, Roy Foster, and Vera Kreilkamp, amongst many others.[3] And, while not all of these scholars have engaged directly with the thorny issue of terminology, their assessments of 'the Irish Gothic' mutually, if implicitly, support the idea of a literary tradition, passed from generation to generation of Anglo-Irish writers and traceable from

Regina Maria Roche's *The Children of the Abbey* (1796) and Charles Maturin's *Melmoth the Wanderer* (1820) through to Sheridan Le Fanu's *Uncle Silas* (1864) and Bram Stoker's *Dracula* (1897). If, in this roll call of names and titles, 'tradition' seems to shade into 'canon', it is because attempts to define 'the Irish Gothic' as peculiarly Protestant in nature all too easily fall prey to accusations of canonization, as was the case with *The Field Day Anthology*'s section on 'Irish Gothic and After'. Edited by another contributor to this volume – W. J. Mc Cormack – 'Irish Gothic and After' represents a seminal piece of scholarship on the literary gothic in Ireland, but, as another of our contributors has pointed out, its 'list of writers looked to some to be a ready-made Irish canon'.[4] Mc Cormack was, in fact, and continues to be, driven by a scepticism about the very idea of an Irish gothic 'tradition', and his recovery, in 'Irish Gothic and After', of little-known works such as Mrs F. C. Patrick's *The Irish Heiress* (1797) and *More Ghosts!* (1798) gestured towards the wonderful richness and expansiveness of the literary gothic in Ireland, as highlighted in later years by the work of Rolf and Magda Loeber.[5] Nevertheless, his selection of titles and authors seemed, to critics of the Field Day project at large, the result of a process of canonization.

In answer to the problematics of both 'tradition' and 'canon', Haslam and Siobhán Kilfeather, amongst others, have explored the possibilities afforded by terms such as 'mode' and 'register'. Employing Aristotelian categories as he does in the essay included in this volume, for instance, Haslam plainly states that 'Irish Gothic is more conceptually plausible when envisioned as a mode rather than tradition'.[6] Kilfeather, in turn, powerfully suggests that the literature produced in post-1798 Ireland was a literature of terror that mobilized the tropes made familiar in popular contemporary fictions such as Ann Radcliffe's *The Mysteries of Udolpho* (1794) and Matthew Lewis's *The Monk* (1796) in order to 'describ[e], enumerat[e], and commemorat[e] [the] acts of atrocity' recently witnessed by the Irish people.[7] Repeatedly and insistently merging 'the irreducible realities of facts and figures with the powerful unreality of poetic language', post-1798 Irish literature attests to the ways in which all forms and genres of writing became gothicized precisely because the language of the literary gothic allowed writers to register atrocity, in the sense both of enumerating or recording actual acts of atrocity and of 'record[ing] or 'becom[ing] aware of' the effects of those atrocities on Irish reality.[8] For Kilfeather, then, Irish literature across the genres in the late eighteenth and early nineteenth centuries is fundamentally gothic in nature. Jarlath Killeen makes a similar point about the universality of a gothic 'mode' or 'register' in eighteenth- and nineteenth-century Irish literature, arguing that, since characteristic gothic themes and tropes seem to manifest themselves in most modern Irish literature, 'the Irish Gothic is a canon, a tradition and a mode all at once'.[9]

Lest this troublesome terminology start to take on a peculiarly Irish emphasis, it is worth noting that the dispute over the genealogy, authorship, and makeup of Irish gothic literature finds its parallel in larger discussions about the literary gothic as a whole. Indeed, the brackets surrounding 'the Irish Gothic' are equally germane to 'the Gothic' and 'the Gothic novel'. As David Punter notes, 'what constitutes Gothic writing is a contested site',[10] even if, as Punter elsewhere writes, gothic literature seems, at first glance at least, to be immediately recognizable.[11] What makes gothic so familiar and therefore so easily identified? For Robert Miles, it is the 'plots, motifs and figures [that are] endlessly recycled' in text after text. The literary gothic, Miles suggests, relies on tried and tested thematic and narratological stratagems, never daring to move outside the parameters established by early practitioners such as Horace Walpole (1717–97), Ann Radcliffe (1764–1823), and Matthew Lewis (1775–1818): 'A strain of the novel', Miles contends, 'the Gothic emerged in the mid-eighteenth century and since then has hardly changed'.[12] Our expectations for gothic literature are, therefore, relatively simply stated. A 'gothic' text combines, among other things, supernatural figures and events with medieval Catholic Continental settings, an interest in the Burkean sublime, and a beleaguered heroine seeking release from the imprisonment – physical and otherwise – of a depraved and tyrannical male family member.

If, however, as Punter maintains (and Miles suggests with his wry tone), the literary gothic initially seems 'to be a relatively homogenous body of writing, linked stylistically, thematically and ideologically [. . .] closer inspection [shows] the illusion fall[ing] away, revealing a very disparate collection of works'.[13] This is so not just because of variations introduced by what are sometimes understood as different 'schools' of gothic writing – male/female, terror/horror, explained/unexplained supernatural – but also by the gothic's tendency to infiltrate all genres of literary production. It has generally been accepted that the literary gothic that began to develop in the latter half of the eighteenth century drew inspiration from a wide variety of genres, texts, and traditions. Devendra Varma, for instance, early noted the omnivorous origins of the literary gothic in 'the supernatural realm of the ballad, and all that was mysterious and eerie in epic and the drama', as well as '[t]he traditional lore of old, heathen Europe, the richness and splendor of its mythology and superstitions, its usages, rites, and songs'.[14] Yet, for Varma and other pioneering scholars of gothic literature, the wide-ranging beginnings of the gothic combined to create a single entity: 'the Gothic novel'. The underlining assumption that the literary gothic is primarily fictional in nature, 'a strain of the novel' as Miles puts it, is suggested by scholarly works such as Montague Summers' *The Gothic Quest: a History of the Gothic Novel* (1938), Punter's *The Literature of Terror: a History of Gothic Fictions from 1765 to the Present Day* (1980; repr. 1996), Frederick Frank's *The First Gothics: a Critical Guide to the English Gothic Novel* (1987), Maggie Kilgour's *The Rise of the Gothic Novel* (1995), and Emma Clery's *The Rise of Supernatural Fiction, 1762–1800* (1999), among many others.

Against this privileging of the novel, Anne Williams persuasively contends that early gothicists routinely worked across literary genres, producing poetry, drama, and short stories in addition to the novels for which they are now principally known.[15] Matthew Lewis, for instance, wrote several dramas that rely on the same themes and tropes popularized in his more familiar novel, *The Monk*, including *The Castle Spectre* (1797) and *Adelmorn the Outlaw* (1801). The same is true of Horace Walpole and Charles Robert Maturin, both of whom wrote gothic dramas that have tended to fall by the wayside in consideration of *Otranto* and *Melmoth the Wanderer*, and both of whom routinely translated the spectacle of drama into their fiction. Emma McEvoy contends, for instance, that *The Castle of Otranto* is 'notable for its use of a very theatrical mode of display and soliloquy rather than internal cogitation'.[16] Maturin's fictional *oeuvre* similarly displays a keen awareness of theatre, performance, and spectacle, featuring several actress-heroines as well as a tendency to vivid – his critics might say histrionic – language and effect that effectively shrinks the distance between drama and prose. Tellingly, Walter Scott's review of Maturin's fourth novel, *Women; or Pour et Contre* (1818), praised the novel largely by reference to and publication of several occluded scenes from Maturin's earlier tragedy, *Bertram; or, the Castle of St. Aldobrand* (1816), the name of which was also used to identify the author on the novel's title page.[17]

Scott's intent may have been to applaud the 'moral' nature of *Women*, produced by Maturin's toning down of the 'supernatural horrors' on which he was wont to rely, but his inclusion of the scenes omitted from *Bertram* on his own advice both undermines Scott's disregard for these 'horrors' and collapses the distance between drama and prose. More than that, Scott's repeated praise of Maturin's writing style – both prosaic and dramatic – as 'poetical' forcefully underlines the fundamental hybridity of genres in the Romantic period.[18] Indeed, Maturin's fiction, like that of his contemporaries, was very often described as 'poetical', not least because it reflected its author's parallel poetic output but also because it was itself fundamentally imbued with poetry, featuring poetic epigraphs and excerpts of poetry, original and otherwise, scattered throughout its pages. Such insertions may represent nuanced attempts on the part of Maturin and other gothicists such as Radcliffe, Lewis, Charlotte Smith (1749–1806), and Mary Robinson (1756/8?–1800) to masculinize and/or legitimize the novel in an atmosphere of continued critical contempt for it and its practitioners,[19] but they also validate Williams's contention that 'Gothic prose of the 1790s is [...] disturbingly "poetic"'.[20] What is so disturbing about these works and their fusion of prose and poetry is, as Williams maintains, their problematization of any neat conceptualization of gothic fiction as a debased form of Romantic literary production that bears no real resemblance to contemporary poetry.[21] Instead, as is the case with drama and fiction, poetry and fiction frequently merge in the production of the literary gothic in the late eighteenth and early nineteenth centuries.

That the essentially hybrid nature of the literary gothic was clearly understood by contemporary readers and writers – if less so by more modern scholars – is evident from Alicia Le Fanu's 1816 novel, *Strathallan*, which refers to a list of 'modern Horrors' striking in its transgeneric nature. Gathered around the fireside engaged in charitable works, Le Fanu's various female characters amuse themselves with recitations from

> Lenora, Donica, the Grim White Woman, the Little Grey Man, the second book of the Last Minstrel, the Eve of St. John, the Haunted Beach, selections from Otranto, Udolpho, Montorio, whatever was calculated to inspire, on the timid or imaginative, the deep, nameless feeling of terror, unfounded, undefined.[22]

Featuring a mixture of drama, poetry, short fiction, and novels, *Strathallan*'s list speaks compellingly to the multi-generic nature of gothic literary production in this period and invites us to revisit some of the restrictions inherent to thinking about gothic literature in Ireland and elsewhere by way of exclusive terms such as 'tradition', 'canon', 'genre', and even 'form', 'mode', or 'register'.

* * *

At its heart, this collection is about such rethinking and revisiting. Rather than offer further definitions and delimitations of 'the Irish Gothic' and, indeed, 'the Gothic novel' or 'the Gothic' more widely, it proposes instead a de-limitation of gothic literary production in Ireland over the course of the eighteenth and nineteenth centuries. In other words, each of the essays gathered here opens up the study of Irish gothic literature by pushing the terminological limits imposed by restrictive notions of traditions, canons, genres, and even modes, registers, forms, and styles. Excavating the works of a diverse group of eighteenth- and nineteenth-century Irish authors, this collection contests the omission of such texts from current scholarly consideration of the literary gothic, bringing powerfully into focus the multi-generic, cross-sectarian nature of Irish gothic literature. In this, it seeks to produce what Williams calls '[a] thoughtful analysis of "Gothic"' by 'challeng[ing] the kind of literary history that organizes, delineates, and defines: a literary history that also confines us within some inherited literary concepts, particularly ideas about genre, that can be as confusing as Udolpho's amazing structures'.[23] Instead, each of the essays that follow reaches for new, more nuanced perceptions of the literary gothic by celebrating, rather than decrying, multiplicity. While there may be, as Punter points out, 'many uncertainties' about exactly what constitutes 'the Gothic' in Ireland and elsewhere, these essays adopt Punter's further contention that it is perfectly plausible 'to view this uncertainty about the field of Gothic writing as, if not exactly a virtue, at least a significant resistance to canonisation'.[24] In fact, this collection begins with what Suzanne Rintoul calls the '[scholarly] inability to define the Gothic' and proceeds, as she suggests gothic criticism should, '[to use] this inability to arrive at a number of workable modes of interpretation'.[25] Hence our pluralized title, 'Irish Gothics', as well as the decision not to impose a collection-wide policy on capitalization or terminology when referring to the literary gothic: this collection is about *interpretations*, rather than interpretation, of the literary gothic in Ireland.[26]

Accordingly, the authorial opinions in this collection often diverge as much as they meet. Christina Morin begins the collection by interrogating the supposed confessional nature of Irish gothic literature. In line with recent nuanced scholarship, Christina Morin argues against the exclusivist notion of Irish gothic literature as the spectral imagination of Protestant Ascendancy fears. Rather, she posits, the literary gothic readily accommodated itself to, and appealed to, the constituents of often antithetical bodies – be they organized along the lines of class, gender or religious allegiances. Morin argues the case for the gothic as a felt numinous register, one that chose genre according to taste, moment, or perceived audience. Drawing attention to Mary Delany's short tale 'Marianna' (first drafted 1759), Thomas Leland's *Longsword* (1762), and Elizabeth Griffith's *Amana* (1764), Morin seeks to dispel the notion of Irish gothic literature as an offshoot of the eighteenth-century novel tradition. Instead, she argues, it arose concurrently with, if not antecedent to, Horace Walpole's purportedly foundational text, *The Castle of Otranto* (1764), and was both multi-generic and multicultural in nature.

Diane Long Hoeveler continues Morin's probing of the importance of Protestant confessionalism in Irish gothic literature, examining one of the most critically accepted practices of Irish gothic literature – its use as a vehicle for the dissemination of anti-Catholic polemic. Focusing on the Methodist Dublin printer Bennett Dugdale (d. 1826), Hoeveler demonstrates the interesting ways in which certain actors within the Dublin literary marketplace treated those gothic narratives produced primarily for the lower end of the English market. In the simple act of importing these narratives into Ireland, Dugdale and printers like him changed these texts significantly. From being literary artefacts consumed in an often passive manner in a predominantly Protestant country, these chapbooks, in crossing the Irish Sea, became part of the vicious confessional debates that scarred Ireland in the post-Union period. The literary gothic in Ireland, Hoeveler intimates, rather than being an entertaining or reflective mirror, was often an explosive object thrown for deliberate effect into the heavily politicized public sphere.

In various ways, Niall Gillespie's piece both valorizes Hoeveler's notion of the literary gothic as a potent political weapon and illustrates Morin's thesis – that gothic written by Irish political radicals in the post-Bastille era eschews the privileging of one genre in favour of a multi-generic approach. This occurred not because of an overdeveloped aesthetic sensibility, but rather out of necessity. The contingencies of the times often determined what genre would best facilitate political propagandizing. Likewise, the Irish Jacobins did not employ the gothic to call up the unreal, but rather they turned to the gothic as it best allowed them to describe the very real actualities of the period.

If a collective traumatic event can indelibly mark a nation's literature for successive generations, then the defeat of the democratic idealism intrinsic to the 1798 rising undoubtedly cast a long pall over the cultures of the Presbyterian, Episcopalian, and Catholic communities. In the immediate aftermath of reaction's victory, much of the imaginative literature produced in Ireland (both gothic and otherwise) was directed at explaining, rationalizing, celebrating, or lamenting insurrection's failure. Jim Shanahan's incisive essay shows the degree to which the gothic suggested itself very naturally to a variety of authors operating independently of each other and possessing very different political creeds. The literary gothic seemed eminently suited to relating the very recent violent history that was being narrativized (and marketed) within a remarkably short period after the rebellion. As with Gillespie, Shanahan believes the literary gothic to be a heightened form of Irish realism but points out, too, the problem with this crossover of fiction and reality – the gothicized portrayal of a perceived historical truth often seems to negate its own veracity.

This question of truthfulness is picked up by Anne Markey as well. Focusing on an anonymously published collection of supposed Irish folk stories, *Tales of the Emerald Isle* (1828), Markey details the ways in which pre-Famine nineteenth-century writers frequently presented their material as not unduly sullied by authorial invention. In purporting to be based on authentic folkloric tales, the author of the *Emerald Isle* presented a gothicized version of Irish history that sought to paper over the explosive contradictions that left Ireland deeply unsettled in the post-Union period. In this sense, the literary gothic is used not to terrorize the reader, but rather to reassure them that the Irish population was, despite obvious appearances, fundamentally happy with the paternalistic leadership of a deeply sectarian Irish polity.

Richard Haslam returns us to the paternal by arguing for Charles Maturin as the origin point of the Faustian pact within Irish gothic literature. In spite of Maturin's apparently deep hostility to Catholicism, his most prominent heirs include those of a creed never accustomed to sitting in his pews. It is undoubtedly an irony that Maturin may not have appreciated, but in the gothic tale, heirs often turn out rather differently to their dead progenitors, and Haslam richly illustrates the need to rethink current criticism's emphasis on Protestant confessionalism as the root of the literary gothic in nineteenth-century Ireland.

Elizabeth Tilley considers Sheridan Le Fanu as both editor of, and contributor to, the *Dublin University Magazine* (*DUM*) in the year 1864. She suggests that Le Fanu, anxious to keep the periodical financially afloat, was equally nervous to ensure that his own fiction was seen in the tradition of Walter Scott, rather than being thought of as the offspring of the sensationalist novels that then dominated the popular market. This tension between the editor, author, and perceived readership inflected Le Fanu's concept of what the literary gothic should be. If, however, asserting a firm morality within the boundaries of well-written fiction was a formula Le Fanu glorified, it was one to which he did not always consciously conform, as is made clear by the sometimes contradictory takes on popular fiction produced in the essays, fiction, and poetry published in the *DUM* in 1864.

W. J. Mc Cormack follows Tilley's assessment of the hesitancy towards questions of literary genre evident in the *DUM* with an innovative annotation of the fourth chapter of Le Fanu's *The House by the Churchyard* (first serialized 1861). Arguing that, in writing *The House by the Churchyard*, Le Fanu embedded his text with a species, if not a style, of cryptic annotation, Mc Cormack explores the ways in which 'gothic' and 'historical' fiction merge as Le Fanu simultaneously exposes, and attempts to exorcize, those ghosts that frustrated the Protestant Ascendancy's doomed attempt to consolidate their declining cultural and political power in the mid-to-late nineteenth century. From Mc Cormack's astute analysis and annotation, it is clear that Le Fanu not only recognized the violent origins of his ancestors' power but also ruefully acknowledged the continuing impact upon Irish politics of the French Revolution, which had just vigorously renewed itself in the foundation of the Irish Republican Brotherhood (IRB) in 1858.

This radical new politics finds itself echoing through Bram Stoker. Jarlath Killeen presents us with that side of Stoker often ignored – Stoker the Home Ruler, Stoker the promoter of the Gaelic Athletic Association (GAA), and Stoker the devotee of Michael Davitt, the IRB organizer and Land League leader. In his reading of Stoker's novel, *The Snake's Pass* (1890), Killeen shows that in their search for the lost gold of the French republican army that had aided the Irish democrats in 1798, the characters of the novel regenerate themselves physically, and (what was analogous for Stoker) morally. The literary gothic, in Stoker's mind, presents an ideal forum in which to discuss the regressive impediments to modernity in Ireland by way of a contrast between a monstrous and atavistic past represented by weak and effeminate male characters, on the one hand, and, on the other, a glorious future of Irish national influence and power manifested in the strength and vigor of athletic 'muscle men'.

Luke Gibbons closes this collection by focusing, like Killeen, on an often overlooked dimension to Stoker – the novelist as both devotee of Abraham Lincoln and apologist for racial supremacist views and genocidal imperialist expansion. Beginning with Stoker's description in *The Mystery of the Sea* (1902) of a vista of races condemned by social Darwinism to extinction, Gibbons explores the ideas of progress, evolution, and 'Manifest Destiny' in several of Stoker's less well-known novels, including *The Snake's Pass* and *The Shoulder of Shasta* (1895). In so doing, Gibbons documents the mixed fascination and angst with which Stoker celebrated the triumph of inexorable capitalist development in the face of gothic recidivism (racial, social, and economic).

*   *   *

While it would be wrong to perceive too much common agreement as to what constitutes Irish gothic literature in this collection, it would be disingenuous to amplify the differences artificially. What all of the essays in this edition demonstrate is a distinct awareness of the need to problematize notions pertaining to the limits that can reasonably be imposed when identifying and describing the literary gothic in eighteenth- and nineteenth-century Ireland. Such nuance ought ultimately to lead to greater clarity rather than confusion. In this regard, this book of essays seeks to further the recent trend that foregrounds the complexity of Irish gothic literature and to lay the groundwork for future research in this area. This can be done by taking into greater account the literary gothic as it manifested in poetry and drama, not just novelistically. Likewise, an account of the contribution made by 'minor' writers (who often had large contemporary audiences) deserves further attention. Canonical authors, too, need to be re-evaluated. Stoker's lesser-known works, for instance, merit more minute scrutiny, as suggested by the rich essays by Killeen and Gibbons published here. Similarly, Le Fanu's more familiar texts necessitate detailed glossing (as Mc Cormack does in his essay), and a greater acknowledgment of the role played by marketplace choices (in terms of production, medium, audience, and anticipated reception), which Tilley's contribution accomplishes admirably.

Like many a gothic narrative, this book leaves much unanswered. What is 'Irish Gothic'? Is there even such a thing? If so, is it determined by nationality, by blood, by environment? Is it a genre, a tradition, a mode, or all three intersecting variously? Is it, as Terry Eagleton has posited, intrinsically bound up with the political economy of underdevelopment?[27] Is it a displaced form of societal interrogation, the only true way of explaining and attempting to address Ireland's colonial condition? Does the European gothic have an Irish origin point in Leland's *Longsword*, or in Edmund Burke's metaphysical concept of the sublime?[28] Did Burke's *Reflections on the Revolution in France* (1790), as Clive Bloom states, redirect the transatlantic gothic into a more serious (and more conservative) channel?[29] What differentiates Irish Gothic from its Scottish counterpart? Is the Irish Gothic predominately a literature of morality or one that riotously enjoys the tale it tells? The editors hope that these essays, in highlighting some of the many possible answers to these questions, will help to produce new clarity precisely by way of embracing multiplicity.

Notes

1. Richard Haslam (2007) 'Irish Gothic', in *The Routledge Companion to Gothic*, eds Catherine Spooner and Emma McEvoy (London: Routledge), pp. 83–94 (p. 86).
2. We are borrowing the term 'fear and desire' from the title of William Patrick Day's 1985 study, *In the Circles of Fear and Desire* (Chicago: University of Chicago Press); Julian Moynahan (1995) *Anglo-Irish: the Literary Imagination in a Hyphenated Culture* (Princeton, NJ: Princeton University Press), p. 116.
3. See Margot Gayle Backus (1999) *The Gothic Family Romance* (Durham, NC: Duke University Press); Day, *In the Circles of Fear and Desire*; Roy Foster (1995) *Paddy and Mr Punch: Connections in Irish and English History* (London: Penguin); Moynahan, *Anglo-Irish*; and Roy Foster (2011) *Words Alone: Yeats and his Inheritances* (Oxford: Oxford University Press).
4. Jarlath Killeen (2006) 'Irish Gothic: a Theoretical Introduction', *The Irish Journal of Gothic and Horror Studies* 1, 1–10 (p. 1). As there are no page numbers in the online edition, we have used those that appear when the article is printed.
5. See, for instance, Rolf Loeber and Magda Stouthamer-Loeber (2003) 'The Publication of Irish Novels and Novelettes, 1750–1829: a Footnote on Irish Gothic Fiction', *Cardiff Corvey: Reading the Romantic Text* 10, n.p. Available online from <http://www.cardiff.ac.uk/encap/journals/corvey/articles/cc10_m02.html>; and Rolf and Magda Loeber (2006) *A Guide to Irish Fiction, 1650–1900* (Dublin: Four Courts Press).
6. Haslam, 'Irish Gothic', p. 89.
7. Siobhán Kilfeather (2004) 'Terrific Register: the Gothicization of Atrocity in Irish Romanticism', *boundary 2* 31.1, 49–71 (p. 71).
8. Kilfeather, 'Terrific Register', p. 71; 'register, v.', *OED Online*, June 2013. Available from <http://www.oed.com>. Accessed 23 August 2013.
9. Jarlath Killeen (2008) 'Irish Gothic', *The Literary Encyclopedia*. Available online from <http://www.litencyc.com>. Accessed 1 August 2013. Elsewhere, Killeen contends that it is still possible to see 'a version of a tradition' in Irish gothic literature, though he also outlines this tradition as comprising 'certain Irish writers [who] pursued similar questions that were historically specific to the Irish situation [...] utilis[ing] the Gothic *mode*'; Killeen, 'Irish Gothic: a Theoretical Introduction', p. 2. Emphasis ours.
10. David Punter (2000; 2001) 'Introduction: *The Ghost of a History*', in *A Companion to the Gothic*, ed. David Punter (Oxford: Blackwell), pp. viii–xiv (p. viii).
11. David Punter (1996) *The Literature of Terror*, 2 vols (2nd ed.; London: Longman Group), 1: 1.
12. Robert Miles (1993) *Gothic Writing 1750–1820: a Genealogy* (London: Routledge), p. 1.
13. Punter, *The Literature of Terror*, 1:7.

14. Devendra Varma (1957; 1987) *The Gothic Flame* (London: Scarecrow Press), pp. 24–5.
15. See Anne Williams (1995) *Art of Darkness: a Poetics of Gothic* (Chicago: The University of Chicago Press).
16. Emma McEvoy (2007) 'Contemporary Gothic Theatre', in *The Routledge Companion to Gothic*, eds Catherine Spooner and Emma McEvoy (London and New York: Routledge), pp. 214–22 (p. 214).
17. See Sir Walter Scott (1818) 'Rev. of *Women; or Pour et Contre*, by Charles Robert Maturin', *Edinburgh Review* 30.59, 234–57.
18. Scott, 'Rev. of *Women; or Pour et Contre*', 253, 254.
19. On this, see, for example, Christina Morin (2011) *Charles Robert Maturin and the Haunting of Irish Romantic Fiction* (Manchester: Manchester University Press), pp. 33–57 and Anna Wierda Rowland (2008) 'Romantic Poetry and the Romantic Novel', in *The Cambridge Companion to British Romantic Poetry*, eds James Chandler and Maureen N. McLane (Cambridge: Cambridge University Press), pp.117–35.
20. Williams, *Art of Darkness*, p. 4.
21. Ibid.
22. Alicia Le Fanu (1816; 2008) *Strathallan*, ed. Anna M. Fitzer (London: Pickering and Chatto), p. 66. Fitzer names the works referenced here as Gottfried August Bürger's 'Leonora' (1774), Robert Southey's 'Donica' (1797), Matthew Lewis's 'The Grim White Woman' (1800), Walter Scott's 'The Eve of St. John' (1800) and 'The Lay of the Last Minstrel' (1805), Mary Robinson's 'The Haunted Beach' (1806), Walpole's *The Castle of Otranto*, Radcliffe's *The Mysteries of Udolpho*, and Charles Robert Maturin's *The Fatal Revenge; or, the Family of Montorio* (1807); see Le Fanu, *Strathallan*, p. 498, n. 61.
23. Williams, *Art of Darkness*, p. 13.
24. Punter, 'Introduction: *The Ghost of a History*', p. ix.
25. Suzanne Rintoul (2005) 'Gothic Anxieties: Struggling with a Definition', *Eighteenth-Century Fiction* 17.4, 701–9 (p. 709).
26. In this introduction, we have chosen to use as much as possible the un-capitalized and (largely) undetermined forms of 'gothic', 'Irish gothic literature', and 'the literary gothic' in order to break down the borders erected by terminological determinates.
27. Terry Eagleton (1995) *Heathcliff and the Great Hunger: Studies in Irish Culture* (London: Verso), pp. 124–5.
28. For the identification of the former two novels as pre-*Otranto* gothic novels, see Loeber and Stouthamer-Loeber, 'The Publication of Irish Novels and Novelettes'.
29. Clive Bloom (2010) *Gothic Histories: the Taste for Terror, 1764 to the Present* (London: Continuum), p. 78.

1
Theorizing 'Gothic' in Eighteenth-Century Ireland

Christina Morin

I perceive you have no idea what Gothic is.[1]

Irish gothic literature has inspired widespread interest and heated debate in recent years. Much of the scholarly work devoted to the subject has focused primarily on two questions: is there such a thing as an Irish gothic 'tradition', and, if so, what are its fundamental characteristics? The conventional answer has been that, if a unique Irish gothic literary tradition does, in fact, exist, it was produced by Anglo-Irish writers concerned with confronting the anxieties induced by their minority position in Ireland. What ties such disparate authors as Regina Maria Roche (c. 1764–1845), Maria Edgeworth (1768–1849), Charles Maturin (1780–1824), Sydney Owenson (c. 1783–1859), Joseph Sheridan Le Fanu (1814–73), Bram Stoker (1847–1912), and Oscar Wilde (1854–1900) together, it is argued, is their shared Protestant confessionalism and an attendant interest in 'the burden of colonial history', which expresses itself in their works via gothic themes, settings, and motifs.[2] As Roy Foster has influentially argued, Irish gothic writers of the eighteenth and nineteenth centuries were motivated by fears surrounding their privileged position as members of the Anglo-Irish Ascendancy. Their 'occult preoccupations', Foster contends, 'mirror a sense of displacement, a loss of social and psychological integration, and an escapism motivated by the threat of a takeover by the Catholic middle classes'.[3] Vera Kreilkamp similarly maintains that nineteenth-century Anglo-Irish writers harnessed the conventions of the gothic novel that had developed across Britain and Europe in the latter half of the eighteenth and the beginning of the nineteenth centuries in order to express 'the reality of Anglo-Irish conditions' in the period following Anglo-Irish Union (1801), when the Ascendancy was increasingly under threat by a growing Catholic middle class and an ongoing campaign for Catholic Emancipation.[4]

Recent scholarship, however, has begun to question the prevailing assumptions that have shaped our understanding of Irish gothic literature. Is it, in other words, an exclusively Protestant form that emerged in an atmosphere of continued angst over a process of marginalization inaugurated by the political disenfranchisement of Ireland's Protestant parliament and exacerbated by a new Catholic social mobility? Answering resoundingly in the negative, Claire Connolly persuasively images the use of the gothic mode in Ireland in the 1820s as essentially cross-sectarian in nature. Rather than emblematize the anxious expression of Anglo-Irish fears, the gothic is, instead, in Connolly's construction, the domain of Protestants and Catholics alike interested in portraying Ireland as 'a place of densely textured and interlocking communities characterised by richly realised belief systems'.[5] Connolly's contentions extend, in a sense, the skepticism presented by Jarlath Killeen when he urges caution in the understanding of Irish gothic literature as a nineteenth-century Protestant response to the loss of power and status associated with Union and impending Catholic Emancipation. Instead, Killeen observes, 'Irish Gothic has a longer history than the nineteenth century, longer, in other words, than the actual marginalization of Protestant interest in Ireland'.[6] For Killeen, the roots of Irish gothic literature may be traced as far back as the mid-seventeenth century and be seen to encompass a wide variety of prose works by Sir John Temple (1600–77), William Molyneux (1656–98), Jonathan Swift (1667–1745), Edmund Burke (1729/30–97), Roche, and Edgeworth, amongst many others.[7]

Although Killeen's focus remains on Anglo-Irish writers, his location of what he terms 'a pre-Gothic aesthetic' in Ireland in the long eighteenth century prompts us to rethink the ideological basis of later Irish gothic literature.[8] Moreover, his attention to an extensive array of fiction and non-fiction invites a reconsideration of current understandings of the novel as the gothic literary form *par excellence*, though Killeen himself does not tease out the multi-generic nature of Irish gothic literary production. Instead, he suggests that seventeenth- and eighteenth-century works such as Temple's *The Irish Rebellion* (1646), Swift's *A Modest Proposal* (1729), and Burke's *A Philosophical Enquiry into the Origins of our Ideas of the Sublime and Beautiful* (1757), simply laid the groundwork for 'a discernible "Irish gothic" canon' in the later nineteenth century. That this 'canon' is comprised, in Killeen's arguments, solely by novels, including Maturin's *Melmoth the Wanderer* (1820), Le Fanu's *Uncle Silas* (1864), Wilde's *The Picture of Dorian Gray* (1891), and Stoker's *Dracula* (1897), lends apparent credence to the current critical tendency to define the literary gothic as almost wholly novelistic in nature. As Anne Williams rightly observes, 'Out of long habit, the word "Gothic" seems most appropriately followed by the word "novel"'. Robert Miles, for instance, defines 'Gothic' as '[a] strain of the novel', and both David Punter and Jerrold Hogle describe the literary gothic as specifically fictional in nature.[9] Working against this mono-generic notion of the so-called 'Gothic novel', this essay explores the emergence of gothic tropes in a cross-generic selection of often overlooked Irish texts, including Mary Delany's unpublished 1759 short story, 'Marianna', Thomas Leland's only novel, *Longsword, Earl of Salisbury* (1762), and Elizabeth Griffith's *Amana. A Dramatic Poem* (1764). As it does so, it seeks to problematize the notable transition from, in Killeen's formulation, a cross-generic 'aesthetic' to a mono-generic 'tradition' or 'canon' over the course of the eighteenth century, proposing instead an understanding of gothic literary production in Ireland, Britain, and Europe akin to that suggested by Timothy G. Jones when he writes, 'Perhaps the Gothic is something which is done rather than something that simply is [...] My suggestion is that the Gothic is a cultural practice that is almost as institutionalised yet adaptable as activities such as "playing a game of football" or "going to church"'.[10]

Jones's notion of the gothic encourages us to view gothic literary production 'not as a set form, nor as a static accumulation of texts and tropes, but as a historicized practice which is durable yet transposable: a habitus that orchestrates the generation of various texts and variant readings over the course of time'.[11] Such a perception constructs gothic literary production as a specific kind of cultural activity, one that was inherently influenced by changing and evolving temporal and cultural conditions over the course of the eighteenth and nineteenth centuries. Moreover, it enforces the fact that gothic literary production is not now nor ever was restricted to a specific genre, an understanding that is, in any case, misleading, given the intrinsic generic instability of the late eighteenth and early nineteenth centuries.[12] The texts analyzed here highlight the importance of thinking across generic boundaries when considering gothic literary production, showing eighteenth-century Irish gothic practice to be, above all else, the product of a particular mode of thinking about the past that filtered into all aspects of cultural production in eighteenth-century Britain and Ireland. In so doing, these works show the folly of thinking about 'Irish Gothic' as a specific 'tradition' or 'canon' precisely because they point to the ways in which Irish authors shared their cultural perception and, therefore, their practice of the gothic not only with each other, regardless of religious and ideological affinities, but also with their contemporaries in Britain, Europe, and further afield. These works, in other words, gesture towards a cosmopolitan conception of gothic literary production wherein questions of religious background, political affinity, geographical location, and literary genre become subsumed within an overarching cultural practice that fundamentally transcends the normative boundaries usually ascribed to 'Gothic' and 'Irish Gothic' literature.

Gothic, gothic, or Gothick? Exploring eighteenth-century conceptions

Current literary criticism more often than not adheres to the belief that 'the gothic novel' as a unique literary genre came into being in 1764 with the publication of Horace Walpole's *The Castle of Otranto*. It is with this premise that most twentieth- and twenty-first-century discussions of gothic literature begin, with particular attention frequently paid to the apparently pioneering subtitle added to *Otranto*'s second edition – 'A Gothic Story'. Yet, it is worth remembering that this putatively genre-founding subtitle was self-consciously chosen by Walpole not necessarily to underline the generic innovativeness of his text but play-fully to engage with several oftentimes competing notions of the term 'gothic' then in dominance in the British popular imagination. That very few writers in Walpole's wake adopted the terminology 'gothic' to describe their works is indicative of the manner in which contemporary perceptions of the term 'gothic' signified not generic novelty or speci-ficity but a particular manner of viewing and relating to the past. Indeed, for eighteenth-century readers and writers the word 'gothic' was sugges-tive of the chronological and social evolution that had helped produce the modern British nation. Accordingly, throughout the eighteenth cen-tury, 'Gothic' – generally with a capital 'G' – was defined as 'uncouth' or 'barbaric' and was applied to the past as a way of indicating 'a dis-tant, non-specific, period of ignorance and superstition from which an increasingly civilized nation had triumphantly emerged'.[13] At the same time, however, 'Gothic' also assumed a particular, and apparently con-tradictory, significance in the emergence of modern Britain.[14] As Clare O'Halloran observes, recourse to the Gothic past provided one means by which British society could imagine an august political inheritance derived from a rather vague set of Germanic and Teutonic tribes, includ-ing the Anglo-Saxons, who, despite their barbarity, were seen as having given birth to modern British liberty.[15] Reference to Britain's Gothic political origins throughout the eighteenth century thus functioned as a method of critiquing current governmental policies and political trends. The so-called 'noble Gothick Constitution' thereby became a far-removed 'fount of constitutional purity and political virtue from which the nation had become dangerously alienated'.[16]

In a related use of the term, architectural treatises propounded upon the link between architecture and Gothic liberty, endowing the Gothic, or broadly if only vaguely medieval, style with roots in the innate political nobility and virtue of the Gothic past. An instructive example of such symbolism occurs in Henry Fielding's *The History of Tom Jones* (1749), as Barrett Kalter points out. In that novel, Squire Allworthy's estate and, accordingly, the gentleman himself, are described in terms of their positively valued 'Gothick' character: 'The Gothick stile of building could produce nothing nobler than Mr Allworthy's house. There was an air of grandeur in it, that struck you with awe, and rival'd the beauties of the best Grecian architecture; and it was as commodious within, as venerable without'.[17] As with other contemporary uses of the term 'gothic', however, Gothic architecture could also be contrastingly understood as inferior, especially in comparison to the classical style, against which it was linked to 'lawlessness' and 'disorder'.[18] In this schema, the Gothic architectural style was seen to suffer from the innate barbarity of its original, medieval setting in contrast to the civilization that produced its opposite, the classical style. Gothic architecture was therefore condemned in the early eighteenth century as 'Dark, Melancholy and Monkish Piles...Mountains of Stone, Vast and Gygantic...but not Worthy the Name of Architecture'.[19]

At issue in these complementary but also internally contradictory understandings of the term 'gothic' – historical, political, and architectural – was a primal disconnect between past and present. In its signification of barbarity and pre-modernity, 'gothic' pointed to an Enlightenment distancing of the past that was key to eighteenth-century British modernity. Similarly if contradistinctively, in its connotation of the past as the ancient if dangerously far removed seedbed of political virtue and liberty, 'gothic' condemned the present as fatally devolved from its noble roots. These equally temporally minded contemporary understandings of the term 'gothic' poignantly highlight cultural concerns over historical transition in the period, anxieties that feed directly into eighteenth-century literature and tend to corroborate the view of gothic literary practice as, in Siobhán Kilfeather's terms, 'more often than not [...] a response to modernisation, a mode of registering loss and suggesting that new forms of subjectivity are necessary to deal with the new forms of knowledge and power that are conquering past systems and beliefs'.[20] Similarly, Killeen compellingly describes the literary gothic as 'a product of a society that is seeking to heal itself from a terrible wound self-inflicted at the moment of modernity, a period of "the imposition of certainty, the rhetorical summation of the absence, or the loss of doubt" '.[21] As such, gothic literature as a whole is best defined, Killeen suggests, by its indeterminacy:

> In responding to the breach of modernity, the Gothic is a 'construct' rather than a completed genre, an interstitial form in an interstitial period, an 'assemblage' of fragments rather than a totalized unity, a form which points backwards to the old world and forwards to the new, in which the old order has been broken down but a new order has not yet been completely realized.[22]

Killeen's arguments emphatically remind us of the false generic and ideological cohesiveness that retrospective understandings of gothic literature seek to enforce upon a body of work that was, in its essence, embryonic. More than that, they direct us to the competition of past and present, as well as anxieties surrounding modernity, evident in several Irish works which not only predate *Otranto* but which also showcase the gothic as a widespread, multi-generic cultural practice in which fears about modern society and its relationship to the past feature prominently. Traditionally, however, the works discussed here have frequently been understood as different in kind from 'the Gothic novel' supposedly inaugurated by Walpole, primarily, it would seem, because of their immediate generic identifications as short stories, children's literature, historical fiction, and dramatic verse. Nevertheless, their evident interest in and direct engagement with contemporary notions of 'gothic' invite us to consider what Jones identifies as the trap into which gothic criticism very often falls: the anachronistic analysis of eighteenth-century gothic practice by way of twentieth- and twenty-first-century gothic practice.[23] The texts discussed here, in other words, highlight the historically specific but also incredibly variable cultural practice of gothic in eighteenth-century Ireland, positioning it as 'a shared way of understanding and "doing" things' that transcends the normative boundaries of generic identifications, in particular, that of 'the Gothic novel'.[24]

Known today as an artist and famed for her paper mosaics of botanical life, Mary Delany (1700–88) was a widely talented woman 'possessed of a punishing work ethic and a truly fearsome ambition, [who] left

behind an impressive corpus of literary and visual art'.[25] Yet, as Lisa
L. Moore notes, Delany's work remains overlooked today because her
art and writing fall into the categories of 'minor genres associated
with women [...] the letter, the memoir, needlework, ceramics, shell-
work, paper silhouettes, collage, landscape drawing, and the copying
of famous paintings'.[26] The comparatively small amount of Delany's
artistic production that survives today, as Moore observes, is frequently
dismissed as little more than a collection of commodified 'female
accomplishments' intended to help Delany successfully compete in the
contemporary marriage market.[27] Yet, as Moore's analysis suggests, a
closer consideration of Delany's *oeuvre* reveals much about mid- to late-
eighteenth-century cultural life in Ireland and Britain. 'Marianna', a
little-known short story written by Delany in 1759 and revised in 1780,
for instance, attests to Delany's keen awareness of notions of the Gothic
past and its relationship to the present. This is an interest made manifest in Delany's extensive correspondence, where, for example, she
speaks scathingly of her visit to the Windsor home of Lord Bateman
in October 1768. With minute precision, Delany details the house after
its refashioning 'from the Indian to the Gothic' style in critical terms
that echo the negative reception of the second edition of *Otranto*, which
famously revealed that the first edition was not in fact an authentic historical artifact but simply a modern production masquerading as one.[28]
Where the first edition, therefore, was praised as an intriguing relic of
the past able to tell modern readers willing to put up with what the
Monthly Review called 'the absurdities of Gothic fiction' much about the
past, the second was condemned for giving credence to the 'preposterous phenomena [...of] a gross and unenlightened age'.[29] At issue,
as Emma Clery suggests, was Walpole's reproduction of the superstitions and waywardness of a premodern society without an explanatory
apparatus that might highlight the rationality and modernity of the
eighteenth century.[30] Delany clearly regarded Lord Bateman's faux-
Gothic house – 'the old monastery (for such it is to represent)' – in
a similar fashion.[31] Having reproduced the relics of the past, Bateman
had neglected to clarify how that past fit in with the enlightened
present:

> You'll say I am satirical, I don't mean to be so, but I was a little pro-
> voked at his chapel [...] There are many crucifixes in it, ivory figures
> of saints, crowns, and crosses set with sapphire, a little case called the
> treasury filled with rosaries, crosses, and a thousand things relating
> to *ceremonies that I don't understand*.[32]

Not understanding either what was represented in the chapel or Lord Bateman's intent in reproducing these ceremonies – 'I don't suppose he desires to be thought a papist' – Delany condemns Bateman's foray into gothic culture as having muddled the difference between past and present, just as the second, inauthentically Gothic edition of *The Castle of Otranto* did.[33]

Yet, despite Delany's obvious attention to distinguishing true Gothic from false, an action necessary, both she and the reviews of *Otranto* imply, because of the need to distance the enlightened present from a barbaric past, Delany portrays in 'Marianna' a British nation still struggling to escape the bonds of an atavistic past. In the tale, as Mark Laird and Alicia Weisberg-Roberts observe, Delany 'marr[ies] a "gothic tast[e]" to an Italianate setting', picturing her young heroine living in 'a very large Old Gothick building'.[34] Delany thus draws on the contemporary architectural Gothic Revival and anticipates the emphasis on architecture in *Otranto*, but 'Marianna''s engagement with the gothic is never simply architectural. Instead, the tale strikingly displays what Diane Long Hoeveler identifies as *the* defining element of gothic literary practice in the late eighteenth and early nineteenth centuries: an exploration of the oftentimes tenuous relationship between rational and numinous.[35] Anxious about their daughter's future, Marianna's parents, Leontin and Honoria, decide to assuage their fears by consulting Hermilia, a wealthy woman of distinction and learning who is renowned for her powers of 'prediction' (p. 250). Leontin, however, finds himself torn between his superstitious belief in Hermilia's ability to foretell the future and the rational thinking prescribed by his social rank:

> Leontin was a little superstitious in his nature, & something enclined him to favour the common opinion of Hermilia's foresight, which made him wish as well as Honoria, to advise with her. But it required some delicacy, & management to bring about, as they could not possibly address her abruptly, as if she was a fortune-teller. (p. 251)

The conflict between an archaic and anarchic past and the enlightened present/future is further emphasized in the outcome of the eventual encounter between Honoria, her daughter, and Hermilia. After due consideration and observation of Marianna, Hermilia cautions Honoria about her daughter's inclination to disobedience, a trait, Hermilia augurs, that may lead Marianna into significant trouble in future. Hermilia is soon proved the 'Oracle' Honoria thinks her when Marianna disobeys her governess's wishes, loses her way, and is abducted by gypsies (p. 252). Two years later, Marianna is reunited with her parents by chance, only to be abducted once more, this time by pirates. Eventually, she is saved by Bellario, Hermilia's son, and reunited once again with her parents, who gratefully consent to Bellario's marriage proposal. Marianna herself at length agrees, but not without first experiencing severe scruples over her apparent misconduct.

Ultimately, Delany's tale ends on a happy note, informing readers that the couple married and continue to live together in harmony to the present day. The narrative's concluding didactic message is clear: disobedience inevitably brings misery and hardship. Intriguingly, however, there is no denial of the superstitions that had lead Leontin and Honoria to fear Marianna's disobedience in the first place. Where Ann Radcliffe, in later years, would famously and assiduously caution readers against the dangers of excessive sensibility and irrationality, Delany not only refrains from reining in superstition but implicitly gives it force by showing it vindicated. In this, Delany seems to fall into the same representational faults for which she criticized Lord Bateman, suggesting both the fraught and the evolving nature of eighteenth-century gothic practice as a particular cultural mode of negotiating the transition from pre-modernity to modernity.

That Delany's short story is only now beginning to receive attention highlights the ways in which the understanding of her *oeuvre* has been circumscribed by modern views not just of 'the Gothic novel' but also of Delany as a particular kind of female intellectual, one with private rather than public interests.[36] Such thinking has ignored Delany's didactic prose, which also included 'An Essay on Propriety' and 'The History of Miss MacDermot' – pieces which went unpublished in her lifetime but which she wrote for her great-niece in 1777 – as well as her keen interest in the links between Gothic and modern temporalities.[37] Accordingly, Delany has been excluded from consideration as a contributor to eighteenth-century gothic literary production in Ireland and Britain. Something similar might be said of the Anglican clergyman and Trinity College Dublin Fellow and Professor of Oratory, Thomas Leland (1722–85), who is now principally remembered as a historian, the author of *A History of the Life and Reign of Philip, King of Macedon* (1758) and *The History of Ireland from the Invasion of Henry II* (1773). Along with his work as a classical scholar in editing, with John Stokes, the Philipic *Orations of Demosthenes* (1754) and translating Demosthenes's *Orations* (1756–60), these histories established Leland as a man of letters with serious scholarly ambition. In this context, Leland's only novel, *Longsword, Earl of Salisbury: an Historical Romance* (1762), is often presented as generically closer to historiography than fiction, an assessment in keeping with Leland's own advertisement of *Longsword* as a kind of history-writing. The preface to the novel, in fact, claims that '[t]he out-lines of the following story; and some of the incidents and more minute circumstances, are to be found in the antient English historians'.[38] Contemporary criticism of the novel eagerly adopted Leland's own emphasis on historical truths, praising the novel's foundation 'on real facts' and dismissing its reference to itself as a 'romance' as generically inappropriate and far too 'modest'.[39]

Set in England and France during the reign of Henry III (r. 1216–72), *Longsword* narrates the experiences of its eponymous hero, the real life William, Earl of Salisbury, as he returns to England after successfully protecting English-held lands in France. Although he expects to return to a native country in which liberty and governmental justice prevail, contrasting strikingly with the lawlessness and corruption he had experienced in France, William finds instead a continuation of the struggles he had undergone abroad. Thanks to the weakness of Henry III, William's castle has been usurped, his wife all but forced into an illegitimate marriage, and his young son sent to a monastery to be guarded by an evil monk. William's return to his castle ultimately sets right the private and public wrongs committed in his absence: not only is his home and family restored to him, but the king correspondingly ousts his controlling counsel and reasserts his proper, liberal sovereignty, providing a narrative conclusion that seems clearly to invite allegorical political readings such as those advanced in recent years by Fiona Price, James Watt, and Toni Wein.[40] Price, for instance, contends that *Longsword* 'uses the reign of Henry III, when territories had just been won in Gascony, to warn George III about the dangers of favouritism and absolutism'.[41] Similarly, Wein reads a 'eulog[y]' of George III as a 'glorious Monarch' in *Longsword*'s treatment of the reign of Henry III, arguing that the novel glorifies present British governance by way of a contrast with the political debasement of the past.[42]

Such arguments are persuasive in their emphasis on *Longsword*'s understanding of the utility of history and its function as an important point of contrast with the present. This is, perhaps unsurprisingly, a perception of relational temporalities *Longsword* shares with Leland's historiographical nonfiction. In its use of recognizable historical figures and events as a method of highlighting the civic advantages to be had from a strict attention to historical precedence, in fact, *Longsword* echoes earlier texts such as *A History of the Life and Reign of Philip*. In that work, Leland traced the cyclical vicissitudes of political liberty and justice in the kingdom of Macedonia over several generations, emphasizing the manner in which just rule proceeds from a keen awareness of both the merits and demerits of preceding sociopolitical constructs. Both texts implicitly underline the progression of modern England from its pre-decessors, representing the ancient, Gothic past as providing a largely negative example for the present. In this scenario, the more romantic and fantastical practices of former ages are depicted as part of the whole 'truth of history' but in such a way as to emphasize eighteenth-century England's advancement from them. Writing of the birth of Philip in the *History of the Life and Reign of Philip*, for instance, Leland observes that Philip's nativity was seen 'as an omen of happy fortune; as the ora-cles were said to have pronounced, that Macedon was to be eminently flourishing under the reign of one of [Amyntas's] sons'.[43] Reproduc-ing a contemporary verse containing this prediction, Leland is careful to insert a cautionary note, downplaying any credibility that might have been assigned to the prophecy by suggesting its rational basis in Amyntas's own political interests:

> [The prophesy] is too clear and explicit not to have been made after the event: however, it still might have been the interest of Amyntas, in a season so critical at the eve of a dangerous and hazardous war, to amuse and encourage his barbarous and ignorant subjects, with predictions and oracles; and to improve this incident, of the birth of his son, into a pledge of future happiness, vouchsafed by heaven itself. (I: 22)

Inserted into a historiographical record specifically meant to distinguish the ordinary 'actions and events' of the past from the 'extraordinary and surprising [...] great and glaring', this apparent divination and Leland's matter-of-fact deflation of it highlight his attention to distanc-ing enlightened present from atavistic past (I:xvii). While his history allows, in other words, for the historic belief in 'extraordinary', 'surpris-ing', and even oracular events, it simultaneously counters them with modern, rational skepticism and explanations.

Such a measured historiographical approach was precisely that which separated Leland's *Longsword* from Walpole's later *Castle of Otranto*, which, as I have noted, courted controversy primarily because it was seen to collapse the temporal and ideological distance between past and present. In contrast to *Otranto*, however, *Longsword* was understood, like the *History of the Life and Reign of Philip* before it, to distance superstition and the supernatural from the present, offering, as Clery puts it ' "the

advantages of history" – an informative picture of the past which illustrated progress while stimulating through its strangeness – but without
corrupting the faculty of judgement with fantastic improbabilities'.[44]
For Clery, the popularity of Leland's novel, as well as its 'universally
favourable and unproblematic' reception, owed chiefly to the author's
'exclu[sion] [of] any hint of the supernatural or marvellous'. In resisting
the lure of the numinous, Leland was able to appeal to and satisfy contemporary taste for 'images of the gothic past as [already evident in the
works of] Macpherson, Walpole and Chatterton' while simultaneously
avoiding the threatening suggestion of the present age's regression to or
lack of progression from former unenlightened superstitions or religious
dominance.[45]

It is also, however, this dedication to 'the truth of history' that per-
petuates *Longsword*'s exclusion from consideration in the historiography
of the literary gothic. Seen by contemporaries as generically closer to
a factual history than to the fantastical, hybrid romance presented by
Walpole, *Longsword* continues to be assessed today as different in kind
from *Otranto* – an example of 'historical' rather than 'gothic' fiction.
Richard Maxwell, for instance, calls *Longsword* 'the first real English historical novel', and Fiona Price names Leland a significant 'historical
novelist' of the 1760s and 1770s.[46] Yet, as I have discussed elsewhere,
Leland's novel contains several subtle suggestions of the threatening
hold of the Gothic past on the present, even after Longsword himself has returned to England and re-established rightful rule.[47] In this,
Leland's novel might be seen to dissolve the borders between past and
present just as *Otranto* does, with the exception that *Longsword*'s lack
of supernatural content makes this dissolution even more threatening,
precisely because more realistic, than *Otranto*'s. It is worth remembering,
too, that *Otranto*, like *Longsword*, has also sometimes been analyzed as
'historical' in nature. Sir Walter Scott, for instance, praised Walpole's tale
for its 'accurate display of human character' and faithful depiction of
'such a picture of domestic life and manners, during the feudal times, as
might actually have existed'.[48] 'Gothic' and 'historical', in other words,
pointedly converge in *Longsword* and *Otranto*, highlighting the inherent overlap of these terms as well as the modes and, indeed, genres of
writing that they represented in eighteenth-century society.[49]

Where the examples of *Longsword* and 'Marianna' make it clear
that eighteenth-century gothic practice in Ireland encompassed a wide
variety of prose, Elizabeth Griffith's dramatic poem, *Amana* (1764),
suggests that literary engagement with notions of the Gothic past per-
meated eighteenth-century prose, poetry, and drama alike. As is the case

with both Leland and Delany, Griffith's gothic practice has suffered at the hands of contemporary and posthumous receptions of her work. Although a prolific writer who produced a variety of translations, poetry, short stories, epistolary novels, and critical essays, Griffith is best known today for her career as a playwright and for productions such as *The Platonic Wife* (1765), *The Double Mistake* (1766), *The School for Rakes* (1769), and *A Wife in the Right* (1772). This renown owes, in part, to the striking popularity of *The Double Mistake* and *The School for Rakes*, but also to the controversy Griffith excited with her proto-feminist views and transgression of normative gender roles. *Amana*, for instance, was scathingly condemned upon publication because its 'lady' author presumed '[to fancy] herself a POETESS, and her performance [...] a dramatic poem'.[50] *The Platonic Wife* was similarly censured by outraged male critics not just for its self-proclaimed female writer but also for its none-too-gentle support for equitable relationships between husbands and wives.[51]

Although little read today, Griffith's fictional works fared better, if only because they adhered to contemporary norms of female literary production. *The History of Lady Barton* (1771), for instance, was deemed an 'equally ingenious and sentimental' tale, which distinguished itself from the usual 'mean performances which flow annually from the press, under th[e] character [of romance]' by its 'natural delineation of the passions' with laudable 'propriety'.[52] In very similar terms, *The Story of Lady Juliana Harley* (1776) was commended for its 'elegance of style, chasteness of sentiment, and moral tendency' and was described as 'a very decent story, interspersed with just and wholesome observations, which sufficiently evince the ingenious Writer's knowledge of human nature'.[53] Indicative of the genres and modes of writing considered acceptable for female authors in this period – novels, romances, and didactic fiction chief among them – the reviews of Griffith's novels contrast markedly with those of her dramas and, correspondingly, suggest the reasons for current, albeit limited, attention to Griffith's prose fiction in gothic criticism. Assessed as 'sentimental' by contemporary reviewers, works like *The Delicate Distress* (1769), *The History of Lady Barton*, and *The Story of Lady Juliana Harley* underscore the close relationship between sentimental, historical, and gothic modes in this period, as noted by Ian Campbell Ross.[54] It is on the basis of their sentimental content, in fact, that these works have been described by Kilfeather as containing 'early gothic scenes', which situate them at the start of '[a] history of Irish gothic fiction'.[55] Yet, as is clear from analysis of *Amana*, Griffith's consideration and use of contemporary notions of the Gothic past is both less tangential and more multi-generic than Kilfeather's analysis suggests.

Published in 1764 but never performed, *Amana* retells, with several significant revisions, a tale that had first appeared in *The Adventurer* in 1753.[56] In that piece, the reader is presented with the tragic story of Amana, a beautiful young woman who, whilst drawing water from a well, is rudely accosted by Caled, the servant of a rich merchant, Nouraddin, who, intervening, falls in love with Amana and proposes marriage. On the day of their wedding, however, Amana is seized by servants of the Egyptian caliph, Osmin, whose insatiable sexual appetite is to be temporarily appeased with a competition to find the most beautiful virgin woman in Egypt. As Amana thereafter fights off Osmin's lascivious advances, Nouraddin wishes that he could trade places with Osmin, who, in turn, finding himself scorned by Amana, laments that he is not Nouraddin. Both are spectacularly granted the means temporarily to become their rivals by a mystical 'Genius' and both immediately take advantage of their interchange.[57] Disguised as Nouraddin, Osmin approaches his own castle only to be fatally assaulted by Caled. Meanwhile, Nouraddin, in disguise as Osmin and forgetting that Amana cannot recognize him as her lover, accepts from her a drink that she has poisoned with a toxic powder that magically appeared in her hand moments earlier when she had wished for the means to kill Osmin. Nouraddin soon after dies, having revealed to Amana the ruse by which he had gained access to the castle. Distraught, Amana attempts to escape but is detained by Osmin's men, who believe she has murdered their king and who promptly put her to death.

Intriguingly, Griffith's version of the tale omits all element of the supernatural and focuses instead on the difference between 'Gothic' Egypt and enlightened England, reworking the tale, in Griffith's own representation, for 'a British audience'.[58] To do so, Griffith excludes all mention of 'genie's [*sic*]' and 'superior agents', claiming that 'Shakespear alone could *call spirits from the vasty deep*' (p. iii). Such omissions allow Griffith to focus more particularly on a commentary on 'the miseries of those nations which are subject to despotic power' in contrast to 'the peculiar blessings of liberty, that we enjoy in these thrice happy kingdoms!' – an idea she claims to have been inspired with upon first reading the original tale in *The Adventurer* (p. iv). Although she outlines the moral of her revised narrative as '*To shew the folly of human wishes and schemes for correcting the moral government of the world*', her real interest appears to lie in assessing the moral worth of contemporary British governance. Indeed, as Griffith herself maintains, her desire is 'to contribute my grateful mite of praise to those laws, and to that government, under which our superior advantages are established, defended, and preserved' (p. iv). Her method of doing so is to contrast the British present with an eastern, 'Gothic' past presented as antithetical to British modernity (p. 35).[59] Accordingly, Griffith's text strikingly images the necessary overthrow of tyranny, engaging as it does so in thought-provoking musings about the nature of just rule. As Nardic, Osmin's prime minister, ponders:

> [Is there] no way to blend
> Prerogative with liberty? To poise
> In equal scales, the prince and people's rights,
> And make them mutually suspend each other? (p. 21)

Later, after the death of Osmin and the subsequent suicides of Amana and Nouraddin – in Griffith's version of the tale, Amana drinks the poison herself, prompting Nouraddin to stab himself with his sword – Amana's father, Abdallah, laments,

> heaven's avenging hand
> Hath struck this heavy blow – The Sultan's vice
> Hath earned his fate – For tyranny should bleed!
> But these unhappy innocents were doomed
> For my foul crimes, my vile apostasy;
> For quitting heaven, and native liberty –
> Let those who dwell in Albion's happy land,
> Grateful acknowledge heaven's most bounteous hand. (p. 54)

The apostasy of which Abdallah speaks is his renunciation of both nation and faith for his foreign wife, now dead. The events of the play confirm for Abdallah his belief that his daughter '[i]s marked a victim for her father's crime', and, in so doing, corroborate his perception of Britain as the seat of munificent justice and liberal rule (p. 18). More than that, Abdallah's concluding encomium supports Britain's active role in brokering peace outside of its national boundaries, praising England's 'protector' as one

> Who not in Britain's cause alone sustains
> The toils of council, and of hostile plains:
> The world's great champion, born for all mankind,
> In whom the oppressed a certain refuge find:

Whose sword, but like the lancet, wounds to heal,
Where moral lenitives can naught avail;
Whose olive bearing laurel peace restores,
And calms the discord of contending powers. (p. 54)

In this, *Amana* appears to call upon a rhetoric of patriotism both to validate British intervention in international conflict and to reassure readers
of British greatness during a time of continued concern over France, following the Seven Years War, and of increasing conflict with the colonies
in America. Accordingly, *Amana* might be considered a dramatic version of what Watt calls 'the Loyalist Gothic romance', a literary form
he sees as encompassing works such as *Longsword* and Clara Reeve's *The
Old English Baron* (1778). Both of these novels, as Watt contends, use the
Gothic past in order to 'provide a reassuring moral and patriotic fable
during a period of national crisis', much as *Amana* might be seen to do.[60]
At the same time, however, *Amana*'s praise of Britain serves as a veiled
warning to England's 'protector' – presumably George III – about the
dangers of British failure to 'calm the discord of contending powers' –
religious recusancy, political tyranny, and social discord. Again, this is
an argument made recently in reference to Leland's *Longsword*, which, as
Price maintains, deploys negative depictions of the French villain, Mal-
leon, not so much to malign France but to warn George III of 'the danger
of corrupted values should Britain fail to keep the balance of power in
Europe'.[61]

The striking parallels between *Amana* and *Longsword*, in combina-
tion with their shared engagement with the Gothic past, compellingly
speak to eighteenth-century gothic literary practice's cross-generic roots
in Ireland. Traditionally excluded from the history of Irish, but also
British and European gothic literary production, the works discussed
here demand reconfiguration of the generic parameters usually ascribed
to late-eighteenth-century gothic literature. In particular, they invite us
to set aside our current attention to 'the Gothic novel' and think instead
of eighteenth-century gothic literary production in terms of a multi-
generic cultural practice informed by contemporary conceptions of the
Gothic past. More than that, they underline the fruitfulness of considering Irish writers' gothic practice as less a codified tradition, genre, or
mode peculiar to a fragment of the national population and more a
manner of thinking, perceiving, and writing that these writers shared,
not just with each other, regardless of religious or political affiliations,
but also with contemporaries across Britain and Europe. In the democratic realm of gothic literary practice, in other words, the boundaries

we have traditionally relied upon in our assessments of both 'the Gothic novel' and 'Irish Gothic' literature – genre and religious affiliation, but also gender and political allegiance – begin to break down, and the richly cosmopolitan and generically diverse nature of a transnational eighteenth-century gothic habitus begins to emerge.

Notes

1. Sir Horace Walpole to Sir Horace Mann, 27 April 1753, in Peter Sabor (ed.) (1987) *Horace Walpole: the Critical Heritage* (London: Routledge), p. 239.
2. Jarlath Killeen (2006) 'Irish Gothic: a Theoretical Introduction', *The Irish Journal of Gothic and Horror Studies* 1, 1–10 (p. 2). As there are no page numbers in the online edition, I have used those that appear when the article is printed.
3. Roy Foster (1995) *Paddy and Mr Punch: Connections in Irish and English History* (London: Penguin), p. 220.
4. Vera Kreilkamp (2006) 'The Novel of the Big House', in *The Cambridge Companion to the Irish Novel*, ed. John Wilson Foster (Cambridge: Cambridge University Press), pp. 60–77 (p. 66).
5. Claire Connolly (2011) *A Cultural History of the Irish Novel, 1790–1829* (Cambridge: Cambridge University Press), p. 167.
6. Killeen, 'Irish Gothic: a Theoretical Introduction', p. 3.
7. See Jarlath Killeen (2005) *Gothic Ireland: Horror and the Irish Anglican Imagination in the Long Eighteenth Century* (Dublin: Four Courts Press) and Killeen, 'Irish Gothic: a Theoretical Introduction'.
8. Killeen, *Gothic Ireland*, p. 25.
9. Anne Williams (1995) *Art of Darkness: a Poetics of Gothic* (Chicago: The University of Chicago Press), p. 2; Robert Miles (1993) *Gothic Writing 1750–1820: a Genealogy* (London: Routledge), p. 1; David Punter (1996) *The Literature of Terror*, 2 vols (2nd edn; London: Longman Group), I: 1; and Jerrold E. Hogle (2002) 'Introduction: the Gothic in Western Culture', in *The Cambridge Companion to Gothic Fiction*, ed. Jerrold E. Hogle (Cambridge: Cambridge University Press), pp. 1–20 (p. 1).
10. Timothy G. Jones (2009) 'The Canniness of the Gothic: Genre as Practice', *Gothic Studies* 11.1, 124–33 (p. 126).
11. Jones, 'The Canniness of the Gothic', p. 127. Jones here is working from Pierre Bourdieu's notion of 'habitus'; see Pierre Bourdieu (1972; 1990) *The Logic of Practice*, trans. Richard Nice (Stanford: Stanford University Press).
12. David Duff convincingly contends, for instance, that Romantic-era writers, though traditionally understood as anti-generic, were, in fact, hyperconscious about issues of genre, not least because they understood that genres always involved a certain innate hybridity. This acute awareness of hybridity, Duff maintains, expressed itself in Romantic-era works in a variety of ways, including various degrees of mixing and manipulation of generic characteristics; David Duff (2009) *Romanticism and the Uses of Genre* (Oxford: Oxford University Press), pp. 161, 45.

13. James Watt (1999) *Contesting the Gothic: Fiction, Genre and Cultural Conflict, 1764–1832* (Cambridge: Cambridge University Press), p. 14. Throughout this study, I use 'gothic' with a lower case 'g' to distinguish between the term's modern application to literary works of terror or horror and contemporary use of the term 'Gothic' as connotative of Britain's social, cultural, and political heritage. In this, I follow the example of Robert W. Rix, who makes the same distinction in his recent article in *Gothic Studies*: Robert W. Rix (2011) 'Gothic Gothicism: Norse Terror in the Late Eighteenth to Early Nineteenth Centuries', *Gothic Studies* 13.1, 1–20 (p. 16, n. 4).

14. W. S. Lewis (1964) Introduction, in *The Castle of Otranto*, by Horace Walpole, ed. W. S. Lewis (London: Oxford University Press), p. x.

15. Clare O'Halloran (2004) *Golden Ages and Barbarous Nations: Antiquarian Debate and Cultural Politics in Ireland, c. 1750–1800* (Cork: Cork University Press and Field Day), pp. 41, 56.

16. William Molyneux (1698) *The Case of Ireland, Stated* (Dublin); quoted in O'Halloran, *Golden Ages and Barbarous Nations*, p. 57; Watt, *Contesting the Gothic*, p. 14.

17. Henry Fielding (1749; 1985) *The History of Tom Jones* (New York: Penguin Books), p. 85; quoted in Barrett Kalter (2003) 'DIY Gothic: Thomas Gray and the Medieval Revival', *ELH* 70.4, 989–1019 (p. 997).

18. Kalter, 'DIY Gothic', p. 997.

19. Roland Freart and John Evelyn (1707) *A parallel of the ancient architecture and the modern...by Roland Freart...made English...to which is added an account of architects and architecture* (2nd edn; London), pp. 9–15; quoted in J. M. Frew (1982) 'Gothic is English: John Carter and the Revival of the Gothic as England's National Style', *The Art Bulletin* 64.2, 315–19 (p. 316).

20. Siobhán Kilfeather (2006) 'The Gothic Novel', in *The Cambridge Companion to the Irish Novel*, pp. 78–96 (p. 83).

21. Killeen, *Gothic Ireland*, p. 18.

22. Killeen, *Gothic Ireland*, p. 21.

23. As Jones aptly puts it, 'Gothic criticism of historical texts sometimes runs the risk of failing to unpick itself from its own contemporary Gothic habitus, from the Gothic as it appears now'; Jones, 'The Canniness of the Gothic', p. 128.

24. Jones, 'The Canniness of the Gothic', p. 127.

25. Lisa L. Moore (2005) 'Queer Gardens: Mary Delany's Flowers and Friendships', *Eighteenth-Century Studies* 39.1, 49–70 (p. 49). Delany (née Granville) was originally of English background but traveled extensively in Ireland in 1731, after being widowed for the first time. In 1742, she married Patrick Delany, a senior fellow at Trinity College Dublin, and thereafter lived with him in Ireland, primarily at his estate in County Dublin and also at his deanery in Downpatrick, County Down. She moved back to England after Delany's death in 1768 and died there in 1788. Her correspondence reveals a deep interest in Ireland and Irish affairs, and the short story discussed in this essay was first written while Delany lived in Ireland.

26. Moore, 'Queer Gardens', p. 49.

27. Moore, 'Queer Gardens', pp. 49–50.

28. Mrs Delany to Miss Dewes, 10 October 1768, in R. Brimley Johnson (1925) *Mrs. Delany at Court and Among the Wits* (London), p. 214. The first edition of *Otranto* claimed to be 'an ancient Italian manuscript' purportedly written by 'Onuphrio Muralto, Canon of the Church of St. Nicholas at Otranto' and later discovered, translated, and printed by 'William Marshal'; Horace Walpole (1764; 1964) *The Castle of Otranto*, ed. W. S. Lewis (London: Oxford University Press), p. 1.

29. *Monthly Review* 32 (February 1765), 97–9; *Monthly Review* 32 (May 1765), 394.

30. E. J. Clery (1995) *The Rise of Supernatural Fiction, 1762–1800* (Cambridge: Cambridge University Press), p. 54.

31. Mrs Delany to Miss Dewes, 10 October 1768, in Johnson, *Mrs. Delany at Court and Among the Wits*, p. 214.

32. Mrs Delany to Miss Dewes, 10 October 1768, in Johnson, *Mrs. Delany*, pp. 214, 215. Emphasis mine.

33. Mrs Delany to Miss Dewes, 10 October 1768, in Johnson, *Mrs. Delany*, p. 215.

34. Mark Laird and Alicia Weisberg-Roberts (eds) (2009) *Mrs. Delany and her Circle* (Yale: Yale Center for British Art), p. 250; Mrs [Mary] Delany (1759; 2009) 'Marianna', in *Mrs. Delany and her Circle*, ed. Mark Laird and Alicia Weisberg-Roberts (Yale: Yale Center for British Art), pp. 250–61 (p. 251). Future references are to this edition and are given parenthetically in the text.

35. See Diane Long Hoeveler (2010) *Gothic Riffs: Secularizing the Uncanny in the European Imaginary, 1780–1820* (Columbus, OH: The Ohio State University Press).

36. 'Marianna' first appeared in print in 2009, following the exhibition of *Mrs. Delany and Her Circle* at the Yale Center for British Art from 24 September 2009 to 3 January 2010, and, later, at the Sir John Soane's Museum, London from 18 February to 1 May 2010. A short bibliographic précis of the tale is also available in Rolf and Magda Loeber (2011) 'New Findings: Addendum to the *Guide to Irish Fiction 1650–1900* for the Period Between 1674 and 1830', *Irish University Review* 41.1, 202–15 (pp. 208–9).

37. For 'An Essay on Propriety' and 'The History of Miss MacDermot', see Johnson, *Mrs. Delany at Court and Among the Wits*, pp. 277–83.

38. Thomas Leland (1762) *Longsword, Earl of Salisbury: an Historical Romance*, 2 vols (Dublin), I:[iv]. Future references are to this edition and are given parenthetically in the text.

39. *The Critical Review* 13 (March 1762), 252–7 (p. 252). For a similarly positive assessment, see *Monthly Review* 26 (March 1762), 236–7.

40. See Fiona Price (2001) 'Ancient Liberties? Rewriting the Historical Novel: Thomas Leland, Horace Walpole and Clara Reeve', *Journal for Eighteenth-Century Studies* 34.1, 19–38; Watt, *Contesting the Gothic*, Chapter 2; and Toni Wein (2002) *British Identities, Heroic Nationalisms, and the Gothic Novel, 1764–1824* (Basingstoke: Palgrave Macmillan), pp. 4–5.

41. Price, 'Ancient Liberties?', p. 22–3.

42. Wein, *British Identities, Heroic Nationalisms*, p. 5.

43. Thomas Leland (1758) *The History of the Life and Reign of Philip, King of Macedon*, 2 vols (London), I: 21. Future references are to this edition and are given parenthetically in the text.

44. Clery, *The Rise of Supernatural Fiction*, p. 60.

45. Ibid.
46. Richard Maxwell (2008) 'The Historical Novel', in *The Cambridge Companion to Fiction in the Romantic Period*, eds Richard Maxwell and Katie Trumpener (Cambridge: Cambridge University Press), pp. 65–87 (p. 67); Price, 'Ancient Liberties?', p. 20. For the recent identification of *Longsword* as an earlier Irish gothic novel than *Otranto*, see Rolf and Magda Loeber (2006) *A Guide to Irish Fiction 1650–1900* (Dublin: Four Courts Press), pp. 748–9, and Rolf Loeber and Magda Stouthamer-Loeber (2003) 'The Publication of Irish Novels and Novelettes, 1750–1829: a Footnote on Irish Gothic Fiction', *Cardiff Corvey: Reading the Romantic Text* 10, 1–24 (p. 9). Available online from <http://www.cardiff.ac.uk/encap/journals/corvey/articles/cc10_n02.html>. As there are no page numbers in the online edition, I have used those that appear when the article is printed. For the description of *Longsword* as integral to the establishment of 'the Loyalist Gothic romance', see Watt, *Contesting the Gothic*, p. 47.
47. See Christina Morin (2011) 'Forgotten Fiction: Reconsidering the Gothic Novel in Eighteenth-Century Ireland', *Irish University Review* 41.1, 80–94 (pp. 84–6).
48. Sir Walter Scott (1825) *Lives of the Novelists*, 2 vols (Philadelphia, PA), II: 120, 128. For a more modern assessment of *Otranto* as a historical novel, see Ruth Mack (2008) 'Horace Walpole and the Objects of Literary History', *ELH* 75.2, 367–87 (pp. 370–3).
49. The overlap of gothic, historical, and sentimental modes in eighteenth-century Irish fiction has been noted by Ian Campbell Ross; see Ian Campbell Ross (2006) 'Prose in English, 1690–1800: From the Williamite Wars to the Act of Union', in *The Cambridge History of Irish Literature*, eds Margaret Kelleher and Philip O'Leary, 2 vols (Cambridge: Cambridge University Press), I: 232–81 (I: 273).
50. *The Critical Review* 19 (March 1765), 235 (p. 235).
51. Betty Rizzo (ed.) (2001) *Eighteenth-Century Women Playwrights: Volume 4: Elizabeth Griffith* (London: Pickering and Chatto), pp. 4–6.
52. *The Critical Review* 32 (November 1771), 372–7 (pp. 377, 372, 377).
53. *The Critical Review* 42 (August 1776), 155 (p. 155); *Monthly Review* 55 (September 1776), 238–9 (p. 239).
54. Ross, 'Prose in English', I: 273.
55. Siobhán Kilfeather (1994) 'Origins of the Irish Female Gothic', *Bullán* 1.2, 35–45 (pp. 37, 38). See also Kilfeather, 'The Gothic Novel', pp. 80–1.
56. See *The Adventurer* 72 (July 14, 1753), in *The Adventurer. In Four Volumes* (Dublin, 1793), III: 185–7; and *The Adventurer* 73 (17 July, 1753), in *The Adventurer. In Four Volumes*, III: 188–90.
57. *The Adventurer* 73 (17 July, 1753), III: 189.
58. 'A Lady' [Elizabeth Griffith] (1764) *Amana. A Dramatic Poem* (London), p. iii. Future references are to this edition and are given parenthetically in the text.
59. Osmin's Egyptian castle is specifically described in the stage directions as *'A Gothic building, representing the palace of Sakara'* (p. 35).
60. Watt, *Contesting the Gothic*, p. 49.
61. Price, 'Ancient Liberties?', p. 23. That Ireland forms part of 'the discord of contending powers' of which George III needed to be aware is clear from Griffith's dedication of her work to Elizabeth Percy, Countess of

Northumberland, whose husband acted as Lord Lieutenant of Ireland from 1763 to 1765. In her dedication, Griffith calls on Percy to remember her noble ancestors' dedication to 'Liberty' (p. [v]), suggesting the author's desire to persuade the Countess to look favourably upon Edmond Pery (1719–1806) and other parliamentary patriots, whose demands for constitutional concessions such as an Irish Habeas Corpus Act, reform of the pensions list, and a dramatic overhaul of the treasury system applied to Ireland, were proving increasingly irksome to the Lord Lieutenant.

2

The Irish Protestant Imaginary: the Cultural Contexts for the Gothic Chapbooks Published by Bennett Dugdale, 1800–5

Diane Long Hoeveler

What vanity and presumption! that man should suppose he can pardon the sins of others, and yet have the weight of so many on his own head! Why did he not stay in the land of superstition? – I should blush at seeing an Englishman on his knees to you, – more than I should at hearing a long catalogue of transgressions. It is more excusable to fall down before a crucifix – it might convey to the mind an idea of a great transaction. – But to kneel to such a man as that, is to pay adoration to the representative of folly and inconsistency – for the Romish priest is no better than his neighbours. – May the supplications of mankind be ever and only addressed to that Being who is placed far above all principality and power, – and might, – dominion – and every name that is named, not only in this world, but that which is to come.[1]

The historical context

Perhaps it is just a coincidence, but when the former Catholic priest Antonio Gavin (1680–?) decided to flee Spain he headed first to London and then finally to Ireland, where the Dublin publisher George Grierson produced his diatribe against the Catholic Church, *The Great Red Dragon; or The Master-key to Popery* (1724). Twenty years later an anonymous and mean-spirited satire on Catholic doctrines was published by James

Carson in Dublin: *Purgatory Prov'd: Illustrated and set forth, in a clear Light. By Father Murtagh O'Lavery. Priest of the Parish of St. John's Dromore, and Macherlin. In a Funeral Sermon, upon the death of one of his parishioners* (1746). Using an exaggerated Irish dialect that mocks the lower-class origins of the priest, the anonymous satirist has Fr O'Lavery refer to Purgatory as 'de Turd Plath'.[2] And then in 1773 Elizabeth Bonhôte (1744–1818) first published her vindictive attack on Catholic priests in *The Rambles of Mr. Frankly, Published by His Sister* in Dublin with Messrs Sleater, Lynch, Williams, Potts, Chamberlaine, excerpted in the epigram above. There is also a very early gothic monk villain in *Longsword, Earl of Salisbury* (1762), written by the Anglo-Irish clergyman and historian Thomas Leland and published in its first Dublin edition by George Faulkner (1762). Generally discussed as a pre-gothic novel in the Loyalist tradition,[3] this historical romance features an evil monk named Brother Reginald who domineers over the local monastery where the besieged heroine Ela's son has been sent by the usurping villain Raymond (much of this plot would be repeated later in slightly altered form in Matthew Lewis's popular gothic drama *The Castle Spectre*, 1797). Reginald is such an odious character that Mary Muriel Tarr observes, 'it is significant that Reginald's conduct is exceptional and that [...] his brothers detest him and try to control his excesses'.[4] Matthew Lewis's anti-Catholic tome, *The Monk* (1796), was published in Dublin for the first time in 1796 by P. Wogan (and then reprinted by various houses in 1797 and 1808), while *The Adventures of Signor Gaudentio di Lucca*, a sensationalistic Inquisition trial account, was published in Dublin by J. Carrick in 1798. The Dublin publisher Arthur O'Neil produced the anonymous and blatantly anti-Catholic chapbook *Mystery of the Black Convent,* based on *The Monk* in 1814.[5] Finally, one could mention the Dublin-born Anglican minister Charles Maturin, descended from Huguenots, who published his *Five Sermons on the Errors of the Roman Catholic Church* in Dublin with William Curry in 1824.

My point in listing these examples of only a few of the hundreds of anti-Catholic texts that appeared in Ireland during this period is to suggest that there were a number of publishers in Dublin who were interested in and committed to publishing some of the most extreme anti-Catholic propaganda being written during the eighteenth and nineteenth centuries.[6] And while we may now think of Ireland, and in particular Dublin, as a dominant Catholic culture, we would be mistaken to assume that such was the case for the eighteenth century. At that time a minority Anglo-Irish ascendancy dominated the religious, social, and political life of Ireland, while the majority Roman Catholic population struggled to maintain a cultural presence in proportion to their numbers. Certainly there were Irish Catholic publishers producing Catholic religious works,[7] and there was a strong nationwide Catholic Committee campaign as early as 1792 which published widely, as historians like James Kelly, Kevin Whelan, and Thomas Bartlett have noted.[8] Men like Hugh Fitzpatrick, John Coyne, and Richard Coyne were active in publishing Catholic texts, but each one of them was supported at one point or another by 'ecclesiastical authority'.[9] Apart from these early efforts, however, more aggressive and propagandistic responses by Catholic publishers did not become overtly antagonistic until 1823, when W. J. Battersby started his own press specifically designed to counter the productions of Protestant publishing houses. In 1825 he wrote to a friend, 'I agree with you that the Biblicals are industrious in disseminating their pestiferous tracts and the Catholics are grossly negligent in counteracting their efforts. I have at my own personal risk published the works you see marked in the catalogue'.[10] One of those 'Biblicals', I would contend, was Bennett Dugdale, Methodist publisher.

It is not, I think, unfair to state, as Foster has,[11] that the Irish Protestant imaginary was well aware of its own acts of usurpation and that this violation of a land and its indigenous heritage found literary expression in the sense of being haunted by a repressed and threatening Catholic majority population. But another explanation is possible as well. Memories of Catholic atrocities committed against Protestants in Ulster and beyond were continually revived in the Protestant Imaginary, Richard Musgrave's (1746–1818) *Memoirs of the Different Rebellions in Ireland* (1801) being just one recent example. Musgrave's text was a pro-Loyalist history that linked the failed Irish rising of 1798 to a longer and more complicated tale of Catholic crimes against Protestants.[12] Hence what I am calling the 'Irish Protestant Imaginary' manifests itself as what we would recognize as textual displays of anti-Catholicism, and is composed of equal parts of guilt, anxiety, fear, and disdain for the native religion of the majority population.[13]

It is revealing that defenses of Catholicism tended to be published in places like Cork, for instance, by the Cork publisher John Connor who published in 1813 *Plain Facts*, by Eneas MacDonnell, a defense of Catholics in the face of Protestant agitation against the Catholic Emancipation bill. Connor was, according to Rolf and Magda Loeber, 'the single most important publisher in Ireland of original fiction at the time when reprints of English authors prevailed'.[14] The full title reveals the pamphlet's position: *Plain Facts, demonstrating The Injustice and Inconsistency of Anti-Catholic Hostility, fairly illustrated in a letter to the Rev. J. Coates, Vicar, Chairman of the Meeting of Clergy, Gentry, and Inhabitants of Huddersfield and Vicinity, who have resolved to petition Parliament against the Roman Catholic Claims* (original pamphlet in Cambridge University Library). Clearly, Catholics were on the defensive. The fact was that until the 1778 and 1782 Relief Acts they were restricted as to property ownership, they could not vote, and could not work for government except as cannon fodder and in lesser offices. And then during this decade the gothic novel became all the rage in England, France, and Germany.

The anti-Catholic tone of the majority of gothic works in the European imaginary has been extensively documented and explored in a number of scholarly studies published during the past 30 years.[15] And scholars of the Irish literary tradition have certainly noticed the trend as well.[16] This essay will focus on a question that has not to my knowledge been explored: what can we learn about specific Dublin publishers by looking at the titles they chose to publish as revealing the ideological content of their catalogues? In short, were publishers who produced gothic materials operating according to purely financial motivations as has usually been asserted,[17] or did they have an ideological (political and religious) agenda in their choice of works to reprint from London? Although we know a few tantalizing facts about only a handful of these men working in Dublin and Cork, we do have catalogues of their published works to guide us in making some judgments about their intentions, and, by extension, about the characteristics of the book trade in Ireland at this time. Using a sampling of the gothic chapbooks published by the Dublin Methodist Bennett Dugdale (1771–1826),[18] this essay will examine the larger historical and cultural contexts associated with four of the 19 titles in his catalogue of published chapbooks: *Father Innocent* (1803), *Phantasmagoria* (1803), *Amalgro & Claude* (1803), and *The Secret Tribunal* (1803), all of them anti-Catholic gothic chapbooks that he issued in collaboration with the London-based publishing house of Tegg and Castleman under the direction of Thomas Tegg. Although Loeber and Loeber discuss this collaboration and have documented that 19 chapbooks originally published in London by Tegg were produced in collaboration with Dugdale, they have not been able to prove that the chapbooks were exported to Dublin for circulation.[19] I would state here that, given what we know of Dugdale's religious sympathies, that is, that he blocked the sale of a Methodist chapel to Jesuits and his biographer labeled him as 'bigoted',[20] it is difficult not to believe that these particular chapbooks were very specifically selected for their anti-Catholic contents and that they were intended for a Methodist and Church of Ireland readership keen to have their prejudices and fears about Roman Catholicism confirmed. I make this assertion (rather boldly) because Tegg himself had a history of publishing anti-Catholic chapbooks and, in fact, he had gone so far as to appropriate the identity of a notorious Irishman, George Barrington, in order to claim that Barrington was the author of an anti-Catholic chapbook that Tegg himself published in London in 1803.[21] If the chapbooks were not intended for circulation in Ireland, why was Dugdale involved in their production?

By way of additional historical background, it is important to note that in 1793 the Irish Parliament, at the direction of Pitt's government, passed a Relief Act that gave Irish Catholics the right to vote. The earlier Relief Acts of 1778 and 1782 allowed Catholics the right to own property outright, as long as such property did not automatically confer on the proprietor the right to select a Member of Parliament. And in 1801 the Anglo-Irish Union established formal governmental ties between England and Ireland, thereby adding some three and a half million Irish Roman Catholics to the population of the United Kingdom (raising their numbers to 30 per cent). Traditionally, the Act of Union that went into effect on 1 January 1801 has been seen as having a devastating effect on publishing in Ireland because it extended English copyright law to Ireland, thereby curtailing the ability of Irish publishers to pirate English books.[22] Although Maureen Wall and others have claimed that the atmosphere in Dublin was increasingly less anti-Catholic as their numbers grew in the city after the Act of Union, the publishing climate was another matter.[23] Between 1801 and 1823, there were a number of Dublin publishers producing anti-Catholic propaganda and the gothic's popularity gave Protestant publishers like Dugdale an opening: they could propagandize against Catholicism at the same time that they entertained and titillated the lower and middling classes with their profitable anti-Catholic gothic chapbooks. After 1823 there was an Irish Catholic Association, led by Daniel O'Connell, working in concert with the priests of Ireland in order to influence local elections of Members of Parliament and to call up public demonstrations of 5000 men in a very short order.[24] O'Connell's election to Parliament for County Clare in 1828 is generally recognized as the tipping point in putting pressure on the Wellington Tory administration to finally pass the Emancipation Act in 1829, but clearly the way had been paved by recognizing the constant need of the British government for Irish Catholic soldiers to shore up its far-flung imperialistic ventures in the British colonies of the Americas and India.

Throughout the sixteenth and seventeenth centuries, tales of Popish atrocities focused on the Marian persecutions and evolved into folklorish witch tales about 'Bloody Mary' Tudor. 'Bloody' was a word routinely associated with the religion,[25] no doubt recalling the reign of Mary Tudor, as well as the St Bartholomew's Eve massacre in France in 1572, the Irish 'massacres' of 1641, and the Great Fire of London in 1666, laid at the feet of Catholics. In fact, as late as 1830, the Monument to the London fire carried an inscription stating that it had been started by 'the treachery and malice of the popish faction'. As Linda Colley has noted, 'outlandish' was another word that was frequently attached to Catholics because they were 'out of bounds, did not belong, were suspect'. The religion was linked to Rome, France, and Spain, England's traditional enemies and potential invaders. Colley also observes that during the Gordon Riots Catholics were frequently dunked in rivers in exactly the way that reputed witches had been: 'in times of danger or insecurity, Catholics – like witches – became scapegoats, easy targets on which their neighbours could vent fear and anger'.[26] 'Swimming' people suspected of witchcraft occurred in Suffolk as late as 1795,[27] so clearly the belief in the power of witches and other manifestations of 'magical' beliefs was rife in popular, lower-class consciousness during the height of the gothic ideology. From viewing Catholics as witches who need to be confronted and destroyed, it was but a short step to understanding the popularity of gothic works that prominently feature witches, like George Walker's *The Three Spaniards* (1800), James Norris Brewer's *The Witch of Ravensworth* (1808), and Quintin Poynet's *The Wizard Priest and the Witch* (1822), just to name a few. And it is certainly instructive that the origin of the word 'coven' is the same as for 'convent'.[28]

Clearly, if there was a historical residue that haunted the conscious and unconscious British psyche, it was the specter of Roman Catholicism, in all its garish, violent, corrupt, and nostalgic splendors. And so it is not difficult to see the emergence of the gothic as a form of remediation, a textual reinterpretation of Britain's historical past, as a literary response or what we might recognize as an imaginative engagement with an ambivalent history that all classes had a difficult time understanding or intellectually processing. Hence the events of the recent and more distant past become so much representative fodder for the public imagination to turn around in its hands so to speak, bring its materials into the glare of the light, look at from different directions and perspectives in order to more fully comprehend and thereby control and contain.

Another way of approaching this question is to note that at the same time as a lower-class imaginary was emerging in Great Britain, a nationalistic and politicized form of Protestantism was institutionalizing itself and infiltrating the newly developing public sphere through the proliferation of a number of Protestant societies, all of which sponsored their own publication houses. For instance, the Society for the Preservation of Christian Knowledge (SPCK; founded in 1699) printed a number of 'anti-Catholic chapbooks' for the lower classes, as well as *A Protestant Catechism: Shewing the Principal Errors of the Church of Rome* (1766), 24 pages, and written at the level of a child's understanding in a question and answer format.[29] The SPCK kept up its publications for more than 200 years, often serving as the front line in its war on Roman Catholicism, a war that continues to be fought even today in the work of someone like Ian Paisley. For more sophisticated readers there was the work of John White, who originally produced the very long anti-Catholic work *The Protestant Englishman Guarded against the Arts and Arguments of Romish Priests and Emissaries* (1753). But faced with the need to reach the masses with these warnings, the book was reissued in 1755 as *A New Preservative against Popery*, much abbreviated in size and cost, with simpler content, and intended for dispersal 'among the lower People'.[30] This virulently nationalistic form of Protestantism served as one of the primary unifying and identificatory totems around which the modern nation state of 'Great Britain' organized its sense of itself as an isolated island besieged on all sides by the forces of reactionary Catholicism.

William III's Popery Act of 1698 (passed by Parliament in 1700), made worship in a Roman Catholic Church illegal, while the penalty for a priest saying mass was perpetual imprisonment. The act effectively placed a bounty on every priest's head, promising £100 to anyone who could capture a 'Popish Bishop, Priest or Jesuite' who had said 'Mass or exercised any other Part of the Office or Function of a Popish Bishop or Priest within these Realms'.[31] Conversion to Popery became an offense, as did the sending of children abroad to Catholic countries for their educations. Further, under this act Catholics at the age of 18 were required to take the oaths of allegiance and supremacy and to renounce distinctively Catholic doctrines, most importantly transubstantiation. If they refused, their estates were to be inherited by their next Protestant relatives. As Haydon has noted, had this requirement been rigorously enforced, 'Catholic landholding, and consequently seigniorial Catholicism, would soon have been a thing of the past; but various legal subterfuges had been found to evade the clause'.[32]

Within this extremely tense religious atmosphere, the flames of prejudice were fanned by what Habermas has labeled the newly developed bourgeois public sphere. For instance, by 1770 there were several religious debating societies which 'appear to have helped in communicating hatred of Catholicism to the lower orders, even bridging the gap between the literate and the illiterate',[33] while Methodists took a large part 'in perpetuating anti-Popish prejudice in the latter half of the century'.[34] The notorious anti-Catholic informer, William Payne, had Methodist connections, and John Wesley was involved in attacks on popery and in the agitation that followed the passage of the first Catholic Relief Act (1778). In fact, the caption on a print circulated after the Gordon Riots presented Wesley as a reactionary fanatic: 'Religious strife is raisd to Life, / By canting whining John; / No Popery he loud doth cry, / To the deluded throng'.[35] As George Rudé has noted, the Gordon Riots 'drew on a long radical-Protestant tradition and were inspired (if not promoted) by the most radical elements in the city', men like the Baptist alderman Frederick Bull, a close friend and ally of Lord George Gordon in the anti-Papist cause.[36] More moderate Anglican clergymen feared this sort of religious extremism, knowing it could alarm the populace and lead to the sort of civil disturbances that wracked England during the Tudor dynastic struggles. This new tolerance toward Catholics seems to reveal what historians claim was a softening in attitudes towards them after large numbers of Scottish and Irish Catholics served with distinction during the Seven Years War and in India and the West Indies.[37] While there was a growing spirit of tolerance during George III and George IV's reigns leading to the eventual passage of the Catholic Emancipation Act in 1829, there is no denying the fact of the Gordon Riots in London in 1780, nor the continued whipping-up of fear and anxiety toward Catholics as 'Others' that appears almost unabated in gothically inflected texts throughout the nineteenth century. [38] Even though there were no riots on the scale of what happened in 1780, there was an anti-Catholic rally attended by 60,000 people in Kent after the passage of the 1829 Act: 'such protests – which were a nationwide phenomenon and have never been properly investigated – confirm yet again just how important Protestantism was in shaping the way that ordinary Britons viewed and made sense of the land they lived in'.[39]

In the midst of these religious disputes, as well as heated political, military, and economic debates about the status of religion in the national character, the ghost of Roman Catholicism continued to haunt the British Protestant imaginary. We can see manifestations of this ghostly presence writ large in the hundreds of gothic chapbooks and novels that seized the imagination of the lower- and middle-class Briton, while the longer and more expensive three-volume novels written by Ann Radcliffe, Matthew Lewis, Charles Maturin, William Henry Ireland, Edward Montague, and Thomas Isaac Curties Horsley peddled very much the same representations and scenarios for a more well-heeled reading population. In fact, it can be argued that the Whig ascendancy self-consciously employed the gothic in its campaign to demonize and scapegoat Catholics in the public consciousness. Relying on by now stereotyped tropes that had circulated for more than 200 years in anti-Catholic propaganda and pornography – like the tyrannical and hypocritical Inquisitor, the lecherous monk, or the lesbian nun – anti-Catholic gothics enlisted the familiar conventions from a variety of discourse systems intended for the lower and middling classes.[40] As Robert Darnton has observed, while the sophisticated and ironic classic of anti-clerical pornography *Thérèse Philosophe* (1748) may have been read primarily by the elite 'Champagne-and-oyster' crowd,[41] its source materials were distilled into cheap, wordless chapbooks that circulated to the lowest level of readership, the poor and illiterate, in order to spread the same tale of clerical seduction.[42] Relying on the fact that all levels of reading audiences would have been familiar with the staples of the anti-Catholic agenda, the gothic novelist could use them almost as shorthand for conveying in a few dramatic strokes all that threatened the beleaguered British Protestant nation. By the late eighteenth century through to 1829, Britons were looking for a scapegoat and one came ready-made and uncannily familiar in the figure of the Catholic.

In an era that was characterized by the production of pornographic mockery, biting satire, and worse, anti-Catholic texts proliferated and invaded the British Protestant consciousness at all class levels. One of the most virulent and influential texts, as I mentioned earlier, was written by the apostate Antonio Gavin and titled *The Great Red Dragon; or The Master-Key to Popery*, becoming a bestseller that continued to be printed throughout the nineteenth century. A former Spanish priest who fled in disguise to England and eventually settled in Ireland, he preached as a Church of Ireland minister in Gowran, Cork, and Shandon, eventually dying in Ireland 'somewhat forgotten'.[43] Gavin traded in the most outrageous gossip and stories about the Catholic clergy, including one of the famous tales that purported to expose officials of the Inquisition who filed charges against beautiful women in order to have them arrested and held as a private 'ecclesiastical harem' behind the walls of the Inquisition. This vignette has had such a long shelf life that it was recently used as the basis for the film *Goya's Ghosts* (Miloš Forman, 2006) which advertised the events depicted in the movie as 'true'.

In addition to the religious condemnation of the clergy, monks and nuns in particular, there was a sudden uptick in the depiction of Catholic clergy in provincial British newspaper stories that date back to the 1745 uprising to restore the Stuart line to the throne. At this particular time a number of 'circulated horror stories about the intentions of Papists in different parts of the kingdom' began to proliferate.[44] We also know that a variety of anti-Catholic popular publications featuring foolish or lecherous monks were widely available throughout Europe and England since the Reformation, for instance Pierre du Moulin's *The Monk's Hood Pull'd Off: or the Capucin Fryar Described* (1671), about group flagellation and the over-zealous friar who castrated himself, and the ballad 'The Lusty Fryar of Flanders' (1688), based on the saga of Cornelius Adriaensen (1521–81), a Franciscan in Bruges who specialized in whipping his nude female followers.[45] All of these middling- and lower-class texts would have produced in the Protestant imaginary a very real tendency to see Catholics as 'foreign' and dangerous in a traitorous manner, with monks in particular being represented as secretive, sexually deviant, and mysterious.

These examples of anti-Catholic polemic verged close to the pornographic from their inception because a large part of the Protestant case against Catholicism included sexual issues, in particular, clerical celibacy. To the Protestant mind, clerical celibacy was unnatural, perverse, and doomed to fail and, in doing so, to cause incalculable damage to both the clergy and their victims. In *A Short History of Monastical Orders* (1693) we are informed that 'Nuns[,] to conceal from the World their Infamous Practices, made away secretly their Children; and this was the Reason, why at the time of the Reformation, so many Bones of Young Children were found in their Cloisters, and thrown into places where they ease Nature'.[46] This accusation surfaces in any number of gothic novels, most strongly in *Maria Monk* (1836). Other examples of this kind include *Nunnery Tales Written by a Young Nobleman* (1727), a three-volume French novel published in England as *Nunnery Tales* by the pornographers John and William Dugdale; and John Fairburn's *Atrocious Acts of Catholic Priests, who have lately committed the most Horrid and Diabolical Rape and Murders in Ireland and France* (1824), and his *The Rape and Assassination of Marie Gerin by Mingrat, a French Catholic Priest* (1824), the latter two volumes culled from articles in French and Irish newspapers.

The chapbooks

I think it is no coincidence that Matthew Lewis served one term as a Whig Member of Parliament, while Horace Walpole's father Robert was the first Whig Prime Minister of England. Lewis also was one of the earliest and most vehement practitioners of the anti-Catholic gothic, although Ann Radcliffe's three major gothic novels all contain vignettes or 'type scenes' of an anti-Catholic nature: i.e., the suffering nun and the evil abbot in *A Sicilian Romance* (1790), the convent kidnapping and abbey persecution of Adeline in *The Romance of the Forest* (1791), and the evil abbess and Inquisition scenes in *The Italian* (1797). Lewis's *The Monk*, however, was the mother lode of anti-Catholic propaganda, and its subplots, particularly those featuring Raymond and Agnes and the Bleeding Nun, were mined for decades as the source material for chapbooks, novellas, penny dreadfuls, ballads, operettas, melodramas, and even paper dolls that were sold for children.[47] The novel's popularity was so immense that it spawned a virtual publication industry, and was the basis of the majority of the imaginative content of chapbooks that concerned the Catholic monk and his nefarious activities. The novel was so sprawling that there were at least three separate tales within it, each of which could be focused on as the content for an entire chapbook. The first and perhaps the most popular excerpt from the novel concerned the tale of the 'Bleeding Nun', derived from German sources and adapted by Lewis to supplement the story of Raymond and Agnes, the pregnant nun held captive below the Convent of St Clare. But, while the emphasis in the Bleeding Nun tale appears to be horror and the fear of the dead walking, the story also relies on the familiar tropes of the profligate nun, the unchaste and undead Sister who continues to seek out male victims for her unsated lust, much like a proto-vampire. For instance, the Preface to one of the chapbook editions of *The Monk*, *The Castle of Lindenberg; or the history of Raymond & Agnes, a Romance* (1799), states the ideological agenda quite clearly:

> The subject of the following pages is founded on those remoter days of our ancestors when, blinded by superstitions, they sacrificed their dearest interest to the will of monastic fanatics who, under the pretence of religion, committed the most cruel actions; and with a zeal, deaf to all those tender feelings which distinguished a true Christian, let fall their revenge on all those who were so unfortunate as to deviate from the path they had drawn out for them to pursue.[48]

We do know that Bennett Dugdale had parents in England and that he traveled there frequently to visit family.[49] When the Copyright Act went into effect on 2 July 1801, the 'Dublin reprinting of current works was virtually stopped and the booksellers had to look to London and Edinburgh for much of their supply'.[50] It is precisely at this point that Dugdale began a collaboration with the London publishing firm of one Thomas Tegg (1776–1846), himself an unscrupulous London publisher who, in fact, had attributed one of his own books, *The Biographical annals of suicide* (1803), to the notorious Irishman George Barrington (c. 1758–1804), the 'celebrity convict', pickpocket, and thief who once escaped Ireland dressed as a Catholic priest (shades of Gavin) and was now living as a transported felon in New South Wales. I bring in the 'young genteel Irishman' because he is such a perfect representation of the cross-cultural hybridized construction of Irish and English culture existing at this time.[51] Both historically 'real' and a fantasy construct of the English imagination, this Irishman became famous in England as the 'Prince of Pickpockets', and the supposed author of *A Voyage to New South Wales* (1795), as well as a variety of other books about spies and suicides (both extremely popular topics in early nineteenth-century British culture). Barrington actually wrote nothing except letters continually asserting his innocence of charges of theft, yet he is identified as the author of a number of books published by any number of British publishers, Tegg being just one of them.[52] Tegg was as prolific and successful a publisher of reprints, remainders, and cheap reading materials intended for the lower and middling classes in London as Dugdale was in Dublin. In many ways their publishing collaboration made eminent sense, and both of them appear to have been nothing if not ruthless in their publication schemes. At one point in his reprinting career, Tegg simply ripped off the conclusion to Milton's *Paradise Lost* in order for it to fit into its page allocation.[53]

As his contemporary biographer has shown, Barrington could not have been the author of any of the books attributed to him.[54] His name, notorious and widely recognized as it was with the lower and middling classes as something of a folk hero, was simply appropriated by the book's publisher Tegg in order to sell books to salvage his struggling publishing house (he was parting ways with Castleman at exactly this time). The full title of the original work is *The Biographical annals of suicide, or Horrors of self-murder, whether impelled by love, penury, depravity, melancholy, bigotry, remorse, or jealousy,* and it consisted of a series of 23 stories that he claimed to have uncovered during his extensive travels. When it was reprinted as a chapbook in 1804 in another Tegg production, *The Marvellous Magazine*, only four tales were selected, three of which featured detailed descriptions of the evil deeds of Catholic clergy as causing the suicides of young and beautiful people.[55] The first two tales concern Clementina and Eliza, while the third focuses on a Frenchman who is bankrupted and forced into suicide by a corrupt Abbé who is intent on lavishing money on his mistress. Garvey speculates that Tegg himself, rather than Barrington, was the author of these tales, and this is what is most important, I think, for my argument.[56]

The first tale concerns Clementina Pellegrini, consigned to a convent at the age of six when her Genoan father loses his estate to a kinsman, the Marquis Abruzzo. After many years of unhappiness in the convent, Clementina has finally reached the age where she is to be forced to take her final vows and on her final night of freedom, she meets and falls instantly in love with her cousin Jeronymo Abruzzo, the son of her father's old enemy. He instantly proposes marriage, and then convinces his father that in marrying Clementina, they can right the wrongs the family committed years earlier in seizing Pellegrini's fortune. Abruzzo obtains an immediate release of Clementina from the convent, and they rush there the next morning to perform a surprise wedding rather than the long-scheduled vows ceremony. Amid much jubilation, however, the evil and haughty Abbess, descended from an old Genoan aristocratic family, seems perturbed and slighted, perhaps even jealous. Without thinking, Clementina accepts a glass of lemonade from the Abbess's hands, and it is not long before she is dead, poisoned by the drink. When the Abbess's family is able to use its wealth and influence to have her released from a prison sentence, the Abbess is attacked during a public procession and stoned to death by the population. And the dramatic denouement of the tale occurs when Clementina's coffin is carried through the streets of Genoa in a procession to the cemetery. As it passes below him, Jeronymo flings himself onto it, 'dashing his brains out and scattering them on the black pall' (p. 82), dying instantly, to be buried with his bride in the same tomb.

In the second tale about 'Eliza or the Unhappy Nun', we learn of a young British girl forced into a French convent by her fanatical Catholic father from 'S—d [Sheffield], in the north of England' (p. 87). Here we are given an anglicized story of Mme Genlis's 'Cecilia, the Beautiful Nun' or Clementina, a direct and fearful confrontation of the British Protestant imaginary with the religious tyrannies practiced in the Roman Catholic convent (see Figure 2.1).

Figure 2.1 Chapbook version of 'George Barrington', *Eliza, the Unhappy Nun*
(London: Thomas Tegg, 1804)
Source: Reproduced courtesy of the Sadleir-Black Collection, University of Virginia Library.

There are hints that the Abbess who presides in this convent is not just cruel, but the suggestion is that she is also a lesbian (much like the Abbess in 'Clementina') who jealously wants complete control and dominance over her young charges. Further, we are told that below the convent there are two underground prison cells strewn with the bones of other unlucky nuns, a veritable chamber of horrors.

In this brief tale, all of the familiar tropes are brought out and used to great effect: a cultured and cosmopolitan British man is traveling in the south of France during 1791, and he hears a tale about a British woman who had been killed in a convent by a cruel Abbess more than 30 years earlier. As he inquires in the village about the convent and the history of the beautiful but tragic British nun, he learns that the revolutionary troops are preparing to descend on the town, attack the convent, and murder the Abbess, all of whom agree has been a tyrant and oppressor for decades. Taken on a tour of the ruined and burned convent, the nameless narrator finds a handwritten testament composed by Sister Eliza, and we have a first-person narration of how one British woman found herself in a convent's underground dungeon, where she was 'buried alive', starved, and eventually committed suicide by slitting her wrist with a razor (p. 87), as shown in the illustration above (Figure 2.1).

The action of the inset narrative takes place in 1759, when the 15-year-old Eliza H is forced by her cruel father to take vows as a nun in a small convent outside of Nice. Her only friend is a Sister Madeleine who has been forced into the convent as well, this time by a stepmother who did not want her to marry a distant relative. When Eliza appears as a nun in her first religious procession on the feast day of St Philip, she is spotted by Charles de R..., a handsome young man who falls instantly in love with her and proposes marriage via letters smuggled into the convent. Through her network of spies, the jealous Abbess discovers these letters and sentences Sister Eliza to banishment below the convent, where she is slowly starved to death. Her final act is to leave a written testament, to be given to her father on her death, before she slits her wrists and bleeds to death. This nun's tale, which in various versions we find throughout gothic novels like *The Monk*, *The Abbess* (1799), and *Legends of a Nunnery* (1807), stands as a curious hybrid: a denunciation of the worst abuses of the French convent system, justifiably destroyed by the French Revolution. And yet the British Protestant imaginary that reveled in these tales was not politically radical, nor was it in sympathy with the principles or the spread of the French revolutionary ideals onto British soil. This confused ideological agenda accounts, I think, for the critical splits in trying to decipher the use that the gothic makes of Catholic religious tropes.

Four of the 19 gothic chapbooks that Dugdale and Tegg published are anonymous and clearly anti-Catholic productions: *Amalgro & Claude; or the Monastic Murder, Father Innocent, The Secret Tribunal; or, The Court of Winceslaus,* and *Phantasmagoria, or the Development of Magical Deception,* and most of them conform to the pattern described by Loeber and Loeber in that they 'were illustrated with a frontispiece representing a terrifying or crucial scene from the narrative',[57] while they promulgate a 'discourse which associates monstrosity, Catholicism, and sublimity [for] the Irish Anglicans attempting to come to terms with the "enemy" in their midst'.[58] They are all, in fact, virtual miniature plagiarisms of their source texts, either *The Monk* for *Amalgro & Claude* and *Father Innocent,* or Friedrich Schiller's *The Ghost-Seer* (1789; translated into English 1795) for *Phantasmagoria,* or Christiane Naubert's *Hermann von Unna* (1788; translated into English 1794), a novel purporting to expose the workings of 'secret tribunals' at the corrupt aristocratic court of the Emperors Winceslaus and Sigismond in Westphalia, for *The Secret Tribunal.*

There is no question that *Hermann* was extremely popular in Britain and has long been recognized as an important influence on Radcliffe's depiction of the Inquisition in *The Italian.* In addition, James Boaden virtually plagiarized the work as his gothic drama *The Secret Tribunal* (Covent Garden, 1795), while a redaction of the novel appeared as an 1803 chapbook (see Figure 2.2). Felicia Hemans later adapted the legend as the basis for her long narrative poem *A Tale of the Secret Tribunal* (comp. early 1820s; publ. 1845), citing Madame de Staël's *De l'Allemagne* (1813) as her source. Walter Scott also drafted a Tribunal play himself, 'The House of Aspen', based on Veit Weber's *Sagen der Vorzeit* (1787–98) in 1799.

Friedrich von Schiller's *Der Geisterseher,* translated into English as *The Ghost-Seer or the Apparitionist,* was the major Germanic source for both *The Monk* and *Melmoth the Wanderer,* as well as a number of German necromancer novels, most famously K. F. Kahlert's *Der Geisterbanner* (1790) (*The Necromancer,* trans. Peter Teuthold, 1794) and its chapbook redaction *Phantasmagoria. The Ghost-Seer* is a scathing portrait of the real-life Masonic charlatan, Count Cagliostro, a Sicilian who performed across Europe in the late 1780s as a fortune teller and séance leader and was eventually executed by the Inquisition in Rome in 1795. He was rumored to be a member of the Illuminati, a revolutionary group of Freemasons who used a number of sensory tricks (magic

Engraved by Holber from a Drawing by Craig.

THE SECRET TRIBUNAL.

London Published 1ʳᵗ May 1803. by Tegg, & Cᵒ.

Figure 2.2 Frontispiece to Anon., *The Secret Tribunal; or, The Court of Winceslaus* (London: Thomas Tegg, 1803)

Source: Reproduced courtesy of the Sadleir-Black Collection, University of Virginia Library.

lanterns, exploding powders) to gain power over their gullible victims. The Freemasons' aim was to assume control over the property of their bamboozled adherents (usually convents of easily duped nuns). By extension, fear of the Illuminati was based on the belief that they could use these same techniques on powerful 'Princes' in order to gain power over nation states. Schiller's short mystery was also supposedly modeled on yet another contemporary historical figure, the third son in line to the dukedom of Würtemberg, whose family was Protestant but who was himself rumored to be considering the idea of converting to Catholicism. *The Ghost-Seer* tells the tale of a young German prince driven by a mysterious monk first to religious skepticism, then to libertinism, and finally to murder in the religiously paranoid atmosphere of Venice. Raised in a strict Protestant society, the Prince's naturally good feelings and impulses are corrupted so thoroughly that he easily falls prey to the superstitious mysteries and displays that the mysterious Armenian monk offers to him. *The Ghost-Seer* is almost a textbook study of the 'explained supernatural', except that all of the supernatural powers of the so-called 'Incomprehensible' Armenian monk are finally not explained fully, nor is the work finished. Influenced by the Swabian pietism of his youth, Schiller focused on a depiction of God as a punishing force and his *Ghost-Seer* returns repeatedly to exploring the unfortunate connection between freethinking and damnation, skepticism and credulity. The use that these two chapbooks make of the themes of political revolution, upheaval, and invasion would have been particularly anxiety-producing in an Anglo-Irish reading population at this time. With the failure of the 1798 uprising, the French invasion at County Mayo and its defeat in September, and then the attempted invasion with the involvement of Wolfe Tone later that same year, the Anglo-Irish Protestant majority would still have been anxious and would have feared yet another imminent invasion, particularly after Bonaparte's coronation in December 1804.

The two gothic chapbooks based on *The Monk* – *Amalgro & Claude* and *Father Innocent* (see Figure 2.3) – are both hyperbolic texts full of events that feature elaborate costuming, excess, and the sort of displays of clerical corruption and wealth that the Methodist mentality would have found deeply disturbing and offensive. *Amalgro & Claude* is 40 pages long and focuses on retelling the banditti inset tale in conjunction with the Bleeding Nun narrative, while *Father Innocent* is a 72-page novella concerned with the Ambrosio and Matilda story. As Cooney has shown, the Irish Methodists recruited their membership from the Church of Ireland and nonconformists, people who were artisans and

52

Engraved by J. Walker from a Drawing by J. Hamilton

FATHER INNOCENT.

London Pub.d by Tegg. and C.o April 1st 1803

Figure 2.3 Frontispiece to Anon., *Father Innocent* (London: Thomas Tegg, 1803)
Source: Reproduced courtesy of the Sadleir-Black Collection, University of Virginia Library.

'upwardly aspiring commercial classes', particularly characterized by their industry, thrift, and hard work.[59] Such a description accurately characterizes Bennett Dugdale, who converted to Methodism after hearing John Wesley preach in Dublin during his fourteenth visit to the city in 1773. Before long, Dugdale was a 'prominent member' of the Primitive Wesleyan Methodist Society, frequently preaching at the Methodist chapel and spearheading the drive to raise funds in order to build a new and large assembly hall for the Methodists.[60] As a publisher we know that he was particularly interested in producing anti-slavery tracts, Methodist hymnals, and religious pamphlets, in addition to these five anti-Catholic gothic chapbooks.[61] In short, he was not simply a 'pious publisher' as Cooney states, or just an ambitious Dublin-based collaborator of Thomas Tegg, as Loeber and Loeber suggest. He was also a Methodist propagandist who used his publishing firm to produce the sort of works that he and his associates thought would best advance the cause of Methodism in Ireland. To extrapolate from that conclusion, we might very well conclude that many of the publishing houses in Dublin during this period had unspoken but very clear political and religious agendas that can be discerned by a careful reading of their publication lists.

Notes

1. Elizabeth Bonhôte (1773) *The Rambles of Mr. Frankly, Published by His Sister*, 2 vols (Dublin: Messrs. Sleater, Lynch, Williams, Potts, Chamberlaine), I: 67.
2. Anon. (1746) *Purgatory Prov'd: Illustrated and set forth, in a clear Light. By Father Murtagh O'Lavery. Priest of the Parish of St. John's Dromore, and Macherlin. In a Funeral Sermon, upon the death of one of his parishioners* (Dublin: Carson), p. 6.
3. James Watt (1999) *Contesting the Gothic: Fiction, Genre and Cultural Conflict, 1764–1832* (Cambridge: Cambridge University Press), p. 47.
4. Mary Muriel Tarr (1946) *Catholicism in Gothic Fiction* (Washington, D.C.: Catholic University Press), p. 64; see also Christina Morin (2011) 'Forgotten Fiction: Reconsidering the Gothic Novel in Eighteenth-Century Ireland', *Irish University Review* 41.1, 80–94.
5. Rolf and Magda Loeber (2003) 'The Publication of Irish Novels and Novelettes: a Footnote on Irish Gothic Fiction', *Cardiff Corvey: Reading the Romantic Text*, 10, n.p. (p. [26]). Available online from <www.cardiff.ac.uk/encap/journals/corvey/articles/cc10_n02.pdf>. Accessed 1 May 2012.
6. Cooney notes that 'in 1787 there were 53 printers in the city [of Dublin]. Bookbinders were rather fewer, but of booksellers there were in 1790 a total of 65. [...] In these circumstances, the Dublin book trade flourished. These halcyon days, however, were coming to an end' with the passage of the Act of Union; Dudley Levistone Cooney (2001) *The Methodists in Ireland: a Short History* (Blackrock: Columba Press), p. 78. Pollard notes a steep decline in

publishing output in Dublin after 1793, but notes that there was an almost double rise in importing books from England during the 1790s; Mary Pollard (1989) *Dublin's Trade in Books* (Oxford: Clarendon Press), pp. 154–5.

7. Charles Benson (2011) 'The Dublin Book Trade', in *The Irish Book in English 1800–1891*, ed. James H. Murphy (Oxford: Oxford University Press), pp. 27–46 (p. 30).

8. For further historical context to this issue, see James Kelly (1992) *Prelude to Union: Anglo-Irish Politics in the 1780s* (Cork: Cork University Press); Kevin Whelan (1998) *Fellowship of Freedom: the United Irishmen and 1798* (Cork: Cork University Press); and Thomas Bartlett (1992) *The Fall and Rise of the Irish Nation: the Catholic Question, 1690–1830* (Dublin: Gill and Macmillan).

9. Benson, 'The Dublin Book Trade', p. 32.

10. Quoted in Benson, 'The Dublin Book Trade', p. 35.

11. Foster has noted that major Irish gothic novelists like Maturin, Le Fanu, and Stoker all shared 'occult preoccupations [that] surely mirror a sense of displacement, a loss of social and psychological integration, and an escapism motivated by the threat of a takeover by the Catholic middle classes'; Roy Foster (1995) *Paddy and Mr Punch: Connections in Irish and English History* (London: Penguin), p. 220.

12. Fenning has traced in detail the conditions of Catholic bishops and laity in Ireland during the eighteenth century, particularly with regard to the passage of a series of bills that gradually restored voting and property rights to Catholics. As he observes, in 1707 there was only one Catholic bishop in Dublin and he was in prison; Hugh Fenning, OP (2002) 'A Time of Reform: From the "Penal Laws" to the Birth of Modern Nationalism, 1691–1800', in *Christianity in Ireland*, pp. 134–43 (p. 135). When *The History of Andrew Dunn, an Irish Catholic*, a religious fiction about the conversion of a man from Protestantism to Catholicism was published anonymously in 1814 by the Religious Tract Society, it was published in London. See Rolf and Magda Loeber (2006) *A Guide to Irish Fiction 1650–1900* (Dublin: Four Courts Press), p. 688 for bibliographical details.

13. My book from the University of Wales Press, *The Gothic Ideology: Religious Hysteria and Anti-Catholicism in British Popular Fiction, 1780–1880* (2014), examines in much greater depth the complex and convoluted sources of anti-Catholicism in British gothic texts.

14. Rolf and Magda Loeber (1998), 'John Connor: a Maverick Cork Publisher of Literature', *18th–19th Century Irish Fiction Newsletter* 5, n.p.

15. See Irene Bostrom (1963) 'The Novel and Catholic Emancipation', *Studies in Romanticism* 2, 155–76; Victor Sage (1988) *Horror Fiction in the Protestant Tradition* (London: Macmillan); Susan Griffin (2004) *Anti-Catholicism and Nineteenth-Century Fiction* (Cambridge: Cambridge University Press); Diane Long Hoeveler (2012) 'Anti-Catholicism and the Gothic Imaginary: the Historical and Literary Contexts', *Religion in the Age of Enlightenment* 3, 1–31; Diane Long Hoeveler (2013) 'Demonizing the Catholic Other: Religion and the Secularization Process in Gothic Literature', in *Transnational Gothic: Literary and Social Exchanges in the Long Nineteenth Century*, ed. Monika Ebert and Bridget Marshall (Aldershot: Ashgate), pp. 83–96.

16. Loeber and Loeber, 'The Publication of Irish Novels and Novelettes', p. 29.

17. In 1810 Walter Scott famously claimed that the gothic was an 'unthinking mass production [done by] hack writers [...] writing solely for gain'; Michael Gamer (2002) 'Gothic Fictions and Romantic Writing in Britain', in *The Cambridge Companion to Gothic Fiction*, ed. Jerrold Hogle (Cambridge: Cambridge University Press), pp. 85–104 (p. 91).

18. What we know about Dugdale's personal and religious history and his professional activities as a publisher has been summarized in the biographical articles by Cooney and Pollard; see Cooney (2002), 'Irish Methodism', in *Christianity in Ireland*, ed. Brendan Bradshaw and Daire Keogh (Dublin: Columba Press), pp. 144–54 (p. 78) and Mary Pollard (2000) *A Dictionary of Members of the Dublin Book Trade, 1550–1800* (Cambridge: Bibliographical Society), pp. 172–3.

19. Loeber and Loeber, 'The Publication of Irish Novels and Novelettes', p. 26.

20. Cooney, *The Methodists in Ireland*, pp. 53, 98.

21. Loeber and Loeber ('The Publication of Irish Novels and Novelettes', p. 20) comment on the use that Dublin publishers made of works pirated from London, as well as the opposite occurrence, the pirating of an Irish author's work by London publishers. Given the revisions in copyright law that occurred throughout the eighteenth century, copyright infringement was not rigorously enforced, although publishers themselves tended to work to ostracize a particularly egregious offender. Haywood and Groom both provide detailed overviews of the culture of literary piracy and the issue of spurious authorship of books during this period; see Ian Haywood (1987) *Faking It: Art and the Politics of Forgery* (Brighton: Harvester), esp. pp. 21–70, and Nick Groom (2002) *The Forger's Shadow: How Forgery Changed the Course of Literature* (London: Picador).

22. Loeber and Loeber, 'The Publication of Irish Novels and Novelettes', p. 22.

23. See Maureen Wall (2001) 'The Age of the Penal Laws', in *The Course of Irish History*, ed. T. W. Moody and F. X. Martin (Cork: Mercier Press), pp. 176–89.

24. Albert D. Pionke (2004) *Plots of Opportunity: Representing Conspiracy in Victorian England* (Columbus, OH: Ohio State University Press), p. 54.

25. Colin Haydon (1993) *Anti-Catholicism in Eighteenth-Century England, c. 1714–80: a Political and Social Study* (Manchester: Manchester University Press), p. 42.

26. Linda Colley (1992; 2009) *Britons: Forging the Nation 1707–1837* (New Haven, CT: Yale University Press), p. 23.

27. Nicholas Rogers (2004) 'Popular Culture', in *The Enlightenment World*, ed. Martin Fitzpatrick, Peter Jones, Christa Knellwolf, and Iain McCalman (London: Routledge), pp. 401–17 (p. 408).

28. The association of Catholicism with witchcraft, black magic, and diabolical sorcery goes back to the Reformation period (Spencer's Duessa in *The Faerie Queene*, Milton's Dalila in *Samson Agonistes*). See Deborah Willis (1995) *Malevolent Nurture: Witch-Hunting and Maternal Power in Early Modern England* (Ithaca, NY: Cornell University Press) for further examples of this association.

29. Haydon, 'Anti-Catholicism', pp. 41, 58.

30. Haydon, 'Anti-Catholicism', pp. 42, iv.

31. *Statutes of the Realm*: volume 7: 1695–1701 (1820), pp. 586–7. Available online from <http://www.british-history.ac.uk/report.asp?compid=46963>. Accessed 15 August 2013.

32. Haydon, 'Anti-Catholicism', p. 68.
33. Haydon, 'Anti-Catholicism', p. 60.
34. Haydon, 'Anti-Catholicism', p. 60.
35. The print is available in the British Museum, Department of Prints and Drawings, 5,685; quoted in Haydon, 'Anti-Catholicism', p. 65.
36. George Rudé (1971) *Paris and London in the Eighteenth Century: Studies in Popular Protest* (New York: Viking), p. 139.
37. Colley, *Britons*, p. 332.
38. The most extensive discussion of the class motivations of the people who participated in the Gordon Riots can be found in Rudé, *Paris and London*, pp. 268–92. While the initial participants of the demonstration appear to have been tradesmen, the ranks soon swelled with weavers from Spitalfields and an 'inferior set' shouting 'No Popery!' The first building to be attacked was the private chapel of the Sardinian embassy and the next was the chapel attached to the Bavarian embassy. Both chapels were known to have been frequented by aristocratic British Catholics; Rudé, *Paris and London*, p. 271.
39. Colley, *Britons*, p. 337.
40. Huxley notes that the gulf between official Catholic teaching and practice by individual ecclesiastics was 'enormous' during the early modern period: 'it is difficult to find any medieval or Renaissance writer who does not take it for granted that, from highest prelate to humblest friar, the majority of clergymen are thoroughly disreputable. Ecclesiastical corruption begot the Reformation, and in its turn the Reformation produced the Counter Reformation'; Aldous Huxley (1952) *The Devils of Loudon* (London: Chatto and Windus), p. 6. For a survey of dozens of historical incidents involving eighteenth-century Spanish priests who had affairs and illegitimate children with their female confessors, see Stephen Haliczer (1996) *Sexuality in the Confessional, A Sacrament Profaned* (Oxford: Oxford University Press). Several of these affairs, in which both participants were denounced to the Inquisition and forced to stand trial, read as the historical source material for any number of gothic novels by Ireland and Montague.
41. Karl Toepfer (1991) in *Theatre, Aristocracy and Pornocracy: the Orgy Calculus* (New York: PAJ Publications), makes the same sort of distinction in his study of *ancien régime* Enlightenment theater, contrasting the open and democratic aspect of carnivalesque excess and the secret, closed, and exclusive quality of libertine orgies practiced by the aristocracy (pp. 10–13).
42. Robert Darnton (1982) *The Forbidden Best-Sellers of Pre-Revolutionary France* (London: HarperCollins), p. 107.
43. Henry Spencer Ashbee (1879; 1962) *Centuria Librorum Absconditorum*, vol. 2 (London), p. 121.
44. Haydon, 'Anti-Catholicism', p. 38.
45. Roger Thompson (1979) *Unfit for Modest Ears: a Study of Pornographic, Obscene and Bawdy Works Written or Published in England in the Second Half of the Seventeenth Century* (Totowa, N.J.: Rowman and Littlefield), pp. 147, 142.
46. *A short history of monastical orders in which the primitive institution of monks, their tempers, habits, rules, and the condition they are in at present, are treated of* / *by Gabriel d'Emillianne* [pseudonym of Antonio Gavin, fl. 1726] (London: Printed by S. Roycroft, for W. Bentley, 1693), pp. 133–4.

47. Diane Long Hoeveler (2010) 'More Gothic Gold: the Sadleir-Black Chapbook Collection at the University of Virginia Library', *Papers on Language & Literature* 46, 164–91.
48. *The Castle of Lindenberg; or the history of Raymond & Agnes, a Romance* (London: Fisher, 1799), p. 1.
49. Cooney, *The Methodists in Ireland*, p. 87.
50. Benson, 'The Dublin Book Trade', p. 40.
51. Nathan Garvey (2008) *The Celebrated George Barrington: a Spurious Author, the Book Trade, and Botany Bay* (Potts Point, Australia: Hordern House), p. 2.
52. In addition to Garvey on the contested biography of Barrington, see Sheila Box (2001) *The Real George Barrington? The Adventures of a Notorious London Pickpocket, later Head Constable of the Infant Colony of New South Wales* (Melbourne: Australian Scholarly Publishing), pp. 11–25. Both Frank and Mulvey-Roberts mistakenly identify Barrington as the author of *Eliza, The Unhappy Nun*; Frederick S. Frank (1987) *The First Gothics: a Critical Guide to the English Gothic Novel* (New York: Garland), p. 22, and Marie Mulvey-Roberts, 'Biographies of Gothic Novelists'. Available online from <http://www.ampltd.co.uk/digital_guides/gothic_fiction/biographies.aspx>. Accessed 1 May 2012. Summers describes Tegg's production of chapbooks, stating 'there was no busier house in this particular trade than that of Thomas Tegg, No. 3 Cheapside, and it may be remarked that his bluebooks are far better printed than the majority of these miniature romances'; Montague Summers (1938) *The Gothic Quest: a History of the Gothic Novel* (London: Fortune), p. 83.
53. James J. Barnes and Patience Barnes (2000) 'Reassessing the Reputation of Thomas Tegg, London Publisher, 1776–1846', *Book History* 3, 45–60 (p. 48). Tegg's publishing career is analyzed in a good deal of detail in Barnes and Barnes, who note that he was known in London as 'the broom that swept the booksellers' warehouses', a reference to the fact that he successfully exploited the reprint and remainder trade. At his death his obituary identified him as the single most prolific publisher in London; Barnes and Barnes, 'Reassessing the Reputation', p. 45.
54. Garvey, *The Celebrated George Barrington*, p. 154.
55. 'Barrington, George' [Thomas Tegg?] (1803), *Eliza, or the Unhappy Nun, exemplifying the unlimited tyranny exercised by the abbots and abbesses over the ill-fated victims of their malice in the gloomy recesses of a convent. Including the Adventures of Clementina...* (London: Tegg). Rpt. *Marvellous Magazine* (1804), III: 83–94. Subsequent page-number references to this work will be made in parentheses in the main text.
56. Garvey, *The Celebrated George Barrington*, p. 159.
57. Loeber and Loeber, 'The Publication of Irish Novels and Novelettes', p. 18.
58. Jarlath Killeen (2005) *Gothic Ireland: Horror and the Irish Anglican Imagination in the Long Eighteenth Century* (Dublin: Four Courts Press), p. 131.
59. Cooney, 'Irish Methodism', p. 146.
60. Cooney, *The Methodists in Ireland*, p. 81.
61. Pollard, *A Dictionary of Members*, pp. 172–3.

3
Irish Jacobin Gothic, c. 1796–1825

Niall Gillespie

On 23 May 1794, the preeminent republican body in Ireland, the United Irish Society, was forcibly dissolved by the Dublin Castle administration. The era of associational, pacific, constitutional, and civic republicanism in Ireland effectively ceased. A year later, in the autumn of 1795, the United Irish Society reorganized itself into an illegal underground entity, one which overlaid military structures onto civilian ones. Its class composition changed substantially. With its proscription, much of its middle-class membership fell off, and it became increasingly an organization drawn from the peasantry and skilled and semi-skilled labourers of the manufacturing sector. The United Irish leadership formally requested French military co-operation, and, by December 1796, the French revolutionary regime had sent to Ireland a large invasion fleet, which failed to land due to severe weather. In the immediate aftermath of this, Irish republicanism had gained critical mass in quantitative terms (with the United Irishmen boasting, in mid-1797, over 200,000 adult male members) and in terms of its ability to challenge the prevailing intellectual and cultural orthodoxies emanating from the Dublin Castle-sponsored press. To counteract this consolidating Jacobin threat, the Irish government, which was in essence a dependent executive outpost of Pitt's Westminster regime, dropped its prior conciliatory policies in favour of mass coercion. Thus, from Fitzwilliam's departure (1795) to the Act of Union (1800), the Irish government relied more and more on state violence to subdue its rebelling subjects.[1]

In essence, a severe de facto martial law was applied to Ireland. The methods to pacify the country were particularly brutal, even by the standards then prevailing in war-torn Europe. Collective punishment was the norm (General Lake opined 'nothing but terror will keep them in order'), and the civilian population was indiscriminately targeted, with little attention paid to guilt or innocence.[2] With habeas corpus suspended and the magistracy indemnified, Ireland's judicial protections (never particularly strong) were obliterated. Central to Dublin Castle's policy of coercion were five groupings: the regular standing army; a mercenary force drawn from continental Europe; and three indigenous bodies, the yeomanry (effectively the propertied in arms), the militia, and the Orange Order (an organization founded on the principles of supposed racial and sectarian supremacy and possessing, by early 1798, the tacit support and financial sponsorship of government). These entities, under full or partial state control, were increasingly used to disarm and harass the popular oppositional forces (the Jacobins and advanced Whigs). The disarming was savage – the Lord Lieutenant, Camden, had told his underlings in late 1797 to 'strike terror', and, with relish, they did.[3] The most common methods used, as contemporary loyalist sources inform us, were picketing (where the sufferer was forced to stand barefoot upon a sharp object), triangling (the whipping of a bound man), pitch capping (the pouring of a dome of burning tar onto the head, which, when cooled, was removed, tearing off the hair and scalp), roasting (the burning of flesh), pricking (non-fatal bayoneting), the salting of raw wounds, rape, gang rape, extrajudicial execution, half-hanging, hanging, digital mutilation, the cropping of ears, and what we now term waterboarding.[4] Lighter measures included impressment into the navy and forced internal banishment or external repatriation. The destruction of fixed property was also rather routinely undertaken. Government also forcibly closed down the democratic press – the *Northern Star* in May 1797 and the *Press* and *Harp of Erin* in March of 1798.

This extensive violence turned the Irish landscape into a gothic landscape, and it was as a gothic landscape that it was perceived by both Irish Jacobins and advanced Irish Whigs. English Jacobins perceived this gothicization of the Irish landscape too, and for good reason. They feared that what was occurring in Ireland was a preparatory laboratory that Pitt had engineered for importation into the Home Counties. Coleridge, on 17 January 1798, stated that Ireland's situation was worse than that of the Vendée, while Southey, in July of the same year, stated that 'torture has been to all intents introduced in that country'.[5] Likewise, Thomas Holcroft believed Pitt was carrying out a reign of terror against the Irish.[6] In late January 1798, the London Corresponding Society issued an address to Ireland on the events, stating that there were 'few in Britain who do not shudder with horror at a recital of the sufferings of the Irish people'. The address further berated the 'sanguinary malice' of Pitt's Irish administration.[7]

Prior to this coercive campaign, that is, prior to 1795, the literature of the Irish Jacobins made use of a variety of modes and genres. At the more elite end of the spectrum they frequently employed the proclamation, Platonic dialogues, catechistic responses, the pastoral, the elegy, the neoclassical, etc. At the more popular level, they utilized the most commonly established forms of the Irish literary marketplace – coffee-house satire, ballads, squibs, handbills, broadsheets, etc. These popular forms tended to the comic, the humorously lewd, the ludicrous, the anarchic, and the carnivalesque. However, with the onset of the coercive campaign, Irish Jacobin writing found these forms increasingly inadequate. The objective situation on the ground changed dramatically. Radicals were being physically targeted by the state, and republicans, ill-armed, were forced on the defensive. In 1795, the radicals of the province of Connaught were effectively neutralized as the armed forces of government, often acting illegally, swept the western counties with much brutality.

The most established genre in the Irish market that could mirror this torturous situation was the gothic, which, as the Loebers have demonstrated at the bibliographical level, had a solid tradition within the Irish literary marketplace.[8] Before assessing the use of the gothic by the Irish Jacobins, it may be useful to provide a sample of their more lurid writing. The following anonymous ode was printed in Arthur O'Connor's enormously popular periodical entitled the *Press* (1797–8) and typifies the minor poetry of that sheet:

> Hark! heard ye not those dreadful screams?
> And heard ye not that infant cry?
> 'Tis sure, some neighbouring cot in flames
> Which with crimson tints the sky.
>
> Oh God! An aged corpse I see
> Naked, wounded, stained with gore,
> Hanging on a blasted tree
> Before the burning cottage door.
>
> [...]
>
> But see untouch'd yon palace stands
> While all around the hamlets burn;
> And lo! those military bands
> Back to the flames their victims spurn.[9]

Prose likewise manifests this gothic tone: 'Bloody is the field where she lies, and her garments are weeping with blood – for the wounds of her sons are streaming around her, and the ghosts of her heroes are screaming for vengeance. But Erin has not awakened – no! she still sleeps [...] wives and virgins violated by miscreants, on whom the blood of their husbands and relatives still smoked [*sic*]'.[10]

And finally, the well-known poem the 'Wake of William Orr' (1797), which was composed by Ireland's last great Augustan poet, William Drennan:

> Hunted thro' thy native grounds,
> Or flung *reward* to human hounds;
> Each one pull'd and tore his share,
> Heedless of thy deep despair.

> [...]

> Monstrous and unhappy sight!
> Brothers blood will not unite;
> Holy oil and holy water,
> Mix, and fill the world with slaughter.

> Who is she with aspect wild?
> The widow'd mother with her child,
> Child new stirring in the womb!
> Husband waiting for the tomb.[11]

Quite clearly all of these pieces draw on the sensationalist literature and gothic register that predated and ran concurrent with the government's coercive campaign, a literature that Niall Ó Ciosáin has identified in the inexpensive contemporary Irish chapbook and trial book forms.[12] These pieces also draw on that literature at the more expensive end of the market, that is, the well-developed late-eighteenth-century Irish gothic novel tradition as isolated by Jarlath Killeen and Christina Morin, as well as on the archetypes present in the English gothic novel.[13] English gothic novels of the late eighteenth century are often referenced by United Irishmen. A central text in the United Irish canon was Godwin's *Caleb Williams* (1794), to which Ulster United Irishman Henry Joy McCracken turned when describing the horrendous conditions of his imprisonment. Thomas Russell, one of the formative ideological progenitors of the United Irishmen, read the novels of Ann Radcliffe, appropriately enough, while incarcerated. The first substantial dramatic adaptation of Godwin's gothic classic *St. Leon* (1799) was by a United Irishman, John Daly Burk, who remodelled the novel into a United Irish allegory.[14] Quite demonstrably, the Irish Jacobins had enough familiarity with the gothic genre to mobilize it for popular political purposes.

Clearly the gothic presented Irish republicans with a language in which to describe the military and paramilitary outrages that the state was spreading throughout the nation. But this adoption of the gothic was a major break with prior Irish republican forms. Irish republicanism had, in its constitutional phase (that is, prior to May 1794), insisted on the rational, the reasonably argued, the discursive practices of the classical. In the constitutional phase, when outrages were described, it was in the language of the legal, the objectively statistical, or the polite but firm remonstrance. The United Irish of the pre-1795 period prided themselves on privileging the reasoned above the emotional, the intellectual above the somatic. With their adoption of the gothic, such Enlightenment rationality lost its priority and the previously under-utilized melodramatic medium assumed a more central position. The pieces quoted above were all printed in the *Press* newspaper, the central Irish Jacobin periodical in the years 1797 and 1798. As it progressed it became increasingly graphic, to the extent that it was, with reason, called a blood-sheet in government circles. One of the more lurid pieces happened to be the product of the then young radical, Thomas Moore, who the paper published on 19 October 1797, signaling, if only symbolically, the Jacobins' incomplete move from the clarity of the Enlightenment to the subjectivities of the Romantic.[15]

If the Irish Jacobins used the gothic, they did not use it without questioning it or without remoulding it to their purposes. While the gothic proved useful to Irish Jacobins it did not prove unproblematic. In general, at the ideological level, English gothic of the late eighteenth century unleashes the forces of the despotic (whether monarchic or aristocratic) only to effect closure by taming these forces. The heroine vanquishes the feudal, breaks medieval social relations, and asserts the morality of middle-class commercialism. The ideology espoused by the heroine is, in general, Whiggish, whether of the Old or New Whig variety. It is the cementing ideology of the British state, the ideology of the Glorious Revolution of 1688. In Ireland such Whig ideology had never gained majority acceptance – in fact it was noticeably an ideology held only by a small minority (principally the Anglo-Irish Ascendancy and the beneficiaries of their patronage). That this ideology was never mentally ratified by the Irish was not surprising. The Glorious Revolution discriminated against, and penalized, Ireland's two major religious blocs, the Catholics and the Presbyterians, neither of whom were allowed to participate fully in the polity. Thus in contrast to English gothic normatives, in Irish Jacobin gothic, the medieval terrorizers are those of an Anglican state (and its clergy who doubled as magistrates); the gothic landscape is located in the North and West, not in the Catholic South. State-sponsored Anglicanism, rather than Catholicism, is figured as villainous, superstitious, corrupt, irrational, and tyrannical. Added to this, Irish Jacobin gothic questioned the imperializing agenda of the gothic; it sought to decenter the British state's sense of itself as the ideal governing standard. Irish republican gothic was a de-imperializing gothic – it figured colonization as hell. Not for nothing did John Philpot Curran proclaim Ireland 'to be the spectatrix of her own funeral, and the conscious inhabitant of her own sepulchre'.[16] One final major difference between the generalized norms of the English gothic and Jacobin gothic is in the realm of narrative closure. Typically, in English gothic (though exceptions naturally exist), closure is affected through marriage – the heroine is domesticated, she comes into money (through marriage or fortuitous inheritance), and her circle is narrowed to that of the private sphere. In Irish Jacobin gothic, the typical narrative is one where the domestic sphere is destroyed by government forces, the victim's accumulated capital and means of production are damaged, and the protagonist is forced into the public sphere – he or she is politicized. Much English gothic immobilizes its female subject politically. Jacobin gothic, conversely, is geared towards revolutionary praxis. And one final difference: Jacobin gothic was not an attempt at fabulist fiction – it sought to relate the actual. The horror it described was not of the imaginative variety; it was what the Jacobins perceived Ireland to be at that moment. It was an attempt, however flawed, at realism, at reportage – it mobilized the gothic to portray authentically an authentic reality. Hence the radical William Hamilton Drummond stated in his 1797 gothic pamphlet poem, *The Man of Age*, thus: 'The following little production is not altogether the suggestion of fancy. The evils complained of here are not children of the brain; – they are the legitimate offspring of too convincing reality'.[17] More often than not, this attempt at realism collapsed into the bathetic and melodramatic. The gothic had its limits, and the portrayal of a very real and violent actuality was one of them. Part of this collapse into the bathetic most probably stems from the fact that the Irish radical authors were attempting to utilize (and thus validate) a gothic register that they seemed not wholly to either trust or be at ease with.

By 1797 it was evident to the radicals that they would either have to surrender in the face of the government's coercion campaign or fight back through the use of physical force. Government had intensified its campaign and the options left to the radicals were narrowing. On 13 May 1797, 25 people were massacred by the Ancient Britons and the Yeomanry near Crossmaglen, and this was but one atrocity among many. To prepare the Irish population for the counteroffensive, the Irish democrats put onto the literary market a selection of short, intense tracts written in the gothic register in an attempt to anger, and thus mobilize, the people. Among these were the anonymous 1797 pamphlet poem *Lysimachia*, William Hamilton Drummond's bloody chapbook poem *Hibernia* (1797), and the writings of Ireland's preeminent female radical poet, Henrietta Battier.[18] Battier, who claimed to have been an intimate of Samuel Johnson, exemplifies the transition of many Irish radical authors. The work she published in the early to mid-1790s tended to the domestic, or, when addressing public issues, the satiric. But, with the harsher conditions of the late 1790s, she recognized the truth of Jean Paul Marat's dictum – satire had a tendency to deflate the very anger that it sought to harness.[19] Whereas previously she had mocked, jibed, and lampooned her reactionary opponents, she now, in her 1798 version of the pamphlet poem, *The Lemon*, forged violent images in order to generate an energy of political revenge:

> Thy tears, Green Erin, have increased the flood!
> Thy fields are fatten'd with thy children's blood!
> Thy gates are desolate! thy works forlorn!
> Thy priest and virgins are with anguish torn!
> Rape, murder, sacrilege, and torture join,
> To prove our Executive Pow'r, Divine![20]

By detailing such atrocities in fictive form, Battier was attempting to rouse her passive readership into a position of active politicized revolt. And in reproducing such horrific scenes (most notably the lines that show the Orange Order immolating pregnant women), Battier was obviously not working within the gothic register for any purely aesthetic reasons or merely to entertain her audience. The ultimate goal was that of praxis. Literature was only valuable in so far as it produced a kinetic response in the reader, so far as it pushed a reader into active moral or physical opposition. Similarly, the United Irishman, Edward John

Newell, in writing his autobiography, sought to alienate his readership from government and add their person to the mass of insurgents. Newell had turned informer in 1797 and his testimony had been instrumental in providing Dublin Castle with evidence allowing them to round up at least 100 radicals. Regretting his new alliance, Newell returned to the radical camp and provided the United Irish with the specifics of his perjured testimony to government. His autobiography details what occurs to the individual when he fraternizes with the 'blood-thirsty Cannibals [...] [the] fiends of Hell' that were government agents. Somewhat like Caleb Williams, Newell descends into the 'madness' of a torturing subjectivity brought on by those who have access to the polity's policing instruments.[21] Newell's *Life* was a substantial departure for the Irish radicals, for their literature, when not comic, had, in the main, kept within the perimeters prescribed by that strand of Enlightenment discourse which had privileged the rational, the empirically verifiable, the reasoned. Such literature had avoided the subjective and psychological, viewing these perspectives as undemocratic and excessively prone to an almost aristocratic hyper-individualism. The Jacobin movement was an idealistic endeavor to unify the nation politically and it sought to homogenize its public voice. Only its enemies, it suggested, used their words to individuate and fragment discourse in order to perpetuate selfish interests. The fact that Newell chose an intensely subjective first-person narration demonstrates the degree to which the demands of the gothic pressured the Jacobins into reconfiguring their normative practices.

The 1798 rebellion began on 23 May. Lasting about 120 days, it ended in failure for the Jacobins. Ill-trained rebels armed with pikes and antiquated or defective arms stood little chance against the modern armaments and well-disciplined soldiers of the British Empire. Conservatively, it is estimated that at least 25,000 people died in the rebellion.[22] The violence was overwhelmingly that of the state, with at least 90 percent of the casualties being rebels or perceived rebel sympathizers. To appreciate the scale of this, roughly the same amount of people were killed in absolute numbers, and in a shorter period of time than during the terror in France (a nation that had at least five times Ireland's population). It was also a particularly brutal affair, Pitt's regime adhering little to the rules of war, regarding the insurgents as rebels against the crown rather than legitimate belligerents. Massacre of civilians by the state was widespread. On 24 May, the state murdered 40 civilians at Dunlavin, and a week later the army executed 40 more at Carnew. On the 25th of that month, over 200 civilians and rebels were burned alive in their cabins by the military in Carlow town, while on 29 May, about 350 rebels who had surrendered on guarantees of clemency were massacred by government forces at Gibbet Rath. Pitt, Castlereagh, Edward Cooke, and the ultra-reactionary speaker of the Irish House of Commons, John Foster, were intent not only on quelling the immediate rebellion, but on ensuring that Irish Jacobinism had no prospect of ever reviving again in any form. Post-rebellion, the atrocities committed on both rebels and non-combatants would provide much material for those radicals who survived the onslaught.

Likewise, the rebellion fed into anti-Jacobin gothic fiction. The insurrection became a standard warning in Irish and British conservative literary circles as to what would happen in England were the English Jacobins to triumph. English anti-Jacobin literature of the Minerva Press gothic-shocker variety, as Jim Shanahan has observed, frequently introduced the rebellion into its narratives.[23] Examples range from Charles Lucas's *Infernal Quixote* (1801), to Bullock's *Dorothea* (1801), to Caroline Lamb's tediously overwrought *Glenarvon* (1816). In each of these novels, the rebel was figured as deluded at best, monstrous and satanic at worst. Quite naturally, the British state pacified the gothic landscape of the rebellion, restoring it back to the idealized Burkean paradise of contented peasants and suitably servile townspeople. Unsurprisingly, no genuine attempt was made to understand the grievances of the radicals or the material conditions that shaped their Jacobin ideology.

Much post-rebellion Jacobin literature was, thus, an attempt to counter the proliferation of anti-rebellion texts then entering the literary marketplace. Immediately following the rebellion, radicals attempted to counter this anti-Jacobin narrative by denying that the rebels were gothic villains, by insisting on their humanity, and by making monsters of those who labored for the state. Thus, the radical, Thomas Ledlie Birch, publishing in Philadelphia in 1799 one of the first histories of the rebellion, gave those American republicans who purchased his book a tale full of government-sponsored atrocities.[24] Following in his wake, William Sampson described Kildare as a landscape terrorized by government demons, while William Duckett's historical poetry, printed in Paris, versified the plight of those Irish people who had been disemboweled by the military.[25] Villains were named and made monstrous. In 1799, a pamphlet poem, *Monody Sacred to the Memory of Lord Edward Fitzgerald*, was published anonymously by an author who claimed to have been present at Fitzgerald's midnight funeral procession. The poet, under the shadow of the Genius of Erin, demands justice be meted out on the celebrated informer, Thomas Reynolds, a state employee 'thirsting for blood yet fearful of the day'.[26] Mary

Wollstonecraft's protégée, the United Irishwoman Margaret Moore, writing in the same year, figured the recently victorious colonial state as the 'suckers of Irish blood'.[27] The positioning of the state agent as gothic villain suggested, if it did not presuppose, the rebel as human. This humanizing was notable in Bernard Dornin's biography of Samuel Neilson, the proprietor of the *Northern Star* and one of the founding members of the United Irish Society. Dornin's Ireland was one where the '[Anglican] priests of the hierarchy, like those of Odin, hunt[ed] on these miscreants [loyalists] to blood and rapine'. Neilson the rebel was fully humanized – he is characterized as the enlightened child of Montesquieu, Mably, and Locke. Imprisoned by the monstrous Pittite regime,

> Eighty pounds of iron fastened him to the floor of the dungeon – no ray of light or of heat ever cheered its wall. It was deep, and damp, and dismal. The face of humanity was never seen, nor was its voice ever heard within it. A monster, in the form of a man, but without a heart was its keeper [...] a refinement in cruelty that would not have disgraced a Caligula.[28]

Dornin's Neilson is the typical gothic sufferer – bound, imprisoned, subject to mental torture, in fine, undeserving innocence suffering at the whip of the damned.

The Irish Act of Union was implemented in 1801, and the last significant expression of Irish Jacobinism broke out in Dublin in 1803 in the form of Robert Emmet's insurrection. The rebellion was a disaster, but its legacy was important. An international cult developed around Emmet, one that strongly romanticized his life and figured him as an idealistic young man, an ethereal celestial wisp, rather than the hard-headed, pragmatic strategist that his colleague and co-conspirator Miles Byrne demonstrated him to be.[29] Most writers within the Emmet cult gave to his existence an atmosphere of the gothic. To an extent, Emmet's life and actions invited this reading. His own celebrated court speech had focused on his impending burial and his epitaph:

> My lamp of life is nearly expired; my race is finished; the grave opens to receive me, and I sink into its bosom. All I request then, at parting from the world, is the charity of its silence. Let no man write my epitaph, for as no man who knows my motives dare vindicate them, let not prejudice or ignorance asperse them; let them and me repose in obscurity and peace, and my tomb remain uninscribed, 'till other times and other men can do justice to my character.[30]

Further, the gothic nature of his demise was amplified after his death when his heart was purportedly removed from his body and burnt. Emmet himself had written four poems in the gothic register, 'Arbour Hill', 'Genius of Erin', 'Help from Heaven', and 'The Coming Discord'.[31] Very soon after Emmet's death, poems were being written about the young republican, the victim of a gothic state. An anonymous handbill circulating in Dublin in 1803 imagined the blood of Emmet's 'headless form' crying for vengeance.[32] In the same year, William Drennan circulated a manuscript of an untitled 12-line poem. The poem was yet another blood poem – its central fiend being the one-time liberal William Plunket who had worked for the prosecution during Emmet's trial:

> When Emmet, self-convicted, stood,
> In fate, already hung,
> Plunket still longed to taste the blood
> And piked him, with his tongue.[33]

Perhaps the most famous of all the Emmet poems, excepting those of Robert Southey and Thomas Moore, is that written in 1812 by Percy Shelley, then flirting somewhat tentatively with United Irish ideology, shortly before he came over to Dublin. It is entitled 'The Devil's Walk':

> Fat – as the Death-birds on Erin's shore,
> That glutted themselves in her dearest gore,
> And flitted around Castlereagh,
> When they snatched the Patriot's heart, that his grasp
> Had torn from its widow's maniac clasp,
> And fled at the dawn of day.[34]

The degree to which pre-apostasy English Romanticism was influenced, positively or negatively, by Irish Jacobinism still remains as yet an underdetermined question. But what ought to be noticed is the degree to which many of the Romantics heroized Emmet in the period immediately after his death. Southey and Coleridge both sympathized with his fate and appeared to displace their political unease onto the finality of his career. With Napoleon's dictatorial tendencies showing themselves clearly post-Union, and with France's increasingly despotic treatment of its satellites (especially Switzerland), both Irish and English Jacobins were searching for a figure who would embody the unadulterated republicanism of their minds. Emmet provided this, and his failure neatly reflected the defeated atmosphere of English radical circles in the years following the banning of the London Corresponding Society and the successful anti-Jacobin campaigns of Reeves, Hannah More, and the Minerva Press, while simultaneously proclaiming that an uncorrupted republicanism still existed.

A further example of Emmet's attractiveness to radicals is furnished by the compendium of gothic stories printed in the two-volume horror tome, *The Terrific Register, Or, Record of Crimes, Judgements, Providences, and Calamities* (1825).[35] It contained a variety of self-contained, anonymously written short stories (both factual and fictional) that showed, in the main, the trajectory of the villain's progress from crime to providential punishment. The wicked are caught, and the law and ordered society prevail (the title page boldly proclaimed – 'God's revenge against Murder'). In the second volume of this work is a short anonymous story entitled 'The Midnight Assassination'. Above the title to this story is a striking illustration of a night scene – forked lightning rends the darkness and illuminates an open grave in which is laid a female corpse. The story itself begins in the Galway cabin of an Irish peasant family. A father and mother care for their engaged daughter. Their desperate poverty is repeatedly emphasized and blamed by the author upon English colonial misrule. One night Robert Emmet visits the family and persuades the father and his daughter's fiancé to join in his rebellion plans. They do so, and take part in the insurrection with desperate courage. The prospective son-in-law is killed in the fighting. The father escapes, and after witnessing Emmet's trial and hanging, becomes a hardened 'dæmon'. He returns home to find his daughter dying from the effects of poverty. In order to supplement his income, the father had rented space in his cabin to a female domestic. Desperate for money to cure his daughter, the father makes a plan to murder the lodger in order to take possession of her savings, a mere guinea. In the nocturnal gloom, the father and mother go to the domestic's room, plunge a dagger into the sleeping female, and bring the body outside and dump it face upwards in a pre-prepared grave. The night sky illuminated by lightning, the parents realize to their horror that they have mistakenly murdered their daughter. In the shock, and believing she has seen a spirit, the mother falls down dead on her daughter's corpse. The authorities arrest the father and try him. Before being hung, the guilty man 'confessed the share he had taken in the rebellion and the nature of his connexion with Emmet, but solemnly persisted in affirming that he was driven to rebellion and murder by the miseries of his country, and the unexampled indigence of his own family'.[36] The story ends, rather fittingly for one about one of Emmet's disciples, with a description of the man's grave. Avoided as the abode of 'unholy spirits', it is situated at a short distance from the main road, between a dark forest and the limitless expanse of a wasteland bog. The author completes the piece by writing an epitaph of sorts for the father: 'It is known as the grave where the murderer reposes, and the liberal-minded people, when they shudder at the crimes of him who sleeps below, curse in the bitterness of their hearts the apostates who caused such guilt by the miseries they have entailed on their country' (p. 23).

'The Midnight Assassination' is clearly the work of either a rather advanced Whig sympathetic to Emmet's designs, or a Jacobin tempering his politics to induce sympathy for Emmet in an audience that would have included many loyalists (the fact that the author unreservedly celebrates popular mobilization would suggest a Jacobin). Besides two factual errors, or perhaps two incidences of poetic license (the rebellion occurs in autumn, rather than summer; it is not possible to travel from Galway to the east coast in a night), the author demonstrates a clear understanding of the rebellion and a comprehension of Emmet's ideology. Importantly, the story differs significantly from the other tales included in *The Terrific Register*. The pattern established in *The Terrific Register* is one where villainy exists in and of itself. Generally, the villain is given no extenuating circumstances that would attenuate his guilt. In 'The Midnight Assassination', however, the rebellion and the murder are expressly given as the natural consequences of government persecution: 'the English military oppressed the unfortunate Irish with the most unexampled tyranny. The whole of the lower classes, on whom the yoke fell the heaviest, determined at last to struggle for the recovery of their freedom, and wisely resolved to take the first opportunity of exerting their energies' (p. 19). Again, while in general the other stories describe the deeds of people almost genetically evil, and society's revenge on them, the murderer in 'The Midnight Assassination' is portrayed sympathetically. The murder is palliated by the fact that he kills a daughter who was already dying of state-induced poverty – his crime was but to hasten the inevitable. The father's resistance to the state is justified, and his daughter's fiancé is described as having 'died in the cause of liberty' (p. 21). Likewise, Emmet's purity of character and nobility of purpose remain unquestioned; he is a victim rather than a villain: 'If he has erred, let his errors be imputed to the more daring treason of those doubly-damned apostates, who have sacrificed every liberal principle at the bloody shrine of Moloch' (p. 21). Written nearly a generation after the 1798 rebellion, 'The Midnight Assassination' is quite typical of later Irish Jacobin writing, which went on the offensive in the post-Waterloo period. The rebellion was figured as the good fight, and the agents of the state were portrayed as the real-life incarnations of the specters and monsters that populated the gothic. The republican programme was predicated on exorcizing these malevolent spirits.

Irish Jacobin fiction, of whatever genre, was, in general, only ever produced in so far as it witnessed an actuality, in so far as it delineated societal relations of exploitation, in so far as cultural production could aid radical political mobilization. Generic choice, therefore, was rarely an anticipation of marketplace demand, but rather political contingencies determined generic selection. Naturally, aesthetics was a secondary consideration; instruction and propaganda were the aims.

In the early 1790s, Irish republican writers sought to create a discursive space that was predicated on rationality, order, and polite reasoning. Until the banning of the United Irish Society by the Pitt regime, this space paid sparse attention to a gothic genre that seemed to promise it little in terms of propagandizing potential. The government's coercive campaign, begun mid-decade, changed this. The fictional gothic appeared to offer Irish Jacobins the closest literary reality to their actual circumstances. They borrowed from the gothic its standardized vocabulary and tropes, its reliance on sensual responses and sentimentality, co-opting the traits of the gothic genre to describe a militarized actuality. But transferring a fictional form onto a present reality meant that it was not adopted without additions and subtractions. The underpinning ideological framework of the gothic was also interrogated and transformed. And it was these transformations that allowed Irish Jacobinism to appropriate the gothic genre.

Notes

1. Fitzwilliam was dismissed as Lord Lieutenant of Ireland because he sought to promote a type of liberal agenda that Pitt could ultimately not countenance. In the aftermath of Fitzwilliam's dismissal, Westminster abandoned conciliatory measures in favour of subduing Ireland through the rigorous implementation of state-sanctioned violence.
2. Richard Gott (2011) *Britain's Empire: Resistance, Repression and Revolt* (London: Verso), pp. 133–4.
3. Quoted in Nancy Curtin (1998) *The United Irishmen: Popular Politics in Ulster and Dublin, 1791–1798* (Oxford: Clarendon), p. 89.
4. Ruán O'Donnell (1998) *1798 Diary* (Dublin: Irish Times Publication), p. 16; John D. Beatty (2001) *Protestant Women's Narratives of the Irish Rebellion of 1798* (Dublin: Four Courts Press), p. 18; Archibald McLaren (1798) *A Minute Description of the Battles of Gorey, Arklow, and Vinegar Hill* (Dublin), p. 39; Jonah Barrington (1833) *Rise and Fall of the Irish Nation* (Paris: Bennis), p. 373; James Gordon (1805) *A History of Ireland. Volume II* (Dublin: John Jones),

pp. 377, 462; Francis Plowden (1803) *An Historical Review of the State of Ireland. Volume II. Part II* (London: T. Egerton), p. 705; Ivan F. Nelson (2007) *The Irish Militia, 1793–1802* (Dublin: Four Courts Press), p. 135; Joseph Stock (1800) *A Narrative of What passed at Killala, In the County of Mayo* (Dublin: E. Mercier), pp. 155, 163; Francis Rawdon Hastings (1798) *The Speech of the Right Honourable Earl of Moira* (Dublin: P. Byrne), pp. 8–12. The pre-1834 texts are all the works of loyalists.

5. David V. Erdman (ed.) (1978) *The Collected Works of Samuel Taylor Coleridge. Volume III* (London: Routledge & Kegan Paul), pp. 11–12; Kenneth Curry (ed.) (1965) *New Letters of Robert Southey. Volume I* (London: Columbia University Press), p. 171.

6. William Hazlitt (1816) *Memoirs of the Late Thomas Holcroft. Vol. III* (London: Longman), p. 17.

7. *The Beauties of the Press* (London, 1800), p. 510.

8. Rolf and Magda Loeber (2006) *A Guide to Irish Fiction, 1650–1900* (Dublin: Four Courts Press), *passim*.

9. *The Beauties of the Press*, p. 311.

10. *The Beauties of the Press*, pp. 18, 502.

11. *The Beauties of the Press*, pp. 375–7.

12. Niall Ó Ciosáin (2010) *Print and Popular Culture in Ireland, 1750–1850* (Dublin: Lilliput Press).

13. Jarlath Killeen (2005) *Gothic Ireland: Horror and the Irish Anglican Imagination in the Long Eighteenth Century* (Dublin: Four Courts Press, 2005); Christina Morin (2011) *Charles Robert Maturin and the Haunting of Irish Romantic Fiction* (Manchester: Manchester University Press).

14. John Daly Burk (1807) *Bethlem Gabor, Lord of Transylvania* (Petersburg, VA: J. Dickson).

15. Moore's poem had first appeared anonymously in the Belfast-based periodical, the *Northern Star*, on 12 May 1797. After a brief flirtation with Jacobinism, Moore, post-rebellion, slid into a fairly polite Whiggism.

16. John Philpot Curran (1795) *A Letter to the Right Honourable Edmund Burke* (Dublin: J. Chambers), p. 5.

17. William Hamilton Drummond (1797) *The Man of Age. A Poem* (Belfast), unpaginated memorandum. Post-rebellion, Drummond lost his radicalism for a tepid liberalism.

18. Anon. (1797) *Lysimachia. A Poem. Addressed to the Orange and Break-of-Day Men in the Counties of Armagh and Down* (Belfast); William Hamilton Drummond (1797) *Hibernia, A Poem* (Belfast: Northern Star Office).

19. Clifford D. Conner (2012) *Jean Paul Marat: Tribune of the French Revolution* (London: Pluto), p. 66.

20. Henrietta Battier (1798) *The Lemon, A Poem* (Dublin), p. 15. The first version of Battier's *Lemon* was published in 1797.

21. Edward John Newell (1798) *The Apostasy of Newell, Containing the Life and Confessions of that Celebrated Informer* (Belfast), pp. 9, 26. This pamphlet was published in April or May of 1798.

22. For the debate as to casualty numbers see Thomas Bartlett, David Dickson, Dáire Keogh, Kevin Whelan (eds) (2002) *1798: a Bicentenary Perspective* (Dublin: Four Courts Press). This volume represents the finest scholarship on 1798 to date.

23. Jim Shanahan (2006) *An 'Unburied Corpse': the 1798 Rebellion in Fiction, 1799–1898* (unpublished PhD thesis, Trinity College Dublin).
24. Thomas Ledlie Birch (1799) *A Letter from an Irish Emigrant, To his Friend in the United States* (Philadelphia).
25. William Sampson (1812) *Trial of Captain Whitby* (New York: Gould, Banks & Gould), p. 34; William Duckett (1822) *To My Country, A Dithyrambic Ode* (Paris: David).
26. Anon. (1799) *Monody Sacred to the Memory of Lord Edward Fitzgerald* (Dublin), p. 6.
27. Incidentally, the state as vampire was an image used rather frequently by radicals – Wolfe Tone talked of the members of the polity as 'insatiable vampires', Charles Teeling spoke of 'those vampires [of government]', while an anonymous poem of late 1803 celebrating Bartholomew Teeling cursed the 'foul vampires of the state'. See especially Margaret Moore (1799) *Reply to a Ministerial Pamphlet* (Dublin), p. 17. For the figure of the vampire in radical fiction, see Peadar Bates (1998) *1798 Rebellion in Fingal* (Loughshinny), pp. 146–7; Charles Hamilton Teeling (1828) *Personal Narrative of the 'Irish Rebellion' of 1798* (London), p. 135; Theobald Wolfe Tone (1796) *An Address to the People of Ireland* (Belfast), p. 14.
28. Bernard Dornin (1804) *A Sketch of the Life of Samuel Neilson, Of Belfast, Ireland* (New York: Bernard Dornin), pp. 9–10.
29. Miles Byrne (1863) *Memoirs of Miles Byrne. Volume I* (Paris: Gustave Bossange).
30. Henry Brereton Code (1803) *The Insurrection of the Twenty-Third July, 1803* (Dublin: Graisberry & Campbell), p. 97.
31. Thomas Emmet (1915) *Memoir of Thomas Addis and Robert Emmet. Volume II* (New York: Emmet Press), pp. 15–20.
32. Marianne Elliott (2004) *Robert Emmet: the Making of a Legend* (London: Profile), p. 105.
33. Jean Agnew (ed.) (1999) *The Drennan-McTier Letters. Volume 3, 1802–1819* (Dublin: IMC), p.157.
34. Percy Shelley (1812) 'The Devil's Walk'; quoted in Paul O'Brien (2002) *Shelley and Revolutionary Dublin* (London: Redwords), pp. 198–9.
35. *The Terrific Register; Or, Record of Crimes, Judgments, Providences, And Calamities. Vol. II* (London: Sherwood, Jones, & Co, 1825).
36. *Terrific Register*, p. 23. All further references to this tale will be cited parenthetically.

4
Suffering Rebellion: Irish Gothic Fiction, 1799–1830

Jim Shanahan

> A storm without doors is, after all, better than a storm within; without we have something to struggle with, within we have only to suffer.[1]

Towards the end of John Banim's novel, *The Boyne Water* (1826), Grace Nowlan recalls how she witnessed her lover and child being burnt alive by her own brothers: 'I heard the little cries of my child – the hissing of flesh and the crackling of bones, until my hoarse shrieks died away in mute madness, and hell – real and eternal hell was round me, and I thought it was my doom and punishment to see, and hear, and suffer without a tear or groan'.[2] She does not, however, continue to suffer in silence. Seemingly driven insane by this horrific sight, her screech becomes a leitmotif of the story, heard whenever something particularly ghastly or dramatic occurs to the two families – the Protestant Evelyns and the Catholic M'Donnells – at the heart of the novel. Grace's personal trauma ultimately manifests itself as a 'mute madness', but the trauma of others induces a gothic screech. In Irish gothic, the appropriate response to one's own suffering and guilt is silence. For most of the novel, Grace Nowlan is known only as 'Onagh of the cavern', a mysterious Sibyl who plays a prominent role in imbuing *The Boyne Water* with a supernatural and gothic atmosphere. Abandoned by her lover, Donald M'Donnell, and then punished by her own brothers, Nowlan vows revenge on the remaining M'Donnell family by frustrating their attempts to marry.

The story of Grace Nowlan's transformation from 'the handsomest maiden in her country' (III: 409) to a bitter and deranged virago plotting revenge on the family of her seducer is set against a background of political, social, and religious turmoil, massacre, starvation, and war, that has all the characteristics of the classic gothic novel. But *The Boyne Water* is supposedly a historical novel outlining the cause and consequences of the Williamite wars, and its purpose is to make a plea for religious toleration (meaning Catholic emancipation) in 1820s Ireland. Grace Nowlan's troubling presence is only one element of a tale into which the monstrous and the seemingly supernatural constantly intrude. From the perspective of plot there is no real need for Nowlan's experience to be quite so horrific or so graphically described. The abandonment and ostracism she suffers would be reason enough for her to desire revenge on the M'Donnells – especially as it is not clear whether she has actually been driven insane (indeed, in what may be a further level of discomfort for the reader there is considerable evidence to suggest that she has not). Nowlan's particularly gory description could be seen as a gratuitous addition to the plot itself were it not for the fact that it serves a clear purpose by revealing something about the Irish historical experience. Although the gothic element may be partially ascribed to Banim's slavish imitation of Walter Scott – particularly Scott's *The Bride of Lammermoor* (1819), with which *The Boyne Water* shares some similarities – the gothic continually surfaces in the tale, and *The Boyne Water* is perhaps the clearest example of the fact that the gothic cannot be separated from the historical in an Irish context in this period.[3] *The Boyne Water* is considered by many as the finest Irish historical novel of the nineteenth century, but it is also a gothic novel.

This is not altogether surprising. The Irish historical experience, already a gothic nightmare as a result of the traumas of the seventeenth century, was given a fresh gothic injection by the shock of the rebellion of 1798. The gothic is a consistent element of Irish reality, and therefore an essential component of a specifically Irish realism. An Irish version of the emerging realist novel, therefore, was invariably maimed at the beginning by the need to incorporate this gothic element. Grace Nowlan's shocking description of the death of her child echoes a long Irish tradition of what James Kelly has termed 'emotive atrocity literature' produced by Catholic and Protestant alike, but which is mostly associated with an enduring Protestant belief in an Irish Catholic desire to massacre all Protestants and to exterminate all 'heretics' which stretches from accounts of the 1641 Rebellion through the seventeenth and eighteenth centuries up to the 1798 Rebellion.[4] Indeed, when *The Boyne Water* was first published the most recent 'massacre' crisis had barely passed: the so-called 'Pastorini' prophesies. Promulgated by an English Catholic priest in the 1770s and reputedly believed by many of the Irish Catholic peasantry, these 'prophesies' had foretold that 'Lutheran heresy' would be finally destroyed in 1825. Many Protestants took this to mean they were all to be massacred, a foreboding not alleviated by the fact that the 1820s and '30s in Ireland saw an escalation in the level of Rockite agrarian insurgency and tithe disturbances that could be construed as a Catholic war against Protestants. Jarlath Killeen has argued that the Monstrous, fragmented, and unstable narratives, cannibalism, a terror of the Irish landscape, and the shadow of the past are characteristics of Irish Anglican gothic writing, and that Irish gothic writing generally is a Protestant genre.[5] But all of these elements are also present in *The Boyne Water*, suggesting that Catholic and Protestant gothic preoccupations were not all that different. While Irish Catholic writers may not have set out to write gothic novels, the gothic nevertheless features heavily in Catholic fiction.

The tendency of the gothic to surface in other modes of writing is symptomatic of a generic promiscuity characteristic of Irish fiction writing in this period and contributes to the problematic nature of the Irish historical novel, most specifically in the way that it subverts other Irish literary modes. As well as the gothic and the historic, *The Boyne Water*, for example, has elements of a frustrated national tale as one of the proposed 'national' marriages (in this case between the Protestant Esther Evelyn and the Catholic Edmund M'Donnell) does not occur and the other (between Robert Evelyn and Eva M'Donnell) has to overcome tremendous obstacles and misunderstandings, not the least of which are the ferocious religious and political animosities unleashed by the Williamite wars. By the end of the novel Esther Evelyn has died of starvation during the siege of Derry, and Edmund M'Donnell has chosen exile, while the liberal Protestant Robert and the Catholic Eva feel like strangers in their own country, as the guarantees given to Catholics in the Treaty of Limerick are not honoured. But it is in the figure of Grace Nowlan that *The Boyne Water* makes connections with both the national tale and the gothic. Her name is not dissimilar to Maria Edgeworth's heroine Grace Nugent, the epitome of genteel and chaste Irish womanhood in *The Absentee* (1812), while John Banim would subsequently use the Nowlan surname again as the title for a heavily gothic novel in which the main character, John Nowlan, also seems to suffer a mental breakdown. Moreover, Grace Nowlan's description of the burning of her lover and child has strong echoes of the Spanish Catholic Alonzo Monçada's nightmare of being burnt by the Inquisition in the most famous Irish gothic novel of this period, Charles Robert Maturin's *Melmoth the Wanderer* (1820). Monçada's fantasy that, engulfed in flame, 'my muscles cracked, my blood and marrow hissed, – my flesh [was] consumed like shrinking leather',[6] has its counterpart in 'the hissing of flesh and the crackling of bones' of Grace Nowlan's account. Both Monçada and Grace Nowlan are victims of their own families, as Monçada is forced by his parents into a Madrid monastery against his will. In both cases, too, questions of legitimacy are involved, and these issues – legitimacy and oppression by one's own – become consistent elements of an Irish gothic aesthetic.

Taking Maturin's *Melmoth the Wanderer* as typical would suggest that the content of Irish gothic writing of this period reflects much of the external paraphernalia and preoccupations of the wider British gothic tradition. A selective canon of exemplary Irish gothic stretching from Regina Maria Roche to Bram Stoker, and including Maturin and Sheridan Le Fanu, would do little to challenge this impression. The gothic texts of these writers can be read as 'Irish', of course, but this is only one dimension of these works. Some recent scholarship has argued that 'Irish gothic' may not just be an offshoot of the gothic but may have its own distinctive points of origin, influence, and development. The gothic, in fact, lies at the very core of Irish literature in English. Jarlath Killeen has identified the 1641 Rebellion, and the memory thereof, as both the site of origin of Irish Protestant Gothicism and 'what has been baldly termed "Anglo-Irish literature" '.[7] Violence, horror, and atrocity therefore were encoded into Anglo-Irish writing from the start. Christina Morin in turn has identified an Irish gothic tradition in fiction that (just) predates the generally accepted point of origin for British gothic, Horace Walpole's *The Castle of Otranto* (1764).[8] In pointing out that many of the new forms of Irish fiction writing that prevail in the nineteenth century – the regional novel, the national tale, and the historical novel – actually develop out of the gothic novel aesthetic, Morin demonstrates that Irish gothic fiction of the eighteenth century shares many of the characteristics and concerns identified here as being typical of that of the nineteenth century. Indeed, in creating an eighteenth-century Irish gothic tradition that both attempts to vindicate Ireland and yet also reveals an anxiety and uncertainty about its creators' own security and status in Irish society, as Morin argues these writers do,[9] they also manage to provide a template for the first Irish Catholic gothic writers, who emerge in the early nineteenth century. Thus, in arguing for a distinctive genealogy, set of concerns, content, and development, it is possible to talk of an Irish Gothic, rather than merely an Irish gothic, tradition. This essay intends to build on these ideas and argue that Irish Gothic fiction, if it has any claim to distinction in the decades after the 1798 Rebellion, is most accurately characterized by a view that suffering is ever-present and fresh suffering always imminent, and that this manifests itself most obviously in a concomitant fear of rebellion and rebelliousness, and a craving for their opposites, respectability and conformity. These are not particularly Irish concerns, but for good historical reasons they are perhaps more immediately pressing in an Irish context.

Where Irish Gothic differs from Irish gothic and the gothic in general is the manner in which traditional gothic fears are explored. Irish Gothic's main characteristics are its focus on the internal rather than the external and in the fact that it was written in the wake of real and recent, rather than some imagined or remote, trauma. Silent suffering and internal conflict rather than external demonstrations of grief and anguish characterize Irish Gothic: Grace Nowlan's traumatized silence says more than her melodramatic screech. In discussing the development of Irish Gothic fiction in the 1799–1830 period we must make a necessary distinction therefore between Irish novels written in a gothic mode and those which can be seen as written in an evolving Irish Gothic mode. This distinction is important because the arguments contained in this essay center around the idea that Irish Gothic is less a series of tropes and conventions and more a register, a tone, and a set of concerns, which finds its way into all kinds of Irish fiction in this period. As Siobhán Kilfeather observes, 'For most of the nineteenth century, Irish Gothic cannot be defined so much in terms of a subgenre as much as in terms of an extra dimension apparent in many works of Irish fiction'.[10] Irish Gothic can thus be seen in the writing of that supposed arch-rationalist Maria Edgeworth, and in the romantic national tales of Sydney Owenson (Lady Morgan) and, of course, Charles Maturin. But it also finds its way into the writing of the Catholic novelists of the 1820s, intruding, as we have seen, into the historical novels of the Banim brothers as well as into their novels of Catholic life and those of their contemporary, Gerald Griffin. The defining characteristic of Irish Gothic therefore is that it does not confine itself to a gothic subgenre of its own, but periodically interrupts and always haunts other subgenres of Irish writing. As such it is one of the factors – perhaps the crucial factor – in the generic instability of Irish fiction writing, and a contributor to the so-called failure of the realist novel in Ireland. No matter what a text may initially appear to be, in Irish writing the gothic is likely to intrude at any time. Although the atrocities, injustices, and traumas of the Irish past are never far away, Irish Gothic is not so concerned about the distant past and imaginary fears, but is better understood as a kind of hyper-realist technique that periodically reveals the truth by laying bare the awful reality behind Irish life and the Irish historical experience. Irish realism, therefore, has a strong gothic element. Seeing Irish Gothic in this way also allows us to move beyond the idea that Irish Gothic is an exclusively Protestant mode of writing, and helps to highlight a common thread between Protestant Gothic writing and an emerging Catholic Gothic aesthetic in this period.

Although it is by no means characteristic, therefore, it seems entirely appropriate to begin any examination of the precise nature of Irish Gothic and the way the gothic featured in Irish fiction of the post-1798 period by referring to Maturin's *Melmoth the Wanderer*. As the quotation at the top of this essay suggests, Maturin was aware of the necessity to externalize trauma and fear in order to expunge or exorcize it. In this context, the 'storm without doors' corresponds to the traditional gothic conventions and paraphernalia usually seen in a gothic text, whereas 'the storm within' more accurately reflects the Irish Gothic reality. But Maturin also, in the shape of the wanderer, creates a character for whom escape from the consequences of his actions – in this case his Faustian pact – can only be effected by another's willingness to take on his burden. This is an implicit recognition that *someone* must suffer. While today *Melmoth* may appear to be the last and most extreme example of a hysterical gothic tradition beginning with Walpole's *Otranto*, it is useful to remind ourselves that, on its appearance, the *Edinburgh Review* had no doubts that *Melmoth* was typical of an exclusively Irish strain of writing, itself the product of an undisciplined and undeveloped country:

> Whatever be the cause, the fact, we think, cannot be disputed, that a peculiar tendency towards this gaudy and ornate style, exists among the writers of Ireland. Their genius runs riot in the wantonness of its own uncontrolled exuberance; – their imagination, disdaining the restraint of judgement, imparts to their literature the characteristics of a nation in one of the earlier stages of civilisation and refinement. The florid imagery, gorgeous diction and Oriental hyperboles [...] become cold extravagance and floundering fustian in the mouth of a barrister of the present age; and we question whether any but a native of the sister island would have ventured upon the experiment of their adoption.[11]

The 'cause' alluded to here can be attributed subsequently to a particular historical experience that would be associated with the Irish Gothic – that strange sense of being both oppressor and oppressed, conqueror and conquered, victim and victimizer; of being both powerful and powerless. Luke Gibbons, in his analysis of Irish Gothic, refers to Leslie Fiedler's idea that the gothic typically recounts the story of someone 'who begins by looking for guilt in others and ends up finding it in himself'.[12] This element has a special significance in Irish Gothic. The attraction therefore of reading *Melmoth* as an allegorical exploration of the hidden fears and repressed guilt of the Protestant Anglo-Irish and their troubled relationship with their Catholic compatriots is obvious, but it is also fraught with potential difficulties, not the least of which was that Irish Gothic tends to internalize rather than externalize. The manifest externality of *Melmoth* confirms that it is primarily a European gothic novel. As perhaps the most 'gothic' of gothic novels, *Melmoth* reflects the excesses of the gothic imagination and the conventional tropes and preoccupations of the British and European gothic to such an extent that it can be difficult to identify any exclusively Irish elements. In addition, the conventional view of Ireland itself as a gothic space, so central an idea to Irish Gothic, Romantic, and anti-Jacobin thought about Ireland, means that almost any gothic text can be read allegorically as being about Ireland. These two factors – *Melmoth* as an *über*-gothic text and Ireland itself as a gothic space – mean that readers searching for ways to read Ireland into *Melmoth* will find plenty of material and ways of doing so. But if we are looking for texts that might aid us in identifying a specifically Irish strain of gothic at this time, and not least if one is looking for evidence that Irish Gothic in this period is not just a Protestant Anglo-Irish phenomenon, then Maturin and *Melmoth* are not the best place to start. Even within Maturin's *oeuvre*, his earlier novel *The Milesian Chief* (1812) is much more representative of Irish Gothic in the way that it uses gothic tropes and plots, and in the way it telescopes the nightmares of the recent and the distant past and presents them as a constantly recurring trauma. As the Anglo-Italian heroine of *The Milesian Chief*, Armida Fitzalban, explains, 'the past has been all suffering – the future is inscrutable'.[13] Her pessimism about the future extends to her doomed lover Connal O'Morven, the rebel leader:

> Often I think that such are his talents and virtues, that their weight will drag down the scale against a country's force and wrongs, and heaven, even by a miracle, will justify its favourite on earth: but much oftener I feel a boding, an inward and unuttered prophesy of a heart inspired by grief, that murmurs talent and virtue are in vain, and heaven has determined mankind shall receive the example of his sufferings, not his virtues. (III: 130)

The fear is 'inward and unuttered'. Moreover, the rhetoric of suffering feeds into the fact that the particularly Irish Gothic element of *The Milesian Chief* lies not so much in the gothic landscape, buildings, and plot of the novel, or indeed in the plot's evocation of 1798 and the more distant atrocities of 1641, but in the depressing fact that the rebellion which occurs is *not* 1798. In *The Milesian Chief* O'Morven leads yet another rebellion, one that is compared by Connal himself not to 1641 or 1798, but to Emmet's uprising of 1803. On the surface this is because, like Emmet's rebellion, it is an event seemingly orchestrated and inspired by one man, but its real significance lies in that it is a post-Union rebellion, an indicator that Union has not brought peace and justice to Ireland and that rebellion can still erupt at any time.

Although *The Milesian Chief* may be the better example, this does not change the fact that *Melmoth* remains most definitely an Irish Gothic novel, even if it is not necessarily representative of Irish Gothic writing in this period. Despite its multi-tale form and its use of exotic locations, *Melmoth* is firmly rooted in Ireland. It begins and ends in Ireland, the title character is Irish – indeed, explicitly Anglo-Irish – and, as has often been remarked, the tales are regularly punctured by remarks that deliberately bring us back to Ireland and serve as periodic reminders both of the wanderer's Irish origins and the fact that the tale, however fantastic it may appear, does have its root in Irish realities. Appropriately enough, the Irish Gothic element is most prominent in the footnotes, which often back up what might otherwise be seen as the more preposterous – and gothic – incidences in the novel with real examples from Irish history and folklore.[14] A characteristic of the footnotes is that it is here that Maturin utilizes his own gothic experiences: many of the footnotes contain information from Maturin's own reading and personal knowledge.[15] This has a double effect, reminding the reader that *Melmoth* is a fiction and yet at the same time adding veracity to what might otherwise be seen as the less believable parts of the tale. The overall effect is a disturbing one, and suitably gothic. It is also Maturin's way of articulating his own fears: by using the footnotes he is both telling, and, in another sense, not telling.

Despite (or because of) the lurid nature of much of the gothic elements in *Melmoth*, it is often not so easy to make out the Irish Gothic tree in the midst of all the gothic wood, but the novel does reflect one of the major preoccupations of the Irish Gothic: the distinction between property and home, or inheritance and entitlement. Christina Morin has observed that Irish gothic writing of the eighteenth century is characterized by an 'ongoing uncertainty about the safety and security of their characters' Irish homes', and *Melmoth* follows in that tradition.[16] In the framing narrative of the novel, John Melmoth is the ultimate inheritor of his uncle's rundown house and estate, and, as if to destabilize or problematize this fact, the theme of inheritance and of frustrated inheritances runs through the various stories told in the text. Reinforcing these themes of dislocation and the fear of dispossession, concerns shared by Irish Protestants and Catholics alike, it is not insignificant that the very last word in the novel is 'home', a word that in the context of *Melmoth*, has little of the homely about it. The tale itself is framed by the wanderer's homecoming: he has returned 'home' to Ireland to commit suicide by throwing himself off a cliff, and in the concluding sentence of the novel his descendant John Melmoth and the Spanish Catholic Alonzo Monçada, having guessed what has happened, exchanged 'looks of silent and unutterable horror' and then 'returned slowly home' (p. 542). Here, the gothic and the Irish Gothic overlap: generally speaking, it is precisely the function of the gothic to explore the 'silent and unutterable', and here, too, 'home' is anything but welcoming and homely. Indeed, in *Melmoth* and the gothic in general, the word 'home' seems to have become detached from any comforting connotations, and in so doing raises the possibility that John Melmoth, and by extension the Anglo-Irish in general, are, like his restless ancestor, condemned to be eternal wanderers, not at home anywhere. Considering *Melmoth* in an Irish Gothic vein, the Anglo-Irish are most obviously represented by the wanderer himself, who was the first-generation Irish descendant of Cromwellian conquerors, and therefore representative not just of the Melmoth family, but of an entire caste. In keeping with the hybrid nature of the Anglo-Irish identity, however, there is a sense in which the mythologized Anglo-Irish experience is most effectively represented here by the Spanish Catholic, Monçada. Having been imprisoned and oppressed by a form of Roman Catholic tyranny, Monçada reveals in his narrative how he is forced into an alliance with an unsavory and untrustworthy figure in order to secure his escape through the secret passages underneath the monastery where he is a captive. Monçada's fate is thus tied to a man known solely by the crime he has committed – parricide – who is also the most wretched kind of Roman Catholic: a Roman Catholic without faith. The parricide, by his own admission, has no religion, no God, and no creed, but has 'that superstition of fear and of futurity'. 'I am convinced', he explains to Monçada,

> that my own crimes will be obliterated, by whatever crimes of others I can promote or punish [...] Mine is the best theology, – the

theology of utter hostility to all beings whose sufferings may miti-
gate mine. In this flattering theory, your crimes become my virtues, –
I need not any of my own [...] your guilt is my exculpation, your
sufferings are my triumph, I need not repent, I need not believe; if
you suffer, I am saved, – that is enough for me. (pp. 224–5)

'Your crimes become my virtues, – I need not any of my own' translated into an Irish situation suggests a view that being the lesser of two
evils is some kind of moral validation, one that both justifies and reveals
the anxieties surrounding Protestant hegemony in Ireland. Equally however, from a Protestant perspective it can be a criticism of the more
Jesuitical elements of Roman Catholic morality. So here one can trace
not just some of the worst, most secret fears about Irish Roman Catholics
(especially of the lower orders) but also an implicit acknowledgment
that the Anglo-Irish may have sins for which they too must atone. Like
Monçada, the Anglo-Irish have an invidious choice to make: they can
choose separation, exile, and ultimate damnation; or, like Monçada,
they can put their faith in the untrustworthy and religiously repugnant
Other. Both of these options have consequences. In choosing the former they, like Melmoth, are condemned to become eternal wanderers,
whereas in opting for the latter they can engage in what would literally be for them an unholy alliance with Catholic Ireland, and risk
their own ultimate destruction as a people. But there are always two
sides to the Irish Gothic coin. Protestant fears of union are reflected
in a concomitant Catholic fear. Thus in *Melmoth*, the parricide says to
Monçada: 'Our situation has happened to unite very opposite characters in the same adventure, but it is an union inevitable and *inseparable*.
Your destiny is now bound to mine by a tie which no human force can
break, – we part no more forever [...] We may hate each other, torment each other, – worst of all, we may be weary of each other, (for
hatred itself would be a relief, compared to the tedium of our insep-
arability), but separate we must never' (p. 187). The parricide here is
voicing both Protestant *and* Catholic fears. Both sides could say the
same about the other, and the notion that being 'weary' of each other
would be the worst of all fates has a ring of Irish realpolitik about it.
For the general gothic reader, the gothic elements of this episode of
the book are the dark passages, the fear of getting lost, and the discovery and story of the skeletons of two lovers left to starve to death
under the monastery. The Irish Gothic element is the fear of being condemned to put one's fate in the hands of a despised and mistrusted
fellow traveller.

Even more specifically from an Irish perspective, the parricide's view that in punishing the sins of others he is somehow ameliorating his own is a clear echo of some of the ultra-Protestant accounts of the motivations of the Catholic rebels during the 1798 Rebellion. In these accounts the rebels are portrayed as being on a religious crusade to exterminate all Protestants. Some ultra-Protestant accounts of 1798 stress that the superstitious beliefs of the Catholic peasant rebels led them to believe that their priests were protected by God, and that they in turn were invulnerable if they wore scapulars and other religious paraphernalia. In the case of the piking to death of Protestant prisoners on Wexford Bridge, one of the worst rebel atrocities of the Rebellion, some conservative Protestant propaganda put forward the notion that the Catholic peasantry understood the 'MWS' seen on some banners to stand for 'Murder Without Sin'. In other words, it was a justification, indeed a license, to indiscriminately kill Protestant 'heretics' that mirrors that found in any gothic novel.[17] For Protestant propagandists, this was further evidence that the Catholic rebels' flawed religion encouraged them to ensure their own salvation by killing others.

However, the danger of portraying the Catholic rebels as wretches was that it inevitably raised the uncomfortable question as to why they were quite so wretched. Seeing Catholicism as a flawed and oppressive religion provided an answer but also presented a dilemma. The usual gothic portrayal of Catholicism as a tyrannical religion may have had traction in novels set in Catholic Europe, but it had rather less valency in a country like Ireland where Catholics were the more obviously oppressed party. The only mitigating circumstances that could be put forward for that particular treatment was the view that Catholics, given the opportunity, would oppress and ultimately exterminate Irish Protestants. Anti-Catholicism in Irish Gothic novels therefore served the purpose of justifying and reinforcing conservative Protestant policy in Ireland, but did so at the cost of raising the twin specters of perceived Catholic atrocities of the past and of state oppression of Catholics in the present. In the context of attempting a distinction between gothic and Irish Gothic it can be argued that the memory of Catholic atrocities of the past is characteristic of the gothic, whereas the uncomfortable awareness of the contradictions of contemporary Protestant oppression is a characteristic of the Irish Gothic.

No fiction written in the period 1799–1830 could be more gothic in effect than many of the histories or 'factual' accounts written at this time. Propagandists on all sides vied to establish the moral high ground by portraying their own side as particularly victimized. Early accounts of the 1798 Rebellion by Sir Richard Musgrave, Charles Jackson, George Taylor, James Alexander, and others described scenes of the massacre of Protestants in lurid detail, while Catholic apologists such as Francis Plowden, Edward Hay, and the *Irish Magazine* of Walter (Watty) Cox responded with graphic descriptions of atrocities perpetrated upon an innocent Catholic population by government and ultra-Protestant forces. In such a polarized atmosphere, where the side perceived as having suffered the most was the most virtuous, and the sufferings of the other side were dismissed as having been brought upon themselves or as a punishment from God, Irish Gothic fiction served an important role in revealing the anxieties that lay behind this partisanship. Irish Gothic is primarily an exploration of unacknowledged guilt and insecurity, and an exercise in self-contradiction, a state akin to that described by Monçada in *Melmoth* as a 'haunting of yourself by your own spectre, while you still live' (p. 236).

All Irish writing in this period is written in the shadow of the 1798 Rebellion, itself a perfect gothic moment, and its effects found their way into every aspect of Irish life. But further evidence that gothic tropes do not necessarily an Irish Gothic novel make can be seen in a series of anti-Jacobin novels, presenting the 1798 Rebellion in gothic terms, published in England in the early 1800s and aimed at an English reading public.[18] While these may be gothic in appearance, and may feature Ireland, they are not Irish Gothic – and not just because they are not written by Irish writers, but because anti-Jacobinism was in many ways the antithesis of Irish Gothic. Whether they truly felt it or not, anti-Jacobin writers affected an absolute assurance of their own moral rectitude, and their novels reflected this certainty. In contrast, Irish Gothic in this period is characterized by doubt and contradiction, reflecting the secret fears and uncertainties of those who outwardly professed to *know*. It is this characteristic more than any other that allows us to make a connection between Anglo-Irish (or Protestant) Gothic and an emerging Catholic Gothic first glimpsed in the late 1810s but seen most clearly in the 1820s.

The immediate aftermath of the 1798 Rebellion provides evidence for the emergence of a particular Irish Gothic sensibility that would ultimately come to be shared by Protestant and Catholic writers alike. The gothic and the Irish Gothic can be seen side by side in the earliest text to be considered in this period, the anonymously penned *The Rebel* (1799). This work is anti-Jacobin in sentiment, but contains that element of uncertainty and internal contradiction characteristic of Irish Gothic. *The Rebel* is interesting for many reasons, not the least of which is the fact that it appears to have been started almost immediately after the Rebellion was over, and when its horrors and anxieties were fresh in the mind. Written from a loyalist Protestant perspective and replete with massacre, murder, torture, dismemberments, and burnings alive, it manages to combine elements of anti-Jacobin sensationalism with images drawn from the 1641 Rebellion – the last great Irish atrocity. These Irish sources are combined with more conventional gothic tropes. While the rebels, like Radcliffian banditti, roam the country, we discover that Mr Hamilton, the patriarch of the loyal Hamilton family at the center of the novel, has been keeping his estranged wife, long thought to be dead, a prisoner in a secret room underneath the house. Hamilton, therefore, has a double, contradictory, identity. In the context of a conservative Protestant interpretation of the 1798 Rebellion, Hamilton is clearly one of the oppressed Protestants; but he is also, in his unjust treatment of his wife, an oppressor. This is the most gothic of all the guilty secrets of the Hamilton family, but all of the major characters in *The Rebel* are hiding moral, social, or political transgressions. The only character not harboring a guilty secret is the rebel of the title, who is a victim of coercion and calumny. His 'guilt' is all too public, until in the course of the novel he demonstrates that he was, in fact, 'a loyalist in my heart'.[19]

These guilty secrets tormenting the main characters of *The Rebel* are symbolic of a broader unease related to Irish Protestant anxiety about the precise nature of their role in the Irish historical nightmare. For instance, George Hamilton, Mr Hamilton's son, who has taken an active part in fighting the rebels, describes Wexford as 'a desert', writing that 'scarcely a cabin remains inhabited, or inhabitable; and the inhumanity of their proceedings are horribly dreadful' (I: 83). This sentence, intentionally or not, is ambiguous as it stands. Hamilton does not specify whose 'proceedings' he is referring to, but the politically conservative reader would assume he is referring to the devastation wreaked by the rebels. But why would the rebels raze the cabins of the peasantry? In these circumstances, it would be more likely that this was the work of avenging government forces than of the rebels. This sense of ambiguity is heightened by the fact that George Hamilton follows this by observing, 'there is a grand fault somewhere, but I am silent' (I: 83). Hamilton's silence here is deafening. In *The Rebel*, all the main characters are attempting to forget or atone for some past indiscretions, but even at the end of the novel, when all outwardly seems to be well, we are told that 'The retrospection of the past would sometimes cause to each an involuntary shudder [...] and each tried to cast in oblivious darkness, the recollection of that which would give them pain'

(II: 245). This tendency to allow repressed doubt and guilt to bubble up through silence, ambiguity, contradiction, or, more drastically, by seeming to sabotage the plot and structure of a text is a characteristic of Irish Gothic. In a gentler way, the same kind of undermining of plot and character occurs in one of the most famous Irish novels of the early nineteenth century, Sydney Owenson's *The Wild Irish Girl* (1806). In *The Wild Irish Girl*, the willingness of the Gaelic and Catholic O'Melvilles to harbor a mysterious gentleman even though they suspected him of being a 1798 rebel was a risky device in a work intended to present a positive picture of the Gaelic Irish to an English readership. In addition, when the hero 'Horatio M' dreams of the beautiful features of the 'wild Irish girl', Glorvina O'Melville, transforming into the face of a gorgon before his eyes, he is surely revealing a fear that, despite all that he had seen and experienced, behind the civilized and exotic façade, the native Irish remained essentially monstrous.

It is precisely this very sense of repressed doubt and guilt that ultimately enables an Irish Gothic sensibility that would be common to both Protestant and Catholic writers to emerge. Again, the legacy of the 1798 Rebellion meant that Catholic fiction was, from the very earliest texts, obsessed with the notion of respectability and the need to disassociate respectable Catholics of the middle ranks from those lower orders who seemingly comprised the main body of rebels in 1798. One of the earliest works of fiction by a Catholic writer, Eliza Kelly's *The Matron of Erin* (1816) – a pointed deconstruction of Owenson's *The Wild Irish Girl* – is very careful to draw a distinction between those who practiced a rational and enlightened version of Catholicism and those whose religion was comprised largely of superstition and folk practices. The last thing Kelly wished to do was to exoticize Catholicism in the way Owenson does in *The Wild Irish Girl*.

The anxieties of *The Wild Irish Girl* and *The Matron of Erin* notwithstanding, it is not until the 1820s that we can see a form of Catholic Gothic constructed around anxieties concerning the true nature of Catholic respectability. Just as Irish Protestants might be secretly fearful that they are more oppressor than oppressed, respectable Catholics were traumatized by the fear that beneath the middle-class exterior, there still lurked an atavistic, barbaric, sectarian rebel. Novels such as John Banim's *Croohore of the Billhook* (1825), his brother Michael's *The Croppy* (1828), and Gerald Griffin's *The Collegians* (1829), for example, all reflect this anxiety. While these novels may not necessarily conform to the traditional notion of a gothic text (although all have clearly gothic elements to them), they do point the way to a more deeply psychological and nuanced form of gothic that makes its way into the gothic mainstream over the century. Irish Catholic Gothic tended to be more internal than external, with the emphasis more on psychological breakdown than supernatural terrors. In general, Irish Gothic writers – Protestant or Catholic – did not need the paraphernalia of the gothic, for the very reason that the tension between competing versions of a traumatic history and the political, religious, and social tensions of everyday Irish life ensured that the gothic, in some form or other, was always with them.

Fear of the atavistic Catholic therefore, was not just a Protestant concern, but features prominently in Catholic writing of the 1820s. It can be clearly seen in Gerald Griffin's *The Collegians*, a novel in which the Catholic middle-class antihero, Hardress Cregan, implicitly encourages his servant, Danny Mann, to rid him of the young woman he had rashly married. The fear in *The Collegians* is not so much that for every Kyrle Daly (the other 'collegian' of the title and the very epitome of the respectable Catholic middle-class gentleman) there is a Danny Mann; but the fact that in Hardress Cregan, who combines the best and worst of Daly and Mann, we see respectability struggling and failing to overcome the primitive. Ultimately Hardress Cregan proves to be more Danny Mann than Kyrle Daly. Similarly, in John Banim's *The Nowlans* (1826), the central character's Catholicism and his inability to come to terms with the choices he has made is the cause of his gothic torment and mental breakdown. As with Hardress Cregan, John Nowlan cannot triumph over the primitive, and his passions get the better of him. Although he wants to be a priest, he is drawn towards women. Eloping with the Protestant Letty Adams, Nowlan marries her in a Protestant ceremony his Catholic convictions can neither accept as a valid marriage nor reconcile with his vows as a Catholic seminarian. One possible compromise, to become a Protestant clergyman, is not a realistic option in a novel aimed at a Catholic readership in the confessional Ireland of the 1820s. In a country still riven with sectarian tension, apostasy would be an even greater disgrace. John Nowlan represents the Irish Catholic psyche under pressure in an exaggerated form. We are told that he 'felt remorse for the past, despair of the present, terror of the future',[20] an emotional state not a million miles away from Armida Fitzalban's previously mentioned sense of the past being suffering and the future inscrutable in *The Milesian Chief*. Behind John Nowlan is an unarticulated fear – here, a Catholic fear – that perhaps Catholicism, in forcing these impossible choices upon him, *is* a repressive and unreasonable religion. In an entirely different but equally traumatic way to that experienced by Protestants in gothic literature, John Nowlan is tormented by the Catholic religion, and his predicament reminds us that perspective, as discussed below, is another important element of Irish Gothic.

The Nowlans is, in many obvious ways, a traditional gothic novel. It has terrifying villains, outlaws, murders, abductions, attempted rapes, midnight meetings, doppelgangers, pseudo-supernatural events, monstrous faces at windows, and so on. But perhaps the real gothic element for the contemporary Irish Catholic reader (apart, of course, from John Nowlan's mental breakdown) is the presence of the characters Peery Conolly and Kitty Carey. Tolerated by the respectable Nowlans, the sinister Conolly is a disruptive and chaotic presence in the novel, facilitating both good and evil. A morally ambiguous figure, he embodies many of the classic stereotypical characteristics of the Irish peasant – he is intemperate, emotional, and loyal, but also reluctant to inform on anyone to the law. His silence in this regard is an act of rebellion. When a magistrate makes the observation that Peery must have deserted from 'Captain Rock' (II: 352), Conolly, and by association the Nowlan family, are explicitly linked to contemporary insurgency and implicitly associated with 1798 and, indeed, 1641. Kitty Carey, the mother of John Nowlan's illegitimate cousin Maggy Nowlan, is an even more sinister and troubling figure. She represents the worst, most fearful, kind of Irish resistance to authority. When Carey is convicted of murder and sentenced to death, her pulse is described as 'steady and regular as that of innocence at rest' (II: 358). Together the unrepentant Carey and the unpredictable and morally ambiguous Conolly are symbolic revenants from a past that is undead: totems of an older, atavistic, barbaric Irish Catholic psyche that no veneer of middle-class respectability can entirely obscure from view. In a religiously divided Ireland Carey and Conolly are inevitably perceived to be part of the society in which even respectable Catholics are required to move and live. It is a suitably gothic touch that the main narrative of *The Nowlans* ends with the disturbing image of a defiant Carey being led to her fate. Her silence is terrifying. It is a clear reminder that despite the low-key optimism of the end of the novel, the old gothic Ireland that middle-class Catholics long to consign to the past continues to exist and to intrude into the present. *The Nowlans*, therefore, is very much an Irish Catholic Gothic novel for an Irish Catholic readership, playing as it does on Catholic middle-class fears about aspects of their own religion and coreligionists. But in *The Nowlans* we can also see other traits shared with Irish Protestant Gothic, especially the notion of being in the position of not just being the victim but also the agent and perpetrator of injustice and atrocity.

Not the least of its other traits is that, as stated above, Irish Gothic is often a matter of perspective, and that in a polarized society the gothic is often in the eye – and mind – of the reader. This is particularly relevant in relation to the emerging Catholic strain of Irish Gothic, which may not appear to be gothic in the traditional sense of the term. But perspective *is* important in Irish writing, not least because of the contested nature of the Irish past and its subsequent influence on the present. Thus, a novel which reads as a tale of empowerment to one section of society may be read as a sinister, indeed a nightmarish, threat to another. For example, the anonymously penned *The United Irishman, Or, The Fatal Effects of Credulity* (1819) may initially appear from its title to be a late anti-Jacobin text, warning of the disastrous effects of naïve faith in impractical political ideals. But the credulity referred to in the title is that of a Catholic landowning family who, precluded by penal legislation from holding their land in their own name, disastrously entrust it to an unscrupulous Protestant upstart instead. Although the novel is politically conservative in general, and therefore respectable to a degree, the ambivalent and unrepentant attitude of Gerald O'Brien, the United Irishman of the title, to his involvement in the 1798 Rebellion would be troubling, perhaps even shocking, to a conservative reader. Even more disturbing would be the fact that the structure of the novel itself reflects the transfer of power most dreaded by Protestant conservatives. Initially the novel mirrors the classic national tale, beginning as a series of letters written by an Englishman traveling in Ireland, in which he recounts his experience of the country and the life story of O'Brien. However, an indiscretion of his youth – the memory of killing his best friend in a duel – comes back to haunt the narrator during his time in Ireland, resulting in him losing his sanity, and the concluding sections of the novel are narrated by O'Brien. The appalling vista of O'Brien, the unrepentant rebel, taking narrative control of the text is compounded by the fact that it was through the political influence of the English narrator and some loyal members of the nobility that O'Brien obtained an official pardon. In *The United Irishman* it is the English traveler, a liberal Protestant, who is punished for an offense regarded by many as a moral rather than a criminal indiscretion. Although this might not seem particularly gothic in the traditional sense, it does have a more conventionally gothic counterpart in *Melmoth*, when the Englishman Stanton finds himself unjustly incarcerated in a madhouse surrounded by insane rebels. As Luke Gibbons has remarked, in *Melmoth* it is the liberal Englishman who suffers, and not the unrepentant rebels.[21] *The United Irishman* also raises the specter of the unreconstructed rebel.

O'Brien matter-of-factly admits that, 'Had our men conducted them-selves with the least prudence, we would eventually have been masters of Ireland. But they unfortunately intoxicated with success, began to drink and commit outrages disgraceful to humanity'.[22] The word 'mas-ters' here would have been particularly alarming for a Protestant reader, and the clear inference is that it was only the indiscipline of the rebels that saved conservative – and by implication Protestant – Ireland. Para-doxically, therefore, it is the barbaric and undisciplined nature of the Catholic Irish that on the one hand threatens, and on the other, guar-antees Protestant safety and hegemony. This is the precarious position that Irish Protestants find themselves in. Such a situation has a parallel in *Melmoth* when Monçada describes his feeling in the company of the parricide as 'a kind of doubtful security' (p. 187). O'Brien also has an unsettlingly deterministic view of his own role in the Rebellion: 'Great as my misfortunes have been [...] they did not proceed from any fault of mine; if it was wrong to be an United Irishman, I was one from prin-ciple, and no man can be accountable for his feelings' (II: 13). Even more unsettling, perhaps, is the threat from within. O'Brien's younger brother Diarmuid – an even more ardent patriot – has married into the Protestant nobility at the end of the novel, but this is no guarantee that he has changed his opinions: one of the English narrator's last observa-tions is, 'I cannot discover whether Diarmuid's principles are changed; on politics he never speaks' (II: 236). Just as George Hamilton's silence on the question of who is to blame for the Rebellion in *The Rebel* is significant, for an insecure Protestant reader, Diarmuid O'Brien's silence here speaks volumes. Read in this way, the rise of Daniel O'Connell, and the prospect of a disciplined and constitutional Irish peasantry was a more terrifying prospect than the 'doubtful security' of a barbaric and undisciplined one.

This notion of perspective as an Irish Gothic trait can be applied even more generally. *The United Irishman* makes an interesting contrast with *The Rebel*. Both feature rebels seeking forgiveness, and both rebels at the center of the text receive official pardons. The more obviously gothic text pardons moral transgressions but not political ones (with the notable exception of the title character), whereas in *The United Irishman*, rebellion is forgiven but the moral weakness of the English narrator is punished. Which of these novels is ultimately more psy-chologically disturbing depends on where the reader is on the political and religious spectrum. But both novels, as with all of the texts con-sidered here, have that Irish Gothic quality of continually undermining assumptions and revealing contradictions, discordances, disturbances, and anxieties about not just the Other, but the Self, and the confessional group to which one belongs. The Catholic Monçada, in so many ways the cipher for Anglo-Irish sensibility in *Melmoth* (which is itself a contradiction) proclaims that 'I am what they have made me' (p. 168); and the same can be said of Grace Nowlan, John Nowlan, Hardress Cregan, and a whole series of rebels from Connal O'Morven to Gerald O'Brien. The realization that they are products of a contentious and traumatic Irish past and, by extension, a problematic relationship with the Other is both a source of strength and a source of anxiety. But guilt and internal conflict at least have the mitigating qualities of being conventional gothic emotions: in Irish Gothic the fact that for every tormented O'Morven or Nowlan there also lurked an unapologetic Peery Conolly, Saunders Smiley, Danny Mann, or Kitty Carey was likely to have been, for the Irish reader of this period, the most gothic terror of all.

Notes

1. Charles Robert Maturin (1820) *Melmoth the Wanderer*, 4 vols (London), I: 4.
2. [John Banim] (1826) *The Boyne Water, A Tale*, 3 vols (London), III: 413; further page references will be included parenthetically in the text.
3. For the influence of the gothic on the writings of Scott, see Fiona Robertson (1994) *Legitimate Histories: Scott, Gothic and the Authorities of Fiction* (Oxford: Clarendon).
4. James Kelly (2003) ' "We Were All to be Massacred": Irish Protestants and the Experience of Rebellion', in *1798: a Bicentenary Perspective*, eds Thomas Bartlett et al. (Dublin: Four Courts Press), pp. 312–30 (p. 313).
5. See Jarlath Killeen (2005) *Gothic Ireland: Horror and the Irish Anglican Imagination in the Long Eighteenth Century* (Dublin: Four Courts Press).
6. Charles Robert Maturin (1820; 1998) *Melmoth the Wanderer*, ed. Douglas Grant (Oxford: Oxford University Press), p. 236; further page references will be included parenthetically in the text.
7. Killeen, *Gothic Ireland*, p. 12.
8. Christina Morin (2011) 'Forgotten Fiction: Reconsidering the Gothic Novel in Eighteenth-Century Ireland', *Irish University Review* 41.1, 80–94.
9. Morin, 'Forgotten Fiction', p. 83.
10. Siobhán Kilfeather also identifies 1798 as a crucial watershed in the development of Irish Gothic. See Kilfeather (2006), 'The Gothic Novel' in *The Cambridge Companion to the Irish Novel*, ed. John Wilson Foster (Cambridge: Cambridge University Press), pp. 78–96 (p. 86).
11. 'Melmoth, the Wanderer', *Edinburgh Review*, 35:70 (July 1821), pp. 353–62 (pp. 355–6).
12. Luke Gibbons (2004) *Gaelic Gothic: Race, Colonization, and Irish Culture* (Galway: Arlen House), p. 87.
13. [Charles Robert Maturin] (1812) *The Milesian Chief. A Romance*, 4 vols (London), III: 129; further page references will be included parenthetically in the text.

14. One of the more obvious of these footnote reminders in *Melmoth* is when a reference to the fact that the wanderer taught the naïve and innocent Immalee the 'wild and sweet songs' of 'his native country' is footnoted with a single word: 'Ireland' (p. 334).

15. For example, see the footnote recounting the murder of Lord Kilwarden, which marked the beginning of Emmet's rebellion in 1803, a story Maturin claims was 'related to me by an eye-witness', and the traumatic effect the event had on another eyewitness (p. 257n.). Another scene in the novel, where Monçada describes the death of a man tormented by guilt, is footnoted with the comment, 'Fact, – me ipso teste [*sic*]', suggesting that the recollection was from Maturin's own personal experience (p. 200n.).

16. Morin, 'Forgotten Fiction', p. 83.

17. See, for example, the account of the massacre on Wexford Bridge quoted in Sir Richard Musgrave (1802) *Memoirs of the Different Rebellions in Ireland*, 2 vols (3rd ed; Dublin), II: 16. Lending some credence to this view is the fact that it is still unclear what the 'MWS' stood for.

18. The prime examples are Charles Lucas (1801) *The Infernal Quixote: a Tale of the Day*, 4 vols (London); Mrs Bullock (1801) *Dorothea; Or, A Ray of the New Light*, 3 vols (London), and Robert Bisset (1804) *Modern Literature: a Novel*, 3 vols (London). For an article on anti-Jacobin novels featuring the 1798 Rebellion, see M. O. Grenby (2007) 'Rebels Denied a Cause: Fiction, Anti-Jacobinism and the Irish Rebellion', in *Reactions to Revolutions: the 1790s and their Aftermath*, eds Ulrich Broich, H. T. Dickinson, Eckhart Hellmuth, and Martin Schmidt (Berlin: Lit Verlag), pp. 61–83.

19. 'A Lady' (1799; 1801) *The Rebel: a Tale of the Times*, 2 vols (repr.; Dublin), I: 26; further page references will be included parenthetically in the text.

20. [John Banim] (1826) 'The Nowlans', in *Tales by the O'Hara Family. Second Series. Comprising The Nowlans, and Peter of the Castle*, 3 vols (London), vols 1–2 (II: 40); further page references will be included parenthetically in the text.

21. Gibbons, *Gaelic Gothic*, p. 87.

22. Anon. (1819) *The United Irishman, Or, The Fatal Effects of Credulity; A Tale Founded On Facts*, 2 vols (Dublin), I: 198–9. Further references will be included parenthetically in the text. The novel was later reissued in 1821 as *The Cavern in the Wicklow Mountains, or; Fate of the O'Brien Family. A Tale Founded on Facts*, 2 vols (Dublin). It is mentioned under this name by Siobhán Kilfeather in 'The Gothic Novel', p. 81.

5
The Gothicization of Irish Folklore

Anne Markey

Drawing attention to their shared association with superstition, transgression of rationality, fascination with the supernatural, and repetitive recourse to familiar tropes and formulaic narrative conventions, critics have repeatedly argued that folklore is a significant source for Gothic tropes and themes. Jason Marc Harris, for example, claims: 'the Gothic and other literary traditions of fantasy and the fantastic have extended and stylized motifs and metaphysics that were long-standing in folklore to begin with'.[1] Attributing the virtual absence of ghosts and phantoms in early-eighteenth-century literature to the dominance of the supremely rational worldview of the Augustans, David Punter argues: 'But they started to reappear with the Gothic revival, occurring often in the old ballads and from there they moved into Gothic fiction'.[2] Elizabeth MacAndrew, meanwhile, points to the creative encounter between individual imagination and communal lore presented in Gothic fiction, which 'gives form to amorphous fears and impulses [...] using an amalgam of materials, some torn from the author's own subconscious mind and some the stuff of myth, folklore, fairy tale, and romance'.[3] From these critical perspectives, Gothic fiction feeds on older narrative forms, including folklore, which in turn inform and haunt a newer literary mode whose central preoccupations revolve around a contested power dynamic between past and present. At the same time, though, folklore and Gothic fiction are perceived as being separate discourses, but it must be remembered that this distinction may not have been immediately apparent to readers in the period before the term folklore was coined and defined. As conventions regulating the collection and presentation of folk narratives did not emerge until the end of the nineteenth century, early readers would have found it difficult to ascertain whether a story with elements of terror and supernatural intervention was a traditional tale or original fiction. A critically neglected volume, *Tales of the Emerald Isle; or, Legends of Ireland*, written by 'A Lady of Boston' and published in New York in 1828, casts intriguing light on the fluidity of genre in the early decades of the nineteenth century while also highlighting some complexities of the early relationship between folklore and Gothic fiction. An analysis of this collection illuminates contemporary cultural values, debates, and anxieties about such varied yet connected issues as the construction of Irish national identity, the proprieties of female authorship, and the vagaries of the American literary marketplace.

The title and subtitle of *Tales of the Emerald Isle; or, Legends of Ireland* suggest that the volume contains a number of authentic – and specifically Irish – folktales and legends. Passing to the contents, the reader sees that the collection consists of seven stories – 'Tradition, or St Kevin's Bed'; 'Carol More O'Daly, or The Constant Lover'; 'Humble life, or The Sycamore Tree'; 'Retribution'; 'The Victim'; 'Mystery, A Modern Story'; and 'Bran, The Bloodhound' – the titles of which serve to reinforce the impression that this is a collection of Irish folk narratives. However, this is far from being the case. In the only recent critical commentary on the book, Charles Fanning describes it as 'a curious collection of early fiction based on Irish folklore', and claims that four of the stories 'have their origin in folk materials'.[4] He identifies those stories as 'Tradition', 'Carol More O'Daly', 'Humble Life', and 'Bran, the Bloodhound'. In fact, only the first three have any kind of verifiable connection with Irish folklore, because despite its clear allusion to the faithful hound (and cousin) of the legendary figure of Fionn mac Cumhaill, hero of the Ulster Mythological Cycle, 'Bran, the Bloodhound', which Fanning calls 'a Gothic production', is entirely attributable to authorial invention.[5] The remaining three stories are similarly Gothic in tone and set in the recent past in romanticized, but recognizable, Irish locations. Effectively, then, what purports to be a collection of Irish legends is actually a work of Gothic fiction in which three literary versions of authentically traditional material are followed by four original stories of suspense, terror, and romance.

To anyone at all familiar with the conventions of folklore as an academic discourse in the twenty-first century, *Tales of the Emerald Isle* appears an aberration, because the Lady from Boston not only presents original fiction as authentically legendary material but also fails to provide sources for any of the actual legends she recounts, adopts a literary tone in the presentation of those legends rather than replicating the words of storytellers representative of the 'folk' amongst whom she

claims the stories circulate, and makes no attempt to place her material within a comparative or scholarly framework. Given that the word
'folklore' was not coined until 1846, when it was used in a letter published in the *Athenaeum* from the English antiquarian W. G. Thoms
to describe 'the manners, customs, observances, superstitions, ballads,
proverbs, &c of the olden time', it would be anachronistic to expect earlier collectors, such as the Lady of Boston, to approach their material in
ways that reflected later understandings of the term or that adhered to
subsequent standards guiding the collection and publication of folk narrative.[6] In order to place the actual, rather than apparent, peculiarities
of *Tales of the Emerald Isle* in context, it is therefore necessary to trace
the emergence of popular tale collection in nineteenth-century Europe.

Although collections of folktales and legends began to appear in the
1780s, the enterprise really took off with the publication of Jacob and
Wilhelm Grimm's *Kinder- und Hausmärchen* [*Children's and Household
Tales*] in 1812. In an attempt to undermine the dominance of French
Enlightenment values, the Grimms hoped to establish the importance
and worth of German culture by collecting examples of indigenous
folk literature. Claiming that this material was still plentiful but under
threat from foreign influence and the forces of modernity, Jacob Grimm
argued for the necessity of collecting and faithfully recording folktales
and legends: 'it is important that these items be recorded in the most
exact and detailed fashion from the mouth of the informants, faithfully and truthfully, without any cosmetic touch-up or addition, and
where feasible in and with their own words'.[7] In the preface to *Kinder-
und Hausmärchen*, the Grimms insisted: 'We have tried to collect these
tales in as pure a form as possible. No details have been added or
embellished or changed, for we would have been reluctant to expand
stories already so rich by adding analogies and allusions'.[8] A comparison between the original manuscript and the first edition, however,
shows that the Grimms shaped and polished the narratives for publication, while revisions to subsequent editions included the deletion of
stories that did not seem sufficiently German and the addition of others,
as well as stylistic changes to the texts of the tales themselves. Despite
their claim to have reproduced 'these tales in as pure a form as possible', the Grimms' editorial practices reveal that the collection was never
an authentic replication of folk narrative. From the outset, then, literary
representations of folklore raised issues related to national identity, literary taste, and editorial or authorial subterfuge. *Kinder- und Hausmärchen*,
a work inspired by cultural nationalism, was reprinted in seven revised
editions during the Grimms' lifetime, and first translated into English

by Edgar Taylor as *German Popular Stories* in 1823. Its success inspired the production of other collections of folktales across Europe.

As a result of both the influence of the Grimms and the rise of anti-quarianism in Ireland, Irish folklore increasingly became the focus of research and scholarship over the course of the nineteenth century. In 1825, the Commissioners of Irish Education reported that *The Royal Hibernian Tales; being a collection of the most entertaining stories now extant* was being used in hedge schools in Ireland. No copies of that early edition have been traced, but versions were reprinted in Belfast in 1832 and in Dublin in 1835. Another, more influential, volume of traditional stories, *Fairy Legends and Traditions of the South of Ireland*, which was later revealed to be have been compiled by Thomas Crofton Croker (1798–1854), was published in London in 1825. Fancifully illustrated by woodcuts taken from drawings by William Henry Brooke, cousin of Charlotte, the first volume of Croker's *Fairy Legends* contains an original introductory poem dedicated to Lady Chatterton of Castle Mahon, and 27 legends, which are bookended by extracts from *Paradise Lost* and *A Midsummer Night's Dream* and accompanied by commentaries glossing Irish-language expressions and giving analogues in classical and medieval sources. Although Croker claimed that the stories were 'written in the style in which they are generally related by those who believe in them', they were highly stylized literary productions in which an erudite narrator sets the scene and, condescendingly, if occasionally affectionately, introduces an array of quaint Irish characters who believe in fairies of various denominations.[9] A second series of *Fairy Legends*, bearing Croker's name and dedicated to Walter Scott (1771–1832), was published in London in 1828. Croker's attitude to the material he presented in both collections is revealed in his condemnation of the superstition of the Irish peasantry, which, he claims, served 'to retard the progress of their civilization'.[10]

The first edition of *Fairy Legends* met with widespread acclaim, including praise from the Grimm brothers who, despite Wilhelm's reservations about the style and language used to present apparently genuine legends to a general readership, translated it into German in 1826. In John Hennig's view, the Grimms valued Croker's work 'as a means of acquiring some knowledge of Ireland'.[11] Jennifer Schacker has convincingly argued that Croker invited 'English readers, regardless of education, class or age, to direct a critical and patronizing gaze on their Irish objects'.[12] Folklore, then, was perceived as giving insights into national character, but while the Grimms built on that perception to vindicate German culture, Croker presented Ireland as a place bemired in ignorant superstition. In 1849, he revealed that the first volume had been published anonymously because it was a collaborative effort to which a group of friends 'tendered their friendly assistance' and for which they 're-wrote some of the tales'.[13] It later transpired that they not only rewrote legendary tales that genuinely circulated in Ireland, but that one of his collaborators, Thomas Keightley, took a legend – 'The Peasant and the Waterman' – from the Grimms' *Deutsche Sagen* [*German Legends*] (1816), renamed it 'The Soul Cages', relocated the action to Clare, and presented it to Croker, who went on to include it in the collection as an authentic Irish legend. Given that tales which appeared in *Fairy Legends* were filtered through the literary lens of a group of educated men, one of whom admitted to fabrication, the insights offered by the collection into Irish national character were highly dubious. The years following the success of Croker's *Fairy Legends* witnessed the publication of various memoirs and sketches which drew on Irish folklore. These included *Tales of the O'Hara Family* (1825) by John and Michael Banim, Gerald Griffin's *Tales of the Munster Festivals* (1827), and Caesar Otway's *Sketches in Ireland* (1827). Similar issues relating to authenticity of material, editorial intervention and authorial manipulation arise in relation to these volumes, which, Seamus Deane claims, were indistinguishable from Irish fiction both in purpose and quality.[14] The intermingling of folklore and fiction in these volumes, all of which were originally published in England, facilitated the presentation of varying constructions of Irish national character to readers in Ireland and elsewhere.

In summary, by 1828 the term folklore had still to come into being and there was as yet no consensus on how traditional tales should be collected or presented. The guiding principles that the words in which stories were originally told should be preserved and that sources should be provided had still to be generally accepted and adopted. There was a market for collections of Irish folklore, in which traditional narratives and legends of the supernatural were presented as authentic, without proffering any evidence of their authenticity. These collections were perceived as providing insights into national character, but the version of national character they portrayed reflected the prejudices and opinions of the collector, so could be either sympathetic or hostile or lie somewhere in between. The only collection of Irish folklore readily available to American readers was an 1827 Philadelphia edition of Croker's first volume of *Fairy Legends*, which presented the Irish as superstitious and culturally backward. While this viewpoint may well have bolstered an English reader's sense of national superiority, its appeal to an American readership was far less certain. Over 400,000 emigrants from Ireland had settled in America by 1815, while the following 30 years witnessed the arrival of an estimated 100,000 others.[15] It was against this background of a burgeoning expatriate Irish readership and lack of consensus on how folk narrative should be presented that the New York firm of W. Borradaile published *Tales of the Emerald Isle; or, Legends of Ireland*, by 'A Lady of Boston', in November 1828.

The opening three stories are based on authentic legendary material presented in a stylized, literary fashion, which was not at all unusual for the time. What was unusual was that Gothic elements are superimposed on two of these legends, and that the remainder of the stories are original Gothic fictions, masquerading as traditional tales. In a preface addressed to the public, the Lady of Boston claims that in works on Irish history 'romance and fable [are] so closely blended with historical fact, that it would be a most difficult task to separate fact from fiction'.[16] In the stories that follow she similarly interweaves folklore and Gothic fiction to present positive representations of Ireland and the Irish. The sequencing of the collection is important because it serves to elide the distance not only between Ireland's Gaelic past and colonial present but also between the Catholic peasantry and the Protestant Ascendancy of the contemporary moment. Readers are introduced to Irish national character through a legendary prism which emphasizes a Gaelic tradition of loyalty, endurance, honesty, and self-sacrifice, while the Gothic stories with which the volume concludes reinforce the continuing attribution of these positive traits to Anglo-Irish people in more recent times. Overall, then, the collection vindicates the civility of Irish national character while downplaying social, religious, and political differences. That vindication, however, does not amount to a justification of Ireland's right to self-governance or even to a sustained critique of the injustice of the penal laws under which Catholics and Protestant dissenters were excluded from participation in public life. Instead, the Lady of Boston presents Ireland as a place threatened less by external forces than by internal manifestations of fanaticism and eruptions of a desire for domination. Her sympathy extends to the Catholic peasantry but her allegiance lies with the Protestant Ascendancy, whose virtue always triumphs over adversity.

So, the collection opens with 'Tradition, or St Kevin's Bed', introduced by a quotation from Macpherson's *Works of Ossian* (1765), which praises the beauty of the bereaved lover, Malvina, while drawing attention to her melancholy. Accordingly, the quotation establishes a tragic context for the legend that follows. The story itself provides a romanticized account of the sixth-century saint's attempts to escape the unwanted attentions of Kathleen O'Donnell, 'the fair-haired, white-bosomed maid of Clohogue' (p. 3). The legend was a familiar one, not least because it provided the basis for Thomas Moore's 'By that lake whose gloomy shore', which had appeared in various editions of *Irish Melodies*, including one published by Mathew Carey in Philadelphia in 1815.[17] Indeed, lines from Moore's poem are quoted in the story, where, in keeping with other versions of the legend published over the course of the nineteenth century, the saint's piety eventually wins through. Here, though, the landscape is presented as a Gothic terrain:

> The figure of the holy man seemed, in this situation, a mere atom in creation. On arriving at the top of the dizzy cliff, he knelt down, and looking over into the abyss beneath, observed that there was a slight opening on the side of the declivity towards the lake. (p. 11)

There, Kevin makes a bed, believing that he will be able to elude Kathleen. Less a seductress than an innocent maiden who 'was too chaste, too modest, to tell how she loved' (p. 4), she pursues him even to this secluded spot. Her obsessive love is presented as a form of madness: 'the hapless girl grew more wretched till reason at length forsook its throne. She could no longer feel the relief of tears, for her brain seemed as if on fire' (p. 8). After Kevin unwittingly pushes Kathleen to her death from the cliff, he is overcome with love and remorse. The story ends with the haunted figure of the repentant saint and the ghostly specter of the spurned maiden:

> He mourned her with tears and fasting, so long as he lived, and praying that she might not be entirely lost to his sight. The saints granted his prayer, and the Irish peasantry still assert that her blessed spirit floats on the dusky waves of the lake, to guard weak maidens against the approach of the wily god of love. (p. 14)

Both Kathleen's innocence and the saint's humanity are stressed throughout. The compassion of her affectionate parents, who possess 'that tact peculiar to the Irish' (p. 8), is also highlighted, so the Lady of Boston portrays these traits as representative of Irish character. Significantly, however, she Gothicizes an authentic legend to provide a sympathetic portrayal of the Irish, but also to suggest that fanaticism, whether it take the form of all-consuming love or excessive religiosity, is the greatest threat to their happiness and continued existence.

'Carol More O'Daly, or The Constant Lover' is another Gothic retelling of an authentic Irish legend, which recounts how a young chieftain from the time of Elizabeth I dresses as a harper to rescue his beloved Ellen Cavanagh from an arranged marriage. The opening quotation from Macpherson's 'The Songs of Selma', which presents Colma lamenting the death of Salgar, introduces the theme of familial opposition to the alliance of offspring of warring families, and establishes the fidelity and integrity of the thwarted lovers. That constancy is further reinforced by the later citation of the first stanza of 'Come o'er the Sea', which was included in several versions of Thomas Moore's *Irish Melodies*, including Mathew Carey's 1815 American edition. Carol More O'Daly, the eponymous hero of the story, also features in 'The Legend of Knockfierna', which appeared in the first volume of Croker's *Fairy Legends*, but there, instead of being a chieftain, he is a 'strapping young fellow up out of Connaught', known as 'Devil Daly'.[18] Fearless to the point of being foolhardy, Croker's O'Daly throws a rock down a hole in a mountain that is reputed to lead to a fairy castle. The rock comes back up and hits him in the face, leaving him not only chastened but also disfigured for life. In a note, Croker states: 'Carroll O'Daly [*sic*], the hero, is much celebrated in Irish song and tradition. The popular melody of *Ellen A Roon* is said to have been composed and sung by him when he carried off Miss Elinor Cavanagh'.[19] Instead of recounting that legend, in which O'Daly is a brave and heroic figure, however, Croker presents one in which O'Daly is a rash young man who gets his comeuppance and is punished for his folly. The Lady of Boston, by contrast, presents him as the 'constant lover' of her version's subtitle, who falls for the beautiful daughter of his father's greatest rival and enemy. Donogh More O'Daly, the young hero's father, we are told, 'was wealthy, powerful, and overbearing, and had long been the terror of the neighbouring chieftains, on whose estates he permitted his numerous train of followers to commit many depredations' (p. 15). This tyrant lives in an impregnable castle, set against a majestic and menacing landscape:

> It was a large, but low, stone castle, that covered an extensive spot on the banks of Lough Rhea. On one side arose an immense rock, which completely concealed that part of it from human sight, and was an invincible barrier to the foe. Behind Balclutha was a high and inaccessible mountain; on the western side was Lough Rhea; but the castle was situated on a bold, projecting cliff, whose extremity hung beetling over the lake in a threatening manner, looking as if it would fall, bearing death and destruction in its course. On the south front

of the castle was a deep moat, and a drawbridge, which was let up and down at leisure. This moat was surrounded by ramparts. So well was it protected by nature and art, that the idea of obtaining redress was a thing abandoned and hopeless; and the lion crouching in his lair, bade a bold defiance to his injured neighbours, and almost held the whole province of Connaught at bay. (pp. 15–16)

Enraged by her dalliance with the son of their sworn enemy, Ellen Cavanagh's father and scheming brother, in cahoots with her confessor, lock her in a turret and force her to accept the odious attentions of one of their loathsome associates, 'the stern and gloomy Chief Gilpatrick MacCormac' (p. 30). The innocent girl is powerless to resist: 'Bitterly did poor Ellen mourn over the tyranny she could not escape' (p. 29). On the day arranged for her marriage to Gilpatrick, 'the pale and fainting Ellen Cavanagh, dressed in virgin white, with bunches of scarlet arbutus and dark green myrtle mingled amid her flaxen hair, looked more like a lamb decorated with flowers for a sacrifice than a bride for the altar of Hymen' (p. 32). Carol More O'Daly, disguised as a harpist, turns up in the chapel and elopes with his beloved. In this Gothic rendition of an authentic Irish legend, the young lovers overcome parental opposition and general treachery to ride off into the sunset together. Before that happy conclusion, though, their happiness is threatened by internal rifts in Irish society that are fueled by a desire to dominate. As constancy and fidelity enable O'Daly and Ellen Cavanagh to triumph over adversity, the suggestion is that these Irish qualities transcend the divisions that threaten Ireland's wellbeing.

'Humble Life; or, the Sycamore Tree' is the only story in *Tales of the Emerald Isle* that does not contain Gothic elements. A literary rendition of an international folktale about a man who dreams of treasure and finds it at home (classified under the internationally recognized Aarne/Thompson/Uther system as tale type 1645), it concerns Philip Alanson, who lives with his wife Norah, and their clutch of children, in a humble but spotless cottage 'in a remote part of the County of Galway' (p. 35). The narrator explains, 'Much has been said of the filthy condition in which the lower classes keep their cabins, and from such high authority as Lady Morgan and Miss Edgeworth' (p. 35), but goes on to undermine these negative reports by insisting that the Alansons 'always looked, as the neighbours said, that is, *clane* and *dacent*', and that 'their establishment was the admiration of all the strangers who travelled in those parts' (p. 36). A series of misfortunes befall the Alansons, and they find themselves threatened with eviction by an agent, 'who, like all the agents of Irish absentees, showed no more compassion to their tenantry than negro drivers on a plantation in the West Indies do to the slaves' (pp. 38–9). On three consecutive nights, an angel appears to Philip in a dream, telling him to go to the bridge at Lough Corrib and await his reward. Philip duly goes, and meets a woman who tells him that she had a dream in which she was told that she would find treasure under a sycamore tree outside a cabin belonging to one Philip Alanson. Philip goes home, digs under the tree, finds the treasure, and lives happily and prosperously ever after. Years later, Norah wonders why the angel didn't just tell him to dig under the tree, and Philip replies, 'I learned from that very circumstance a lesson that should be impressed upon the minds of all; it is this: that we have no right to expect favours or fortune, unless we take pains to seek them, and that reward is consequent upon patience and perseverance' (p. 48). In this story, the Alansons, and by extension, the Irish peasantry, are hard-working, god-fearing, honest, and persevering, so the positive portrait it paints of Irish character serves as a correction to other, less flattering descriptions of the Irish. The opening quotation from *A Winter's Tale* – 'The self-same sun that shines upon a court/Hides not his visage from our cottage,/But shines on both alike' (p. 41) – establishes a continuity between all classes of Irish society and suggests that traits such as integrity and persistence are shared by both powerless and powerful alike. At the same time, however, the actions of the agent reveal that the Irish are not uniformly admirable. Here, the desire to dominate results in tyranny, threatening social harmony and stability. The moral, said to be taken from Goldsmith, with which the story concludes, addresses all ranks of society: 'Let us be but steady and inflexible in the path of virtue and industry, and we shall be eventually both fortunate and happy' (p. 48).

The three stories based on genuine legendary material vindicate the general civility of pre-Norman, Elizabethan, and contemporary Ireland, but also portray this civility as threatened by aberrant yet ongoing fanaticism and the desire to dominate. The remaining four stories, although presented as legends, are all original, authorial fictions. Written in the Gothic mode, they celebrate industry, honesty, and respect for others, and present these traits as a necessary foundation for religious tolerance and harmonious relationships between different Irish social, political, and religious groupings. Rather than being portrayed as representative of any one such grouping, the villains in these stories are deviant individuals. By contrast, the heroes and heroines share common characteristics that transcend social and religious divisions, and so these Gothic fictions complement the positive construction of Irish national character presented in the legends. The continued use of quotations from Macpherson's *Ossian* contributes to this ongoing presentation of a unified Irish identity. Quotations from other authors as varied as the Scottish poet and dramatist James Thomson (1700–48), the English poet, Edward Young (1681–1765), the American writer, Frederic Stanhope Hill (1805–50), and the Irish-born Oliver Goldsmith (1730–74), meanwhile, further testify to Irish civility and refinement.

'Retribution' opens with an observation that implies that the story is an authentic legend: 'There is, perhaps, no country on the face of the earth more fruitful of legendary lore than Ireland' (p. 49). Nonetheless, the story which follows has no affinities with Irish folklore. Instead, it recounts the adventures of the entirely fictional Mr Mountjoy, 'a pious clergyman of the Episcopal persuasion' (p. 50), who gets lost in Wicklow on a stormy January evening and so is forced to seek the hospitality of strangers. He initially looks for shelter in a house where 'a large silver crucifix, and a picture of the holy mother' are the first sights to greet his eyes. The owner, Mr Fitzgerald, tells him that the house is full and suggests that he seek accommodation in an inn about a mile away. Mr Mountjoy is relieved, rather than distressed, by this lack of hospitality because 'Ireland was on the eve of a rebellion, when the animosity of the catholics against the heretics, as they termed the protestants, was drawing to a crisis' (p. 52). The inn turns out to be 'a hovel more fit for the reception of swine than human beings' (p. 52), but Mountjoy is warmly welcomed by the Catholic host, Dermot, who tells him about the nearby castle of Duncraig. Local wisdom has it that the present owner of the estate murdered the last Countess of Duncraig, who now haunts the gloomy mansion. Anxious 'to exorcise the troubled spirit' (p. 54), Mountjoy offers money to Dermot to bring him to Duncraig, and Dermot, whose landlord has promised him three guineas if he can prevail on anyone to spend the night there, agrees to do so. At this point, the Lady of Boston is at odds to dispel any negative impression Dermot's actions might create in the mind of her reader: 'Gentle reader, do not, if you please, infer from this, that "mine host" of the Brown Jug was mean or covetous; he was poor, he was oppressed; to sum up all, he was an Irishman. This includes all the suffering that the human race are subject to' (p. 55). A little later, she praises Dermot's kindness, describing it as 'a distinguishing trait in the Irish character' (p. 57). Echoing 'Humble life; or, The Sycamore Tree', these observations convey sympathy for a beleaguered Catholic peasantry, while eliding religious difference in the presentation of Irish character.

On arrival at Duncraig, Mountjoy opens the 'lock of the Gothic entrance' (p. 57), and enters the desolate mansion, where he sees, 'hung over the Gothic mantelpiece', the portrait of a beautiful lady: 'The face, with the exception of the eyes, was Milesian; but these, instead of being of a soft grey were dark, large and expressive of tenderness; the hair was also dark and very luxuriant, the complexion dazzlingly fair, but rather pale' (p. 59). The use of the term 'Milesian' is politically charged, as for centuries hostile commentators had claimed that the Irish were of Scythian descent, and therefore barbaric, while more sympathetic observers insisted that the Irish were descended from Milesius of Spain, and therefore possessed a pedigree of ancient civility. The lady, who is Arabella, Countess of Duncraig, is thus presented as an emblem of Ireland, past and present. Her spirit appears to a terrified Mountjoy, and leads him under a low archway at the end of a dark corridor, to point at the earth beneath a withered hawthorn tree. The following morning, aided by Dermot and his brother-in-law who dig under the tree, Mountjoy finds the body of the Countess. It transpires that she was murdered at the instigation of her fanatically bigoted, Catholic uncle, Hugh Fitzgerald, because she converted to Protestantism on her marriage to Edward Augustus Hamilton. On hearing that the steward who killed Arabella spared the life of her young son, the villainous Fitzgerald had immured his servant in a small cell in the castle, where he died of starvation. Fitzgerald, the man who refused hospitality to Mountjoy during the storm, is convicted of his crimes, and dies 'a sincere penitent' (p. 74). In this story, an Episcopalian clergyman is aided by the Catholic peasantry to avenge the murder of a Milesian beauty who personifies Irish civility, by her fanatical uncle, whose evil deeds are inspired by an 'unrelenting spirit of bigotry' (p. 74). By extension, the Lady of Boston reveals how the true Irish spirit of integrity and cooperation, which transcends social and religious divisions, is challenged by, but eventually overcomes, an uncharacteristic attitude of sectarian prejudice.

'The Victim' recounts how Arabella Fitzgerald met and married Edward Augustus Hamilton, and ends with the restoration of their son, Augustus, to the estate of Duncraig. This story again highlights the disastrous consequences of sectarian tensions and religious bigotry. The only surviving child of the widowed Malvina, young Arabella is beloved by the children of the peasantry who follow her around and strew wild flowers at her feet. Her maternal uncle introduces her to his aide-de-camp, Edward Augustus Hamilton, who is the youngest son of an English nobleman and who has distinguished himself in the service of the British East India Company. Before they are married, Arabella and her mother 'read a recantation of their belief in the Roman Catholic religion' (p. 79), an act which enrages her paternal uncle, Hugh Fitzgerald: 'so bigoted was he by his prejudices, that he felt as if he were contaminated in their presence' (p. 80). The 'many evil propensities in his disposition' were fanned by his Jesuit education, but the Lady of Boston insists that 'some of the best and most amiable of the human race' are Catholic: 'Hugh Fitzgerald would have been a miscreant under any circumstances; it was not religion that made him thus; it was the total absence of it which rendered him malicious' (p. 80). When Arabella is delivered of a son, Augustus, the tenantry rejoice, but the gloomy Fitzgerald looks 'on the birth of the infant as nothing more or less than an increase of heresy' (p. 82). Following the death of Malvina and the departure of Edward Augustus for England, where he is killed in action, Fitzgerald preys on Arabella, exhorting her to reconvert to Catholicism. When these exhortations fail, he replaces her servants with ones of his choosing, including the steward, Dominic Crosby. While walking in the grounds one day, the distraught Arabella is confronted by a gaunt-looking woman, whose large, dark eyes are sunken in their sockets. This apparition proclaims: 'A blood-thirsty tyrant reigns in the hall of thy fathers – a masked wolf rules the towers of Duncraig' (p. 96). As Arabella attempts to flee the castle, she is murdered by Dominic Crosby, who spares her infant son, entrusting him to the care of the steward's kindly sister. The story ends with the tenantry coming to cheer the restoration of the young heir of Duncraig, who erects a splendid monument in honor of his parents. Here, the Lady of Boston invokes the Gothic tropes of Catholic fanaticism, the persecuted heroine, and the usurpation of power and privilege to present Ireland as a country where the injustices resulting from such sectarianism are equally abhorrent to the peasantry and the ruling class. The account provided of the circumstances leading to the death of the young heir's father, Edward Augustus Hamilton, suggests sympathy for the cause of Catholic emancipation, while revealing that Protestant sectarian fanaticism is every bit as deplorable as its Catholic counterpart:

> Soon after Colonel Hamilton's arrival in England, he was prevailed upon to join the protestant association in presenting a petition to the British House of Commons for the purpose of obtaining the repeal of an act made in favour of the papists. He was afterwards engaged with the military in quelling the alarming riots consequent upon it, in which the conduct of the protestant party was so barbarous as to leave an indelible disgrace upon it. Such was the violence of their

proceedings, that finding the reading of the riot act had not the effect of dispersing the mob, the military were commanded by the Lord Mayor to fire on them; and a returning bullet, discharged at random, pierced the heart of the gallant Colonel Hamilton. There fled one of the best and bravest spirits that ever animated a human breast. (pp. 88–9)

Over the course of the action, though, possession of Duncraig passes from the Catholic, Anglo-Norman clan of the Fitzgeralds to a member of the Protestant Ascendancy, much to the delight of the peasantry, whose putative claims to land ownership and entitlement to political equality are deliberately downplayed. Effectively, the story vindicates the privileged position of the Protestant Ascendancy by presenting the Catholic peasantry as enthusiastic supporters of young Augustus Hamilton and so acquiescent in their own continuing disenfranchisement.

The convoluted plot of 'Mystery, A Modern Story', the longest tale in the collection, revolves around the trials of Jessie Maitland, a destitute, delicate, and beautiful young orphan. Sent from Dublin to Quebec to live with Mrs Beauchamp, a distant relative, Jessie soon finds herself having to cope with the unkindness of her supposed protector, while warding off the sexual advances of Captain Beauchamp. With the help of a young man named Albert, she manages to escape and makes her way back to Dublin. There, she meets and marries Charles Gascoigne Faulkener, but after a blissful honeymoon spent at Leixlip Castle, her tribulations continue as she falls victim to the machinations of a rejected lover and an envious woman. These two see her behaving affectionately to Albert and convince Faulkener that Jessie has been unfaithful. It eventually transpires that Albert is her brother, and that their sibling status has been kept secret to protect Jessie's reputation after he is falsely accused and convicted of killing and robbing Beauchamp. At the end of the story, the Faulkeners are reconciled; Albert's name is cleared; and both brother and sister go on to lead happy, prosperous, and virtuous lives. Mistreated and misrepresented by false friends but ultimately triumphing over adversity, Jessie is an emblem of Ireland, which is apotheosized as follows by the Lady of Boston: 'Ireland, birth-place of my noble ancestors! land of generous hospitality! though borne down by injury, and overwhelmed by injustice and oppression, dear Ireland, I love thee still!' (p. 186).

'Bran, the Bloodhound' features Lord Edmond Mountressor, son of an English officer killed at the Battle of the Boyne, grandson to Sir Walter de Burgo, and so heir to Boyle Abbey, which is relocated from its actual situation in Co. Roscommon to 'a lofty eminence which commanded an extensive prospect of the beautiful but dangerous bay of Carlingford' in Co. Louth (p. 229). With his harpist, Lawrence Maclucan, Edmond delights in visiting 'the gray ruin on the north side of the abbey', with 'its broken shafts, mouldering pediments, and mutilated columns fast crumbling to decay, or covered with the dark moss and ivy' (pp. 229–30). Maclucan has a bloodhound named Bran, which, although ferocious in appearance, is devoted to Edmond. The young hero falls in love with Phillipa DeLacy, 'one of the fairest of Hibernia's daughters' (p. 223), but on a trip to Dublin is robbed, abducted, and locked in a cellar. Thanks to information received from a woman named Biddy, Maclucan, with the aid of Bran, makes his way to the abductor's lair, where Edmond is discovered, surrounded by 'the bones and remains of several human bodies' (p. 249). Once rescued, his marriage to Phillipa goes ahead. As the harpist is the savior of the young lord, whose whereabouts have been revealed by Biddy, the happy ending represents a harmonious reconciliation of Gaelic-Catholic and Anglo-Irish Ireland. Here, again, the Gothic mode is invoked to present deviant behavior as uncharacteristic of the Irish, whose honor and integrity are enthusiastically defended. Hospitality, we are told, 'is a trait so distinguishing in that nation that it has ever involuntarily been awarded to it above all other countries upon the face of the earth' (p. 234). Ireland's claims to cultural prestige, meanwhile, are supported by the assertion that its music 'is excelled by none in its sweetness, pathos, and touching melody' (p. 236).

The portrait of Ireland that emerges from the pages of *Tales of the Emerald Isle* is that of a country whose prosperity is threatened by fanaticism, avarice, and a lust for power which are not representative of the kindness, generosity, and tact that characterize the majority of the population. Throughout, the Lady of Boston is keen to dispel misconceptions about Ireland, by reflecting what she describes in the Preface as 'an intuitive feeling of respect for the Irish', regardless of their class or creed. While the opening stories based on authentic legends testify to the ongoing civility of Gaelic, Catholic Ireland, the Gothic stories with which the volume concludes focus more on the virtues of the contemporary Protestant Ascendancy. Accordingly, the Gothicization of Irish folklore serves to vindicate Irish national character, past and present. The identity of the author remains a mystery; she has been variously identified as Elizabeth H. Stebbins, about whom nothing is known; Rebecca Warren Brown, a prolific writer who did indeed use the pseudonym 'A Lady of Boston', but who had no known connections with Ireland; and Mrs M. A. Weston, a resident of Boston who probably came from Co. Roscommon or Co. Galway.[20] Whoever she was, there were good reasons for presenting a book that throws a flattering light on Ireland and the Irish as a collection of traditional legends.

Concerns about the proprieties of female authorship undoubtedly played a significant role in both the presentation and reception of the book. Instead of identifying herself as the author of a collection of Gothic fiction, a mode of writing associated with political subversion and improper passions, the Lady of Boston adopted a pseudonym to portray herself as the compiler of a collection of anonymously authored, traditional legends. That this tactic was necessary to avoid the type of negative criticism which resulted from the gender expectations of her time is made clear by a contemporary reviewer, who observes: 'the writer is a lady. How far the latter circumstance should operate in softening the rigidity of criticism depends entirely on the nature of the work under review'. He continues:

> In private life, the name of woman should be held sacred; and no eccentricity of conduct on the part of an individual, no strangeness of sentiment, and no departure from the usual characteristics of her sex, while only exhibited in the social circle, can justify her being made the theme of animadversion through the press, in any way that may cause the subject to be recognized [...] When females, however, appear before the public in the character of authors, they not only voluntarily relinquish a part of their claim to the respectful silence of public writers, but, by implication, solicit their notice; and though still; in right of their sex, they should receive the utmost delicacy of treatment, yet the sentiments and opinions advanced in their pro-ductions should be examined by the critic, unbiassed by any extrinsic circumstance, with the same inflexible regard for the same interests of truth and virtue, that ought to characterise all his disquisitions.[21]

The critic then draws attention to the author's inharmonious diction and frequent recourse to mixed and tinseled metaphors, but suggests that these flaws are 'counterbalanced by purity of sentiment' and redeemed by the Lady of Boston's 'fondness for its [Ireland's] natural and national peculiarities'.[22] By presenting herself as the anonymous compiler of a collection of Irish folklore, the author of *Tales of the Emerald Isle* succeeded in escaping the gendered censure typically imposed on female writers who dared to enter themselves as competitors 'in the flowery and crowded walks of fiction'.[23]

Marketability was also an important consideration in the presentation of the collection. Indeed, the Lady of Boston makes the following acknowledgment in the Preface: 'I have been accused of writing books for the purpose of making money; if this be a crime, I plead guilty to the charge in part, as I find that, unless I put my shoulder to the wheel of Fortune, it makes no evolution in my favour' (n.p.). She goes on to draw attention to the dearth of material of Irish interest available to American readers, and clearly indicates that the present volume will go some way towards filling that gap in the literary marketplace. Claiming that it would be as ill-advised to 'essay to convince an Hibernian that the titular bishop of Ireland, his venerated St. Patrick, was an imaginary being, as to attack his national prejudices', she reassures her readers that *Tales of the Emerald Isle* was inspired by, and reflects, 'an intuitive feeling of respect for the Irish people' (n.p.). Implicit in these prefatorial remarks is an admission that the volume is intended to make money by portraying a favorable representation of Ireland and the Irish to American readers who are already well disposed to the country and its people. As pointed out by the contemporary reviewer, the presentation of *Tales of the Emerald Isle* as a collection of Irish legends served to enhance the commercial appeal of the volume to an Irish-American readership:

> [T]hough not entitled to be ranked very high among the productions of modern literature, yet we doubt not that it will find many readers and patrons among that numerous class of the community, to which the nationality of its title alone will be a recommendation.[24]

At the beginning of the nineteenth century, the majority of Irish immigrants to America were Protestant artisans of Scottish and English descent, but by 1830, more than 60 percent of Irish emigrants were Catholics from rural areas.[25] In order to appeal to both communities of potential readers, the Lady of Boston wrote original fictions to complement her literary renditions of genuine legends. This strategy enabled her to construct a positive, cohesive version of Irish identity that downplayed political tensions in Ireland and social differences among the Irish diaspora in America. According to Robert Miles, the mania for Gothic fiction abated in the early years of the nineteenth century, and its market share had dwindled considerably by 1820.[26] By contrast, largely thanks to the translation of the Grimms' *Kinder- und Hausmärchen* into English, the following decade witnessed an increasing interest in collections of national folklore. The decision to present the work of the Lady of Boston as a collection of Irish folklore rather than Gothic fiction, then, reflects an astute appreciation of market forces. As David Duff points out, the picture that emerges from recent work on 'the Gothic novel, or from studies of the day-to-day workings of the publishing industry, is of a dynamic print culture in which genres were more often being exploited than transcended, and in which generic terminology played a key role in both the marketing process and the broader organization of knowledge'.[27] The Gothicization of Irish folklore in *Tales of the Emerald Isle* represents an exploitation of genre attuned to the twin imperatives of marketability and sympathetic elucidation of Irish national character.

Notes

1. Jason Marc Harris (2008) *Folklore and the Fantastic in Nineteenth-Century British Fiction* (Aldershot: Ashgate), p. 19.
2. David Punter (1996) *The Literature of Terror* (London: Longman), I: 11.
3. Elizabeth MacAndrew (1979) *The Gothic Tradition in Fiction* (New York: Columbia University Press), pp. 3–4.
4. Charles Fanning (2000) *The Irish Voice in America: 250 Years of Irish-American Fiction* (2nd edn; Lexington, KY: University Press of Kentucky), p. 11.
5. Fanning, *Irish Voice*, p. 11.
6. *The Athenaeum*, No. 982, 22 August 1846, reprinted in Alan Dundes (1965) *The Study of Folklore* (Englewood Cliffs, NJ: Prentice Hall), pp. 4–5.
7. Jacob Grimm (1811) 'Circular Concerning the Collecting of Folk Poetry' in Alan Dundes (ed.) (1999) *International Folkloristics* (Lanham, MD: Rowan & Littlefield), pp. 1–7 (p. 6).
8. Maria Tatar (1987) *The Hard Facts of the Grimms' Fairy Tales* (Princeton, NJ: Princeton University Press), p. 210.
9. Thomas Crofton Croker (1825) *Fairy Legends and Traditions of the South of Ireland* (London: Thomas Davison), n.p.
10. Thomas Crofton Croker (1828) *Fairy Legends and Traditions of the South of Ireland* (London: John Murray), p. vii.
11. John Hennig (1946) 'The Brothers Grimm and T. C. Croker', *Modern Language Review*, 41:1, 44–54.
12. Jennifer Schacker (2003) *National Dreams: the Remaking of Fairy Tales in Nineteenth-Century England* (Philadelphia: University of Pennsylvania Press), p. 57.
13. Anon. (1849) 'Our Portrait Gallery', *Dublin University Magazine*, August, 202–16, (pp. 206–7).
14. Seamus Deane (1986) *A Short History of Irish Literature* (Notre Dame, IN: University of Notre Dame Press), pp. 94–5.
15. Kerby A. Miller (2003) *Irish Immigrants in the Land of Canaan: Letters and Memoirs from Colonial and Revolutionary America, 1675–1815* (Oxford: Oxford University Press), p. 4; Kerby A. Miller (1985) *Emigrants and Exiles: Ireland and the Irish Exodus to North America* (Oxford: Oxford University Press), p. 193.

16. A Lady of Boston (1828) *Tales of the Emerald Isle; or, Legends of Ireland* (New York: W. Borradaile), p. 1; further references to this volume are given in parentheses in the text.

17. Thomas Moore (1815) *Irish Melodies* (Philadelphia: Mathew Carey), pp. 87–8.

18. Thomas Crofton Croker (1825) *Fairy Legends*, pp. 13–14.

19. Croker, *Fairy Legends*, p. 19.

20. *The Atlas, or literary, historical and commercial reporter*, vol. 1, 1828, 102; the openlibrary catalogue at <http://openlibrary.org/authors/OL525044A/Rebecca_Warren_Brown>; Rolf and Magda Loeber (2006) *A Guide to Irish Fiction 1650–1900* (Dublin: Four Courts Press), p. 1349.

21. Anon. (1829) 'Tales of the Emerald Isle; or Legends of Ireland', *The Critic* 29 November, 68.

22. Anon., 'Tales of the Emerald Isle'.

23. Anon., 'Tales of the Emerald Isle'.

24. Anon., 'Tales of the Emerald Isle'.

25. Stephen A. Brighton (2009) *Historical Archaeology of the Irish Diaspora: a Transnational Approach* (Knoxville: University of Tennessee Press), pp. 41, 43.

26. Robert Miles (2002) 'The 1790s: the Effulgence of Gothic', in Jerrold E. Hogle (ed.) *The Cambridge Companion to Gothic Fiction* (Cambridge: Cambridge University Press), pp. 41–62 (p. 42).

27. David Duff (2009) *Romanticism and the Uses of Genre* (Oxford: Oxford University Press) p. 11.

6

Maturin's Catholic Heirs: Expanding the Limits of Irish Gothic

Richard Haslam

Irish Gothic has become a prominent critical category in Irish and Gothic studies, thanks to pioneering work by Julian Moynahan, Seamus Deane, Roy Foster, W. J. Mc Cormack, Siobhán Kilfeather, and others. However, in accordance with the sacred codes of academic fashion-mongering, the more prominence a category achieves the more questions it receives. Key questions include: is Irish Gothic a mode or a form, a genre or a subgenre, a tradition or an illusion? Are its eighteenth- and nineteenth-century authors solely Protestant? What can Irish Gothic texts reveal about their historical contexts – and vice versa? And which methodologies can best conceptualize the interactions between Irish Gothic and Irish history?[1]

Since these questions are rather broad, it may help us to consult Aristotle's concept of '*phronēsis*' (practical wisdom), which pursues both theoretical 'universals' and empirical 'particulars', and which recognizes that 'the universals are reached from the particulars', not the other way around.[2] My particular focus is to examine how the demonic pact device – central to Charles Maturin's *Melmoth the Wanderer* (1820) – is incorporated and modified for various artistic and ideological purposes in tales by three Catholics – John Banim, Gerald Griffin, and James Clarence Mangan – and one former Catholic – William Carleton. Through this examination, we can determine the degree to which these authors might be considered as Maturin's heirs and the critical implications of expanding the limits of Irish Gothic to include a Catholic component.

'The supposed power of the Evil One'

An early analyst of Maturin's inheritors and of Faustian pacts in Irish Gothic was Roy Foster, whose 1989 essay 'Protestant Magic' sketched out a 'line of Irish Protestant supernatural fiction [...] from Maturin and Le Fanu to Bram Stoker and Elizabeth Bowen and Yeats', in which '[t]he supernatural theme of a corrupt bargain recurs'.[3] (This is certainly true of the first two writers, but not so clearly of the other three.) Five years later, Joseph Spence tracked the same motif in *Melmoth*, Oscar Wilde's *The Picture of Dorian Gray* (1890; 1891), and W. B. Yeats's *The Countess Cathleen* (1899).[4] In claiming that 'Sheridan Le Fanu did not write an Irish Faust legend', Spence overlooked 'The Fortunes of Sir Robert Ardagh; Being a Second Extract from the Papers of the Late Father Purcell', which was published in the *Dublin University Magazine* (or *DUM*) in March 1838, as well as Le Fanu's 1872 reworking of this tale in 'Sir Dominick's Bargain'.[5] Nonetheless, Spence did alert us to two other Faustian narratives in the *DUM* that had not (at that time) received much attention: Isaac Butt's 'Chapters of College Romance. Chapter II. The Murdered Fellow' (1835) and James Clarence Mangan's 'The Man in the Cloak. A Very German Story' (1838).

However, Foster and Spence omitted some significant Faustian pacts from their surveys, perhaps because the narratives containing these pacts did not conform to the Protestant Gothic paradigm embodied in Spence's opening sentence: 'Faust is the pre-eminent Protestant legend'.[6] Our first example from an alternative, Catholic gallery of devil's bargains occurs in John Banim's 'The Fetches' (1825), which was published only five years after *Melmoth*. The narrative provides three perspectives on 'national superstitions'.[7] The first comes from the consumptive student Tresham, who investigates the folklore of the fetch (a spectral double that can predict longevity or imminent mortality for its original) from an academic perspective; the second comes from Tresham's servant Larry, whose viewpoint is shaped by the superstitions he imbibed as a peasant child; and the third comes from Tresham's physician Dr Butler, who is hostile to all forms of superstition. Tresham discusses superstitions with Larry because he wishes 'to have some one to listen to his rhapsodies', but although Tresham is more scholarly than Larry, their metaphysics differ in degree rather than kind: Tresham's 'supernaturals were now systematized so as to suit his intellect and education, while Larry's still lay huddled together in the primitiveness of raw material' (II: 196).[8] We also learn that the two men's fascination with the occult has a common origin. Maria, sister of Anna (the young woman Tresham loves), reveals these shared roots when she tells her fiancé Mortimer that Tresham was '[b]orn in the wildest part of our wild country', where he 'spent a sickly and solitary boyhood among its horrid mountains and forests, and still more horrid peasantry'; thus, when Tresham 'travelled to the continent', he was 'ill-prepared to resist the infatuations' of 'visionary' pursuits (II: 149–50). Later, the narrator reveals that foremost among this 'horrid peasantry' was Larry's mother, 'in whose cabin Tresham, when a sickly child, had [...] received the elements of his present absurdity' (II: 193–4). Under this same 'tutelage', Larry too became 'a firm believer in supernatural agency; nor could the maturity of his natural talent, nor yet his knowledge of the world, remove prejudices thus unconsciously formed and deeply stamped' (II: 193–4). Although words like 'prejudices', 'absurdity', 'visionary', 'infatuations', 'primitiveness', and 'rhapsodies' imply that the narrative takes a strong stance against superstition, this attitude shifts noticeably by the tale's conclusion.

The Faustian sequence commences when we learn that one of Tresham and Larry's common interests concerns 'the supposed power of the Evil One to confer superior knowledge and riches, on certain terms' (II: 197):

> [T]o Larry's view, Tresham pressed the subject too far, and persevered too long and too earnestly in getting an account of all he knew of the advantages derivable in such a case; he had even proposed to his servant such startling questions, as, 'Did he think the individual had ever really appeared at a summons? was it easy to obtain an interview with him? might he be depended on, in a fair bargain? and was it possible to overreach or outwit him?' (II: 197–8)

These questions unnerve Larry so much that, when Dr Butler arrives unexpectedly at Tresham's lodgings, the medic's forbidding appearance leads Larry to suspect he might be the Devil. Realizing this, Butler applies the unorthodox remedy of attempting to frighten Larry out of his superstitions, by commanding the servant to laugh at his own beliefs. When Larry recounts his terrifying experience to his master, Tresham initially hopes to find more evidence for supernatural intervention:

> [Tresham:] 'What! an evil spirit?' [Larry:] 'The ould father o' them all; an' more betoken, he left a message wid me for you; bud am I to keep promise wid the likes of him?' [Tresham:] 'How did your visitant look? what kind of person?' Larry minutely described the face,

figure, and dress of the individual, and Tresham turned away with a 'pshaw!' – disappointed and somewhat humiliated, that in the faithful portrait he could not avoid recognizing his medical attendant and old friend, Doctor Butler. (II: 211)

The next day, Butler discusses his subterfuge with Tresham, emphasizing 'how a weak and contemptible mind can impose on itself' and secretly seizing 'a good opportunity to lecture master and man' (II: 271). Once more, Butler humbles Larry, forcing him again to 'laugh at all the ghosts, my master or myself ever talked of', a barb that causes 'wounded vanity' in Tresham (II: 273–4).

As a doctor, Butler regards Tresham's and Larry's superstitions as a sickness, in which the 'accomplished and respectable man-servant carries the method of the disease to more perfection' (II: 275). Thus, Butler decides to separate Larry, 'of whose hag-ridden superstition he was so well aware, from his master's sight and presence, just as he would have separated the contagious and pre-disposed members of a family amongst whom a raging fever had gained entrance' (II: 301). To treat the ailment, Butler also enlists Maria's fiancé Mortimer. Due to some unsettling recent experiences, Mortimer, like Maria, has begun to wonder whether fetches might actually exist, but under pressure from Butler he appeals to social codes of gender and gentility, telling Tresham his beliefs appear 'incompatible with a strong, masculine mind like his, and unfit for his matured intercourse with serious and accomplished gentlemen' (II: 353). For the sake of Anna's well-being, Tresham finally agrees to renounce his creed, a decision that Mortimer calls 'manly and honourable' (II: 353).

The narrative now seems poised to exorcize the supposedly demeaning and unmanning tendencies of superstitious conviction, but Banim soon leads the skeptical Dr Butler into a zone of doubt that leaves his 'manly indifference' temporarily unsettled:

And now, and not for the first time [. . . Butler] thought, with an irritating and stupefying feeling, of Anna's strange prophecies, and of her assertions with respect to the vision she declared she had seen. Rejecting from the first, with laughter and scorn, every thought of supernatural omen, and crushing it under a load of manly indifference, there now and then stirred, however, in the bottom of the doctor's soul, and under all that philosophical pressure, a something that, like an incipient earthquake at the base of a real mountain, slightly disturbed the mass. But now, after feeling for an instant such an inward motion, Butler grew impatient to acknowledge or yield it place, and at once offering his arm to Tresham, routed the weakness from his mind [.] (II: 358–9)

By concluding the narrative, thirty or so pages later, with the strong implication that fetches do appear and prophesy accurately, Banim leaves the reader in the same zone that Butler temporarily inhabits, a region where – in Tzevetan Todorov's categories – the fantastic shades into the marvelous.[9]

So how might 'The Fetches' be regarded as an heir of *Melmoth*, itself a novel in which fantastic doubt about the Wanderer's existence is soon replaced by marvelous certainty? Like Maturin's novel and Mangan's 'The Man in the Cloak' (and unlike Carleton's 'The Lianhan Shee', Griffin's 'The Barber of Bantry', and Banim's 'The Ace of Clubs'), 'The Fetches' does not ultimately explain away the supernatural. In addition, Banim's story shares other features with *Melmoth*: an interest in Irish folklore, a doomed love affair, a climactic fall from a precipice, the temptation of transgressive knowledge, and – above all – a diabolic pact. Nevertheless, in 'The Fetches' the possibility of a Faustian deal is depicted in a largely comic tone and subordinated to the fetch superstition, whose repercussions are treated tragically. In addition, unlike *Melmoth* and the other four stories, 'The Fetches' does not provide a theologically consoling Christian conclusion, in which evil is punished, good rewarded, and providence vindicated. Banim's young lovers are misguided and impulsive, but they are not Luciferian deceivers like Melmoth. Tresham dies from consumption; Anna dies by throwing herself over a precipice with his corpse; and her family arrive too late to intervene. It is implied but never fully established that Tresham and Anna are Anglo-Irish Protestants, yet the plot includes no clerics and few references to Catholicism or Protestantism.[10] In 'The Fetches', superstitious belief is shared by both educated, upper-class Irish Protestants and uneducated, lower-class Irish Catholics, and it is an emotional state that Banim seeks (for aesthetic and psychological reasons) to evoke in his readers.

'Blood! – broken vows! – ha! ha! ha!'

The case is rather different five years later in Carleton's 'The Lianhan Shee', which first appeared in 1830 in the Reverend Caesar Otway's anti-Catholic *Christian Examiner and Church of Ireland Gazette*. Given that venue, it is hardly surprising that the story exhibits plenty of the orthodox religious attitudes so strikingly absent from the 'The Fetches'.

In addition, its negative representations of Catholicism ideologically align 'The Lianhan Shee' with *Melmoth*. Nonetheless, Carleton – like Mangan – regarded Maturin and his works ambivalently. He writes that as a youth he sought out Maturin to 'satisfy myself as to what a man of genius could be like'; reflecting later on that early encounter, Carleton considered *Melmoth* to be 'a powerful, but gloomy story' and Maturin 'to be as vain a creature as ever lived'.[11]

How, then, might Carleton be an heir of Maturin? 'The Lianhan Shee', like 'The Fetches', selects and recombines elements of character and plot from *Melmoth*, mixing Gothic and Irish folkloric modes. Of course, Maturin was a pioneer of blending these modes, in the opening chapters of *Melmoth* and in his short story 'Leixlip Castle' (1825).[12] In Carleton's modal arrangement, the description of the supernatural persecutor called the Lianhan Shee that emerges from the conversation between the superstitious farmer's wife Mary Sullivan and the defrocked priest Father Philip O'Dallaghy reveals distinct affinities with Melmoth's plight:

> [Father Philip:] 'Pray what do you precisely understand by a *Lianhan Shee*?' 'Why, Sir,' replied Mary, 'some sthrange bein' from the good people, or fairies, that sticks to some persons. There's a bargain, Sir, your Reverence, made atween thim; an' the divil, Sir, that is, the ould boy – the saints about us! – has a hand in it. The *Lianhan Shee*, your Reverence, is never seen only by thim it keeps wid; but – hem! – it always, with the help of the ould boy, conthrives, Sir, to make the person brake the agreement, an' thin it has *thim in its* power; but if they *don't* brake the agreement, thin *it's in their* power. If they can get any body to put in their place, they may get out o' the bargain; for they can, of a sartainty, give oceans o' money to people, but can't take any themselves, plase your Reverence'.[13]

Aspects of Melmoth's personality and biography also infiltrate the protagonists, the former nun Margaret and Philip. The latter seduced Margaret when both were in religious orders, and he believes he killed her with poison many years earlier. The narrative leaves readers in doubt for some time about whether or not the concealed presence on Margaret's shoulders truly is a Lianhan Shee. This rhetorical technique operates by initially whetting the reader's curiosity and by ultimately emphasizing the need to outgrow superstition and Catholicism. Thus, like most of these stories (and like Banim's Dr Butler), 'The Lianhan Shee' employs the risky didactic strategy of using superstition to overcome superstition. (As we have seen, 'The Fetches' takes the opposite course, using superstition eventually to promote superstition.)

Further echoing Maturin's novel, Margaret – like Melmoth – possesses a startling glance (II: 9, 42) and is described as 'the wanderer' (II: 29); like Melmoth too, she can only escape her doom if someone takes her place (II: 28).Whereas Margaret's story incorporates many Faustian pact features, Philip embodies the Wanderer's cynicism, pride, self-loathing, and derisive laughter (as exhibited, especially, in the 'Tale of the Indians' in *Melmoth*):

> [T]he sarcastic lip of the priest curled into an expression of irony and contempt; his brow which was naturally black and heavy, darkened; and a keen, but rather ferocious-looking eye, shot forth a glance, which, while it intimated disdain for those to whom it was directed, spoke also of a dark and troubled spirit in himself [...] 'Ay,' said [...Philip], 'wretches! sunk in the grossest superstition and ignorance, yet, perhaps, happier in your degradation than those who, in the pride of knowledge, can only look back upon a life of crime and misery. What is a sceptic? What is an infidel? Men who, when they will not submit to moral restraint, harden themselves into scepticism and infidelity, until, in the headlong career of guilt, that which was first adopted to lull the outcry of conscience, is supported by the pretended pride of principle. Principle in a sceptic! Hollow and devilish lie! Would *I* have plunged into scepticism, had I not first violated the moral sanctions of religion? Never. I became an infidel, because I first became a villain! [...] Then these hands – blood! – broken vows! – ha! ha! ha! Well, go – let misery have its laugh, like the light that breaks from the thunder-cloud. Prefer Voltaire to Christ; sow the wind, and reap the whirlwind, as I have done – ha, ha, ha! Swim, world – swim about me! I have lost the ways of Providence, and am dark!' (II: 34–5)

Philip returns to his house with Margaret and engages in further Melmoth-like rhetorical outbursts. In a passage reminiscent of the final two chapters of *Melmoth*, he hears 'feet pacing in the room [...] and [...] voices' and believes himself to be 'surrounded by evil spirits' (II: 50). Whereas Melmoth has a dream before his disappearance, Philip's 'state and existence seemed to him a confused and troubled dream'; in addition, both Melmoth's hair and Philip's turn 'white as snow' (II: 53).[14] However, although readers of *Melmoth* are led to believe that the protagonist has been dragged to hell by demons, Carleton's narrator explains that Philip suffers from delusions arising from a guilty conscience

(II: 53). Similarly, Margaret's behavior is attributed to periodic bouts of insanity, and the creature on her back turns out to be the robes she wore and dishonored when a nun. The final rationalization occurs in the endnote Carleton added to the 1833 edition, explaining that any woman who has extramarital sex used to be known as a *'Lianhan Shee'* and that *'Lianhan Shee an Sagarth* signifies a priest's paramour, or, as the country people say, "Miss" ' (III: 447).

'The foul and soul-empoisoning stream'

The explained supernatural returns in Gerald Griffin's 'The Barber of Bantry', published five years after the first publication of Carleton's story. Like Carleton, Griffin laments the prevalence of superstition; like Banim, he believes it affects more than one class:

> At this period the clouds of superstition still rested like a gloomy fog upon the minds of the poorer peasantry (as they do in all countries where education is retarded), nor were there wanting some in the rank immediately above them who participated in their credulity [...I]t was [the Danahers'] wont to [...] interchange their gloomy tales of supernatural agency, while even the youngest members of the group were suffered to drink, undisturbed, at the foul and soul-empoisoning stream, that flowed from the hag-ridden imaginations of the story-tellers. Ghosts, fairies, witches, murderers, and demons, glided with a horrid and hair-stiffening influence through all their narratives, and when the listeners retired for the night, it was to hurry to their beds with alarmed and shuddering nerves, and to supply the frightful fancies of their waking moments, by still more frightful dreams [.][15]

Griffin's terms 'supernatural agency' and 'hag-ridden imaginations' echo the 'supernatural agency' and 'hag-ridden superstition' of Banim's 'The Fetches' (II: 194; 301). Nonetheless, Griffin finds some positive aspects in superstitious propensities, claiming that '[t]he instinct of the supernatural is one, which perhaps nobody, except some conscience-seared criminal, whose heart is hard to every natural feeling, can ever wholly lay aside' and that '[i]t is implanted in us for the best of purposes, and though we may abuse it, as we do the best emotions, to our ruin, it is not the less intended for our good' (III: 277).

Like Banim and Carleton, Griffin employs the supernatural to entice curious readers into the narrative, but ambivalence about this rhetorical tactic surfaces on occasion in his works, for example, in 'The Aylmers of Bally-Aylmer' (1827). His anxiety about introducing superstition and the supernatural appears clearly in his self-censorship of a passage from 'The Barber' that describes in detail a Faustian pact. His brother Daniel speculated that Griffin may have believed 'the parts he cut out were unnatural to the character or that there was something too shocking in the sentiments expressed by the demon', but Daniel found the section of sufficiently 'absorbing interest' to justify restoring it in the multi-volume edition of Griffin's *Works* he edited after his brother died.[16] In the censored passage, the mysterious 'stranger' pledges to save the Barber from his financial plight only if he becomes 'one of us', and he taunts the Barber by declaring, 'He whom thou servest has abandoned thee to want and woe. Continue if thou wilt to worship a neglect-ful master instead of one who is willing to pay thee with abundance' (III: 257–8).

Like 'The Lianhan Shee' (and unlike 'The Fetches'), 'The Barber' ulti-mately explains away its supernatural elements (as also happens in 'The Aylmers'):

> The mode of his detection by Edmund Moynehan relieved the bar-ber from an apprehension which had long sat next to his remorse upon his mind. This was the fancy that he had been haunted by an evil spirit who disturbed him in his sleep, and had on one occasion engaged him in a fatal compact. It now appeared that himself, in his somnambulism, had performed all those feats which had so much perplexed him, and that his midnight excursion to the fir-grove was but a dream to which he would never have paid attention, but for the corroboration afforded to it, by the other mysterious circumstances. (III: 290–1)

'According to his creed'

In a manner markedly different from his earlier 'The Fetches', John Banim's 'The Ace of Clubs' (1838) follows Carleton's and Griffin's route of the explained supernatural. Desperate for money to wed his girlfriend Dora Marum, the shabby genteel protagonist Martin Brophy allows the 'fairy-doctor' Musha Merry to deceive him into believing that he can negotiate a safe Faustian pact, unaware that Merry is pursuing a com-plex, decades-long revenge on the Brophy family.[17] To strengthen his courage before taking the final step, Martin asks his mother to retell him a childhood story of an earlier deal with the devil. Just as in 'The Fetches' and 'The Barber', an adult susceptibility to superstition is alleged to originate in bedtime stories that exhibit poor parenting choices:

> [Martin:] 'Mother [...] tell me some o' your choice old stories about ghosts, and fairies, and Ould Nick.' [Mother:] 'Christ save us, Martin Brophy,' crossing herself. 'Yes, mother; you know you had plenty of 'em for me when I didn't ask for 'em – and never mind the night it is – the blacker to us, the more we want something to put it out of our heads' – he drank another deep draught – 'Come, mother, I remember a capital story of yours that I'll thank you to tell me once again – about old Squire Jarvis, and a friend of his' [.] (III: 281–2)

The narrator's observation that the story 'was an old one; or rather a local version of one, common to every country in Christendom' (III: 282) recalls the opening paragraph of Griffin's 'The Brown Man' (1827), which pictures 'credulity' as 'a sort of mental prism', splitting 'the great volume of the light of speculative superstition' and 'showing only *blue* devils to the dwellers in the good city of London, *orange and green* devils to the inhabitants of the sister (or rather step-daughter), island, and so forward until the seven component hues are made out, through the other nations of the earth'.[18] The story-within-a-story of 'The Ace of Clubs' describes how the destitute Squire – 'a very bad man', who 'led a very wicked life', and 'lived in a lone house' – strikes a deal 'on the usual terms' with a 'dark-complexioned gentleman, decently dressed in black' (III: 282–3). This embedded orange-devil narrative about an upper-class (and, presumably, Protestant) squire provides a distinctive contrast with the green-devil main story concerning the middle-class and Catholic Martin.

An even more illuminating confessional contrast emerges in a passage describing Martin's preparations for sealing the pact. The passage's subject matter and the narrator's reverent tone highlight crucial differences in the attitudes toward Catholicism expressed in Maturin's and Carleton's narratives and those of Banim and Griffin:

> At a certain period of the mass, the priest elevates the consecrated bread and wine, which Roman Catholics believe to be the Real Presence; and Martin Brophy, acting upon Musha Merry's instructions, intended, when this usual ceremonial should occur, to turn his back on the altar, hold up before his eyes, in the hollow of his hand, the Ace of Clubs which his tutor had given him, and bow to it thrice, and worship it thrice, 'in the devil's name': the only concession, he

was assured, required by the great father of riches to give him power over mountains of gold [...] But after he had knelt down, and that mass had begun, the sullen lethargy of Martin's heart became fearfully broken up. The act of apostasy he resolved to commit was, in its form, of no ordinary character; and, further, Martin Brophy believed in the Redeemer, of whose atonement for the sins of the world the sacrament was a memento; nay, still according to his creed, a perpetuation. And this Redeemer, and this sacrament, he came to forswear on his knees, for the worship of the king of hell; – the thought swelled his bosom with tremendous horror [.] (III: 292–3)

Here, unlike in *Melmoth*, or Maturin's *Five Sermons on the Errors of the Roman Catholic Church* (1824), or 'The Lianhan Shee', Catholicism is treated with great respect. And, unlike in 'The Fetches', a theologically consoling conclusion is provided when Dora Marum prevents Martin from performing the final actions of the ritual. After a period of illness and atonement, Martin works hard and earns the money to marry Dora, while Musha Merry is ultimately hanged for robbery.

'A changed man'

Like 'The Ace of Clubs', James Clarence Mangan's 'The Man in the Cloak' weaves a positive representation of Catholicism into its demonic pact reworking. As Patricia Coughlan notes, Mangan's story is a plagiarized adaptation of Balzac's *Melmoth Réconcilié* (1835), which was itself a satirical reworking of Maturin's novel.[19] Making Maturin no doubt spin in his grave, Balzac grants Melmoth a pious Catholic funeral service at home; Mangan goes further, increasing the number of priests in attendance and placing the service in 'the Church of St. Sulpice'.[20] The description of Melmoth's funeral leads to an even more pro-Catholic passage that describes the remorse of Melmoth's successor Braunbrock. The pious intensity of this pro-priest passage is framed with delicious irony when one recalls that Mangan smuggled it into the staunchly Protestant and Unionist *DUM*:

'Invoke the assistance of God, unhappy man!' said the priest.
'Impossible,' answered Braunbrock.
'Can you not call upon God for mercy?'
'I do not know what to say,' replied the German.
'Repeat after me, and with as much sincerity and unction as you can command, O, God, be merciful to me a sinner!'

And Braunbrock repeated the words, *O, God, be merciful to me a sinner!*
'It is enough,' said the priest. 'Rise!'
Braunbrock rose up. 'Go now in peace,' said the priest; 'but return
hither, and be here again on this day week, a changed man – a man
who need no longer shroud himself *in a cloak*.'
[...] Religion and Hope from that hour found their way slowly into
the heart of Braunbrock. (p. 566)

The passage may also function as a counterpoint to a supposed defect
in Goethe's *Faust* that Mangan identified in an 1836 essay in the *DUM*,
'Anthologia Germanica. – No. V. Faust and the Minor Poems of Goethe'.
According to Mangan, Goethe's play 'inculcates nothing either consola-
tory or ennobling [...and] communicates no restorative, no freshening
impetus to the soul of him who, having set out in quest of Truth, droops
by the way-side when storms begin to muster, and clouds first over-
cast the prospect' (p. 86). Spence, in turn, interprets Mangan's *Faust*
essay as a satiric strike against the *DUM*'s ultra-Protestantism. In the passage Spence cites, Mangan claims that 'Faustus' possesses 'too much of
unmitigated selfishness, too reckless a disregard of the Future, too little of that sublime resignation to Destiny which glorifies the sufferer,
too little of a catholic feeling for the afflictions of his species [...] to
accord with our notions of the constituents of a truly estimable character'.[21] According to Spence's perhaps over-ingenious reading, 'Faust
represented the self-proclaimed "cultivated mind" of Anglo-Ireland, but
Mangan spoke for native Ireland'.[22] Whether or not Mangan 'spoke for
native Ireland' in his *Faust* essay, he certainly spoke for Irish Catholicism
in 'The Man in the Cloak'.

'Fully comprehend his method – his means for the effect'

This survey reveals a surprising range of stances towards superstition,
folklore, Catholicism, Faustian pacts, and the explained supernatural. In 'The Fetches', Banim treats the Faust motif in a humorous
tone, heightening the contrast with the tragic outcome for Tresham
and Anna, and refusing to create a didactic conclusion. In 'The
Lianhan Shee', Carleton divides Melmothian features between two
characters and didactically attacks Catholicism and folk superstitions.
In 'The Barber of Bantry', Griffin censors much of his Faustian
sequence, perhaps due to anxiety about blasphemy. In 'The Ace of
Clubs', Banim places at the forefront of the narrative a folklore-
altered Faustian motif, using it to create a positive picture of

Catholicism. And, finally, in 'The Man in the Cloak', Mangan weaves a positive representation of Catholicism into his mainly playful but sometimes somber treatment of the Faustian motif. Out of this gathering, Carleton and Mangan emerge most clearly as Maturin's heirs, although they take his legacy in very different ideological directions.

So, what might be the implications of this overview for the issue of expanding the limits of Irish Gothic? Jarlath Killeen, a contributor to this volume, has engaged in an exchange with me about this topic. He accepts 'that there is a substantial body of Gothic writing composed by Irish Catholics [...]' but insists that

> [n]one of this [...] negates the original point made by McCormack, and rearticulated by myself, which is that Irish Gothic is a Protestant mode because Gothic itself is a Protestant mode. The point being made here is not that Irish Gothic was written only by Irish Protestants (though it mostly was), but that the form itself is Protestant.[23]

As the Robot in *Lost in Space* used to say, 'That does not compute'. If Irish Catholics drew upon the Gothic mode (and here we can see the relevance of substituting the concept of 'the Gothic mode' for 'the Gothic tradition'), then it cannot be a purely (or Puritanly) Protestant one. To be accurate, we must say that the Gothic literary mode, which undoubtedly originated in the work of Protestant authors, was used in Ireland mainly (but not solely) by Protestants in the late eighteenth, nineteenth, and early twentieth centuries, and mainly (but not solely) by Catholics from the mid-twentieth century onwards.[24] It is clear that the employment of an identifiably Gothic mode in the fiction of the Banims, Griffin, and Mangan considerably complicates any generalizing claim that 'Irish Gothic is a Protestant mode'. As with the wording of any Faustian bargain, the devil is always in the details. Thus, we need to consider what Siobhán Kilfeather terms a 'teasing question': 'Is the Gothic always the nightmare of the oppressor, or can it be a vehicle for dissent from below?'[25]

Killeen acknowledges that 'the use by Catholic writers of Gothic motifs and tropes' can be 'a mode of writing back, a kind of reverse Gothic'.[26] However, his assertion that 'when Catholic writers adopt the Gothic they are essentially attempting to appropriate an alien form' neglects the fact that these writers did not just 'attempt [...] to appropriate an alien form' – they actually *did* appropriate it, thereby allowing the alien to become a permanent resident.[27] In addition, we should recognize that the Gothic was only *one* of a range of supernaturalist and quasi-supernaturalist modes (including the ghostly, the folkloric, the psychological, and the theological) interwoven with more naturalist modes in fiction by Irish Protestant and Irish Catholic writers in the nineteenth century. As their tales show, Banim, Carleton, Griffin, and Mangan did not confine themselves within one, monolithic Gothic tradition but rather selected and combined elements from a range of supernaturalist literary modes and expressed them through a range of authorial tones, hoping to create a range of moods (or rhetorical effects) in their readers.[28]

In John Banim's advice to his brother Michael about 'the mode of studying the art of novel-writing' we can see just how intentional this technique was:

> Read any first-rate production of the kind, with a notebook. When an author forces you to feel with him, or whenever he produces a more than ordinary degree of pleasure, or when he startles you – stop and try to find out how he has done it; see if it be by dialogue, or by picture, or by description, or by action. Fully comprehend his method – his means for the effect, and note it down. Write down all such impressions. Enumerate these, and see how many go to make the combined interest of one book. Observe by contrasting characters, how he keeps up the balance of the familiar and the marvelous, humorous, serious, and romantic.[29]

To recognize the fertility and complexity of this splicing of 'familiar [...] marvelous, humorous, serious, and romantic' modes in the tales of both Catholic and Protestant writers of the earlier nineteenth century is at the same time to recognize the need to expand the limits of Irish Gothic.

Notes

1. For explorations of these questions, see Richard Haslam (2007) 'Irish Gothic', in *The Routledge Companion to Gothic*, ed. C. Spooner and E. McEvoy (London: Routledge), pp. 83–94; Richard Haslam (2007) 'Irish Gothic: a Rhetorical Hermeneutics Approach', *The Irish Journal of Gothic and Horror Studies* 2, n.p.; Jarlath Killeen (2006) 'Irish Gothic: a Theoretical Introduction', *The Irish Journal of Gothic and Horror Studies* 1, n.p.; Jarlath Killeen (2008) 'Irish Gothic Revisited', *The Irish Journal of Gothic and Horror Studies* 4, n.p.; and Christina Morin (2011) *Charles Robert Maturin and the Haunting of Irish Romantic Fiction*

(Manchester: Manchester University Press), pp. 4–13, 129–53, and 177–86. All articles from *The Irish Journal of Gothic and Horror Studies* can be found at: <http://irishgothichorrorjournal.homestead.com/Thevault.html>.

2. Jonathan Barnes (ed.) (1984) *The Complete Works of Aristotle: the Revised Oxford Translation*, 2 vols (Princeton, NJ: Princeton University Press), II, sections 1803; 1806. Compare Claire Connolly's advocacy for an 'engagement with the detail' to articulate 'a more nuanced version of the history of the Irish novel'; this involves investigating the formal and thematic 'particularities of a number of fictions' by scrutinizing 'key scenes'; Claire Connolly (2012) *A Cultural History of the Irish Novel, 1790–1829* (Cambridge: Cambridge University Press), pp. 18–19.

3. R. F. Foster (1993) *Paddy and Mr Punch: Connections in Irish and English History* (London: Penguin), p. 220.

4. Joseph Spence (1994) ' "The Great Angelic Sin": the Faust Legend in Irish Literature, 1820–1900', *Bullán: an Irish Studies Journal* 1.2, 47–58.

5. Spence, ' "The Great Angelic Sin" ', p. 53.

6. Spence, ' "The Great Angelic Sin" ', p. 47. In a more recent work, Foster again examines what he terms the 'genre' of 'nineteenth-century Irish Gothic' but still restricts its membership to Protestant writers; R. F. Foster (2011) *Words Alone: Yeats and his Inheritances* (Oxford: Oxford University Press), p. 95.

7. John and Michael Banim (1825) *Tales by the O'Hara Family*, 3 vols (London: Simpkin & Marshall), II: 114. Further volume and page references to this work will be given parenthetically in the main text.

8. Peter Denman usefully connects Tresham's theorizing to 'earlier nineteenth-century arguments concerning hallucinations and kindred manifestations' between supernaturalists like the Rosicrucians and Swedenborgians and materialists like John Ferriar and Samuel Hibbert; Peter Denman (1992) 'Ghosts in Anglo-Irish Literature', in *Irish Writers and Religion*, ed. Robert Welch (Gerrards Cross: Colin Smythe), pp. 62–74 (pp. 64–5).

9. Tzvetan Todorov (1975) *The Fantastic: a Structural Approach to a Literary Genre*, trans. Richard Howard (Ithaca, NY: Cornell University Press), p. 25. Unlike Mark Hawthorne, who argues that Banim deliberately structures the tale so as to leave the reader unclear 'whether the *fetches* are actually present or merely figments of the characters' imaginations', I believe the narrative ultimately implies that the fetches are real; Mark Hawthorne (1975) *John and Michael Banim (The 'O'Hara Brothers'): a Study in the Early Development of the Anglo-Irish Novel* (Toronto: The Edwin Mellen Press), p. 66; see also pp. 66–72. Even though Anna's final sighting is phrased ambiguously ('she saw, or thought she saw'), the narrator does not challenge the strong evidence presented a few paragraphs earlier for the reality of the fetch sightings, some of which were witnessed by people besides Anna or Tresham (II: 91; 388–91). Robert Tracy, too, argues that the fetches 'are real' and that 'the story is partly a psychological study of those who frighten themselves by brooding too much about superstitions', at the same time that 'it partly endorses those superstitions'; Robert Tracy (1998) *The Unappeasable Host: Studies in Irish Identities* (Dublin: University College Dublin Press), p. 45. However, the moral he extracts from the tale – 'Irish superstition is based on ignorance, which in turn is caused by misgovernment. It is as fatal as the diseases which breed in Dickens's slums' – does not accord with the non-didactic atmosphere of

the tale's closing sequence, which focuses instead on frightening readers into believing in fetches, rather than out of that belief (Tracy, *The Unappeasable Host*, pp. 45–6).

10. Kitty, who is in love with Larry, refers briefly to the possibility of 'father [*sic*] O'Shaughnossy' marrying the two of them (II: 247).

11. David James O'Donoghue (1896) *The Life of William Carleton*, 2 vols (London: Downey & Co.), I: 227–8.

12. On Irish Gothic and folklore, see Haslam, 'Irish Gothic: a Rhetorical Hermeneutics Approach'; on folklore and *Melmoth*, see Jim Kelly (2011) *Charles Maturin: Authorship, Authenticity and the Nation* (Dublin: Four Courts Press), pp. 148–74.

13. William Carleton (1830–3; 1979) *Traits and Stories of the Irish Peasantry: Second Series*, 3 vols (New York: Garland), II: 39–40. Further volume and page references to this work will be given parenthetically in the main text. For a detailed examination of differences between the 1830 *Christian Examiner* and 1833 *Traits* versions of the story, see Barbara Hayley (1983) *Carleton's Traits and Stories and the Nineteenth-Century Anglo-Irish Tradition* (Gerrards Cross: Colin Smythe), pp. 75–87. As she notes, Carleton expands the story with additional footnotes and 'long passages of psychological and physical detail about the priest's suicide' (Hayley, *Carleton's Traits and Stories*, p. 87).

14. Charles Robert Maturin (1820; 1989) *Melmoth the Wanderer* (Oxford: Oxford University Press), pp. 538–9; p. 540.

15. Gerald Griffin (n.d.) *The Works of Gerald Griffin*, 9 vols (New York: D. J. Sadlier), III: 273–4. Further volume and page references to this work will be given parenthetically in the main text.

16. Daniel Griffin (1843) *Life of Gerald Griffin Esq.* (London: Simpkin & Marshall), pp. 395–6.

17. John and Michael Banim (1838; 1979) *The Bit O' Writin' and Other Tales*, 3 vols (New York: Garland), III: 272; 277; 290. Further volume and page references to this work will be given parenthetically in the main text.

18. Gerald Griffin (1827) *Holland-Tide; or, Munster Popular Tales* (London: Simpkin & Marshall), p. 297. For a fascinating analysis of the generic, hermeneutic, and rhetorical complexity of Griffin's superficially simple story, see Sinead Sturgeon (2012) ' "Seven Devils": Gerald Griffin's "The Brown Man" and the Making of Irish Gothic', *The Irish Journal of Gothic and Horror Studies* 11.

19. Patricia Coughlan (1987) 'The Recycling of *Melmoth*: "A Very German Story" ', in *Literary Interrelations: Ireland, England and the World*, ed. Heinz Kosok and Wolfgang Zach, 3 vols (Tübingen: Gunter Narr Verlag), II: 181–99 (II: 181).

20. James Clarence Mangan (2002) *Prose 1832–1839* (Blackrock: Irish Academic Press), p. 260. Further volume and page references to this work will be given parenthetically in the main text. Joseph Spence notes how Mangan Catholicizes Melmoth by burying him 'in the Parisian (and Roman Catholic) church of St. Sulpice'; he also mentions that Balzac's *Melmoth Réconcilié* is a reworking of *Melmoth*, but he overlooks how Mangan's story actually plagiarizes from Balzac (Spence, ' "The Great Angelic Sin" ', p. 52; p. 57). For a detailed analysis of 'The Man in the Cloak' and its implications for theorizing Irish Gothic, see R. Haslam (2006) ' "Broad Farce and Thrilling

Tragedy": Mangan's Fiction and Irish Gothic', *Éire-Ireland* 41:3 and 4, 215–44 (pp. 229–38).

21. Mangan, *Prose*, p. 90. Andrew Cusack argues that, in 'Chapters in Ghostcraft' (1842), an essay on ghosts and spiritualism in Germany, Mangan successfully smuggled into the pages of the *DUM* another piece of pro-Catholic propaganda; A. Cusack (2012) 'Cultural Transfer in the *Dublin University Magazine*: James Clarence Mangan and the German Gothic', in *Popular Revenants: the German Gothic and its International Reception, 1800–2000*, eds Andrew Cusack and Barry Murnane (Rochester, NY: Camden House), pp. 87–104 (p. 97).

22. Spence, ' "The Great Angelic Sin" ', p. 51.

23. Killeen, 'Irish Gothic Revisited', p. 6.

24. See Flann O'Brien's *The Third Policeman* (1940; 1967), Brian Moore's *The Mangan Inheritance* (1979), John Banville's *Mefisto* (1986) and *Eclipse* (2000), Seamus Deane's *Reading in the Dark* (1996), Patrick McCabe's *Winterwood* (2007), and Neil Jordan's *Shade* (2005) and *Mistaken* (2011).

25. Siobhán Kilfeather (2006) 'The Gothic Novel', in *The Cambridge Companion to the Irish Novel*, ed. J. W. Foster (Cambridge: Cambridge University Press), pp. 78–96 (p. 91).

26. Killeen, 'Irish Gothic Revisited', p. 7.

27. Killeen, 'Irish Gothic Revisited', p. 8. Defending his stance, Killeen cites Patrick O'Malley's claim that '[i]n its ideological structure, the English Gothic novel, though it typically represents Catholicism, is fundamentally a Protestant genre'; Patrick O'Malley (2006) *Catholicism, Sexual Deviance, and Victorian Gothic Culture* (Cambridge: Cambridge University Press), p. 32 (cited in Killeen, 'Irish Gothic Revisited', p. 7). However, O'Malley is referring to 'the *English* Gothic novel', not the *Irish* Gothic mode.

28. Compare Kilfeather, 'The Gothic Novel', p. 83; pp. 86–7.

29. Patrick Joseph Murray (1884) *The Life of John Banim, The Irish Novelist* (New York: D. & J. Sadlier), pp. 142–3.

7

J. S. Le Fanu, Gothic, and the Irish Periodical

Elizabeth Tilley

Joseph Sheridan Le Fanu bought the *Dublin University Magazine* (*DUM*) in 1861, and controlled its content until he sold his interest in 1869. He had been associated with the journal since the 1830s, and was a seasoned writer of both short fiction and serial novels. However, Le Fanu's editorship of the *DUM* was always unobtrusive. The sort of fanfare that had heralded the appointment of Charles Lever as editor of the journal 20 years earlier did not accompany Le Fanu's arrival on the Dublin literary scene. No 'Address to the Reader', no statement of editorial aim or agenda was discernible, and the Irish 'colour' of the *DUM*, as has been noted elsewhere, was not particularly strong.[1] To find Le Fanu's voice and to understand the journal's response to popular literature, it is necessary to examine the periodicity of the magazine: to read, as its first audience did, laterally.

If the periodical is considered as a whole, at least in terms of its yearly volumes, we ought to be able to expect a version of the same artistic coherence we see in a collection of short stories or poems. Thematic development, repetition of stylistic features, editorial rigor, should all be in evidence. My purpose here is to examine the offerings of the *DUM* from one particular year in order to investigate the issues noted above. The year chosen is 1864, in the middle of Le Fanu's tenure as editor. The year was also the midpoint of the wild popularity of the sensation novel. The *DUM* published that year Le Fanu's best novel, *Uncle Silas*, in monthly parts from July to December, along with a number of literary comments on sensation fiction, as well as short stories and poems reflecting this type of fiction in various ways. The 1864 volume also contained the final chapters of Le Fanu's novel *Wylder's Hand*, the book that came after his agreement with his English publisher (Bentley) not to set his fiction in Ireland and to relate contemporary rather than historical events. The work of two other novelists, Anne Robertson and Mortimer Collins, was also featured. It appears that articles in the volume, with very few exceptions, were written by six individuals, and each seemed to have a specialty: J. W. Cole wrote six articles on Irish actors; Percy Fitzgerald tackled the general interest story; T. C. Irwin wrote on poetry; Patrick Kennedy handled book reviews and Irish folklore; J. A. Scott, Le Fanu's editor, wrote on politics, and Le Fanu himself published on fiction in addition to contributing two novels and two short stories during the year.[2] With so few regular contributors, and with the emphasis on literature over polemic, the 1864 volume was characterized not just by an abundance of fiction, but also by a curious internal discussion on the form and function of popular fiction in general. Again, sensation fiction was the most frequent type produced during the year, both in titles published and in critical articles on the genre in the periodical press. There is a fabric of familiarity woven around these articles, a familiarity produced through repetition of authors as well as repetition of subject matter of and about periodicals. I would like to suggest that the *DUM*, for this particular year anyway, forms an organic whole. There is enough information on the subject of Gothic and sensation fiction to claim that it is discussed in its various different guises, and that run-of-the-mill Gothic is bested through example in the journal. It was only through Le Fanu's influence as editor of the *DUM* that the extended treatment of the genre was possible, and the vast majority of the commentary stresses the difference between the sort of work produced by the year's popular sensation novelists and what the reader could expect from the venerable *DUM*. It was certainly in Le Fanu's own interest to defend his work against the charge of 'sensation'. He believed, and his contributors seconded his belief, that sensation as a driving force of fiction was coming to an end, and that only those authors whose works could claim a more than brief public interest could take their place beside great writers like Scott. The 'cheapening' of fiction that seemed to accompany the appearance of sensation on the market would also have had an effect on the reputation of the *DUM* if its own fictional offerings were seen as part of this trend. It is a pity, then, that Le Fanu was ultimately unable to dissociate himself from what had quickly become a 'women's' genre, and he shared the fate of later obscurity with the vast majority of them.[3] What follows is an examination of the stories, poetry, novels, and essays from the 1864 volume that speak about Gothic/sensation fiction or refer to it in an oblique way, with a view towards understanding the response of the *DUM* to what was both a threat and an opportunity.

In an essay on the relationship between Trollope, the *Cornhill*, and ideological formation, Andrew Maunder draws on the work of a number of periodical theorists to suggest that Trollope's novels 'as they appeared in the pages aut the *Cornhill* can be read as reflections of the assumptions and aspirations of a very particular contemporary "community" of readers for which they were produced and by which they were consumed', and that the various elements of each issue of the periodical work together to reflect and produce this community.[4] W. J. Mc Cormack's study of the *DUM* under Sheridan Le Fanu offers another angle on periodicity, or seriality as Mc Cormack calls it, noting that anonymity and a small pool of contributors created a

> complex 'serialism' of magazine reading as such. For the reader did not simply doggedly follow one episode of a fiction with the next: s/he read in an interspersing manner fiction and non-fiction, the work of authors who may have been (in certain cases) one and the same person.[5]

Anonymity or the presence of pseudonymous authors inevitably refers the reader to the internal structure of the periodical itself in order to validate the existence of the repeated voice.[6] I would argue that this process of validation could extend to the assertion of ideologies contained within the various articles of a particular title. The sheer number of references to Gothic/sensation fiction in the 1864 volume of the *DUM* is illustrated below:

January:

- 'Demoniac Ideals in Poetry' (a study of demons in poetry by Milton, Dante, Goethe and others, written by T. C. Irwin)
- *Wylder's Hand*: by the author of *The House by the Churchyard*
- 'Sensation! A Satire' (author unknown)

February:

- Conclusion of *Wylder's Hand*

March:

- 'My Aunt Margaret's Adventure' (anonymous, but by Le Fanu)

April:

- 'Wicked Captain Walshawe, of Wauling' (anonymous, but by Le Fanu)
- 'Earlier Type of the Sensation Novel' (by Patrick Kennedy)

July:

- *Maud Ruthyn*: by J. S. Le Fanu, Author of 'Wylder's Hand', 'The House by the Church-Yard', &c., begins. (The title of the novel is altered several times over the next few months.)

August:

- *Maud Ruthyn and Uncle Silas: a Story of Bartram Haugh*
- 'An Irish Actress – Margaret Woffington' (by J. W. Cole): 'We are not going to draw an ideal heroine, gifted with startling eccentricities, in the vain hope of emulating the effect of a "Woman in White", an "Aurora Floyd", or any other fashionable focus of excitement. We have no wish by ingenious sophistry to make vice appear virtue'.[7]

September:

- *Maud Ruthyn and Uncle Silas: a Story of Bartram-Haugh*   (name of house hyphenated)

October:

- *Uncle Silas and Maud Ruthyn: a Story of Bartram-Haugh*
- 'Charles Lever's Essays' (no author attributed by *Wellesley*, but likely Patrick Kennedy). This is a review of Blackwood's 1864 edition of Lever's *Cornelius O'Dowd*. The article begins: 'The Essayists have obtained a hearing again, and it is a hopeful sign. It appears to show that Sensationalism is a vein worked out. The excitements of the *fast* novel have lost their power by repetition' (p. 459). The article looks back both to Kennedy's own 'Earlier Type of the Sensation Novel' in April and also the footnote appended to the final chapter of Anne Robertson's *Yaxley and Its Neighbourhood* (serialized in issues from January to October) that claimed the originality of bigamy as a plot device in the novel.

November:

- *Uncle Silas and Maud Ruthyn: a Story of Bartram-Haugh*

December:

- *Who is the Heir?* (anonymous novel by Mortimer Collins begins and takes over the opening slot)
- *Uncle Silas and Maud Ruthyn: a Story of Bartram-Haugh* (novel concludes)

Wylder's Hand, the last few instalments of which were contained within the early issues of the 1864 volume, was the first of Le Fanu's novels that appeared after his agreement with Bentley not to use Ireland as the setting for his work, and to set his plots in modern times. That plot, as Victor Sage has noted, is a fairly complicated murder mystery involving inheritance, Dickensian villains, and isolated women. What it lacks, and again Sage has noted this, is an omniscient narrator.[8] As a result, the reader is frequently in the same emotional space as the characters who fear what they do not comprehend. These narrative gaps, or lacunae, are also discernible in *Uncle Silas*. The ultimate satisfaction of domesticating the threats to self is left unfulfilled at the end of the novel, and its main characters simply glide away from the narrator, as his final paragraph indicates:

> Some summers ago, I was, for a few days, in the wondrous city of Venice. Everyone knows something of the enchantment of the Italian moon, the expanse of dark and flashing blue, and the phantasmal city rising like a beautiful spirit from the waters. Gliding near the Lido – where so many rings of Doges lie lost beneath the waves – I heard the pleasant sound of female voices upon the water – and then, with a sudden glory, rose a sad, wild hymn, like the musical wail of the forsaken sea: –
> The spouseless Adriatic mourns her lord.
> The song ceased. The gondola which bore the musicians floated by – a slender hand over the gunwale trailed its finger in the water. Unseen, I saw. Rachel and Dorcas, beautiful in the sad moonlight, passed so near we could have spoken – passed me like spirits – never more, it may be, to cross my sight in life. (p. 196)

The structure of the average sensation novel is violated here; neither Rachel nor Dorcas is a criminal, and neither deserves such isolation at the end, but there is no resolution to their sadness, and the narrator – who might have spoken to them and thus concluded the novel more neatly – stays silent. Both women are tainted by their association with criminals and as such have stepped outside the boundary of the commonplace. The linear quality of realist fiction is also violated, and the reader is simply dismissed as a result of a conscious choice on the part of the narrator *not* to ask more questions, to solve such puzzles as still remain. In other words, authorial intention is removed from the narrative space; as such, the story is highly suitable for the periodical. *Wylder's Hand* may have ended, but it is contained within an environment that includes a number of other opportunities for reader satisfaction. Its genre, and the manner in which the story reaches its audience, supplies the place of narrator.

The February issue of the *DUM*, besides concluding *Wylder's Hand*, continued the second part of Anne Robertson's sensation novel, *Yaxley and Its Neighbourhood*, which ran until October. At the conclusion of its final instalment, Robertson (or Scott, or Le Fanu) felt it necessary to append a footnote: 'Lest it might be considered that there was a want of originality in introducing into the story of "Yaxley" the subject of bigamy, lately so much the fashion among novel writers, the author wishes to observe that the tale was finished, just as it stands at present, in February, 1861' (p. 386). The note does not apologize for the use of what had become by 1864 a fairly common plot device, nor for the fact that bigamy itself might not be the most morally uplifting of subjects. Its purpose seems simply to claim precedence, and its appearance here further muddies the waters in terms of the attitude displayed in the *DUM* towards sensation in general. Is the reader to glory in the *DUM* having hit upon this sort of plot first? The answer is to be found, again, in reading laterally.

Andrew Maunder, in his recent edited collection of women's sensation fiction, reprinted an eight-stanza poem entitled 'Sensation! A Satire' from the January 1864 issue of the *DUM*. Maunder notes: 'Are we meant to take it as a mocking attack on the public's love of sensationalism? Or is it a parody of the kinds of objections raised by conservative critics?'[9] It seems to me that the position of the *DUM* is more complicated than this, and its various responses to the fiction of the day (beyond this poem) reflect the angles from which the question – what is *good* fiction – is examined.

In a long series of rhyming couplets, the unknown poet of 'Sensation! A Satire' produced a pastiche of an eighteenth-century diatribe against fashion in prose. The naming of seemingly discarded novelists of the

previous generation – Burney, Edgeworth, even Gaskell – provided the
reader with examples of morally upright, serious artists. Taking their
place were the fashionable writers, and Braddon's *Lady Audley's Secret*
(1862) was presented as nothing more than a rather disorganized pot
of 'fierce ingredients': 'Soon will the book through ten editions fly, /
Great Mudie smiles, and eager thousands buy' (p. 86). Though she out-
sold Thackeray, Bulwer, Dickens, and Scott (all named in the poem),
Braddon's claim to be considered an artist was denied; she was indissol-
ubly linked with Mudie, the circulating library bookseller, who was in
turn castigated for fanning the flames of sensation for profit. The poet
backtracked slightly, as he noted that it is not so much the presence
of sensational events that cheapens these novels but rather the crudity
with which they are put together. The reader was then reminded that
none of this was new, that material had always been culled from penny
sheets and crime papers. So the complaint was against bad, immoral
writing rather than inappropriate material. Dumas and Ainsworth, for
example, were offered as successful romancers, novelists who worked
their material 'with skilful hand and nervous force' (p. 87). By the 1860s
public entertainment had begun to partake of the craze for sensation,
and sensation fiction was seen as part of a larger mania for overblown
emotion and spectacle. So the Victorian theatre and its most successful
productions – Boucicault's *Colleen Bawn* (1860) and *The Corsican Brothers* (1852) – were linked in the poem with the aerial feats of Blondin
the tightrope walker, with trapeze artists, and with viewings of famous
prostitutes riding in Rotten Row. All were emblematic of

> A sweet republic, where 'tis all the same –
> Virtue and vice, or good, or doubtful fame.
> [...]
> These are thy freaks, SENSATION! where they tend
> No modest eye can see – nor mark the end! (p. 89)

The poem as a whole was a denunciation of the perceived cheapening
of the novel as an art form, most particularly through allying it (as the
sensation novelists seemed to be doing) with the penny press. Le Fanu's
anxiety about the classification of his own work had, therefore, both
an economic and theoretical basis. He was emphatic about the identification of his novels as romances in the style of Scott. But he was also a
businessman, and the readership of the *DUM*, as well as the ordinary circulating library patron, formed his client base. It would not do to accept
that the magazine, through the printing of the editor's own fiction, was

cheapening itself or betraying its roots. If the serial novel was supposed to produce a 'community of readers', Le Fanu's journal was particularly at risk, because this was not the sort of community the *DUM* was after.[10] As he could not really change his own style of writing, what Le Fanu did was try to argue that his work was not really sensation or Gothic fiction at all.

This point makes the decision to satirize sensation fiction through the medium of poetry an interesting one. The formal, stylized language of the poem suggests a seriousness and erudition that is belied by its content. The interpretive gloss provided at the side of the verses again points out the uneasy juxtaposition of content and style, but offers at least the ghost of a 'reading' of sensation fiction to be supplied through accepting the judgments of the poet regarding the works exposed in this way. Linda K. Hughes makes a strong case for the inclusion of poetry as part of a study of discourse in the periodical, and she notes the ways in which the subject matter of a poem is often picked up by the articles that surround it.[11] Her argument regarding the careful physical placement of poetry – often in the center column of a three-column page of a daily or weekly paper – can be adapted to fit the circumstances of the *DUM*. 'Sensation! A Satire', rather than acting as the still point around which a swirl of complementary information is positioned, is set apart from its fellows, and though a poem, is given the physical status of an article. Hence its 'message' carries a weight equivalent to longer prose articles and fiction on the subject.

In March, Le Fanu published a story of his own entitled 'My Aunt Margaret's Adventure'. It was placed just before the continuation of Robertson's *Yaxley and Its Neighbourhood*, which had taken up the main fiction position after the conclusion of *Wylder's Hand* in February. Le Fanu's story is very much in the style of Gaskell's *Cranford*, serialized by Dickens in *Household Words* from 1851 to 1853. Like the ladies of Cranford, or even Dickens's Mr Pickwick, Aunt Margaret is subjected to misinformation, misunderstanding, the vagaries of servants, and the perfidy of men. Throughout her adventure she keeps by her side what the narrator calls her 'confidential handmaid' (p. 209), whose main function is to act as a silent audience (mimicking the reader?) and to look surprised when required. There is, of course, in addition an aged, rascally hired man, named Tom Teukesbury, whose enormous lies and excuses for incompetence form the comedic effect of the story. It is indeed an adventure, but with a rather mundane economic motive: Aunt Margaret is a landlord in a small way (she owns one and a half houses – a tobacconist and half a tailor), and she sets off to a neighboring town, Tom and Winnie the handmaid in attendance, to collect out-standing rent from the recalcitrant tobacconist. Inevitably, the party gets lost, as Tom, according to the narrator, fell to 'groping in a geographical chaos' (p. 272).

The structure of this story is familiar, and Gothic: a journey under-taken, an incompetent guide, two defenseless women. By rights, the carriage should be set upon, and bandits should rob and threaten the women; the driver should be killed, and the journey, of course, should be undertaken in the Alps, or at least in northern Scotland. What *does* happen is an inversion of the classic Gothic plot. Margaret is the narrator's aunt, a solid, unexcitable, comfortable spinster, and Winnie the maid is half-witted and portly. As an advisor to the heroine, Winnie is severely lacking. Tom the driver is marvelously characterized as a smart-talking, though geographically challenged, underling. The narrator supplies a typical interchange between Aunt Margaret and Tom:

> 'There's a man coming', said Tom hopefully.
> 'Good gracious!' cried my Aunt.
> 'No, there aint', said Tom, dejectedly. (p. 272)

Eventually the three come upon an inn in the middle of the heath, mis-called 'The Good Woman'. The chambermaid of the place is, of course, Irish. There being no room for Tom, he is sent back to an alehouse for the night, and the two ladies are admitted alone. The narrator sets the scene through asking the reader to imagine previously encountered sit-uations in literature: 'I don't know whether my Aunt had read *Ferdinand Count Fathom* or ever seen the *Bleeding Nun* performed on any stage, but if she had I venture to say she was reminded of both before morning'.[12] Even references to Austen's *Northanger Abbey* (1818) are here. Before retiring, Aunt Margaret makes an inventory of her room at the inn, looking in drawers and cupboards but finding only 'an old black glove for the left hand' (p. 277). The room looks down on a courtyard, and as Aunt Margaret is peering out of the window, Nell, the Irish cham-bermaid, looks over her shoulder and gives her a terrible start – but it is irritation at the familiarity of a servant that Aunt Margaret feels, not fear. She *is* terrorized by the maid, but entirely through the verbal audac-ity of the woman, and by her refusal to observe the conventions of the mistress/servant relationship.

Wandering about in the middle of the night, ensuring that her belong-ings are not being ransacked, Aunt Margaret loses her way in the dark and ends up in the wrong bedroom; she is discovered the next morning lying next to a dead body. The mystery is soon cleared up, and the dead man turns out to be the inn's insolvent landlord, who had been hiding from his creditors and had died of catarrh. Even after his death, the people of the house were afraid of the law and had been living with the body in a state of siege until they could dispose of it during the night. The narrator is careful to provide an economic tragedy as the background to the landlord's tale: he had lost his livelihood when a new road, and a newer railway line, bypassed his inn. No forged wills, no murderous villains lurk in his past, and one last reference to the chambermaid emphasizes the extent to which the creation of apparent mystery and horror lie with her:

> The Irish maid, whose head was full of the disguises and stratagems of which she had heard so much in her own ingenious and turbulent country, was, for a while, disposed to think that the unseasonable visitors were myrmidons of the law in disguise. (p. 280)

In other words, the inn's inhabitants were as frightened of Aunt Margaret as she was irritated and annoyed by them. The difference between this story as Gothic or sensation fiction and gentle satire lies both in the attitude of the narrator, whose light tone keeps the narrative comic, and in the description of the main characters, whose age and intelligence (or lack of it) removes them from danger. Everything about the plot line, though, and the atmospheric rendering of darkness and anxiety, is concomitant with Gothic fiction.

In the April issue, Le Fanu published another of his own stories, entitled 'Wicked Captain Walshawe, of Wauling'. The story is narrated, as in 'My Aunt Margaret's Adventure', by a relative, and the tone of the narrator is similar. To an unseen audience the narrator says, 'A very odd thing happened to my uncle, Mr. Watson, of Haddlestone; and to enable you to understand it, I must begin at the beginning' (p. 449). The veracity of this story, as of that of Aunt Margaret, is asserted, as Uncle Watson 'was a truthful man, and not prone to fancies' (p. 452). Both stories were published anonymously in the magazine, but their proximity, tone, and gentle satire are alike, and it is not unreasonable to assume that readers of the *DUM* would also have noticed the similarities between them. However, 'Walshawe' is set in the past – 1822 – the year of the protagonist's death at the age of 81, so the events narrated take place well within the eighteenth century, and we are in fact given an exact starting date for them: 1766, when he was 25 years of age. A recent removal from the Army, and a spate of debts to discharge meant that the Captain turned to a common means of settling his affairs;[13] that is, he eloped with and married an heiress. While the Captain was English, the story begins in Ireland, Clonmel to be exact, where he was quartered, and his future wife (appropriately named Peg O'Neill) was a pensioner at the local nunnery:

> In England there are traditions of Irish fortune-hunters, and in Ireland of English. The fact is, it was the vagrant class of each country that chiefly visited the other in old times; and the handsome vagabond, whether at home or abroad, I suppose, made the most of his face, which was also his fortune. (p. 449)

When the pair soon decamps to Lancashire, Peg's Irish maid goes with them, and stays on after Peg's fortune is squandered; Peg is neglected, and is finally harried into her grave by the rake. The Irish aspect to the story seems incidental until the point at which Peg's body is laid out. It is here that the narrative turns from one like 'Aunt Margaret' – slight and gently humorous – to a decidedly sinister, ghostly tale that hinges entirely on a series of clichés surrounding both the Irish and Catholicism. The narrator, clearly unfamiliar with the last rites, notes that the Captain

> found some half-dozen crones, chiefly Irish, from the neighbouring town of Hackleton, sitting over tea and snuff, &c., with candles lighted round the corpse, which was arrayed in a strangely cut robe of brown serge. She had secretly belonged to some order – I think the Carmelite, but I am not certain – and wore the habit in her coffin. (p. 450)

The order of nuns is unimportant to the narrator; what *is* important is the fact that the Captain knocks a burning candle out of the folded hands of the corpse, drawing down on him the curses of the Irish maid and an assertion that Peg would be lost between this world and the next as a result of his action. Not liking quite to destroy the candle, the Captain throws it in a cupboard and apparently forgets about it. When he too dies – 40 years later – it is revealed that Uncle Watson is his heir. The lack of a will and the belief on the part of Uncle Watson that certain leases have been removed ushers in a vital piece of information about him: he is a member of a 'sect who by no means reject the supernatural, and whose founder, on the contrary, has sanctioned ghosts in the most emphatic way' (p. 452). That Uncle Watson is a

Swedenborgian is not made explicit, but it is likely. If I am right, this factor connects Le Fanu's story to the ideology at the centre of *Uncle Silas* (as well as 'Green Tea'), where Maud's father's belief in the tenets of Swedenborg provides an exotic element to the sort of plot previously enriched through being set in a foreign country. In any event, Uncle Watson spends the night in Wauling, and it is, of course, a stormy night, necessitating a candle, which he procures from the same cupboard in which the Captain had thrown Peg's wake candle so many years previously. It is placed on a table, the legs of which bear a resemblance to satyrs, beside the bed. Somehow, the candle calls into being the figure of the Captain, who expands from the size of a thumbnail to his living height, and then ages before Uncle Watson's eyes, to the extent that the last glimpse we have of him is as a corpse, his shroud alive with grave worms. Eventually the spirit is drawn towards the fire and

> It seemed to my Uncle that the fire suddenly darkened and the air grew icy cold, and there came an awful roar and riot of tempest, which shook the old house from top to base, and sounded like the yelling of a blood-thirsty mob on receiving a new and long-expected victim. (p. 455)

Le Fanu gives the story a final twist, as it appears that the missing leases are revealed by the ghost (who had been about to burn them in life) in a secret drawer at the back of a chest in the room.

Again, the ghost story elements are familiar: a curse, a removal in time, a family mystery, an evil villain, Catholicism as a plot device, an Irish element providing religious superstition, and an honest narrator whose own religious proclivities are left rather uncertain. This is not sensation fiction, at least in the manner familiar to readers by 1864; rather it forms part of the complementary discourses surrounding longer works that interrogate the Gothic and attempt a re-education of the *DUM*'s readers away from lesser genres back towards something Scott would have recognized.

It is tempting to see the exploitation by Captain Walshawe of an innocent Irish heroine as indicative of a larger comment on relations between Ireland and Britain. However, we know nothing about the Irish heiress, other than the ease with which she was lured away from the protection of the convent and separated from her fortune. The main characters of this story are not allowed a voice; the narrator interprets at a double remove from the action, and the force of the plot is strangely split – as in 'My Aunt Margaret's Adventure' – between traditional Gothic and Victorian realist fiction.

Besides 'Wicked Captain Walshawe, of Wauling', the April issue of the *DUM* included an eight-page essay by Patrick Kennedy entitled 'Earlier Type of the Sensation Novel'. The first sentence announced that, as the sensation novel was clearly fading away, readers might like to understand the profound difference between the productions of lesser authors in that vein and the sort of fiction they were presented with in the *DUM*:

> The mere sensational novel, which we would gladly see devoted to the waters of the infernal Lethe, lays no claim to truthful delineation of character, to moral teaching, to sympathy with the outward and inward manifestations of nature, nor pleasing social pictures, nor genial gushes of humour, nor healthy exercises of thought. Its sole merit consists in keeping the mind in painful suspense, exciting sensations of horror, or terror at least, and surrounding vice with a lurid splendour. The novel that excites a lively interest in the fortunes of its good characters, even though united with the excitement of suspense and mystery, is not the thing against which we protest, if it possesses the desirable qualities we have named. (p. 460)

What Kennedy then supplied was a potted history of Gothic, noting that the height of immorality came with M. G. Lewis, that the air was cleansed with the productions of Edgeworth, Austen, and Scott, and that poor Maturin, trying his best, 'came too late, however, to do much harm' (p. 461). In other words, the present mania was to be considered nothing new, and also nothing much to worry about as the current crop of novels 'will, in turn, be thrown over and flung out of doors, but not till they have accomplished their share of mischief' (p. 461). And yet the essay is a long one, and it consists chiefly of translated quotations and paraphrases from a French sensation novel written by Marie Aycard.[14] The title of the novel summarized is not given, as Kennedy's assumption is that it is irrelevant; all such works are equally poorly plotted, and all rehearse the same domestic dramas. Kennedy cannot stop himself offering asides:

> She saw her talking to Mons. Ernest de Meyran and Charlotte his sister under a large tree; and, as frequently occurs in French fiction, she placed herself behind the thick trunk, to ascertain whether the young lady favoured the pretensions of the young gentleman in company. (p. 462)

Though the novel is facile, it is of 'an unobjectionable character, and a date anterior [c. 1848] to the Lady Audley school' (p. 469). Kennedy's detailing of the plot is exhaustive, and he emphasizes the morality of the majority of the characters, together with an ending that sees the reconciliation of an estranged married couple. The tone of the article is odd, though, as Kennedy seems half condemnatory of the novel and half laudatory of its middle-class moral patina.

In the article, Kennedy mentions only one periodical offering such fare: this is the *Keepsake,* a respectable annual containing highly competent steel engravings and verse by the best poets of the day, including Moore and Wordsworth; crucially, it had ceased publication in 1857.[15] The choice is not a random one. Kennedy fastens on a particularly horrible story from the *Keepsake* (supplying no date of publication), within which a young woman is revealed to have, instead of a left hand and arm, a 'hissing serpent', which she is condemned to feed. The climax comes as she is revealed pleading with the serpent to spare the life of her betrothed. Kathryn Ledbetter and Terence Hoagwood note that

> *Keepsake* publishers were fiscally conservative and serious about their position as moral guardians, yet they challenged the boundaries of propriety by promoting a highly successful commercial product targeted to middle-class female readers, one that competed with poetry volumes and other ostensibly serious literature for an equal share of the literary market.[16]

In other words, the aims of business and the protection of moral rectitude in publishing are presented as not necessarily incompatible. Context is everything, and the placement of this article in an issue that offers so many variations on the Gothic/sensation plot has the effect of complicating reader response to the fiction, and contradicting the 'official' response offered both by the *DUM* as a whole and by Kennedy here. Though Kennedy does not say so, the essay suggests that the discerning reader will be able to tell the difference between literature that enriches, and literature that aims only to shock. The implication is that the sort of prose contained within the *DUM* belongs to the former category. The final paragraph of the essay places Aycard's story and asserts its difference:

> Our object being to present a sensation French story of an unobjectionable character, and a date anterior to the Lady Audley school, we have spared our readers everything in the shape of criticism. Being

destitute of the evil qualities so dear to the admirers of the wicked works of Feydeau, Sue and Co., it has missed such popularity as is enjoyed by their writings, and will, therefore, as we hope, possess the virtues of novelty for many of our readers. (p. 469)

My final example from the 1864 volume comes from the conclusion in December of Le Fanu's novel *Uncle Silas*. Neatly contained within one volume of the magazine, the novel was, physically at least, always a separate entity. Its first appearance coincided, as we have seen, with the high point of the sensation novel, and Le Fanu's awareness of the apparent timeliness of his work was not completely happy. Bentley published the first edition of the novel in December of 1864, just as the serial version of the story was completed in the *DUM*. Le Fanu provided a 'Preliminary Word' to this edition, meant to be read before the novel and to act as a corrective to those who might mistake the genre to which *Uncle Silas* belonged. However, in the serial version of the novel, this 'Preliminary Word' was appended to the last instalment as 'A Postscript'. We can assume that it was just that, a response by Le Fanu to contemporary reactions to his work as a whole, as well as a slightly exasperated final defense of this novel. Le Fanu noted firstly, and in order to avoid the charge of plagiarism, that *Uncle Silas* was a vastly expanded version of an earlier short story of his (published anonymously in the *DUM* in 1838) entitled 'A Passage in the Secret History of an Irish Countess', and that the story had again appeared with the title altered, in a separate volume of stories.[17] The remainder of the Postscript was a vigorous denunciation of the

> promiscuous application of the term 'sensation' to that large school of fiction which transgresses no one of those canons of construction and morality which, in producing the unapproachable 'Waverley Novels,' their great author imposed upon himself. (p. 679–80)

Le Fanu then offered the reader a fair number of examples of the frequency of death, crime, and general mystery in Scott's novels, calling his work 'tragic English romance' and asserting that *Uncle Silas*, though clearly inferior in execution, used incident in the same way that Scott did, and with the same 'moral aim'.

The Postscript is important, I think, as its content is not only applicable to Le Fanu's novel, but also, as we have seen, to a number of other stories and articles in the 1864 volume. The point is not so much that Le

Fanu's works are *not* Gothic, but that Scott's *are*, and that the imprimatur of Scott surely legitimizes Le Fanu's fiction.

The discussion surrounding genre is one that, I would argue, appears coherent only after the fact. The echoes, repetitions, and competing discourses that occur in the 1864 volume are ones that impress as a result of their sheer weight, but that are only obvious through lateral reading. A small number of contributors, a particular type of fiction valorized, a declaration of the worth of the definitions offered, all add up to a branding for the Le Fanu years that is not often seen during the tenure of other editors of the *DUM*. Behind the declarations regarding the proper use and form of fiction is the added value accrued through the thirty-odd years of the existence of the *DUM*. That is, opposed to new magazines like *Temple Bar* the *DUM* offered itself as a serious literary and political voice, as weighty perhaps as the frequently invoked reputation of Scott. It is impossible to speculate about the readership of the magazine during the 1860s, and Le Fanu's apparent determination to keep his presence as editor very low-key means that clues to an editorial voice and worldview must come from study of the placement and content of articles. However, I do not believe that a clear set of guidelines regarding what constitutes good literature is provided by the material examined above. Contradictions within and between individual statements – whether in prose or fiction – reveal a curious hesitation and confusion about the subject as a whole. Ultimately the absence noted so often in Le Fanu is here as well, and the reader, like many of Le Fanu's characters, is referred back to the periodical itself as a source of meaning, to form as a substitute for completion.

Notes

1. The critical literature available on the *DUM* begins with Michael Sadleir's 1937 essay delivered to the Bibliographical Society of Ireland (published in 1938); see Michael Sadleir (1938) *Dublin University Magazine: Its History, Contents and Bibliography; a Paper Read Before the Bibliographical Society of Ireland, 26 April 1937* (Dublin: Juverna Press). Wayne Hall's *Dialogues in the Margin: a Study of the* Dublin University Magazine (1999) is the latest long study of the magazine.
2. See *The Wellesley Index to Victorian Periodicals, 1824–1900*. Available online from <http://wellesley.chadwyck.co.uk/home.do>.
3. Suzanne Clark (1991) *Sentimental Modernism: Women Writers and the Revolution of the Word* (Indiana: Indiana University Press): 'The modernist exclusion of everything but the forms of high art acted like a machine for cultural loss of memory' (p. 6).

4. Andrew Maunder (2000) ' "Monitoring the Middle-Classes": Intertextuality and Ideology in Trollope's *Framley Parsonage* and the *Cornhill Magazine'*, *Victorian Periodicals Review* 33.1, 44–64 (p. 45).

5. W. J. Mc Cormack (1996) ' "Never put your name to an anonymous letter": Serial Reading in the *Dublin University Magazine*, 1861 to 1869', *The Yearbook of English Studies* 26, 100–15 (p. 105). See also Mc Cormack's *Sheridan Le Fanu and Victorian Ireland* (1980; Dublin: Lilliput Press, 1991).

6. Mc Cormack, ' "Never put your name to an anonymous letter" ', p. 105.

7. 'An Irish Actress – Margaret Woffington', *Dublin University Magazine* (August, 1864), p. 180. Further references to the *DUM* will be contained within the text.

8. See Victor Sage (2004) *Le Fanu's Gothic: the Rhetoric of Darkness* (Basingstoke: Palgrave), p. 77.

9. Andrew Maunder (ed.) (2004) *Varieties of Women's Sensation Fiction, v. 1: 1855–1890* (London: Pickering and Chatto), p. 88.

10. See Deborah Wynne (2001) *The Sensation Novel and the Victorian Family Magazine* (Basingstoke: Palgrave), p. 5 and *passim*.

11. See Linda K. Hughes (2007) 'What the *Wellesley Index* Left Out: Why Poetry Matters to Periodical Studies', *Victorian Periodicals Review* 40.2, pp. 91–125.

12. This is Tobias Smollett's 1753 novel, *The Adventures of Ferdinand, Count Fathom*. Scott had said that Smollett had painted a 'complete picture of human depravity'. The *Bleeding Nun* was an adaptation of an incident in M. G. Lewis's *The Monk* (1796).

13. We are told that the title of 'Captain' is one of courtesy, 'for he had never reached that rank in the army list' (p. 449).

14. Marie Aycard (1794–1859) was the author of some 22 novels and six plays, most of a sensational character.

15. *The Keepsake* ran from 1829 to 1857. 'Keepsake proprietor Charles Heath was careful to market his book in advertising and prefaces as an exclusive, hand-crafted book of fine literature, but the essential focus on women readers and the means of its production places *The Keepsake* squarely in the mainstream of nineteenth-century middle-class consumerism, oppositional to exclusivity'; Terence Hoagwood and Kathryn Ledbetter, 'L. E. L.'s "Verses" and *The Keepsake* for 1829' at <http://www.rc.umd.edu/editions/lel/keepsake.htm>. Accessed 31 July 2013.

16. Hoagwood and Ledbetter, 'L. E. L's "Verses" and *The Keepsake* for 1829'.

17. Mc Cormack notes that the novel is also a reworking of another of Le Fanu's stories entitled 'The Murdered Cousin', published in 1851; see W. J. Mc Cormack (1993) *Dissolute Characters: Irish Literary History Through Balzac, Sheridan Le Fanu, Yeats and Bowen* (Manchester and New York: Manchester University Press), p. 69.

8

'Whom We Name Not': *The House by the Churchyard* and its Annotation

W. J. Mc Cormack

Towards history, not trauma

I have long wanted to edit Sheridan Le Fanu's last Irish-set novel. However, the miserable condition of publishing, and the academic profession's even more parlous state, cancels the wish in current circumstances. The text is both lengthy and dense, requiring a vast corpus of annotation with a counterbalancing discreetly critical essay. Beyond these relatively hum-drum aspects of the project lies a topic difficult to summarize, easier to demonstrate. That is to say, *The House by the Churchyard* incorporates a species – even a style – of annotation, cryptic perhaps, yet communicative with the reader. Indeed, its procedures may amount to a kind of self-interpretation, employing an intermittent but distinctively 'intransitive' grammar. Thus, the task of comprehensive annotation could become thematic.

Perhaps the notion, in its crudest form, is vindicated by reference to the authorial footnotes in Charles Robert Maturin's *Melmoth the Wanderer* (1820). In turn, these might compare with similar apparatus in Maria Edgeworth's *Castle Rackrent* (1800) which certainly is no Gothic tale: on the contrary, it mocks the Gothicizing habits and tastes of a stratum in Irish landownership at the end of the eighteenth century. To be honest, I remain sceptical about Irish Gothic – Maturin, Le Fanu, and Stoker hardly amount to a subtradition, and much of Le Fanu's work lies quite outside any definition of the Gothic. The closer examination of Chapter IV from *The House* will generate an alternative case for this fiction (or at least Le Fanu's) as forms of historical writing.[1] This should hardly surprise readers who have noted Le Fanu's keen response to Gilbert's *History of the City of Dublin* (the first volume, 1854).[2]

The 1860s saw the emergence of historical work in greater quantity than hitherto, led by the first volume (1860) of *The Calendar of State Papers: Ireland,* followed by W. E. H. Lecky's 'Declining Sense of the Miraculous' (1863) and J. P. Prendergast's *Cromwellian Settlement* (1865). In step with these, the once popular genre of historical novel gradually lost its appeal, while new commercial forces came to influence literary publication: much of this can be traced in Le Fanu's career, even in his first 1860s novel. Legislation on issues of land tenure, small-scale military efforts at separation from Britain, and drastic changes in church–state relations combined in a decade of anxiety. Ireland was on the move – in several directions.

As good timing would have it, the present undertaking allows for some reflections on Conor Carville's *The Ends of Ireland* (2011), which treats at length the work of Seamus Deane, Luke Gibbons, David Lloyd – and myself. Carville is rightly cautious about Irish Gothic, limiting it to the trope of ruination (in Edmund Burke.) What is more germane to the present essay is his account of origination as such, with particular reference to Gibbons and Mc Cormack. In the second connection, the object under discussion in *The Ends* is the Protestant Ascendancy, taken as a dominant social constituency or class flourishing in the eighteenth century and persisting less confidently up to the 1860s or later. As *The House* was published in that decade but set 100 years earlier, it conveniently acts as litmus paper (in 3 vols) for the wider argument.

Carville acutely observes that Freudian *Nachträglichkeit* appeals to Irish Studies people, notably Gibbons and Virginia Crossman.[3] In summary, their account of Irish culture demands a traumatic origin, occasionally identified as the trial and execution of Fr Nicholas Sheehy (1766) or the somewhat larger Famine catastrophe (1845 onwards). Other moments of origination have been detected, Parnell's death in 1891 (for Yeats), the Easter 1916 Rising (for all and motley), and even Bloody Sunday of January 1972 (for Gibbons). *Nachträglichkeit* in these theorizations of Irish culture relates a lost or 'unspeakable' history. Several problems require teasing out, but first let us admit that *The House* does indeed concern itself with nocturnal reburial, a smudged tombstone, and other elusive remote secrets or objects. 'The blank leaf of his master's letter' (Chapter XI) is a very minor detail, yet representative.

Laplanche and Pontalis hardly support the Irish Studies deployment of a 'term frequently used by Freud in connection with his view of psychical temporality and causality: experiences, impressions and memory traces may be revised at a later date to fit with fresh experiences or with the attainment of a new stage of development. They may in that event be endowed not only with a new meaning but also with psychical effectiveness'.[4] Doubtless some cases where Freud used the word involved trauma in the strict sense, but it is clear that *Nachträglichkeit* does not absolutely require a traumatic component. Laplanche and Pontalis go to some lengths to indicate that positive results may follow – new stages of development, effectivity, etc.

The second problem is complicit in the first. Classical psycho-analysis dealt with individuals, one by one, or (to be more exact) one in relation to another one. It remained suspicious of group psychology in any sense other than that of observing and receiving the behavior of the individual in groups. In 1920 Freud began to investigate dangerous postwar tendencies in European society – identification with a leader, or bonding with others through group behavior.[5] But Irish Studies leaders (especially Gibbons) posit a sort of communal *and* traumatic reaction to events which in some cases relate to an individual (e.g., Fr Sheehy or Parnell) and in others relate to the experience of thousands or even millions (Bloody Sunday, the Famine, etc.) Communities invoked (that is, called for, or called forth) are, without exception, structured around an amalgam of Catholicity and nationality which might be thought an illustration of Eliot's *Waste Land*, a metaphysical polity 'mixing memory and desire'. Other ingredients rarely figure. Irish Studies has yet to consider the 1641 Rising as a traumatic causative factor in the history of what will lead to Unionism.

The third problem affects me, Le Fanu, and *The House* more directly. Whereas Freud used *Nachträglichkeit* with considerable frequency, there is a related term which he used sparingly – *auxiliäre Moment*, the 'auxiliary moment'.[6] Conor Carville has extended the first term's currency into my own work: I stare that gift horse in the mouth, having chosen not to buy into *Nachträglichkeit* as broadcast in Ireland. An experiment was conducted at the first conference (c. 1985) of the Eighteenth-Century Ireland Society through a paper on the composition of Sir John Temple's *The Irish Rebellion; or an History of the Beginnings and First Progresse of the General Rebellion Raised within the Kingdom of Ireland . . .* (1646), and the successive republications (London, 1679; Dublin, 1698; Dublin, 1713; Dublin, 1716; Dublin, 1724; London, 1746; [Dublin], 1751?; Cork, 1766; London, 1812) of that provocative work. The intention, to show that these periodic re-counts of rebel and Catholic violence in 1641 were auxiliary to an original trauma, was misguided in several respects, notably in assuming that the procedures, observations, and mechanisms employed in the psycho-analysis of a living individual (with whom the analyst has direct and sustained contact) could be readily applied to collective behavior in historical contexts. The paper was neither expanded nor published.

Nevertheless, Freud's auxiliary moment is valuable analogically when one wants to investigate the subterranean history of Protestant Ascendancy or examine in detail works of fiction produced by writers associated with that peculiar institution. I submit that Carville oversimplifies by declaring me 'remarkably specific in dating the origins of the notion of Protestant Ascendancy to 23 October 1868 and Gladstone's address at Wigan'.[7] Instead, I treated that occasion as a crucial stage which *analogically* one might call an auxiliary moment in relation to an earlier one. My former colleague and good friend quotes me additionally: 'as a rallying-point or -cry in the 1790s Protestant Ascendancy did not exist until it was threatened with reform'.

By coincidence or otherwise, Gladstone spoke on the anniversary of the 1641 Rebellion which, according to Sir John Temple's title page was 'raised upon the three and twentieth day of October'. As Prime Minister, Gladstone's immediate predecessors included Henry John Temple, 3rd Viscount Palmerston, who died in 1865. The viscountcy had been created in 1723 for an earlier Temple who took the title from the village of Palmerstown outside Dublin, where the family held lands. Chapter IV of *The House* is entitled 'The Fair Green of Palmerstown'. Chapelizod has a longer history, involving a supposed devotion to Isolde. In more traceable terms, land in and near the village was granted by James II to Sir John Davies (1569–1626), poet and lawyer.[8]

The novel's publication history is complicated. Le Fanu had acquired the *Dublin University Magazine* in July 1861 as proprietor-editor. Serialization began in October, under the pseudonym Charles de Cresseron, running monthly until February 1863.[9] It seems reasonable to believe that composition had begun before the author acquired the means of publishing the novel himself. 'Ghost Stories of Chapelizod' appeared in 1851, and the novelist's wife died in 1858, an event generally accepted as leading into a new phase of writing. When the moment arrived for book publication, Le Fanu found local resources depressingly limited. Consequently, he bore the expenses of buying paper and having the work printed and bound, to sell copies to a London publisher. William Tinsley (1831–1902) had his first commercial success with Elizabeth Braddon's *Lady Audley's Secret* (1862). He insisted on having Le Fanu's novel re-bound, and so its early history involves some ferocious bibliographical problems.[10] Only in three-decker form was it finally accredited to Le Fanu.

Chapter IV: excerpts and commentary[11]

1 There were half-a-dozen carriages, and a score of led horses outside the fair green, a precious lot of ragamuffins, and a good resort to the public house opposite; and the gate being open, the artillery band, rousing all the echoes round with harmonious and exhilarating thunder, within – an occasional crack of a 'Brown Bess', with a puff of white smoke over the hedge, being heard, and the cheers of the spectators, and sometimes a jolly chorus of many-toned laughter, all mixed together, and carried on with a pleasant running hum of voices – Mervyn, the stranger, reckoning on being unobserved in the crowd, and weary of the very solitude he courted, turned to his right, and so found himself upon the renowned fair green of Palmerstown.

ANNOTATION

'**Brown Bess**': the nickname of a musket used extensively in the British Army, and less regularly for hunting. It became a favored weapon of the American rebels.

Mervyn: the reader has already encountered Mr Mervyn in Chapter II, 'a tall, very pale, and peculiar looking young man' who arrived at night in Chapelizod in 1767 to oversee a reinterment. The presiding clergyman Dr Walsingham observed of the stranger, 'He reminded me of him who is gone, whom we name not'. In terms of the fictional plot, the pale young man is traveling under a false name (miserably expanded to A. Mervyn in # 13): ultimately he is revealed to be a Mordaunt, covertly attempting to clear the name of his father, Richard, earl of Dunoran, condemned in May 1746 for a crime he did not commit. But the name begs to be identified as that of Sir Audley Mervyn (d. 1675), colonel of a foot regiment during the 1641 rebellion.

Audley Mervyn carried baggage. His mother conveyed scandal amid serpentine family trees. She was Christian [*sic*] Touchet, born c. 1587, daughter of George Touchet (first earl of Castlehaven in the Irish peerage) and his wife Lucy Mervyn, baroness Audley. Her brother, Mervyn Touchet, (second earl), was executed in May 1631 for grotesque sexual crimes including rape of his second wife, mutual masturbation with a servant named Fitzpatrick, sodomy, and general domestic debauchery. It is accepted that the wife had been Castlehaven's match in immorality. Eleanor Touchet (1590–1652), daughter of George, Baron Audley, (and so sister of the executed earl) married Sir John Davies in 1609: she wrote on prophecy and defended her brother's reputation vis-à-vis the trial.[12]

Walsingham: no vicar of Chapelizod bore this name. The incumbent between 1741 and 1758 (when he died) was John Jourdan, a Huguenot by birth who had served as chaplain to Lord Galway in 1704, and married Blandine Bouhéreau, daughter of another Huguenot, Elias Bouhéreau, first keeper of Marsh's Library, beside St Patrick's Cathedral. The fictitious Walsingham's learning reflects in miniature the scholarly substance of the Bouhéreau circle, including Jourdan. It might also echo the publication (in 1863) of *Historia Anglicana* by Thomas Walsingham (d. 1422). This, like Mervyn Archdall's *Monasticon*, was a religious chronicle. However, the more obvious name-bearer to consider is Sir Francis Walsingham (c. 1530–90), who was (in modern parlance) spymaster to Elizabeth I.

Palmerstown: the name derives from a medieval association with pilgrims (or palmers).

*   *   *

7 Fat, short, radiant General Chattesworth – in full, artillery uniform – was there, smiling and making little speeches to the ladies, and bowing stiffly from his hips upward – his great cue playing all the time up and down his back, and sometimes so near the ground when he stood erect, and threw back his head, that [Dr] Toole, seeing Juno [a dog] eyeing the appendage rather viciously, though it prudent to cut her speculations short with a smart kick.[13]

ANNOTATION

Chattesworth: although three characters in the novel share this surname, it rarely if ever appears in historical records. It echoes, however, that of Lieutenant-Colonel Richard Bettesworth, commander of the Royal Regiment of Artillery in Ireland (based at Chapelizod) whose wife predeceased him in 1784. What it less obscurely conjures up is Chatsworth, the grand Derbyshire residence of the Cavendishes, (dukes of Devonshire). The third duke was Lord Lieutenant of Ireland in the 1730s, and so (in 1755) was his son. The fourth duke, by marrying Lady Charlotte Boyle, acquired Lismore Castle in County Waterford for the family. In the novel, the Chattesworths signal an easy mingling of a military élite among villagers in the fair green.

*   *   *

19 [...] Miss Magnolia not only stood fire like a brick, but with her own fair hands cracked off a firelock, and was more complimented and applauded than all the marksmen beside, although she shot most dangerously wide, and was much nearer hitting old Arthur Slowe than that respectable gentleman, who waved his hat and smirked gallantly, was at all aware [.]

ANNOTATION

Magnolia: MacNamara's mother is also present. The surname is quite common, offsetting the splendid Christian name.

Arthur Slowe: in January 1817, Mary Ann Slowe (aged 37) was buried in Chapelizod. In October 1818, Caroline Slow married Thomas Rogers in the parish church. In the 1590s, John Slowe was a customary tenant in the nearby manor of Crumlin. In relation to Le Fanu's Mr Justice **Lowe**, note the elaborate Lowe family tombstone in Chapelizod is transcribed by F. E. Ball.[14]

*   *   *

20 Everybody knew that Miss Rebecca Chattesworth ruled supreme at Belmont. With a docile old general and a niece so young, she had less resistance to encounter than, perhaps, her ardent soul would have relished. Fortunately for the general it was only now and then that Aunt Becky took a whim to command the Royal Irish Artillery. She had other hobbies just as odd, though not quite so scandalous. It had struck her active mind that such of the ancient women of Chapelizod as were destitute of letters – mendicants and the like – should learn to read. Twice a week her 'old women's school,' under that energetic lady's presidency, brought together its muster-roll of rheumatism, paralysis, dim eyes, bothered ears, and invincible stupidity. Over the fire-place in large black letters, was the legend, 'BETTER LATE THAN NEVER!' and out came the horn-books and spectacles, and to it they went with their A-B ab, etc., and plenty of wheezing and coughing. Aunt Becky kept good fires, and served out a mess of bread and broth, along with some pungent ethics, to each of her hopeful old girls. In winter she further encouraged them with a flannel petticoat apiece, and there was besides a monthly dole. So that after a year there was, perhaps, on the whole, no progress in learning, the affair wore a tolerably encouraging aspect; for the academy had increased in numbers, and two old fellows, liking

the notion of the broth and the 6d a month – one a barber, Will Potts, ruined by a shake in his right hand, the other a drunken pensioner, Phil Doolan, with a wooden leg – petitioned to be enrolled, and were, accordingly, admitted. Then Aunt Becky visited the gaols, and had a knack of picking up the worst characters there, and had generally two or three discharged felons on her hands. Some people said she was a bit of a Voltarian, but unjustly; for though she now and then came out with a bouncing social paradox, she was a good bitter Churchwoman. So she was liberal and troublesome – off-handed and dictatorial – not without good nature, but administering her benevolences somewhat tyrannically, and for the most part, doing more or less of positive mischief in the process.

ANNOTATION

Apart from **Belmont** (see below), this long paragraph hardly calls for specifics. It contributes little to narrative or plot, yet its importance for the novel should not be underestimated. If the dominant force in the fictional village is the Artillery, we find a displacement of its masculinity by Rebecca Chattesworth's various activities directed towards women, the poor, and a few malefactors. If the narrator adopts a supercilious tone, the cumulative effect suggests a rival presidency of communal life. This mildness will contrast sharply with the gradually disclosed undercurrent of perverted justice hinted at through the nocturnal interment of Chapter II, 'The Nameless Coffin'. With the use of proper names perhaps implicating the 1641 Rebellion and the Castlehaven trial, this violence may not be simply personal or individual: it may characterize an entire society, even a polity.

That the Chattesworth home is called Belmont underscores the theme of justice for, in Shakespeare's *Merchant of Venice*, Portia (the heroine) lives at secluded Belmont; in the play's climactic scene, she will disguise herself as a male lawyer to plead eloquently for justice. By occasionally usurping her brother's command, Aunt Becky also plays the male role; with her broth and six-penny dole, she appreciates 'the quality of mercy' if not perhaps delivering much quantity. Belmont chimes with (van) Helmont, a tribune cited by the rector without enough vigor to keep his audience awake. Each in its strikingly different way – the pound of flesh, the healing sword – insists on a focal wound as the site of possible justice and healing.[15] Together they constitute an unresolved rivalry of judgment. Within this contested field, and suspected by villagers of being a **Voltarian** (cf. Voltaire, François-Marie Arouet,

1694–1788, celebrated skeptic and critic of monarchy), Aunt Becky occupies a complex oppositional role. The narrator scarcely dispels the suspicion, offering a social paradox of his own – Becky is 'a good bitter Churchwoman,' meaning one baptized into the Established Church.

* * *

25 Handsome Captain Devereux – Gipsy Devereux, as they called him for his clear dark complexion – was talking a few minutes later to Lilias Walsingham. Oh, pretty Lilias – oh, true lady – I never saw the pretty crayon sketch that my mother used to speak of, but the tradition of thee has come to me – so bright and tender, with its rose and violet tints, and merry, melancholy dimples, that I see thee now, as then, with the dew of thy youth still on thee, and sigh as I look, as if on a lost, early love of mine.

ANNOTATION

Much of this short paragraph seems to be Victorian sentimental nostalgia. Its utterer, however, is a specific elderly narrator, Charles de Cresseron who, as a 14-year-old, visited his uncle (also Charles), then the curate of Chapelizod. The Le Fanus claimed that the first of their family to reach Ireland was a Charles de Cresserons [sic] who fought for King William at the Battle of the Boyne (1690). The paragraph refers to the rector's daughter, **Lilias**, whereas the narrator (see the Prologue) has visited a curate. Her Christian name, we might add, is uncommon in the eighteenth century, a Scottish variant of Lily.

Gipsy Devereux is a greater problem. Although his surname is not uncommon in east Leinster, for Victorians it still retained a high degree of historical resonance. The impetuous English nobleman, Robert Devereux (1565–1601; second earl of Essex), became a favorite of Elizabeth I, and married Frances, daughter of Sir Francis Walsingham (see above) and widow of Sir Philip Sidney. In 1599, Devereux became Lord Lieutenant of Ireland, having earlier been appointed Chancellor of Dublin University. However, his military campaign was poorly conceived and unsuccessful in its principal objective, defeat of the rebel Hugh O'Neill. He was imprisoned by the Privy Council and, after his release attempted a primitive *coup d'état*, leading to his execution for treason. Several nineteenth-century operas build on his career, notably Mercadante's *Il Conte d'Essex* (1833). When the fictitious Gipsy and Lilias converse, they mime the actual union of a Devereux and a Walsingham.

One might note a Major O'Neill among officers under Chattesworth's command, or his sister's.[16]

* * *

39 'So I would – but by means of my example, not my preaching. No: I leave that to wiser heads – to the rector, for instance' – and she drew closer to the dear old man, with a quick fond glance of such proud affection, for she thought the sun never shone upon his like, as made Devereux sigh a little unconscious sigh. The old man did not hear her – he was too absorbed in his talk – he only felt the pressure of his darling's little hand, and returned it, after his wont, with a gentle squeeze of his cassocked arm, while he continued the learned essay he was addressing to young, queer, erudite, simple Dan Loftus, on the descent of the Decie branch of the Desmonds. There was, by-the-bye, a rumour – I know not how true – that these two sages were concocting between them beside their folios on the Castle of Chapelizod, an interminable history of Ireland.

ANNOTATION

Female deference to the paterfamilias hardly deserves notice in a Victorian novel. Reading at the allusive level, we note that Gipsy and Lilias converse under the untroubled eye of her father. He, however, is distracted from immediate concerns through his discussion of historical research. The topic in question relates to the **Desmond** (i.e. Munster) branch of the powerful Fitzgerald family. From 1569, the Desmond rebellions brought conflict, terror and counter-terror, with officially sponsored famine, conditions which gripped the southern province for more than a decade. It is striking that, in the fiction of Palmerstown's fair green, Walsingham and Loftus discuss the relatively peaceful earlier history of the Desmond Fitzgeralds rather than the famous or notorious rebellion and plantation.

Loftus is by no means a casual choice of name. Adam Loftus (c. 1533–1606) and his nephew-namesake Sir Adam Loftus (c. 1568–1643) played major parts in the protestantizing of Ireland. The younger served as Lord Chancellor of Ireland in the 1630s. Edward Loftus was knighted by Robert Devereux in 1597.

The younger Adam's son, Dudley Loftus (1618–95), is directly relevant. Orientalist scholar and nimble lawyer, he returned from Oxford at an inopportune moment and became caught up in the 1641 Rebellion, successfully defending the city of Dublin. He subsequently aligned with each side in turn, including the Cromwellian. Elizabethanne Boran in *DIB* notes his (second) marriage into the Mervyn family as 'scandalous' in contemporary eyes.[17] A daughter of his first marriage married Thomas Bladen, a sometime Independent minister and occasional Dublin printer, whose family contested Lady Loftus's inheritance in actions lasting into the 1720s. Loftus's publications included a defense of Lady Decies (London, 1677).[18] To summarize the Bladen–Loftus marital nexus, the Revd Thomas Bladen married a daughter of Loftus (probably Letitia, though Jane has also been proposed), and then performed (or at least presided over) the marriage between Loftus and his second wife, Elizabeth Ervin or Mervyn.[19]

The fictional 'young, queer, erudite, simple Dan Loftus' is described in Chapter V as 'a good Irish scholar'.[20] The group on the fair green which includes him, Dr Walsingham, Gipsy Devereux, and at a distance Mr Mervyn, constitutes the most extensive, if still implicit, allusion to eminent historical figures. These are not isolated monads: the historical Loftus had written about the Decies branch of the Desmonds; the fictional Loftus listens to Walsingham on the same general topic; the fictional Loftus is at work on 'an interminable history of Ireland'; Marsh's Library preserves manuscript annals of Irish history compiled by Dudley Loftus.[21]

Beyond the earl of Essex and Sir Francis Walsingham, Dudley Loftus deserves critical attention. Among his surviving papers is an extensive record of Dublin courts martial during 1651–3 under the Commonwealth. These show Loftus to be more than scholar turned emergency soldier; he features as a participant observer (often acting as, formally, the informant) in proceedings leading to repeated inflictions of the death penalty.[22] Le Fanu's characters are presented as almost universally benevolent, gentle, and melancholy, where the earl of Essex or the Elizabethan spymaster or the polyglot Doctor of Laws were not known for niceties of that kind.

Thomas Carlyle, briefly

It is possible now to assess the implications of these notes on proper names encountered in Chapter IV of *The House*. Devereux, Loftus, Mervyn, Walsingham (with Bettesworth/Chattesworth more loosely attached, and Sir John Davies an unnamed possessor) constitute a recognizable string of names from the history of Ireland's invasions and wars, during the late Tudor period through to the Commonwealth. How should the manifest difference of temperament between the historical and the fictional bearers of the names be treated? It seems too easy to invoke Victorian pathos as the first stage of outlining major alterations in behavior (especially male behavior) occurring in the passage of two and half centuries – the increased distance between violence of state and domestic living, the impact of evangelicalism on the practice of charity, the rise of the gentleman, the softening of honor into decorum. For the actions recounted in this Victorian novel have occurred in the eighteenth century, at a midpoint between Tudor aggression and Victorian euphemism.

What readers meet is a three-tier representation, in which the narrator (supposedly a Victorian) employs a linguistic register to recount *actions* trivial and jovial, sinister and seductive, occurring within an earlier discourse at once linguistic and social. Some *actors* are nominated in terms of a yet earlier period, emblemized in the insignia found on the nameless coffin and among the unmistakable Elizabethan and Stuart *nomenklatura*. The emphasis on mild temperament is not seamless – Mervyn can look dangerous and Devereux can murmur threats to resume card-play – but it serves the ends of periodization, by which a *cordon sanitaire* is positioned between the originating offense and its reception into public narrative, holding them apart from each other, without any shared boundary. This is hardly Gothic meat and drink.

As a form of indirect historical enquiry, the early chapters not only set up the nominal markers but establish that certain latter-day fictional namesakes (Loftus and Walsingham) are engaged in their own historical enquiries. These time-consuming hobbies are not to be discounted. Yet the events implied do not include the massacres at Smerwick (1580) or Drogheda (1649). Chapelizod is an anomalous village in the late 1750s or '60s, safe in the arms of the Royal Irish Artillery, which in turn is sweetened by the amiable relations existing between the Catholic priest and his Protestant neighbours. The past violence which will ultimately be disclosed is personal, individual, accountable in terms of sin rather than state policy or imperialism. Nonetheless, there is an acknowledgment of changes in social condition, partly mocking: Mrs MacNamara has it that General Chattesworth is descended from an army tailor and is cousin to a butter dealer living in Cork (# 21). Lilias, as if to balance the scales, playfully suggests that Captain Devereux might join the impoverished barber and pensioner in Aunt Becky's dame-school (# 28). Within the apparently secure village world, upheavals from the past, shiftings in condition, rank or 'status', and intrusions by the not-so-distant metropolis indicate a potential for drastic and transformative revelations. For the Victorian reader of such earlier anxieties, they have already happened: witness 'that grim giant factory, now the grand feature and centre of Chapelizod' (Prologue). But for those readers, and for the characters they review, the most profound changes and upheavals still await disclosure.

Within this three-point dialectic, the novel employs forms of verbal slippage, excess, and mutation. The excess – yarns, digressions, song or verse, colorful if inoffensive oaths, gossip – never wearies, yet it suggests intransitively, by displacing a different topic thus avoided or postponed. A convivial scene in Chapter V brings many notables together at a regimental dinner. Learned Dr Walsingham regales the guest of honor:

> There is, my Lord Castlemallard, a curious old tract of the learned Van Helmont, in which he says, as near as I can remember his words, that magnetism is a magical faculty, which lieth dormant in us by the opiate of original sin, and, therefore, stands in need of an exitator, which exitator may be either good or evil: but it is more frequently Satan himself, by reason of some previous oppignoration or compact with witches. The power, indeed, is in the witch, and not conferred by him: but this versipellous or Protean impostor – these are his words – will not suffer her to know that it is of her own natural endowment, though for the present charmed into somnolent inactivity by the narcotic of primitive sin.

The objective here may be to demonstrate the tedium of Dr Walsingham's delivery, his capacity to bore for Chapelizod alongside the small-bore Brown Besses. Indeed, the narrator admits the charge, 'In the doctor's address and quotation there was so much about somnolency and narcotics, and lying dormant, and opiates, that my Lord Castlemallard's senses forsook him, and he lost, as you, my kind reader, must, all the latter portion of the doctor's lullaby'. In its unfinishedness, Walsingham's longer performance recalls the 'whom we name not' condition associated with Mr Mervyn. His denouement is unheard and so unscripted.

Le Fanu's editor will not nod off. He diligently annotates *oppignoration* as 'the act or instance of pawning or pledging'. At the climax of the paragraph, he meets 'the learned Van Helmont' only to find that two men might earn that tribute: Jan Baptist van Helmont (1579/80–1644), a Flemish early chemist, and his son. The passage to which Walsingham alludes can be found in *A Ternary of Paradoxes; the Magnetick Cure of Wounds, Nativity of Tartar in Wine, Image of God in Man*, Written Originally by Joh. Bapt. Van Helmont and Translated, Illustrated and

Amplified by Walter Charleton.[23] In English the work was dedicated to William Brouncker (1620–84), of Lyons, County Dublin, the second Viscount Brouncker.

The above details may recall that 'series of heroic acts of densely intertextual interpretation' Claire Connolly noted in relation to Edgeworth's *Patronage* (1814).[24] The intensive annotation which *The House* requires follows on interpretations built into the novel itself. When Dr Walsingham cites van Helmont, he places Original Sin more centrally than his Flemish source really justifies. If this is good in a churchman, his sleep-inducing rhetoric effects an incomplete reception of the warning. The very title of Le Fanu's novel suggests imperfect alignments of the social (or domestic) and the theological (or eccle-siastical) edifice. Disestablishment gathers less than a decade away. A Gothic emphasis would play up the closeness of living quarters to burial ground. Instead, it is distance which relates the two, not physi-cal distance but the deep if narrow fissure opening up between doctrine and conduct. In 99 chapters, the novel meanders splendidly through subplot and digression without ever casting off the issue deeply etched in the opening pages. This is Le Fanu's significant narrative grammar – intransitive suggestion, a process which omits the object (or accusative) noun, leaving the reader to fill in the suggestion.

The intrepid well-funded annotator will doubtless read van Helmont closely, together with Loftus manuscripts preserved in Marsh's Library. We might cut here and now to the early chapter where Mr Mervyn is first observed by Dr Walsingham, 'He reminded me of him who is gone, whom we name not'. The plural pronoun involves more than the ageing rector: as in the General Confession, silence on the question of naming is general to sinful mankind. The moment of incomplete recollection is paralleled in Chapter XVIII, when Dr Sturk meets Mr Dangerfield ('a face without a date [...] the outlines of a recollection'). In terms both of narrative and plot, these complement each other; Walsingham will not name, Sturk cannot yet name. However, if a more complex reading of the novel is ventured, within which the reader agrees to consult differ-ent levels of textual implication, then a striking detail quickly emerges from outside any admitted frame of reference.

Consider Thomas Carlyle's *French Revolution*, Book 3, Part 4, Chapter 1, dealing with Charlotte Corday's sole remembered deed:

> And so Marat People's-Friend is ended; the lone Stylites has got hurled down suddenly from his Pillar, – whither He that made him does know. Patriot Paris may sound triple and tenfold, in dole and wail;

re-echoed by Patriot France; and the Convention, 'Chabot pale with terror declaring that they are to be all assassinated', may decree him Pantheon Honours, Public Funeral, Mirabeau's dust making way for him; and Jacobin Societies, in lamentable oratory, summing up his character, parallel him to One, whom they think it honour to call 'the good Sansculotte',—whom we name not here.[25]

If this nails a gnomic phrase, it more capaciously vindicates the scarcely novel idea that mid-Victorian anxieties are traceable to the French Revolution or some legacy of it. Le Fanu had cast French characters as agents of evil within the Irish establishment on the eve of a second Revolution. 'Some Account of the Latter Days of the Hon. Richard Marston of Dunoran' appeared in the *DUM* between April and June 1848, its villainess being Eugenie de Barras. In the June issue, Le Fanu also denounced the incendiary John Mitchel while leaning awkwardly on Carlyle; 'he gave us no pompous metaphors, no affected quaintness, no vapid parodies upon the style of "Sartor Resartus"'.[26] But to whom was the author of *Sartor Resartus* alluding when, in his great history of the first Revolution, he wrote 'whom we name not here'?

The expenses of a stratified reading will be rewarded. At his trial, the Jacobin Camille Desmoulins defended himself with pathos by pointing out that he was old as 'the good sansculotte Jesus, a dangerous age for revolutionaries'.[27] Thus at one level, Le Fanu's Walsingham treats the unknown Mervyn, if not as Christ, then as belonging to the typology of Christ. Is it fanciful to see affinities between Dickens's fiction of revolution, *A Tale of Two Cities* (1859) and Le Fanu's – between Sydney Carton and Gypsy Devereux, for example? The *resurgam* motif literally breaks the surface in Le Fanu's next novel, *Wylder's Hand* (1864) when a hand with a ring thus inscribed protrudes from its slipshod entombment. Historians of Irish literature have yet to assimilate the impact of Jules Michelet and Hippolyte Taine on mid-Victorian representations of France.[28]

We should, then, modify the three-tier dialectic outlined above. Somewhere in that model, the great Revolution must be given a role, however ironized. We note its gross intrusion, because it has been present all along, anxiously unnamed. The principal agent is Carlyle, whose views on the Famine years and after had not endeared him to the survivors. In 1858, his *Collected Works* were published (somewhat prematurely) by Chapman and Hall, with the *French Revolution* central to the edition. France, under Napoleon III, had been once again the focal point of insular anxiety. In Le Fanu's novels and stories the French guest, introduced carelessly into a household, proves fatal to domestic happiness, security, and faith itself. Lord Dunoran, which will turn out to be Mr Mervyn's 'true identity' in *The House*, bears a title already associated with the Francophobia in 'Some Account of the Latter Days' (1848). The most obvious French presence in the novel is the narrator Cresseron, followed by the author himself with his Huguenot name. In Le Fanu's father's library (sold off to pay debts), extensive texts by the arch-anti-revolutionary, Joseph de Maistre (1753–1821) occupied a distinctive position.

'The function of the maze is two-fold: to arrest the intruder by confusing him, and to protect the centre from intrusion' (Michael Ayrton).[29] While apt for Le Fanu, the dictum leaves unasked the question of what is or was to be protected amid the frolics and tale-telling. It cannot simply be the crime which Richard, earl of Dunoran, did not commit. His alleged victim, however, was one Beauclerc, French by implication, to whom Mordaunt/Dunoran had lost heavily at cards. Found guilty, the prisoner committed suicide and, though his body was repatriated it could only be buried surreptitiously in consecrated ground. Hence the rector's non-naming him.[30]

This sounds Gothic enough after ninety or so chapters of devious coding and decoding. Apart from suicide, Mordaunt/Dunoran was innocent, and suicide had not prevented Wolfe Tone's interment in Bodenstown churchyard in 1798. The denouement of Le Fanu's novel involves Beauclerc's actual killer, not the man convicted. The villain was Charles Archer, of whom we have heard little or nothing in the course of Charles de Cresseron's narrative. Trepanned, a dying man names Archer as his assailant, and it takes remarkably few pages to identify Archer with Paul Dangerfield, of whom we have heard much. Convicted, Dangerfield cheats the hangman by asphyxiating himself; thus Charles Nutter, wrongly arrested for the assault, is cleared.

Too many Charleses? And how do these relate (if at all) to the prominent surnames deriving from Elizabethan realpolitik? A feature of the paralleling of historical names with fictional ones had been differentiation effected through the Christian name – thus Robert Devereux is echoed dissonantly in Richard Devereux, Francis in Hugh Walsingham and so on. There is, however, one further fictional Charles Archer, a respectable old English art dealer living abroad: it was certification of his death in Florence which authorized or originated the life of Paul Dangerfield.

But the unique feature of Charles Archer, the fictional character(s), lies in the availability of an actual (not quite historical) Charles Archer, a contemporary of Le Fanu's. Let us approach him cautiously. Charles Palmer Archer (1790–1865) took over the bookseller John Archer's failing business in 1810, persisting for about 16 years at 44 Dame Street.[31] Among the publications which, in the imprint, bear Charles Archer's name and Dublin address is J. G. Spurzheim's *Anatomy of the Brain* (translated from French) appearing in 1826. In the same year, Charles Archer also participated in issuing the same author's *Phrenology in Connection with the Study of Physiology*. The fictional incident which drew a man out of coma to name Archer as his assailant involved trepanning, a surgical operation in which pressure on the brain was reduced by drilling the patient's skull. We have not quite finished with Archer and books: in February 1831, he first registered as a reader at Marsh's Library in Dublin, where Le Fanu also read, commencing in June 1845.

Intransitive narration

Some tentative conclusions are overdue. Conor Carville drew attention to the manner in which Protestant Ascendancy comes into existence through an auxiliary moment – 'in the 1790s Protestant Ascendancy did not exist until it was threatened with reform'. This process jeopardizes any notion of fixed origination, for the same phrase could be repeated with a simple change of date 'in the 1860s Protestant Ascendancy did not exist until…'. The threat of course was Gladstone's, delivered on 23 October 1868. Intensively annotated, *The House* could emerge as a preliminary to that threat, couched (Gothically perhaps) as a warning about heroes or antiheroes who achieve or acquire existence by a kind of self-invention in or through profligacy: Mr Mervyn wins Gertrude Chattesworth by virtue of his disgraced noble father who, simultaneously, is redeemed. In a rare invocation of positive Christian doctrine, Le Fanu cites the Old Testament's 'Song of Solomon', to speak of 'the Redeemer the Bridegroom' (Chapter XCIX).

On such a modest citation of the erotic, a modestly Freudian view of the entire novel might be essayed. Further encouragement occurs in Chapter XCVI ('About the Rightful Mrs Nutter') in which minor complications of plot are tidied away. Aunt Becky, finally realizing that her niece and the redeemed Mervyn are lovers, comments on their extreme discretion: 'that censor must be more severe than I, who would say that concealment in matters of the heart is never justifiable'. Freud ascribed the apparently meaningless character of delusions to internal censorship, comparing it to the appearance of newspapers under the Czarist regime – 'words, whole clauses, and sentences are blacked out so that what is left becomes unintelligible'.[32] Le Fanu's grammar of intransitive suggestion resembles such a mechanism, with the Victorian novel's conventions permitting or requiring the eventual filling in of names, blanks, and romantic unions.

The renowned Oedipus complex found a counterpart in Freud's later work, especially *The Future of an Illusion* (1927) where he advances a view of religion based on longing for a father (*Vatersehnsucht*), a term requiring expansion in English to something more like 'dependency on, in the absence of, the father'. But, for the moment let 'longing' serve. The ambivalence involves the coexistence or overlapping of three basic situations – to long for the father, to long for the dead father, to long for the father [to be] dead. Here Le Fanu's intransitive grammar makes a bid for admission to the domain of metapsychology. *The House* may manifestly revolve round the absence of Mervyn's father (in death and in disgrace). But round the novel as a whole spins the inrushing meteor of disestablishment, Lecky's declining sense of the miraculous, and a skepticism about Hell which infiltrated even Trinity College.

Against the Victorian crisis of faith, and Gladstone's plan for the church establishment, Protestant Ascendancy finds itself through what, by analogy, can be termed an auxiliary moment. Such a cultural process amounts to a transvaluation, in which the grubby commercial monopolies of Dublin's craft guilds in the 1790s are replaced by the myriad rolling acres of landed estate, on the edge of its own disestablishment. The 'traumaculture' detected and deconstructed by Carville is, in some telling ways, a Catholic nationalist countermove, not without its Gothic side. Luke Gibbons virtually makes the admission in the title of his short 1998 reflection on Bloody Sunday, 'History without the Talking Cure'. It is noticeable that those politicized intellectuals most engaged with Bloody Sunday were conspicuous by their absence on the occasion. In the older game as introduced by Le Fanu in *The House*, Protestant Ascendancy played off Dudley Loftus with Dan Loftus, the spymaster Walsingham with the abstracted learned cleric, grafting virtue and villainy on to each other to double the family tree, with – equally – harvests of grandeur and duplicity.

Each of these opposed and complementary ideologies supposes a point of origination which, however, can only be authenticated second-hand through its 'repetition'. Origination, consequently, is always the consequence of something which follows it. Both parties invoke land as the grounding of origination in the physical world – the Catholic nationalists working the complaint of confiscated property (under Elizabeth, James, Cromwell, or William), the Protestant Ascendancy exchanging the same property for title to an antecedent cultural eminence. The much sought-after confidence in be-longing raises only specters. To belong *in* a place is to belong *to* it, to be possessed by it (and not vice versa): the longing is a Plato's cave-picture of certified ownership.[33]

Notes

1. Compare Seamus Deane (1997) 'Landlord and Soil; *Dracula*' in *Strange Country* (Oxford: Oxford University Press), pp. 89–94.
2. In 1855 Le Fanu wrote drawing Gilbert's attention to material in the King's Inn Library, Dublin. He added, 'I have myself got a volume of rare tracts relating to Ireland, some of which illustrate Dublin. One, for instance, describes the ceremonial of the entrance of James II., and which I would be most happy to lend you'. See Rosa Mulholland, Lady Gilbert (1905) *Life of Sir John T. Gilbert, Irish Historian and Archivist* (London: Longman), pp. 56–7.
3. Conor Carville (2011) *The Ends of Ireland: Criticism, History, Subjectivity* (Manchester: Manchester University Press), pp. 23–59 (Chapter 2: ' "Keeping that Wound Green": Luke Gibbons, Traumaculture, and the Subject of Exclusion').
4. Jean Laplanche and Jean-Bertrand Pontalis (1988) *The Language of Psychoanalysis*, trans. Donald Nicholson-Smith (London: Karnac), p. 111.
5. Sigmund Freud (1921; 2001) 'Group Psychology and Analysis of the Ego' in *The Standard Edition of the Complete Psychological Works of Sigmund Freud*, ed. James Strachey, vol. 18 (London: Vintage), pp. 65–143. Neo- or post-Freudians took up group psychology in its own right, notably the feminist, Karen Horney.
6. See James Strachey (ed.) (2001) *The Standard Edition of the Complete Psychological Works of Sigmund Freud*, vol. 2 (London: Vintage), pp. 106–24 ('Miss Lucy R. Age 30) and pp. 125–34 ('Katharina—'); see also 'The Neuro-Psychoses of Defence' in *The Standard Edition of the Complete Psychological Works of Sigmund Freud*, vol. 3, pp. 45–61, esp. p. 50.
7. Carville, *The Ends of Ireland*, p. 137; see W. J. Mc Cormack (1993) *Dissolute Characters; Irish Literary History through Balzac, Sheridan Le Fanu, Yeats and Bowen* (Manchester: Manchester University Press), pp. 185–6.
8. On Davies and Chapelizod, see Francis Elrington Ball (n.d.) *The History of the County of Dublin* (Part 4) (Dublin: Thom), p. 165. For a recent account of Davies' writings see Jean R. Brink (2007) 'Sir John Davies: Lawyer and Poet' in *Ireland and the Renaissance, c. 1540–1660*, ed. Thomas Herron and Michael Potterton (Dublin: Four Courts Press), pp. 88–104.
9. Walter E. Houghton (ed.) (1987) *The Wellesley Index to Victorian Periodicals 1824–1900*, vol. 4 (Toronto: University of Toronto Press; London: Routledge), pp. 193–370.
10. See Michael Sadleir (1951) *XIX Century Fiction*, 2 vols (London: Constable), I: 200–3; also Wayne Hall (2011), 'Le Fanu's House by the Marketplace' in *Reflections in a Glass Darkly: Essays on J. Sheridan Le Fanu*, ed. G. W. Crawford et al. (New York: Hippocampus), pp. 174–88.

11. Paragraphs are numbered, preceded by #.
12. See Frances Elizabeth Dolan (1994) *Dangerous Familiars: Representations of Domestic Crime in England 1550–1700* (Ithaca, NY: Cornell University Press), pp. 79–87.
13. The surname Toole or O'Toole (in Gaelic Ó Tuathail) was common in Wicklow; at least four bearers of the name are cited in the courts martial records involving Dudley Loftus; see n. 22 below.
14. Ball, *The History of the County of Dublin*, p. 176n.
15. Van Helmont, a not uncritical disciple of Paracelsus and a practical experimentalist, held that a weapon-salve could cure wounds by being applied to the sword or knife which caused them.
16. During serialization of *The House*, the *DUM* also carried the multi-part 'Story of the First Earl of Tyrone', by H. F. Hore.
17. James Maguire and James Quinn (eds) (2009) *Dictionary of Irish Biography*, 9 vols (Cambridge: Cambridge University Press; Dublin: Royal Irish Academy), V:540–2. Loftus was 75 at the time. George Stokes (1900) *Some Worthies of the Irish Church* (London: Hodder) gives the bride as 'the Lady Catherine Mervyn', but the parish register of St John records the marriage of Dudley Loftus Dr of the Law and Lady Elizabeth Erwin on 11 May 1693: the prebendary, Thomas Bladen, held office from 1660 until his death in 1695.
18. *Lady Decies' Marriage Asserted*, London: [*s. n.*], 1677.
19. While a minister at Drogheda, Bladen had married Catherine Turner in 1657, in St Michan's COI, Dublin.
20. Dudley Loftus had in his possession more than one manuscript devoted to Gaelic and its grammar, e.g. Marsh's Library Ms Z. 3. 4. 19 (Fra Bonaventura, 'Grammaticae Hibernicae Rudimenta', dated 1655).
21. Marsh's Library, Dublin, Ms. Z. 4. 2. 7. The list of Loftus Mss runs to 38 items, some very substantial. Apart from legal, military, and political material, there are files devoted to medicine, philosophy, and languages. Edmund Curtis published 'The Court Book of Esker and Crumlin, 1592–1600' in the *Journal of the Royal Society of Antiquaries of Ireland* 19.1 (30 June 1929), 45–64 and 19.2 (31 December 1929), 128–48, and 20.1 (30 June 1930), 38–51 and 20.2 (31 December 1930), 137–49. In the final instalment he commented on Loftus's ownership of the MS.
22. See Heather MacLean, Ian Gentles, and Micheál O Siuchrú (2011) 'Minutes of Courts Martial Held in Dublin, 1651–1653' *Archivium Hibernicum* 64, 56–165. Many cases were trials of serving soldiers on disciplinary charges, but some others led to sentences of death being passed on civilian women accused of spying.
23. 'Now Satan excites this *Magicall power* (otherwise dormant, and impeded by the *Science* of the *outward man*) in his vassals: and the same awaked into activity serves them instead of a sword, or instrument of revenge in the hand of a potent adversary, that is the *Witch*. Nor doth Satan adser any thing at all to the perpetration of the murder, more then the bare *excitation* of the somnolent *power*, and a consent of the *Will*, which in Witches is for the most part subject to his compulsion: for which two contributions, the damned miscreant, as if the whole *energy* of the act were soly attributary to himself requires by compact, a constant homage, a firme and irrevocable

oppignoration, and devout adoration at least, and frequently a surrender of the very soule into his possession'; Joh. Bapt. Van Helmont [1650] *A Ternary of Paradoxes* (London: Flesher), pp. 58–9.

24. Claire Connolly (2005) ' "A Big Book about England"? Private and Public Meanings in *Patronage'*, in *The Irish Novel in the Nineteenth Century: Facts and Fictions*, ed. Jacqueline Belanger (Dublin: Four Courts Press), 63–79 (p. 68).

25. Thomas Carlyle (1839) *French Revolution* (2nd ed.; London: Fraser), III: 211–12. For discussion of phantasmagoria in Carlyle and Le Fanu, see James Walton (2007) *Vision and Vacancy: the Fictions of J. S. Le Fanu* (Dublin: University College Dublin Press), p. 169.

26. Quoted in W. J. Mc Cormack (1980) *Sheridan Le Fanu and Victorian Ireland* (Oxford: Clarendon Press), p. 105. Le Fanu was to be proved wrong: Mitchel's *Jail Journal* (1854) is composed in a Germanic style of savage irony heavily indebted to Carlyle.

27. Egon Friedell (2009) *A Cultural History of the Modern Age, Baroque, Rococo and Enlightenment* (New York: Transaction Books), p. 383.

28. In *Dublin 1916: the French Connection* (Dublin: Gill and Macmillan, 2012), I suggest that Patrick Pearse's blood-sacrifice rhetoric draws heavily on French right-wing ideology of the 1890s, which in turn mobilizes implications found in Michelet etc.

29. Quoted in David Gates (1984) ' "A Dish of Village Chat": Narrative Technique in Sheridan Le Fanu's *The House by the Churchyard'*, *The Canadian Journal of Irish Studies* 10.1, 63–9 (p. 64).

30. In Chapter XCVI, it is disclosed that no *verdict* of suicide had been returned, the coroner's jury having found the evidence inconclusive.

31. See Maire Kennedy (1996) 'The Domestic and International Trade of a Dublin Bookseller, John Archer' *Dublin Historical Record* 19.2, 94–105; also (under Archer, John), M. Pollard (2000) *A Dictionary of Members of the Dublin Book Trade, 1550–1800* (London: Bibliographical Society). Charles Palmer Archer served as Lord Mayor of Dublin in 1833–4.

32. Quoted in Laplanche and Pontalis, *The Language of Psychoanalysis*, p. 66.

33. Compare Carville, *The Ends of Ireland*, p. 159: 'Mc Cormack errs […] by refusing to grant any conceptual weight to the various forms of belonging'.

9

Muscling Up: Bram Stoker and Irish Masculinity in *The Snake's Pass*

Jarlath Killeen

Masculinity, despite its reputation, is rather a fragile attribute. It is extraordinarily vulnerable to all manner of attack and quite easy to undermine. A given man's grasp of it at any stage of life is precarious to say the least, and most men appear to feel a constant need to assert, defend, apply, and uphold it. As the great historian of masculinity Michael Kimmel puts it, from the start of the nineteenth century at least, men have expended a great deal of energy in a 'relentless effort to prove their masculinity', however that masculinity was defined: 'men have been afraid of not measuring up to some vaguely defined notions of what it means to be a man, afraid of failure'.[1] Fear rather than (or at least, as well as) power has stalked the quest for masculinity, and when fears need to be addressed, the Gothic genre has long been useful as a means by which the cultural and existential battle could be fought. The Gothic genre has been concerned with masculinity since its inception. Horace Walpole's *The Castle of Otranto* (1764) begins with an enormous helmet crushing delicate, weakly Conrad, a poor excuse for a man, as if to warn against alternatives to hegemonic masculinity, and ends with Alphonso the Great assuming gigantic size and asserting the metaphysical power of primogeniture and normativity. Although much critical attention has rightly been paid to what Barbara Creed famously called the 'monstrous-feminine',[2] the way femininity and femaleness has been consistently monstered in modernity, the heroes of the Gothic genre are as likely to be in battle with a degraded and dangerous version of masculinity as they are with a she-beast. Recently, critics (including Creed) have turned to examine the way in which the Gothic interrogates varieties of masculinity,[3] and often pits these versions against one another in a fight to the death.[4] This chapter examines the Gothic treatment of masculinity by one Irish master of the form, Bram Stoker, a self-made

168

man fully engaged in the gender wars of the late nineteenth century, and demonstrates to what extent such concerns were, for him at least, deeply imbricated in national politics.

Look at any photograph of Bram Stoker and one thing is immediately obvious: he was a big man. Bulky, broad-shouldered, barrel-chested and burly, and, standing six feet two inches tall with a thick beard, weighing about 175 pounds, he was an embodiment of a certain raw kind of masculinity (and was very proud of this fact), a 'big, red-bearded, untidy Irishman', as Horace Wyndham called him.[5] As well as being manly himself, Stoker was fascinated with muscles and masculinity, as anyone who reads their way through his 13 novels would attest. Many of the protagonists of his fiction are physically massive men whose impressive physique is symbolic of their profound moral and psychological goodness. Archie Hunter, the hero of Stoker's 1902 novel *The Mystery of the Sea* describes himself as possessing a 'big body', 'athletic powers', and 'naturally vast strength', and throughout the story is given more opportunities to take off his shirt and display his musculature for the appreciation of both the reader and the woman he loves than the average Hollywood action hero.[6] Rupert Sent Leger of *The Lady of the Shroud* (1909) is similarly physically endowed, described as 'in the very prime of life, of almost giant stature and strength [...] inured to every kind of hardship [...] In a word he is a man whose strength and daring fit him for any enterprise of any kind'.[7] Grizzly Dick, of *The Shoulder of Shasta* (1895), is another enormous male specimen, a 'mighty fine figure of a man', 'big and strong', animated by powerful strength and what Stoker calls 'exuberant vitality', a 'splendid specimen of natural manhood'.[8] An Wolf, the hero of Stoker's novel *The Man* (1905) (a revealing title) is 'more than six foot two in height, deep-chested, broad shouldered, lean flanked, long armed [...with an overall] appearance of strength [...] which marks the successful athlete'.[9]

This intense focus on the powerful male can be found even in *Dracula* (1897). Lord Godalming is described as looking godlike when he stakes his vamped fiancée Lucy: 'He looked like a figure of Thor as his untrembling arm rose and fell, driving deeper and deeper the mercy bearing stake'.[10] We are probably not supposed to think that Arthur possesses a physique as imposing as that of Chris Hemsworth, hunky star of the most recent adaptation of the superhero comic, but this is the image that pops into my mind. The exuberant American Quincey P. Morris, who carries a very large bowie knife, not so much a substitute as an extension of his phallic power, is consistently praised for his masculine potency. On first seeing him, Van Helsing announces: 'You're a man, and no mistake [...] God sends us men when we want them'.[11] In *Lady Athlyne* (1908), the male hero is a 'very masculine person' with an enormously 'strong arm', with which he saves Joy Ogilvie from a fall into a ravine.[12] Adam Salton, protagonist of *The Lair of the White Worm* (1911), Stoker's final and most bizarre novel, is also a mighty example of masculinity, possessing a 'strong, mobile face [...] set in flint' and fixed of purpose, and a healthy physique able to cope with long periods of physical stress and activity.[13]

All told, nearly all of Stoker's heroes are muscle men, their bodies often on dramatic display, openly admired by the other characters and clearly meant to be admired by the readers too. However, if muscle men are everywhere in his fiction, this is not because of a merely personal obsession on Stoker's part, but because muscle men were everywhere in late Victorian culture.

To take one, very famous example: in 1877, a striking bronze sculpture was unveiled at the Royal Academy in London. It depicted an extraordinary scene of a man, his large and powerful muscles tensed and flexed to the limits of contraction, an impressive display of what Kenneth Clark calls a 'muscle landscape',[14] struggling with an enormous snake which has coiled itself around his body, the snake's open mouth held away from the man's head only by his muscular outstretched arm. It was called 'Athlete wrestling with a python' and had been sculpted by the President of the Royal Academy, Frederic Leighton. The figure became something of a *cause célèbre* after its first showing as commentators worried about the ultimate victor in the battle between man and serpent. Some were convinced that the snake had the better of the sportsman, art critic and writer John Ruskin certain of the ability of the python to defeat the athlete; more, though, thought the athlete would endure and overcome, seeing in his astonishingly muscular body not simply physical strength but moral and spiritual purity as well, a purity that would prevail over the metaphysical darkness represented by the serpent.[15]

Stoker himself had undergone a struggle not unlike that depicted in the sculpture. Born in Clontarf, then a coastal town outside of Dublin city, he had been extremely ill and physically weak as a child, so ill indeed that he spent a large amount of time laid up in bed. In his volume reminiscing about his boss, the actor Henry Irving, Stoker writes that 'till I was about seven years old I never knew what it was to stand upright'.[16] This period of his life – the first seven years in which he was effectively laid up in bed, (possibly) near to death – must have had an extraordinary impact on Stoker's personal psychology, since, as Barbara Belford points out, it meant that he never went through the normal childhood experiences of learning to walk through crawling and toddling and was instead carried everywhere by others, living on sofas and beds.[17] His early years, then, were those of an invalid, although exactly what was wrong with him remains something of a mystery, but by the time he began his writing career he had miraculously overcome his frail past to become an immensely successful athlete, the 'Athletic Champion of Dublin' while an undergraduate at Trinity College, and an all-round proponent of male physical power. His early life in bed may have made him shy, but he later wrote that his physical prowess and imposing stature helped to overcome any social ineptitude he felt and he became a favourite in the undergraduate community. His status as what we would now call a 'jock' was certainly helpful in terms of popularity and social lubrication.

His athletic achievements while a teenager in Trinity are extraordinary for someone who had been so fragile earlier.[18] There hardly seems to have been a sport in which he did not participate, and he apparently excelled in rugby, walking races, gymnasium, slingshot, high jump, trapeze, and rowing. He was on the rugby team, and in 1867 won prizes for weightlifting and for the five- and seven-mile walks. In *Personal Reminiscences of Henry Irving* (1906), Stoker recalled that he 'won numerous silver cups for races of various kinds' and 'was physically immensely strong': 'In fact I feel justified in saying that I represented in my own person something of that aim of university education *mens sana in corpore sano*'.[19] Although he was academically fine as a student, he was clearly more interested in the athletic scene and distracted by his sporting activities.

Stoker's devotion to the muscular man can also be seen in his simpering fan mail to Walt Whitman, whose too-close-to-the-bone eroticization of the athletic, warrior body in his collection of poems, *Leaves of Grass* (1855) had caused much discomfort in critical circles. In Whitman's poetry, the 'body electric' and comradely love between men was exalted, and he was accused of preaching licentiousness. But Whitman seemed to Stoker to articulate exactly the kind of approbation the male body both needed and deserved. In 1872, Stoker wrote to Whitman himself (though was too shy to post the letter), detailing his athletic achievements and his physical characteristics: 'I am six feet two inches high and twelve stone weight naked and used to be forty-one or forty-two inches round the chest. I am ugly but strong and determined', he insisted, grateful for the chance to speak to a man as straightforward about delighting in the male body as he was himself: 'How sweet a thing it is for a strong healthy man with a woman's eyes and a child's wishes to feel that he can speak so to a man who can be if he wishes father, and brother and wife to his soul'.[20] Stoker later defended Whitman against accusations of indecency at a meeting of the Fortnightly Club, on Valentine's Day 1876, praising Whitman's philosophy of male comradeship. Although psycho-biographers have found plenty of things to say about both Stoker's Whitman-worship and his emphasis on male physicality in his own work, reading them as indicative of incompletely repressed homoerotic desire, what I would say is that Stoker is a good representative of a cultural tendency in this period to fetishize a certain kind of masculine physique, the body that is athletic and active, the body that visually displays its inner power through external muscular prominence. Moreover, Whitman had read Daniel Jacques's *Hints Towards Physical Perfection* (1859) which insisted on a link between healthy physicality and healthy nationhood, and the connection between the individual and the national body made throughout his poetry must have touched a chord in Stoker. In his fiction he often returns to the idea that America represents the future for mankind, a future embodied in the noble physique of her young men. In *Dracula*, Dr Seward remarks of Quincey that 'If America can go on breeding men like that, she will be a power in the world indeed'.[21] But America was not the only nation where the male physique and national future were intimately connected.

Stoker's athleticism and his writing up of the muscular body in his fiction mark him as representative of the fact that, by the 1870s, the muscular body of a male athlete had become something of a Victorian pinup. Indeed, the first manual of physical development for British men, appropriately called *Manly Exercise*, appeared in 1865. The manual advised men to carry out a series of strenuous exercises including the use of dumbbells in order not just to become healthy, but also to signify that internal health through possession of a particular kind of body shape. The sculpture of the athlete struggling with a python was merely imaging in bronze a perfected version of the ideal British male body. Through the movement known as 'muscular Christianity', connected with prominent public figures like Charles Kingsley and Thomas Hughes, and propagated through Young Men's Christian Associations, Working Men's Clubs, and most importantly through the emphasis on sports in the public schools, the built male body had become an iconic image of perfected masculinity, the muscular body transformed into an insignia of what real men should aspire towards. For muscular Christians the brawny male body was considered to embody Englishness itself. The muscular Christian ideal combined the emphasis on perfected physical masculinity found in Greek and Roman sculpture with the Christian concept of the body as the temple of the Holy Spirit.[22]

The important thing to remember is that the athletic man was not simply strong in body, but also strong in mind and morality, which gave him a kind of priestly authority. In battle with a degraded external world, full of moral compromises and depravity, the warrior hero, like Hercules – the mythological champion with great pecs and abs – could achieve greatness. The bigger his chest, the more likely it was that a man would win the moral as well as the physical battles he would face in his life. A very developed muscular body suggested that the man who possessed it had in fact transcended mere physicality itself.[23] The physically weak man, in contrast, was an example of someone who had allowed his own body to defeat him, and you wouldn't want such a man beside you in the battle of life. As the British Empire expanded, the athlete became ever more important as the ideal to which the British male should aspire.

Given the amount of cultural attention it attracted, it is no wonder that Stoker tried to live up to this ideal in his own life as well as lavishing so much attention on it in his fiction, and he was recognized as an example of such moral and physical prowess by his contemporaries. Indeed, when, in September 1882, he memorably risked his own life by rescuing a man who tried to commit suicide by diving into the Thames, *The Entr'acte* congratulated Henry Irving for his fortune in 'having for his manager a muscular Christian like Mr. Bram Stoker'.[24] However, muscles bring anxiety as well as power. One of the great concerns in this period was that there were simply not enough strong men around to prop the empire up. Having read Charles Darwin very carefully, muscular Christians understood the implications of the view set out in *The Descent of Man* (1871) that a race needs to be strong in order to survive – the survival of the (physically and morally) fittest. As a version of social Darwinism took hold of the public mind, a conviction that evolution also contained the possibility of degeneration became very popular. A strong species could deteriorate, become weak and unable to defeat the forces of darkness, best represented by that great icon of depravity, the serpent which tempted man in the Garden of Eden. If the serpent defeated the athlete, then Britain itself would degenerate and the evolutionary drive would be turned back on itself. In life, Stoker had defeated the serpent of sickness that had almost killed him as a child; in his fiction, he constantly returned to the imagery of the athlete battling the snake as if to re-enact his personal battle again and again, and through this personal war represent the cultural anxieties to which he was so attuned.

It is no surprise that *The Lair of the White Worm*, that weird, compelling final novel of his, is built on the struggle between strong men and serpentine evil. The plot – if it has one – concerns the attempt by the hero Adam to banish an ancient evil embodied in his neighbor, Lady Arabella, who can also transform into the White Worm of the title. The central struggle propelling the plot forward is that between an embodiment of Saxon, athletic masculinity and a serpentine malignity for the future of England itself. I read the novel as a narrative version of the sculpture of the athlete struggling with the python. If the hero, Adam, is defeated by the White Worm, then he will have repeated the failure of his biblical predecessor and mankind will fall again into the hands of a satanic menace. Degeneration, one of the great fears of the period, will have won out. As well as being metaphysically evil, the Worm represents the superstitious, pagan past into which Britain could degenerate should it lose the battle to discipline the bodies of its menfolk. Bram Stoker was future-oriented, by which I mean he valued what he considered progressive and was fascinated by technological innovation, agricultural reform, and capitalist economics, and his novels aggressively reject anything considered to inhibit embrace of this future. He hated the 'forces of conservatism'. Things representative of the past, such as the medieval Catholic Dracula, or the pagan White Worm, need to be defeated by strong men fully in charge of the technological tools of tomorrow.

At the heart of the novel I think there is a relatively simple ideological battle going on, and this is the struggle between pre-Christian forces of the ancient past and the future-oriented powers of Protestant Christianity. The struggle of the athlete against the snake in Leighton's sculpture is here a national drama for the redeemed masculinity of the Saxon race. Whether other races and ethnicities could be considered capable of muscular physicality was a serious issue in the late nineteenth century given the belief that perfect physicality was associated so firmly in the public mind with Anglo-Saxon masculinity. Indeed, for an Irishman like Stoker this was even more problematic because far from being imaged as an athlete bulging with muscular power and proportion, Irish nationalist masculinity was often represented as both pagan and serpentine in the English press, and the old story of George and the dragon was resurrected in order to give a narrative coherence to the difficulties in which England found its relations with Ireland.

In *Judy* magazine, 26 October 1881, the forces of the Land League (a nationalist organization agitating for agrarian rights) were caricatured as a serpent against which English law and order were fighting. After the Phoenix Park murders in 1882 (when the Irish Chief Secretary, who represented British power in Ireland, was murdered by a nationalist group called the 'Invincibles'), nationalist violence was depicted as a serpent with the head of Charles Stewart Parnell, on 17 May, also in *Judy*.[25] The challenge for a proponent of muscular masculinity like Stoker, and one who was so obviously Irish (unlike Oscar Wilde, for example, he never gave up his Irish accent, and his red hair and voice left his country of origin easily legible), was to find a way to shift the imagery of Irish manhood from the serpentine to the athletic in as smooth a fashion as possible.

Stoker certainly believed the Irish capable of muscular power. In his address to Trinity College's Historical Society in 1872, 'The Necessity for Political Honesty', Stoker noted that the 'Anglo-Saxon race is dwindling', but believed that 'the Irish race has all the elements of greatness' insisting that 'the Celtic race is waking up from its long lethargy'.[26] This was a position that contradicted dominant cultural versions of Irish masculinity. The snake-like Irish had famously been considered a 'feminine' race, more interested in poetry and superstition than industry and technology, an association not particularly helpful to nationalist modernizers like Stoker who wanted a progressive and transformed Ireland to take a proud place in the British Empire. Moreover, because of their 'feminine' nature, the Irish were not believed to be capable of incarnating that insignia of rational futurity, the proportionate and athletic male body. Gendering the Irish 'feminine' race not only supports the language used in defining the domestic relationship between husband and wife, thus reinforcing sexual relations in the 'home' country, but also justifies the colonial presence in the feminized colony. Colonial rule was thus naturalized as the necessary expression of a naturally gendered cosmos: gender hierarchy and male control were naturalized as the ultimate referents of the colonial mission.

Perhaps the most famous expression of this division is to be found in Matthew Arnold's lectures on Celtic literature, where he claims that 'No doubt the sensibility of the Celtic nature, its nervous exaltation, have something feminine in them, and the Celt is thus peculiarly disposed to feel the spell of the feminine idiosyncrasy; he has an affinity to it; he is not far from its secret [...]'.[27] This stance allowed him both to celebrate the beauties of Celtic literature, but also insist that Home

Rule could never be granted to such an irrational and effeminate race. Such effeminate races and nations were best served by a colonial arrogation of power, where the masculine forces of Britain would lovingly take them in a firm hand and show them how to behave. For many, Ireland was England's rather defiant wife, the Union between the countries being considered analogous to a marriage in which Ireland was always to occupy the passive female role, beautiful Hibernia to England's John Bull. Those who were not typically 'feminine' in Ireland (Irish nationalists, for example) were not granted the tribute of therefore being considered 'masculine', but were rather seen as atavistic and degenerate perversions of the masculine norm, Neanderthal, simian, drunken and randomly violent, figured in the popular press as hairy and degenerate beasts.[28] As expertly anatomized by Joseph Valente, Irish men were trapped between 'the feminizing discourse of Celticism and the bestializing discourse of simianization, which cooperated in representing the "mere" Irish as racially deficient in manhood and so unready for emancipation'.[29]

As an Irish man who supported Home Rule, these kinds of identification must have been worrying for Stoker, and perhaps, in his own struggle with mastery of his body and his attaining of an impressive physique, he believed he had managed to instantiate in himself one means to extricate Ireland from this dilemma. Another was to celebrate and propagandize in favour of alternative versions of Irish manhood which broke free of the emasculated/simian dichotomy, and I think his very early novel, *The Snake's Pass* (1889),[30] tries to do precisely this. It is set in the west of Ireland and concerns the adventures of a young heroic Englishman, Arthur Severn, who helps to destroy a contemporary embodiment of pagan Irishness, the moneylender Black Murdock, who is also a kind of reincarnation of the prehistoric 'King of the Snakes' who had been banished by the Christian Saint Patrick. Along the way Severn falls in love with the native girl, Norah Joyce, as well as the country (and the county) from which she hails. He also encounters different versions of Irish masculinity, and helps to exorcize the country of both the passive and the atavistic caricatures to which Ireland had been subject since the 1860s.

The degraded Irish male is represented by 'Black' Murdock, a caricatured version of a *Punch*-derived caricature, and he is both aggressively masculine and hysterically effeminate, a monstrous hybrid out-of-control. His serpentine atavism is connected to another ophidian presence, the 'shifting bog', to which he appears peculiarly attached. His atavism is indicated not merely by the relative darkness of his skin and the side whiskers referred to throughout the novel as signifiers of his demonic orientation, but to his perverse desire for the bog. In his desperate search for gold lost on the bog during the 1798 rebellion, Murdock comes upon what he thinks is a chest containing the treasure and arranges to have it pulled out. The degradation to which Murdock has sunk is indicated by his reaction to the object retrieved:

> It certainly was most filthy. It was a shapeless, irregular mass, but made solid with rust and ooze and the bog surface through which it had been dragged. The slime ran from it in a stream; but its filth had no deterring power for Murdock, who threw himself down beside it and actually kissed the nauseous mass [...].[31]

An apparently solid surface is a disguise for the mutability beneath, and the bog's connection with Murdock is clear enough: he looks like a solidly masculine figure, but he is really more like Count Dracula, an amorphous mass able to take various shapes, whose ability to metamorphose and become a wolf, or mist, indicates a dangerous lack of physical solidity and medieval contrariness. Murdock, like the bog, is radically indeterminate in physical terms, and it is only right that he ends up being swept into the sea by the shifting bog, ultimately becoming one with it completely.

Murdock is the kind of man the Irish need to be rid of if they are to become engines of modernity. Stoker had Irish men, other than himself, to draw on as potential models for his ideal Irish male. Indeed, he wrote to the nationalist leader, Michael Davitt, seeking his endorsement for *The Snake's Pass* (and probably a good review as well). Davitt is an interesting figure for Stoker to have chosen when looking for support. Like the author, Davitt too had undergone a severe and life-threatening physical struggle in his early life when his right arm was ripped out in an accident in a Lancashire cotton mill in 1857 when he was 12 years old. Despite this physical handicap he had gone on to become the leader of a remarkable mass movement in the 1880s. It is hardly surprising that Stoker should have admired him, and in seeking Davitt's endorsement he indicated that they were essentially part of the same modernizing process. If Stoker admired Davitt's masculine legitimacy, he also appears to have respected the version of masculinity activated by the Gaelic Athletic Association (GAA), or at least he has his protagonist, Arthur Severn, speak approvingly about the physique of the GAA figure gathered with him to listen to the folklore and legends of the King of the Snakes in the Widow Kelligan's shebeen. On hearing how the King of the Snakes demanded the annual sacrifice of a 'live baby', and that the community apparently acquiesced, one customer is outraged: ' "But did none of the min do nothin'?" said a powerful-looking young fellow in the orange and green jersey of the Gaelic Athletic Club, with his eyes flashing; and he clinched his teeth' (p. 12). The player knows what kind of men would allow such a sacrifice to take place, and they are not his type – they are probably the emasculated, effeminate men associated with an Arnoldian version of Irishness.

The GAA, of course, had been set up precisely in order to banish that image of masculine passivity forever. The Association was formed in 1888 by Michael Cusack, who complained vociferously about the weakened build of Irish men since the Famine, describing how, in the words of an article in the *Democrat* in 1893, 'their physique in general had deteriorated and [...] the young men walked with stooped shoulders and a shambling gait'.[32] Cusack accepted that Irishmen had become effeminate versions of men, but also insisted the Irish male could be remade, and the man he took as the model for this remaking was himself. He described hurling – one of the main exercises advocated for the remaking of the Irish male body – as having been invented by 'the most sublimely energetic and warlike race that the world had ever known', a direct reversal of Arnold's notions of the Celt as being close to the secret of femininity.[33] For Cusack, it was important that Irish men would become 'Strong-men' first, before they were able to take on the responsibilities of being 'Freemen'.[34]

In his reference to 'Strong-men', Cusack probably had in mind the emerging 'sport' of bodybuilding fast spreading in popularity through the Continent. The new figure of the bodybuilder was best represented by its most famous advocate. Eugen Sandow was born Friedrich Müller in East Prussia in 1867, and had risen to fame as the first bodybuilder. He traveled all over Europe displaying his 'perfect body' in packed stadia where men and women were invited to simply stare at him as a representative and example of what the male body could (and should) be able to achieve given enough will and concentration.[35] The displayed male body was central to bodybuilding routines, and also to sporting organizations which took some inspiration from the celebration of perfected physicality. Indeed, the displayed and spectacular muscular male body was central to the GAA's definition of itself. Its games were not only for playing but for spectacle: the GAA player was an athlete not only for himself but as a displayed icon for his country. One observer described a typical game in the Irish winter: 'two or three dozen young fellows with naked arms, naked heads, naked feet, and clad only in a light silken jersey and drawers [...] Our young men stripped and fought fiercely for victory, utterly heedless of cold or danger'.[36] It is the muscular display that is important in this description, a display that helped to redefine attitudes to the male body itself. The muscular body is a power symbol, proof that far from being flaccid, the Irish are as muscularly advanced as their English masters. As Valente insists, the GAA must be seen then, not 'as a purely match playing organization, but rather a training ground for the Irish physique'.[37]

Given the kind of body being rebuilt by the GAA, it is understandable that Stoker's hero Arthur should gaze in admiration at the young GAA member in the pub. The player's words suggest that he would have taken care of business had he been around in the days of the King of the Snakes. In what is possibly a subtle reference to Leighton's sculpture, the implication is that this particular athlete would certainly have defeated the serpent. Given the GAA's commitment to Irish self-legitimation, and the long-held association between the muscular male physique and authority, the scene of the Englishman gazing with approbation on the built body of the Irish athlete carries symbolic weight which effectively bolsters the campaign for Irish Home Rule. If the Irish can indeed produce these kinds of bodies, then there is no reason to deny them the right of self-government too. Severn's approval of the Irish athlete's body is echoed by his later admiration for the bodies of the Irish workers who are assisting his friend, Dick Sutherland. They are, he says, 'fine strapping young fellows' who 'seemed interested in the work' – indicating a scientific orientation – and their presence makes the 'contingent strong enough', strength being the important quality here (p. 77).

Although Arthur never describes his own body shape, we understand that he has been a proponent of athletic masculinity from his boyhood since, in a fight with Black Murdock, he uses the skills he developed on the playing fields to his advantage. When Murdock rushes at him, 'with an old foot-ball trick' Arthur tumbles him over (p. 146). Moreover, it is with this display of physical prowess that he convinces Norah's father that he is the right man for his daughter; the father approvingly tells Norah: 'he shtruck a good blow for ye this night' (p. 149). In addition, when he negotiates with Joyce over his marriage to Norah, Arthur insists: 'I am man enough to do what is best for her' (p. 123). Evidence of Severn's physical strength is demonstrated for the reader numerous times in the novel. The ideological implication of such moments is that the GAA member and the public-school-trained athlete have more in common than anything that divides in terms of their place on the evolutionary scale, and also that Ireland's future is safe enough in the hands of such figures as the GAA player who, like St Patrick, are well capable of driving the snakes of Irish atavism out of the country.

Indeed, St Patrick too is presented in the legend as in possession of an impressively sized body, and when he confronts the King of the Snakes, 'his whole forum seemed to swell out an' get bigger an' bigger', like a tumescent penis, confronting a degraded version of the phallus in the shape of the King of the Snakes (p. 13). As Rosalind Miles has emphasized, in the act of building the body's musculature,

> Each [man] becomes a public phallus, huge, rock-hard, gleaming and veined with blood. And as the phallus first stirred and came to life in the primeval swamps of the male imagination, so males above all are uniquely alert to its siren call and baleful power. Becoming an athlete, body-builder, or 'jock' is therefore a clear and overt statement of manhood and male potency, and the clearest possible message to other men.[38]

The novel is rather like an Irish adaptation of Leighton's sculpture as one version of phallic power battles another, one – that found in the King of the Snakes and Black Murdock – being a degraded and indeed demonic masculinity whose strength comes from the powers of darkness, the other – in Arthur and the muscular Irish men – an elevated masculinity which has gained control over the body and built it into a symbol of transcendent power. The GAA member's slight on the men who would permit their children to be sacrificed to the Snake King is a commentary on the kind of men who have previously populated the country, and also a promise that things are going to be different from now on. Irish manhood is being remade. When the men gathered in the shebeen insist that 'we want St. Pathrick to luk in here agin!' (p. 18), they are in part calling for a rebirth of the legendary masculinity that their stories celebrate, and they are in luck because, with the GAA man and Arthur, St Patrick has indeed reappeared.

Given the ultra-masculinity associated with the Saint, it may even be appropriate to reconsider the nationality of Arthur Severn himself. After all, St Patrick, like Severn, was an English blow-in who was eagerly adopted by locals in the west of Ireland (specifically associated, too, with a Mayo mountain, Croagh Patrick), who then went on to become the iconic image of Irishness globally. Severn should certainly be seen as an 'honorary Irishman' at the very least given that his role in the plot is to drive out the reincarnation of the King of the Snakes, Black Murdock, like St Patrick before him. Arthur, although nominally 'English', is almost a cipher at the start of the story, and he certainly feels existentially devoid. His parents died 'when crossing the Channel', in a kind of liminal inbetweenness, and left Arthur in a 'blank' from which he has yet to extricate himself. He admits that he has always felt like 'an outsider' and it is only in the west of Ireland that he is fully accepted (pp. 5–6). Arthur uses his adventures to make himself into a man as well. As Glover argues, by the end of the novel he is 'no longer the ill-at-ease youth he was, but the heroic leader of his adopted country'.[39] In an article on the 1907 International Exhibition, Stoker specifically comments on the 'strenuous, industrious spirit' which would transform the country and effectively make Patrick into a 'new self'[40] – one that, perhaps, looks as much like Arthur Severn as the GAA player, and perhaps also rather looks like Stoker. Given Stoker's own experience of, like Severn, trooping down to remote parts of the Irish countryside (in his role as Inspector of Petty Sessions), and undoubtedly finding himself treated as an exotic (though welcome) visitor, it may be appropriate to see a certain autobiographical element in the representation of Arthur.[41]

If this reading is correct, interpretations of the novel as an imperialist romance will need to be considerably complicated. Most critics have associated Arthur with a colonial project to remake the west of Ireland into a version of the Home Counties, and argue that the novel shifts all blame for Irish underdevelopment onto native rather than imperial forces. For William Hughes the fact that the villain of the novel is a Catholic middleman is significant because it allows Stoker to deflect attention away from the colonial context in which the novel operates and suggest that Irish mismanagement is responsible for the problems of the country: 'The "real" oppressor is structured as a figure indigenous to the community, one whose practices emblematize the stasis of that community and the choking parochialism of its organization. Conventional social, political and racial relationships are thus inverted in order to produce a situation where the Englishman [. . .] is effectively active on behalf of the oppressed populace'.[42] Through Murdock's savagery, 'Arthur's British, imperial alternative is rendered positive'.[43] Likewise, Nick Daly argues that Murdock 'represents the prosperous Catholic middle classes who later become the Revivalists' rivals for the intellectual leadership of the nationalist movement'.[44] These readings configure the novel as a colonialist evasion of the very real questions about land rights and self-government being fought over in the Irish 'land war' of the 1880s and 1890s.

It would be strange, indeed, if Stoker had written an imperialist fantasy and then requested that one of the major figures in an anti-imperialist struggle (Michael Davitt) endorse it. However, far from Murdock representing the rising Catholic middle class, he is precisely a betrayal of this class, and everyone knows it. He is singularly unin-terested in the good of the community and focused only on his own enrichment, and most importantly is prepared to land-grab in order to attain this wealth. Far from being seen as in any way 'representa-tive' of middle-class Catholic farmers, middlemen (gombeen men) like Murdock were the most hated figures in the community – hated par-ticularly by the Irish Catholic farmers upon whom they mostly preyed, and Stoker's implication of the middleman in exploitation is no more of an imperialist evasion than the complaints of the farmers of the period who found themselves at the mercy of these bloodsuckers. According to Bernard H. Becker, the special commissioner of the *Daily News*, in his letters from 1880:

> Among the many spectres which haunt the sadly-vexed West and South of Ireland, there is [...] one ugly shadow, as of an old man filthy of aspect, hungry of eye, and greedy of claw, sitting in the rear of a gloomy store looking over papers by the light of a miserable tallow dip. From the papers the figure turned to a heap as of bank-notes, and there was in the air the chink of money. For the name of this grisly and terribly real spectre is *gombeen*; which, in the Irish tongue, signifies usury.[45]

This is an accurate description of Murdock, a man Arthur designates as a 'sort of usurer' (p. 19). The fact that Murdock is prepared to capitalize on the financial difficulties of Joyce automatically excludes him from the nation idealized by the Land League, which used the ultimate weapon of the boycott against, not only Irish landlords who evicted tenants, but tenants themselves who possessed the property of those so evicted, and it is hardly likely that Stoker would have asked one of the leaders of the League to endorse a novel in which those he represented were depicted as monstrous.

Moreover, rather than Murdock's supposed Catholicism associating him more closely with the west of Ireland farmers than Arthur, it ren-ders his betrayal of these men the more disgusting and worthy of condemnation. Davitt himself had made it clear that Catholics who land-grabbed or squeezed their neighbors for rack rents were far more dangerous than Protestant landlords who at least had the excuse of being denominationally different from those they were exploiting. He had spread the idea that the meeting at which the Land League was established in August 1879, was called specifically because of the behavior of Canon Geoffrey Bourke, a Catholic priest and executor of an estate in Irishtown, Co. Mayo, who was accused of threatening to evict Catholic tenants for failing to pay their rent. In other words, the behavior of a Catholic middleman was the immediate cause of the establishment of the Land League.[46] For Davitt, these men did not represent the future and were atavistic hangovers of an exploitative system. Such middlemen were certainly the target of the League's methodology of intimidation, and therefore there is nothing 'imperialist' about Stoker's establishing a middleman as the perpetrator of abuse. As Samuel Clark emphasizes, 'many tenants' were subject to being boycotted, 'usually for paying their rents or for landgrabbing'.[47] Murdock's Catholicism is, anyway, nominal. Towards the end of the novel he breaks out in profanities, declaring 'God himself – and he particularized the persons of the Trinity – couldn't balk him, and he'd do what he liked' (p. 182).

The GAA and the Land League were both intensely modernizing forces in Irish affairs, rather than representations of atavistic nationalism, despite the way both were represented in the English press, and on the strength of this novel it would appear that Stoker recognized them both as engines for the reconstitution of Irish manhood. The historian Joe Lee has described the Land League as a force of modernization in Irish society,[48] and both it and the GAA focused on the recalibration of Ireland along radically masculine lines: both set about transforming Irish men from slavish and servile weaklings, into self-authorizing, muscular, hard-working, progressive seekers of the future. Stoker's ambivalence about Irish nationalism has been rather too over-emphasized in critical examination, especially given that nationalism in this period was a multifaceted phenomenon. It is certainly true that he saw no future for an Ireland which had broken from the crown, but that hardly justifies seeing him as a representative of the colonial ruling authorities! Like many Irish nationalists, he wished to restore pride in Irish nationhood by reclaiming the warrior masculinity of the Irish past, retrofitting it for an Irish future (though, notably, with a body more suited to the twentieth century than the Celtic twilight). As Lisabeth C. Buchelt has argued, in *The Snake's Pass*, Stoker advocates 'the formation of a [...] community of inclusion in which membership is not determined by race or ethnicity'.[49] It is determined, however, by body type: the hale and hearty are welcome; especially, strong men are necessary, but the emasculated and the simian are both excluded.

Stoker appears to have seen in his own body and that of the GAA athlete the potential future of an Irish nationhood, in the same way that Whitman saw in a healthy American manly physique the future of American nationhood. Through discovering (or rediscovering) and remaking power within the self, Irish men would be able to establish Ireland as a strong nation firmly within the British Empire. In this way, Stoker's novel should be read as a contribution to the kind of 'self help' P. J. Matthews has described as powering the Irish cultural nationalism of the late nineteenth century. Matthews reads the Revival as a 'progressive period that witnessed the co-operation of the self-help revivalists to encourage local modes of material and cultural development'.[50] Such development schemes would surely include those outlined by Dick Sutherland to reclaim the bog – a scheme explicitly configured as manly, requiring what he calls 'heroic measures' (p. 44) – and to make use of the presence of limestone on the hillside of Knockcalltecrore to turn the area into an economic hub, by which Dick insists they can 'supply five hundred square miles of country with the rudiments of prosperity, and at a nominal price' (p. 174). It is no wonder, then, that after the Parnell affair, Stoker turned away from Irish affairs and Irish literature having become thoroughly disillusioned with one of the supposed emblems of future Irish masculinity. As Valente has detailed, Parnell was lionized as a great man by both supporters and enemies, and he was treated by everyone as 'not just an instance but an icon of manly virtue'.[51] His iconic status as a pinup of Irish masculinity was very quickly destroyed in the early 1890s with the revelation of the sexual scandal, and suddenly, after a ruthless 'campaign against his manliness' in the press, his 'long-standing identification with the Irish people-nation' effectively meant that with his public degradation, so too Irish masculinity in general was seriously damaged, and the crusade to remake it was retarded.[52] One of the great 'myths' of Irish history has been that it was the fall of Parnell that drove Irish energies away from politics and towards culture. According to W. B. Yeats, after the fall of Parnell, 'a disillusioned and embittered Ireland turned from parliamentary politics' and focused her energy on cultural nationalism instead.[53] In Stoker's case the opposite may have applied. The fall of an iconic Irish man may have driven Stoker away from investing in the Irish future, because in the Parnell scandal the snake of depravity had clearly defeated the athlete. Stoker had fought too hard to gain muscular mastery over his own unruly body and was not about to let himself become associated with such an emasculating defeat.

Notes

1. Michael Kimmel (2012) *Manhood in America: a Cultural History* (Oxford: Oxford University Press), p. 15.
2. Barbara Creed (1993) *The Monstrous-Feminine: Film, Feminism, Psychoanalysis* (London: Routledge).
3. See Barbara Creed (2005) *Phallic Panic: Film, Horror and the Primal Uncanny* (Carlton, Victoria: Melbourne University Press); Cyndy Hendershot (1998) *The Animal Within: Masculinity and the Gothic* (Ann Arbor, MI: University of Michigan Press); Andrew Smith (2004) *Victorian Demons: Medicine, Masculinity and the Gothic at the Fin-de-Siècle* (Manchester: Manchester University Press).
4. This is a situation literalized by Chuck Palahniuk's *Fight Club* (1996).
5. Horace Wyndham (1923) *The Nineteen Hundreds* (New York: Thomas Seltzer), p. 118.
6. Bram Stoker (1902; 2003) *The Mystery of the Sea*, ed. Carol Senf (Kansas City, MO: Valancourt), pp. 11, 35.
7. Bram Stoker (1909; 2009) *The Lady of the Shroud* (Doylestown, PA: Wildside Press), p. 43.
8. Bram Stoker (1895; 2000) *The Shoulder of Shasta*, annotated and introduction by Alan Johnson (Westcliff-on-Sea: Desert Island Books), pp. 47, 61.
9. Bram Stoker (1905) *The Man* (London: William Heinemann), pp. 3–4.
10. Bram Stoker (1897; 2003) *Dracula*, ed. Maurice Hindle (London: Penguin), p. 230.
11. Stoker, *Dracula*, p. 160.
12. Bram Stoker (1908; 2007) *Lady Athlyne*, annotated and introduced by Carol Senf (Westcliff-on-Sea: Desert Island Books), pp. 73, 75.
13. Bram Stoker (1911; 2006) *The Lair of the White Worm*, in *Dracula's Guest and Other Weird Stories*, ed. Kate Hebblethwaite (London: Penguin), pp. 151–369 (p. 287).
14. Kenneth Clark (1960) *The Nude: a Study of Ideal Art* (London: Pelican), p. 239.
15. For the debate about the meaning of the sculpture for Victorian observers, see Alison Smith (2005) 'The "Snake Body" in Victorian Art', *Early Popular Visual Culture* 3:2, 151–64 (pp. 156–8).
16. Bram Stoker (1906) *Personal Reminiscences of Henry Irving*, 2 vols (London: Heinemann), I: 31.
17. Barbara Belford (1996) *Bram Stoker and the Man Who Was Dracula* (Cambridge, MA: Da Capo Press), pp. 17–20.
18. For the details of these achievements see Paul Murray (2004) *From the Shadow of Dracula: a Life of Bram Stoker* (London: Jonathan Cape), pp. 39–43.
19. Stoker, *Personal Reminiscences of Henry Irving*, I: 31–2.
20. Horace Traubel (1953) *With Walt Whitman in Camden: 21 January – 7 April 1889*, ed. Sculley Bradley (London: Oxford University Press), pp. 181–5.
21. Stoker, *Dracula*, p. 185.
22. For this 'movement' see Norman Vance (1985) *Sinews of the Spirit: the Ideal of Christian Manliness in Victorian Literature and Religious Thought* (Cambridge: Cambridge University Press), and Donald E. Hall (ed.) (1994) *Muscular*

Christianity: Embodying the Victorian Age (Cambridge: Cambridge University Press).

23. Kenneth R. Dutton (1995) *The Perfectible Body: the Western Ideal of Physical Development* (London: Cassell), pp. 21–32.

24. 'Merry-go-Round', *The Entr'acte*, 23 September 1882, p. 3.

25. 'At Last!', *Judy: or The London serio-comic journal* (26 October 1881), 186–8; 'Another Triumph for Jonathan', *Judy: or The London serio-comic journal* (17 May 1882), 234–5. I owe these references to my doctoral student Valeria Cavalli.

26. Bram Stoker (1872; 2002) 'The Necessity for Political Honesty', in *A Glimpse of America, and other Lectures, Interviews and Essays*, ed. Richard Dalby (Westcliff-on-Sea: Desert Island Books), pp. 31–47 (p. 45).

27. Matthew Arnold (1867; 1962) *On the Study of Celtic Literature*, in *The Complete Prose Works of Matthew Arnold. Vol. 3: Lectures and Essays in Criticism*, ed. R. H. Super (Ann Arbor: University of Michigan Press), p. 347.

28. L. Perry Curtis, Jr (1971) *Apes and Angels: the Irishman in Victorian Caricature* (Washington, DC: Smithsonian Institution Press).

29. Joseph Valente (2011) *The Myth of Manliness in Irish National Culture, 1880–1922* (Urbana, IL: University of Illinois Press), p. 11.

30. First appeared as a serial in *The People*, and was published in single volume form in 1890.

31. Bram Stoker (1889; 2006) *The Snake's Pass* (Chicago: Valancourt Books), p. 132. Future page references will be given in parenthesis in the text.

32. Quoted in Patrick F. McDevitt (2005) 'Muscular Catholicism: Nationalism, Masculinity, and Gaelic Team Sports, 1884–1916', in *Bodies in Contact: Rethinking Colonial Encounters in World History*, eds Tony Ballantyne and Antoinette Burton (Durham, NC and London: Duke University Press), pp. 201–18 (p. 208).

33. Quoted in McDevitt, 'Muscular Catholicism', p. 203.

34. McDevitt, 'Muscular Catholicism', p. 204.

35. For the bodybuilding movement, see David L. Chapman (2006) *Sandow the Magnificent: Eugen Sandow and the Beginnings of Bodybuilding* (Urbana and Chicago: Illinois University Press); David Waller (2011) *The Perfect Man: the Muscular Life and Times of Eugen Sandow, Victorian Strongman* (Brighton: Victorian Secrets); John F. Kasson (2001) *Houdini, Tarzan and the Perfect Man: the White Male Body and the Challenge of Modernity in America* (New York: Hill and Wang).

36. Quoted in McDevitt, 'Muscular Catholicism', p. 207.

37. Valente, *Myth of Manliness*, p. 68.

38. Rosalind Miles (1991) *The Rites of Man: Love, Sex and Death in the Making of the Male* (London: Grafton Books), p. 111.

39. David Glover (1996) *Vampires, Mummies, and Liberals* (Durham, NC: Duke University Press), p. 49.

40. Bram Stoker (1907; 2002) 'The Great White Fair in Dublin', in *A Glimpse of America, and other Lectures, Interviews and Essays*, pp. 145–9 (pp. 145–6).

41. This would hardly be a major surprise since, as Jeffrey Richards has argued, Stoker's 'heroes are frequently projections of himself'; Jeffrey Richards (1995) 'Gender, Race and Sexuality in Bram Stoker's Other Novels', in *Gender Roles and Sexuality in Victorian Literature*, ed. Christopher Parker (Aldershot: Scolar

Press), p. 146. Paul Murray argues that most of Stoker's work needs to be read as autobiographical to some extent; Murray, *From the Shadow of Dracula*, pp. 2–3.

42. William Hughes (2000) *Beyond Dracula: Bram Stoker's Fiction and its Cultural Context* (London: Macmillan), p. 63.
43. Hughes, *Beyond Dracula*, p. 67.
44. Nick Daly (1999) *Modernism, Romance and the Fin de Siècle: Popular Fiction and British Culture, 1880–1914* (Cambridge: Cambridge University Press), p. 79.
45. Bernard H. Becker (1881) *Disturbed Ireland: Being the Letters Written During the Winter of 1880–81* (London: Macmillan), pp. 207–9.
46. There is some debate among historians as to whether Davitt was being truthful, but at the time, that the meeting was called in relation to the actions of a Catholic priest was widely believed. See T. W. Moody (1981) *Davitt and Irish Revolution, 1846–82* (Oxford: Clarendon Press), p. 295.
47. Samuel Clark (1979) *The Social Origins of the Irish Land War* (Princeton, NJ: Princeton University Press), p. 313.
48. Joe Lee (2008) *The Modernisation of Irish Society, 1848–1918* (Dublin: Gill and Macmillan).
49. Lisabeth C. Buchelt (2012) ' "Delicate Fantasy" and "Vulgar Reality": Undermining Romance and Complicating Identity in Bram Stoker's *The Snake's Pass*', New Hibernia Review/Irish Éireannach Nua 16:1, 113–33 (p. 113).
50. P. J. Matthews (2003) *Revival: the Abbey Theatre, Sinn Féin, the Gaelic League and the Co-Operative Movement* (Cork: Field Day), p. 3.
51. Valente, *Myth of Manliness*, p. 35.
52. Valente, *Myth of Manliness*, p. 57.
53. W. B. Yeats (1955) *Autobiographies* (Dublin: Gill and Macmillan), p. 559. This is a view that has been challenged by many, especially Roy Foster who rightly points out that far from politics being a spent force in Ireland after the Parnell crisis, constitutional politics remained effective in this period. Roy Foster (1993) *Paddy and Mr Punch: Connections in Irish and English History* (London: Penguin), p. 268.

10

'The Old Far West and the New': Bram Stoker, Race, and Manifest Destiny

Luke Gibbons

> Even in such a time of stress, racial matters were not to be altogether forgotten.
>
> (Bram Stoker, *The Mystery of the Sea*) [1]

The march of progress in the heyday of empire extended not only to this world but also to the next world, as is clear from an early scene in Bram Stoker's *The Mystery of the Sea* (1902). At the opening of the novel, Archibald Hunter, the leading character, stands on a cliff above Cruden Bay in Scotland after a tragedy in which a local fisherman has drowned, and witnesses a grim procession of ghosts from the remote past of others who had died at the spot:

> There was no need for me to judge by the historical sequence of their attire, or by any inference of hearing; I knew in my heart that these were the ghosts of the dead who had been drowned in the waters of the Cruden Skares. Indeed the moments of their passing – and there were many for the line was of sickening length – became to me a lesson of the long flight of time. At the first were the skin-clad savages with long, wild hair matted; then others with rude primitive clothing. And so on in historic order men, aye, and here and there a woman, too, of many lands whose garments were of varied cut and substance. Red-haired Vikings and black-haired Celts and Phoenicians, fair-haired Saxon and swarthy Moors in flowing robes. (p. 38)

The unfolding of time proceeds to ghosts of the Spanish Armada, whereupon 'one of them turned and looked at me': 'it was a glance from the spirit world which chilled me to the very soul' (p. 39). The procession ends with the fisherman whose death had been foreseen by Hunter through the mysterious sense of second sight only a few days before, a gash of blood still on his forehead and beard. This is not a land that time forgot, for hierarchical stages of history hold true even in eternity – a hint, perhaps, that the spirit of progress itself may be a product of the very superstition it purports to dispel in the name of modernity.

It is in this sense that the concept of progress central to capitalist modernity owes as much to metaphysics as to a secular, material view of history. In the eighteenth century, a stadial version of historical development driven by the invisible hand of the market was promulgated not far from the shores of Cruden Bay by the Scottish Enlightenment, giving rise to more powerful idealist conceptions of progress in Kant, Condorcet, and Hegel, and later to more ominous modes of social evolutionism (not always consistent with Darwin's own views). According to these versions of the perfectibility of man, redemption, in however prosaic a form, was to take place in this world as well as the next through the forced march of reason and Western civilization. It is not surprising that this civilizing mission found its most telling expression in the doctrine of 'Manifest Destiny' that presided over the expansion in the United States – a belief in the divinely ordained mission of the so-called Anglo-Saxon race that was a source of both attraction and anxiety, as we shall see, in Bram Stoker's fascination with the United States.

There is a certain irony that the term 'Manifest Destiny' was coined by an Irish-American journalist, John L. O'Sullivan, to justify the initial phase of American expansion into the far west during the Mexican war of 1845–8. The United States' claim to new territories, most notably Texas, was sanctioned by 'the right of our manifest destiny to overspread and to possess the whole continent which providence has given us for the development of the great experiment of liberty and federated development of self government'.[2] Though framed initially in military terms, Manifest Destiny was part of a wider vision which endorsed the inexorable spread of Western civilization through trade, technology, and, not least, perceptions of white superiority over other 'inferior' races. In a famous Currier and Ives print, Fanny Frances Palmer's 'Across the Continent: "Westward the Course of Empire Takes its Way" ' (1868) – one of the emblematic images of nineteenth-century America – modernization is driven by the surge of technology, the 'iron horse', which brings in its train all the more respectable expressions of how the West was won: the public school, the chapel, and the work ethic, exemplified by the display of woodcutters and toilers in the near foreground. The developmental logic of capital quite literally cuts lanes through the desert in order to open it up to the future. As several art historians have shown, the most striking aspect of such pictorial compositions is the spatialization of time, the translation of the flow and contingency of history into an expansive, synchronized vista in which past, present, and future unroll over a vast canvas from the omniscient viewpoint provided by the artist. As the painter Thomas Cole expressed it: 'Looking over the yet uncultivated scene, the mind's eye may see far into futurity. Where the wolf roams, the plough shall glisten; on the grey crag shall rise temple and tower'.[3] It is this God-like view that underpins the metaphysics of the unfolding panorama, as if the westward course of empire was written in the stars, possessing the inexorability and invincibility of fate. Hence the structuring of space between a foreground on a higher prominence, showing work in progress with a figure often surveying the scene; a midground showing the inroads made by cultivation upon nature in the form of homesteads, hamlets, and the ubiquitous train; and then a far horizon constituted by mountains or the wilderness, offering a blank slate for the blueprint of what is to come.

Not least of the anomalies of the flattening out of time is that the future on the remote horizon turns out to be none other than the prehistoric past. As is clear from Thomas Cole's statement, it is the wolf and the gray crag that loom large on the horizon, defining features of a world long left behind by history. The remote horizon is thus a premonition – but also, paradoxically, a flashback, a confrontation with the primitive on the other side of the frontier. In Palmer's print 'Across the Continent', this endangered space wheels round to the right-hand side of the picture – to the river awaiting its steamer, to the woods awaiting the axe, and, of course, to the native Americans awaiting their destruction, engulfed by the billowing smoke from the train. The lone canoe on the river that winds its way into the future is counterpointed on the other side by the wagon train, trailing a path parallel to that of the railway line receding into the horizon. There is no future, clearly, for those on the wrong side of the tracks, and the powerlessness of the Indians, reduced to spectators in the drama of their own extinction, reinforces the invincibility of the forces effecting their removal from history. It is in this sense, as Odo Marquard observes, that 'a futurologist is an antiquarian turned so that he faces the future'. To treat the past as dead and gone is to preempt the future as well: 'When, through the workings of the compulsion to "flee forward", the future becomes reckless toward the past from which it derives [...] they then project futures that will never come, and are thus, in a new way, museumlike'.[4]

It is striking that Stoker's conception of the spread of freedom in the New World, outlined in his public lecture on 'Abraham Lincoln' delivered to audiences in both the United States and Britain in the late 1880s, amounts virtually to a description of Palmer's image of Manifest Destiny. While 'the slave owners of the South kept ever marching Southward towards the Gulf', the free states were also expanding:

> But all this time the great, free North West was developing. The 'song of the broad axe' was heard in the aisles of the forest. Before the march of the pioneer the woods fell back and in his wake were smiling fields of corn. The rivers were explored, the prairies were lined with tracks of caravans of the pioneers. The pioneers were great men, full of daring, full of hope; of great strength and endurance, with self belief and self-reliance unequalled. Whole families of them followed the sunset driving the wolf from the track and the bear from its lair, the Indian from the path, one continuous stream swept into that wild rich North West. Towns and cities sprung up like magic, and began to pour eastwards the fruits of Western enterprise. Such men were by their very nature and needs of their life, free in every instinct. For them slavery was a shameful thing, a taint unendurable; and from them with all the energy of their swift advancing ways cause the thunder of their ideas and the expression of them.[5]

Stoker's hymn to the Republic is intended as a critique of the 'shameful' and 'hideous' practice of slavery that 'smeared' American liberty, and whose very existence obliterated the very first word of the 'self-evident truths' embodied in the Declaration of Independence – 'All men are created equal'.[6] Stoker's objections to slavery were no doubt greatly influenced by his admiration of Walt Whitman and Abraham Lincoln and, as Amanda Foreman has recently pointed out, such views were not as widespread in Victorian Britain as we might like to think: leading liberals such as Gladstone and Lord John Russell supported the slave-holding South, as did powerful manufacturing and financial interests in Lancashire and London.[7] What is of note for the present purposes, however, is the paradox of freedom promulgated by Manifest Destiny: so far from being inspired by opposition to racism, the critique of slavery is *governed* by racist sentiments towards lesser peoples and doomed races, precisely a denial that 'All men are created equal'.

That this dissociation in moral sensibility was by no means confined to Stoker is clear from the contrast in Northern responses to slavery, on the one hand, and to the racism of Indian removal on the other, an ambivalence shared by Stoker's hero Lincoln. As Eric Foner has noted, 'the continuing evolution of Lincoln's attitudes regarding blacks stands in stark contrast to the lack of change when it came to Native Americans'.[8] Though Foner notes that Lincoln was never an Indian-hater, it was on his orders that the largest mass execution took place in the United States, that of 38 Indians following the Santee Sioux uprising in 1862 during the Civil War. Leading generals on the antislavery Union side such as Sheridan, Custer, and Pope made no secret about their willingness to exterminate Indians, Sheridan carrying his scorched-earth policies from the Shenandoah Valley during the Civil War into the elimination of buffalo from the Great Plains during the final conquest of the Indians. The buffalo hunters, he told the Texas Legislature in 1875, 'have done more in the last two years to settle the vexed Indian question than the entire Regular army has done in the past thirty years. They are destroying the Indians' commissary. For the sake of lasting peace, let them kill, skin and sell until the buffalos are exterminated!'[9]

Racism in this case has less to do with skin or 'epidermal schemas' (in Frantz Fanon's terms) than with evolutionary schemes in which the human as well as the animal world was governed by survival of the fittest, the triumph of superior races over lesser breeds. All men may be equal but not all races. Distinguishing between varieties of racism in the United States, Michael Rogin has noted that while the object of racist pathology towards blacks was *the body*, a source of labor and sexuality, Indians were connected to *land*, and the desire for property. Hatred of Indians was not required for their removal: there was admiration and even idealization of their masculine, warrior-like virtues, but this did not count for much when they stood in the way of territorial expansion, or the expropriation of vast reserves of land. Though feared and vilified, the black body was useful and indeed constitutive of forced, slave labor; by contrast, the Indian body was considered useless for labor and hence surplus to requirements, fated for elimination.[10] As Victorian race theorist writers such as J. W. Jackson pointed out, extinction was the pre-ordained fate of 'inferior' races unless they showed an aptitude for labor that facilitated their integration, at however subordinate a level, into the emergent world systems of industry and agriculture.[11] For all the race hatred, the black population was thus likely to survive, as against the imminent disappearance of the American Indian: 'He [the black person] is the labourer of the Tropics, and is not going to perish out, like a wild Indian, because his buffalo grounds have been enclosed by the white faces' (p. 36). The contrast with the fate of the Australian aborigine is even starker:

It is the Oceanic Negro who is the almost irreclaimable savage, while the African is the improvable barbarian type of his race. The former is useless even as a slave, while the latter is eminently valuable because he has been broken to work and obedience, and has that hereditary aptitude for sustained toils of which the utter savage is so generally devoid [...] He has his place on the earth which none can take from him and what we have to attempt is not his extirpation, but improvement. (p. 36)

It is difficult not to think of such cultural obsolescence when presented with the abject condition of Indians in Bram Stoker's fictional foray into the American West, *The Shoulder of Shasta* (1895), set in the mountainous regions of the Californian/Oregon border. The novel deals with the visit of the Elstrees, an English family based in San Francisco, to the airy climate on the slopes on Mount Shasta at the edge of the frontier, to revitalize the ailing health of their daughter, Esse. The Elstrees send their manservant, La Maistre, ahead to make advance arrangements, and when they meet him at the decrepit railway station at Edgewood, his appearance cuts a dash, looking 'like a Western version of an English squire. But his glories entirely paled before the picturesque appearance of his companions':

Some of these were Indians, bronze-coloured, black-haired, high cheek-boned, lithe fellows who made announcement to all men of the fact of their being civilized by the nondescript character of their attire. Some had old red coats of the British infantry, and some the ragged remains of fashionable trousers, but they still wore some of the barbaric feathers, trinkets and necklaces of bone and teeth; and most of them had given themselves a mild coat of paint in honour of the occasion. They were all armed with rifles, and their lassos hung over their arms.[12]

The Indians are decked out as anachronisms, wearing cast-offs from the imperial past and, indeed, barely disguised traces of their own savage state. The degeneration of the Indians is contrasted with the untamed virility of the frontier hero, Grizzly Dick (based on Buffalo Bill, whom Stoker admired and befriended in real life). Traces of empire are also evident in Grizzly Dick's relation to the Indians: 'His proximity kept the Indians in order; for with the dominance of a Caucasian he made himself to some degree regulator of his neighbour's affairs. Indeed, he stood with regard to his Indians somewhat in the relation of a British justice of the peace to the village community' (p. 49).[13] When 'one of the most brainless looking of the tribe' (p. 49), Heap Hungry, creeps up upon Mrs Elstree while asleep in a hammock to test whether her hair really is gold, her terror is not assuaged by Dick's amusement. But Esse Elstree, by contrast, 'got on very well with the Indians' until she began to notice their cruelty 'to their squaws and children, their dogs and their horses' (pp. 51, 52):

> At first they amused her, and then, when she knew them a little better, they disgusted her. In fact, she went with them through some-what of those phases with which one regards a monkey before its place in the scale of creation is put in true perspective [...] So she gradually began to realize that, in spite of the ragged relics of a higher civilization, they were but little better than savages, and with the savage instincts which could not be altered all at once. (pp. 51–2)

Grizzly Dick assures her that the Indian 'ain't so bad as those think that don't know him', but nonetheless there are 'times when the cruelty of that lot to ours makes me so mad, I want to wipe them all out [...] Guess, you're about beginnin' to size up the noble red man without his frills' (p. 52).

At one point, the sensitive Esse strikes up a conversation with Grizzly Dick and asks him, in thoroughly British terms, if he brings his wife with him when he goes to town. Dick replied with 'a loud, aggressive, resonant laugh, which seemed to dominate the whole place':

> The Indians, hearing it, turned to gaze at him, and as Esse looked past his strong face, jolly with masculine humour and exuberant vitality, at their saturnine faces, in which there was no place for, or possi-bility of a smile, and contrasted his picturesqueness, which was yet without offence to convention, with their unutterably fantastic, bar-barous, childish, raggedness, she could not help thinking that the Indian want of humour was alone sufficient to put the race in a low place on the scale of human types. Dick continued to roar: 'My wife', he said, 'my wife. Ha! Ha! Ha! Wall, that's the best joke I heard since I see the Two Macs at Virginia City a twelvemonth ago'. (pp. 40–1)

The 'Two Macs' were an Irish vaudeville act named 'Hilton and Curly' before they changed their names to introduce 'knockabout' comedy – 'split[ting] one another's heads open' (p. 102) – to English and American music halls (it is perhaps just as well the Irish possess a sense of humor to raise them that little bit higher 'on the scale of human types').[14] The question of 'types' is central to Stoker's contention that Irish and Latin emigrants have an advantage in the acting profession in America on account of their demonstrative habits 'of displaying emotion – and in lesser degree thought and intention – through gesture', by contrast with the German or Teuton who 'has a phlegm which negatives [*sic*] such momentary trivialities'. This bodes well for the survival of some lower races:

> In race-fusion the lower as well as the higher races have beneficent part, adding physical strength, endurance, fecundity, though they may lack moral and intellectual strength. But after all, progress does not proceed on a grade of continuous or eternal proportions. There are set-backs as well as sudden propulsions forward; the utmost that can be expected is a tendency to advance.[15]

That this 'advance' does not proceed in a straight line, for all the 'historic order' of Manifest Destiny, is one of the abiding anxieties of Stoker's work. In *The Mystery of the Sea*, a chapter heading 'The Old Far West and the New' suggests that the forces of darkness in the old world – feudalism, Catholicism, Gaelic culture, Royalist Spain – that preoccupied European Gothic, were coming into contact with the others of American Gothic in the new world. The occasion for such transatlantic conflict was the Spanish-American War, prompted by the Cuban war of independence against Spain, and the sinking of the battleship USS *Maine*, imputed to the Spanish, in Havana Harbor in 1898, which brought the United States into the war. The downfall of Grizzly Dick at the end of *The Shoulder of Shasta* coincides with Frederick Jackson Turner's influential speech at the Chicago World Fair in 1893 announcing the closing of the frontier – an end to internal expansion interpreted by others such as Alfred Mahan, Theodore Roosevelt, and John Fiske (cited by Stoker) as a license to pursue new frontiers abroad. The war led to a revitalization in the doctrine of Manifest Destiny, resulting in the annexation of Cuba and Puerto Rico, and the seizure of Guam, Wake Island, and Manila in the Philippines in a protracted and costly Pacific war.

In *The Shoulder of Shasta*, a young Englishwoman, Esse Elstree, ventures into the American Wild West, but in *The Mystery of the Sea*, the situation is reversed as a young American heiress of pioneering stock, Marjory Drake, ends up on another frontier, the Gaelic periphery of Scotland. As if to compensate for the sinking of the USS *Maine*, Marjory's personal contribution to the Caribbean war, as a wealthy benefactor, is no less than a fully equipped battleship, which brings upon her the enmity of Spain. Her retreat to Crom Castle on the edge of the Highlands is due to a desire to hide from Spanish spies, and it is at Cruden Bay, on the Aberdeenshire coast, that she is rescued from a mishap in the sea by Archibald Hunter. Archibald's purchase of an old desk at an auction leads to the discovery of a series of encrypted manuscripts from Elizabethan times which he sets out to decode, using ciphers and secret codes dutifully outlined for the reader in several gnomic appendices at the end of the book. Hunter is also in possession, as noted above, of the gift of 'second sight', which is bound up with the mysterious appearances of an old crone, Gormala MacNiel, who issues eerie prophecies pertaining to the mysteries of the sea, reproduced in the Gaelic 'original' as a frontispiece to the novel. That Gaelic culture shares a lower evolutionary stage with American Indians is clear when the new West meets the old, and the world-wise Marjory scoffs at the old woman's presentiments of doom:

> At last Gormala's temper broke, and she turned on the girl in such a fury that for a few seconds I thought she was going to attack her physically. I stood ready to hold her off if necessary. At the first moment the passion in her was so great that she spoke in Gaelic; blind, white-hot fury will not allow a choice of tongues. The savage in her was speaking, and it spoke in the tongue it knew best. Of course neither of us could understand it, and we only stood smiling [...] Presently, through the tumult of her passion, Gormala began to realise that we did not understand her; and, with an effort which shook her, began to speak in English. With the English which she had, came intention and the restraint which it implies. Her phrases were not common curses, but rather a picturesque half prophecy with a basis of hate. (p. 184)

Marjory Drake turns out to be an exemplar not only of the new frontier ethic ranging abroad but also of the initial westward enterprise of the Anglo-Saxon race undertaken by her ancestor, Sir Francis Drake – at a time when North America was little more than 'the far home of the red man and the wolf and the bison and the bear' (p. 135). It is for this reason that the Native American, as in Stoker's lecture on Abraham Lincoln, is once again linked with the wolf, both being ripe for extinction. That these primitive inhabitants no longer roam the prairies is not only due to natural selection but to the pioneering spirit of Marjory's forbears:

> I come from a race of men who have held their lives in their hands from the cradle to the grave. My father, and my grandfather, and

my great grandfather were pioneers in Illinois, in Kentucky, in the Rockies and California. They knew that there were treacherous foes behind them every hour of their lives; and yet they were not afraid. And I am not afraid either. Their blood is in my veins, and speaks loudly to me when any sense of fear comes near me. (p. 176)

As the Drake connection unfolds, it becomes clear why a ghost from the Spanish Armada accosts Archibald in an eyeball-to-eyeball confrontation at the beginning of the story. The ghost, it transpires, bears a telling resemblance to the absentee owner of Crom Castle, Don Bernardino de Escoban, who is entrusted with restoring family honor by recovering lost treasure from the Vatican – a gift from the Pope of gold bullion and jewels – lost in the shipwreck of the Armada by one of his ancestors off Cruden Bay. The hermetic manuscripts deciphered by Archibald are the key to solving the mystery of the lost treasure, but in the immediate conjuncture of the Spanish-American war, the restoration of the wealth to Don Bernadino is tantamount to providing a war-chest to fund the Spanish war effort, and is staunchly resisted by the patriotic Marjory. Marjory's patriotism is never in doubt, as is evident from her own identification with a resurgent Manifest Destiny, passed from generation to generation:

Our nation is so vast, and it expands so quickly, that there is nearly everywhere a family separation [...] Somehow, the bulk of our young people still follow the sunset; and in the new life which comes to each, whether in the fields or in the city or in the reclamation of the wilderness, the one thing which makes life endurable is this independence which is another form of self-reliance. This it is which enables them to brave hunger and thirst and all danger which comes to pioneers. (p. 139)

Though the narrative relates that the 'swarthy' Spaniard could have stepped straight out of a Velasquez painting (p. 269), the fact that his days are numbered is clear from his resemblance to the wolf in the wilderness. Calling unexpectedly at Archibald's house, he reveals that he has managed to read the deciphered texts revealing the secrets of the treasure stored in Marjory's chamber in Crom Castle (which, after all, he owns):

'Then you have been to the castle again!', I said suddenly. My object was to disconcert him, but it did not succeed. In his saturnine

frankness had been a complete intention, which was now his protection against surprise. 'Yes!' he said slowly, and with a smile which
showed his teeth, like the wolf's to Red Ridinghood. 'Strange, they
did not tell me at Crom', I said as though to myself. 'They did not
know!' he answered. 'When next I visited my own house, it was at
night, and by a way not known, save to myself.' As he spoke, the
canine teeth began to show. He knew that what he had to tell was
wrong; and being determined to brazen it out, the cruelty which lay
behind his strength became manifest at once. (p. 328)

But it is not only the barely concealed connection to his vulpine fore-
bears that seals his fate; his dark complexion also betrays an ancestry
low down on the evolutionary scale:

Somehow at that moment the racial instinct manifested itself. Spain
was once the possession of the Moors, and the noblest of the old
families had some black blood in them. In Spain, such is not, as in
the West, a taint. The old diabolism whence sprung fantee and hoo-
doo seemed to gleam out in the grim smile of incarnate, rebellious
purpose. It was my cue to throw my antagonist off his guard; to attack
the composite character in such way that one part would betray the
other. (p. 328)

The trace of Africa and slavery under the surface of Catholicism – the
Fantee were a source of slaves for western traders – links the 'others'
of the old and new world. In the stand-off between 'types of the two
races whose deadly contest was then the interest of the world' (p. 269),
it is not surprising that the 'Dago lord' Don Bernardino (p. 383), with
his black blood, feels the odds are stacked against him. Later Archibald
explains that it is not only a conflict between two races: 'This is an affair
of two nations, or rather of three: The Papacy, the Spaniard, the Briton.
Nay, it touches another also, for the lady who shares the secret with me
represents the country with which your nation is at war!' (pp. 336–7).
To which the Spanish nobleman, like other species destined for extinction, can only reply: 'I am the last of my race. There is none to inherit'
(p. 333). But the Spaniard does not give up without a fight, and in one
of the most remarkable exchanges in the book, confronts Marjory Drake
with some home truths about the American civilizing mission into the
wilderness, and its Anglo-Saxon ancestry.

Some of these home truths surface at the end when it becomes apparent that the ultimate threat to Marjory's American patriotism derives

not from the enemy without but the African-American enemy within.[16] The association of black skin with sexual violence in the racial fantasies of the Deep South comes to the fore when one of Marjory's kidnappers is revealed as a 'darkey' from 'Noo Orleans' (p. 380), and members of the rescue party express the conviction that her death would be preferable to falling into his hands. Through a vision of second sight bequeathed by Gormala, Archibald has a premonition of Marjory imprisoned in a ship offshore at the mercy of her captors: 'All but one I surveyed calmly, and weighed up as it were with complacency; but this one was a huge coal-black negro, hideous and of repulsive aspect. A glimpse of him made my blood run cold, and filled my mind with hate and fear' (p. 426). 'Hideous' is the term Stoker used to condemn slavery in his lecture on Abraham Lincoln: now Archibald uses it to demean the *victims* of slavery, a clear indication of how racist sentiments can coexist with, and even inform, abolitionism. That this is no incidental usage on Stoker's part is evident in *The Lair of the White Worm* (1911) when the same terminology recurs in a description of the black African native employed as Edgar Caswell's servant to further reinforce evolutionary hierarchies of history:

> [T]he face of Oolanga, as his master called him, was unreformed, unsoftened savage, and inherent in it were all the hideous possibilities of a lost, devil-ridden child of the forest and the swamp – the lowest of all created things that could be regarded as in some form ostensibly human.[17]

In *The Mystery of the Sea*, Archibald swims to the vessel offshore in which Marjory is imprisoned to rescue the maiden from the Gothic villain, and hears footsteps approaching when he discovers her cabin: 'I knew who it was that was coming [...] The negro did not expect anyone, or any obstacle; he came on unthinkingly save for what evil purpose he had in mind' (p. 437):

> [T]he huge negro [...] was callous to everything, and there was such a wicked, devilish purpose in his look that my heart hardened grimly in the antagonism of man to man. Nay more, it was not a man that I loathed; I would have killed this beast with less compunction than I would kill a rat or a snake. Never in my life did I behold such a wicked face. In feature and expression there was every trace and potentiality of evil; and these superimposed on a racial brutality which made my gorge rise. (p. 438)

In his early publication *A Glimpse of America* (1886), Stoker mentions the rough justice found in America 'when some outrage has been committed, particularly when a woman has been the victim. In the latter instance, when a negro has been the delinquent, he is invariably lynched [...] a summary process of the social law not holding a place in our code'.[18] Archibald, though a barrister in English law, might not agree: with a vengeance that would not be out of place in a lynching, he sinks his dagger into the unsuspecting marauder:

> Never before did I understand the pleasure of killing a man. Since then, it makes me shudder when I think of how so potent a passion, or so keen a pleasure, can rest latent in the heart of a righteous man. It may have been that between the man and myself was all the antagonism that came from race, and fear, and wrongdoing; but the act of his killing was to me a joy unspeakable. It will rest with me as a wild pleasure till I die. (pp. 438–9)

It is this racial bloodlust that throws a shadow over the moral righteousness of Manifest Destiny, and liberal conceptions of progress in the heyday of empire. Popular support for American intervention in the Spanish-Cuban war was mobilized by the shrill reporting of Spanish atrocities in the 'yellow press', orchestrated by a circulation war between William Randolph Hearst's *New York Journal*, and Joseph Pulitzer's *New York World* (Hearst's immediate blaming of the Spanish for the sinking of the USS *Maine* extended to illustrations of cowardly saboteurs attaching explosives to the ship). Behind the sensational headlines lay a genuine humanitarian outrage: under the Spanish General 'Butcher' Weyler, over 200,000 Cubans, and a handful of Americans, were rounded up, tortured and starved to death in *reconcentrados*, the precursors of the twentieth-century concentration camps. Not surprisingly, in view of the 'Papist' demonology of the Gothic, this leads Archibald to discern in Don Bernardino's countenance not only vulpine and Moorish survivals but also the persecuting zeal of the medieval church, a favorite trope of the Gothic genre: 'It was borne in upon me by flashes of memory and instinct that the man was of the race and class from which came the rulers and oppressors of the land, the leaders of the Inquisition. Eyes like his own, burning in faces of deathly white, looked on deeds of torture, whose very memory after centuries can appall the world' (p. 271). As if with this in mind, Marjory's 'racial mission' manifests itself (p. 336), discounting Don Bernardino's claims to chivalry as a nobleman of honor. When he states that notwithstanding hostilities between their nations, he has no quarrel with the 'Senora' since she is a woman, she flashes back:

> 'In the *reconcentrados* were as many women as men. More, for the men were fighting elsewhere!' The passionate, disdainful sneer on her lips gave emphasis to the insult; and blood followed the stab. A red tide rushed to the Spaniard's swarthy face, over forehead and ears and neck; till, in a moment of quick passion of hate, he seemed as if bathed in red light [...] Marjory, womanlike, feeling her superiority over the man's anger, went on mercilessly: 'Women and children herded together like beasts; beaten, starved, tortured, mocked at, shamed, murdered! Oh! it is a proud thought for a Spaniard, that when the men cannot be conquered, even in half a century of furious oppression, their baffled foes can wreak their vengeance on the helpless women and children!' (pp. 270–1)

But the Spaniard tartly reminds Marjory that the policies implemented in Cuba did not have to look back to the Middle Ages for their precedents, but had their origins closer to home on American soil, in General Philip Sheridan's murderous military policies:

> 'For such foul acts I have nought but indignation and grief; though in the history of a nation such things must be. It is the soldier's duty to obey; even though his heart revolt. I have memory of hearing that even your own great nation has exercised not so much care as might be' – how he sneered with polished sarcasm as he turned the phrase – 'in the dealing with Indians. Nay more, even in your great war, when to kill was fratricidal, there were hardships to the conquered, even to the helpless women and children. Have I not heard that one of your most honoured generals, being asked what was to become of the women in a great march of devastation that he was about to make, replied, "The women? I would leave them nothing but their eyes to weep with!" But, indeed, I grieve that in this our mutual war the Senora grieves. Is it that she has suffered in herself, or through others dear to her?' (pp. 271–2)

In the *reconcentrados*, in other words, the Spanish were simply following the lead of the Civil War in America in which concentration camps were introduced by both sides to house unprecedented numbers of prisoners under horrific conditions. Such was Sheridan's reputation that reports of German war atrocities during World War One prompted an article in *The*

William and Mary Quarterly to ask, 'Did Grant, Sherman, and Sheridan teach Militarism to Germany?' The article reprinted a letter by the military historian, John Bigelow, to the *New York Times* in 1915 which recounted Sheridan's advice to Bismarck during the Franco-Prussian war of 1870 'to treat a hostile population with the utmost rigour, leaving them, as he expressed it, "Nothing but their eyes to weep with over the war" '.[19] In Stoker's story 'The Squaw' (1893), the Gothic remnants of both old and new worlds – of the Inquisition and Native American cruelty – come back from the past to wreak revenge on an American rancher and Indian fighter, Elias P. Hutcheson, who suffers a fate akin to that visited by the Apaches upon their victims, when he dies in agony in a medieval torture chamber in Nuremberg.[20]

A thin red line between civility and its 'others' haunts Gothic violence in both the old and new world. Archibald's race-hatred could well have been directed at the savagery of the pioneering spirit itself, for the only signs of violence on the black kidnapper in *The Mystery of the Sea* are his frontiersman trappings (which establish affinities with Marjory's Kentucky origins, and the Texan 'hunter' Quincey Morris in *Dracula* (1897)):

> He was armed, as were all the members of the blackmail gang. In a belt across his shoulder, slung Kentucky fashion, were two great seven shooters; and across his waist behind was a great bowie knife, with handle ready to grasp. Moreover, nigger-like, the handle of a razor rose out of the breast pocket of his dark flannel shirt. He did not, however, manifestly purpose using his weapons at present at any rate; there was not any sign of danger or opposition in front of him. (p. 437)

Such ambiguities have led Lisa Hopkins to suggest that 'Marjory Drake is not only the heroine but the enemy' of the novel's charting of racial and gender antagonisms.[21] In Louis B. Warren's fascinating discussion of Stoker's real-life acquaintance with 'Buffalo Bill' Cody, and the strange affinities between the frontiersman from the West and Count Dracula from the East, Stoker's Gothic vision, alert to the return of the repressed in history, is held to be less optimistic than Cody's triumphal version of how the West was won:

> For showman and author both, continual westward expansion and continual race war secured the racial destiny of white people. But they differed, ultimately, on the promise of frontier warfare. Cody believed in it as the salvation of the white race; Stoker's view was

much gloomier, at least in his most famous novel, wherein frontiers become almost as dangerous to the race as vampires themselves [...] such fears informed a gothic frontier myth, featuring not a clear-cut conquest of the wilderness by white settlers but the transformation of the pioneer into something more racially powerful – and infinitely twisted – that threatens the decadent metropole.[22]

Critical debates on Stoker have contrasted the liberal aspects of his vision – the critic of slavery and sympathizer with Home Rule – with the 'Anglo-supremacist' tendencies of his works, but it may be that Stoker's liberalism and racism are not opposed to one another in the end.[23]

Though the romance of late imperial culture was sustained by Gothic demonologies of racism, it also produced its own countercurrents in Stoker's fiction, for the subversion of progress and linear time in the Gothic genre challenged social Darwinism. Gormala's prophecies, and the clairvoyance of second sight, act as if the future is preordained; yet they also introduce degrees of agency and interpretation that break the 'chain of destiny', for foreknowledge allows Archibald to thwart the prophecies of doom. Stoker's story 'The Gypsy Prophecy' (1914) is a chronicle of a death foretold but while the image of the future rings true, the gypsy's reading of it is wrong: 'the gypsy was wonderfully near the truth; too near for the real event now to occur', as the relieved protagonist notes.[24] Likewise, Gormala in *The Mystery of the Sea* foresees Marjory struggling in the water with a floating shroud (p. 185), but the semantic instability of second sight becomes clear when it transpires that it is Marjory's 'loose skirts' that have been abandoned, along with her modesty, to allow her to swim ashore during the rescue (p. 449). It is as if the hermeneutics of history is sufficient to release the future from the predetermined fate of Manifest Destiny. Just as the pursuers of Dracula, as Catherine Wynne has noted, 'must become Dracula in order to destroy him; they must embrace the occult in order to vanquish it', so also it is through a survival from the savage Gaelic culture it seeks to extinguish that civility is rescued in the end.[25] For all the vindication of the 'historic order', the tenacity with which vanished races come back from the dead in the ghostly procession at Cruden Bay suggests that they have not been left behind by history after all.

Notes

1. Bram Stoker (1902; 1913) *The Mystery of the Sea* (London: William Rider), p. 370. Subsequent references will appear parenthetically in the text.

2. Cited in Anders Stephanson (1996) *Manifest Destiny: American Expansion and the Empire of Right* (New York: Hill and Wang), p. 42. O'Sullivan coined the phrase in his short-lived newspaper, *Morning Star*, 27 December 1845.

3. Thomas Cole (1836) 'Essay on American Scenery' (1836), cited in Albert Boime (1991) *The Magisterial Gaze: Manifest Destiny and American Landscape Painting c.1830–1863* (Washington, DC: Smithsonian Institution Press), p. 7.

4. Odo Marquard (1989) 'The End of Fate? (Some Observations on the Inevitability of Things Over Which We Have No Power of Disposition)', in *Farewell to Matters of Principle: Philosophical Studies* (New York: Oxford), pp. 64–86 (p. 81).

5. Robert J. Havlik (ed.) (2002) 'Bram Stoker's Lecture on Abraham Lincoln', *Irish Studies Review* 10.1, 5–27, (p. 12).

6. Havlik, 'Bram Stoker's Lecture on Abraham Lincoln', pp. 12, 11.

7. Amanda Foreman (2011) *A World on Fire: Britain's Crucial Role in the American Civil War* (New York: Random House); Peter J. Parish (1998) 'Gladstone and America', in *Gladstone*, ed. Peter J. Jagger (London: Hambledon Press), pp. 85–103 (pp. 89–98).

8. Eric Foner (2011) *The Fiery Trial: Abraham Lincoln and American Slavery* (New York: W. W. Norton), p. 261.

9. Cited in Peter Cozzens (2001) *Eye-Witnesses to the Indian Wars 1865–1890: Conquering the Southern Plains*, vol. 3 (Mechanicburg, PA: Stackpole Books), p. xxxix. Sheridan's remark was originally reported in John R. Cook (1907) *The Border and the Buffalo: an Untold Story of the Southwest Plains* (Topeka, KS: Crane and Company), p. 113.

10. Michael Rogin (1987) 'Liberal Society and the Indian Question', in *Ronald Reagan, the Movie, and Other Episodes in Political Demonology* (Berkeley: University of California Press), pp. 134–51.

11. Of course, *free* black labor presented a problem to this view, which is why repatriation to the 'homeland' in Africa gained support as a solution to the slave question among prominent figures such as Abraham Lincoln. See George Frederickson (1975) 'A Man but not a Brother: Abraham Lincoln and Racial Equality', *Journal of Southern History* 41.1, 39–58. Frederickson does not mention attitudes towards American Indians in his discussion.

12. Bram Stoker (1895; 2000) *The Shoulder of Shasta*, introduction by Alan Johnson (Westcliff-on-Sea: Desert Island Books), p. 27. Subsequent references will appear parenthetically in the text.

13. These traces also extend to their eating habits: 'The Indians sat on one side of the fire and ate their meat half-cooked – part of a little deer that Dick had shot, on purpose for the meal, just before sunset. Le Maistre and Dick sat together at the opposite side of the fire, and took their dinner with the larger deliberation of the Caucasian' (p. 31).

14. Frederick Boase (1897) *Modern English Biography* (London: Netherton and Worth), p. 1559.

15. Bram Stoker (1909; 2002) 'Americans as Actors', in *A Glimpse of America, and Other Lectures, Interviews and Essays*, ed. Richard Dalby (Westcliff-on-Sea: Desert Island Books), pp. 84–92 (pp. 86, 85–6).

16. Andrew Smith (1998) 'Bram Stoker's *The Mystery of the Sea*: Ireland and the Spanish-Cuban-American War', *Irish Studies Review* 6.2, 131–8 (p. 137).

17. Bram Stoker (1911; 1991) *The Lair of the White Worm* (Dingle: Brandon Books), p. 27.
18. Stoker, *A Glimpse of America*, p. 15.
19. John Bigelow, letter to *New York Times*, 8 June 1915, cited in 'Did Grant, Sherman, and Sheridan Teach Militarism to Germany?', *William and Mary Quarterly* 24.1 (July 1915), 66–72 (p. 68).
20. Bram Stoker (1893; 1979) 'The Squaw', in *The Bram Stoker Bedside Companion: Classic Horror Stories*, ed. Charles Osborne (New York: Taplinger), pp. 116–26.
21. Lisa Hopkins (2009) *Bram Stoker: a Literary Life* (London: Palgrave), p. 101.
22. Louis B. Warren (2002) 'Buffalo Bill Meets Dracula: William F. Cody, Bram Stoker, and the Frontiers of Racial Decay', *American Historical Review* 107.4, 1124–57 (pp. 1129–30).
23. See Joseph Valente (2002) *Dracula's Crypt: Bram Stoker, Irishness, and the Question of Blood* (Urbana, IL: University of Illinois Press), p. 2; David Glover (1996) *Vampires, Mummies, and Liberals: Bram Stoker and the Politics of Popular Fiction* (Durham, NC: Duke University Press), p. 41; William Hughes (2009) *Bram Stoker's* Dracula: *a Reader's Guide* (London: Bloomsbury), pp. 99–100.
24. Bram Stoker (1914; 1997) 'A Gypsy Prophecy', in *Best Ghost and Horror Stories*, ed. Richard Dalby, Stefan Dziemianowicz, and S. T. Joshi (New York: Dover), pp. 233–42 (p. 242).
25. Catherine Wynne (2000) 'Mesmeric Exorcism, Idolatrous Beliefs, and Blood Rituals: Mesmerism, Catholicism, and Second Sight in Stoker's Fiction', *Victorian Review* 26.1, 43–63 (p. 56).

Index

Printed and bound by CPI Group (UK) Ltd, Croydon, CR0 4YY